FIVE MORE DAYS WITH THE DEAD

STEPHEN CHARLICK

DAY 1

Patrick grunted with effort, as the iron bar that moments ago had ended the unnatural existence of the Dead woman before him, pulled free of her now shattered skull, bringing with it more of her ruined brain.

'Is that all of them?' He asked, his breath heavy from the sudden exertion. 'Is everyone okay?'

Using the back of his sleeve to wipe the dark stinking blood that had sprayed over his face with each swing of his weapon, Patrick looked around at his fellow travelling companions. To his left, Ryan was clubbing the last spark of life from the Dead child on the ground. His powerful blows were quickly rendering the child's small head to a pulpy mush, as skin, shattered bone and decaying brain matter became further pounded into the wet mud. With a forceful kick, Ryan began the stamp down again and again on the now headless corpse's back. Even from where Patrick stood, he could hear the brittle snap of child sized bones.

'Ryan,' Patrick said, trying to catch his old friend's attention.

Ignoring Patrick's voice or simply unable to register it, Ryan continued his relentless pointless attack. With each stamp and kick, he fed the compulsion to obliterate this obscenity from the world completely. In that instant, all he could see as his foot rose and fell were the friends and those he had loved that had been taken by the rotting corpses, by these abominations that he had been forced to confront since the beginning of this living nightmare.

'Ryan!' Patrick now shouted, trying to break through his friend's mania.

'Oh, for God's sake,' came an irritated voice over Patrick's right shoulder.

Glancing to his right, Patrick jerked his head sideways just in time, as the dripping clump of wet mud flew through the air towards him. Following the thrown clod of earth with his eyes, Patrick knew where it would finally hit home and sure enough, Leon's aim was spot on, as

1

usual. It was just the right thing to snap Ryan from his episode and as the wet mud struck him hard in the face, Ryan snapped back to the here and now.

'What the fuck?' said Ryan, halting his foot mid stamp and blinking away the muddy water from his eyes.

'It's down, okay,' said Leon, wiping his mudding hands on his trousers. 'I want to get home... so stop pissing around and let's get going.'

With a brief flick of his eyes, Ryan took in the pulped, bloody carnage now spread at his feet. Realising he had drifted somewhere dark during the attack, Ryan stomped past Patrick, avoiding his gaze and pulled open the cart side hatch.

'Ryan?' Patrick asked, reaching for his friend as he hurried past him.

'I'm fine,' was all Ryan could say as he clambered into the cart.

On more than one occasion recently, they had been forced to have this conversation. Over the last three months, Ryan had developed the habit of losing himself at dangerous times. More importantly, during an episode, he would be totally unaware of what was happening around him. Deep down, Patrick knew it was only a matter of time before the day came when Ryan would be unable to find his way back from the nightmares he held within him and he would ultimately end up as one of the Dead because of them. Grumblings of concern had already reached his ears from some of the other members of the community. They now looked with sideways glances at a man who had lived productively among many of them for years. Patrick had seen the growing wariness in their eyes whenever Ryan was around. They now could only see the man who had fought hard and often risked his own life to ensure the safety of theirs, as an out of control liability. Patrick had argued frequently on Ryan's behalf against those who cast doubt on his sanity. After many promises to keep a watchful eye on Ryan personally, much of the grumbling had finally turned into an underlying simmer of unease.

On a rational level, Patrick knew the community had some grounds for concern. When all their lives could be put at risk by a lapse in concentration of just one of their number, it was understandable they came to him, their leader, with demands for something to be done. Patrick knew that if he had to tell Ryan he could no longer be trusted to keep the community safe, it would crush the man and might ultimately be the thing to shatter Ryan's slipping grasp on his sanity. Each time Ryan was consumed by the darkness inside his mind, Patrick could not help but feel guilty. Even though he had done nothing directly to cause these episodes, Patrick believed the birth of his own daughter, Jasmine, three months ago to be the catalyst that sparked the resurface of Ryan's horrors.

When he and Ryan had first met four years ago, Ryan had told him of how he had spent those first few days when the Dead came. Ryan had been a loving father to his daughter, Jenny and an attentive husband to his heavily pregnant wife, who at the time was carrying their second child, a boy. When his wife had begun to bleed late one night, he knew he had to get her to the hospital right away if the baby wasn't to suffocate. Desperate to save his unborn son, Ryan chose to ignore the radio reports about strange riots that had broken out in the town centre and after waking a neighbour to look after Jenny, he had rushed his wife to the hospital through scenes he never thought to see in his home town. Carnage was everywhere he looked. Alarms blared and cars burned unchecked in the streets where they had collided with each other. At one point he had seen blood covered looters smash their way through the front windows of a late night café to attack the cowering people inside. He did not know what madness had taken over these people but he knew he had to keep on driving or fall victim to their rampage himself.

When he reached the alarmingly busy hospital, he finally managed to corner a frazzled and blood splattered doctor to look at his wife. No sooner had the weary man begun the examination than the screaming started. As if from nowhere a wave of panic-stricken people began running down the corridor, trampling over each other in their need to escape whatever was behind them. Suddenly, the wave of terrified people hit them and they were engulfed in the sea of bodies. Ryan fought to stay with his wife, but he was pushed along in their wake and as the bed his wife sat on was over turned, the last vision of his wife was of her clutching her belly with one hand while desperately reaching out to him with the other. Then as a blood covered orderly fell on her, she was lost from sight. When he was finally pushed though the hospital doors, he emerged to a world changed forever. Everywhere he looked, bloody and mutilated people were bringing down and ripping into those who had tried to flee. He battled to re-enter the hospital and finally managed to force open the door to a small office. If he could just wait a few minutes until the stampede thinned, he would be able to rescue his wife and baby. He had tried to convinced himself of that. However, as the minutes turned to hours and the screaming continued, Ryan knew his wife and son were lost to him. By the time the screaming and sounds of carnage had finally stopped, something in Ryan had broken. Over the next few days and weeks, he somehow managed to survive, his mind shutting out the horrors he was forced to witness. Occasionally, he would still wake in the night with snapshots of terrible images dancing at the corners of his memory, just out of reach. Not knowing if what came to him had been his imagination or real, he grasped at those brief images his mind allowed him to see, no matter how horrific they were. Blood covered hospital cots with infant's limbs torn and discarded, his home burning as he wept, engulfed in his loss and the constant running through darkened streets hiding from the Dead, all the stuff of nightmares or the merely shadows of his past, he did not know. He could remember every day of the last four years since he met Patrick and most of the three years that preceded that but he knew he would never truly be able to fill the gap in his memory of those first few months. So when Helen became pregnant and gave birth to a healthy baby girl, Patrick knew it must have affected Ryan on a deeply psychological level. His mind only now allowed the past traumas to surface, albeit briefly.

'Come on, let's just get going,' said Leon, eyeing Ryan's hunched over figure, as he pulled himself up into the box covered cart. 'We'll be back at the Substation in half an hour and I'm hungry.'

'You're always hungry,' Patrick replied, trying to lighten the mood in the cart.

With a flick of the reins, Patrick urged their dark mare, Shadow, forward along the narrow snow dusted lane, leaving the three permanently dead corpses behind them.

The Substation that they had made their home a little over three years ago had proven to be a sustainable and more importantly, a safe home, for the group of twenty survivors. With the high protective fencing that enclosed a large living area now turned over for vegetable growing, the three small breezeblock buildings converted to stables and storerooms and the now useless electric pylon itself, their elevated haven, they had made themselves a home. The Substation had certainly been a lucky find and when they had been joined by Duncan, an engineer, they had improved their find ten-fold. He had helped them make a drawbridge style ramp that allowed them to sleep in safety on the pylon platforms, secure enough that if the Dead somehow managed to breach the fence they would not simply be able to wander up to get at them. He had even developed an escape route for them, should the worst ever happen. Using the thick wires that led from their pylon home to the next pylon, Duncan had suspended small wooden boats they could winch across to safety by hand. He had since moved onto another community though, doing what he could he make lives easier wherever he went. For the last year and a half, Duncan had lived with those at the Lanherne Convent, a mixed group of survivors and a few of the original Carmelite sisters. Like the Substation group, those at Lanherne Convent were doing what they could to make a life in this strange new world. Patrick classed the Lanherne group as trusted friends and they often traded food, information and livestock with them. Six months ago, the Lanherne group had lost their leader, Charlie, when a crazy religious zealot, new to the area, had decided to forcibly take young children and babies from any outposts they came across in an attempt to build their own God fearing utopia. Even though Patrick worried about his friends, he knew Charlie had left behind a legacy of well-trained and more than capable fighters to protect the weaker members living at Lanherne.

'Are all the spy holes closed?' Patrick asked, glancing over his shoulder, as a shiver trickled down his back, 'There's a terrible draft in here.'

'Sorry,' Leon said, sliding back the cover over one of the many holes they used to watch the world go by as they travelled.

Not that it would make much difference to the temperature inside the cart, anyway. At the moment they were travelling into the wind and every so often a gust of wind would hit the cart at just the right angle to dust Patrick through the front viewing slit with a flurry of damp snowflakes.

'I wish it would just snow and be done with it,' Leon continued, hitting his damp gloves against the side of the cart, 'This slush is just a pain in the arse. At least if it snowed proper, we'd stay home instead of getting our damp arses chewed off.'

'Well, we'll have to think about moving everyone off the pylon and into the stable if it does.' Patrick replied, 'Not everyone is as badass as you, Leon. Some of them need solid warm walls around them and as great as the pylon is, the shacks we have up there aren't that great for keeping out the cold when it gets like this.'

'Yeah, I'm badass alright...' Leon mumbled under his breath, lost in his memories as he picked at a loose thread on one of his gloves.

Leon and his crew had been top dogs of the estate. Older people would cross the road to get out of their way, looking at them with fear in their eyes and that's just how Leon and his mates liked it. As a young mixed race teenager growing up with his mum on the rough council estate, Leon knew his teachers had already written him off to a life of gang violence, drugs and ultimately prison. However, he didn't give a fuck what they thought and what did they know about his life anyway. Looking back on it all now, Leon was ashamed of the little shit he'd been. His mother certainly hadn't deserved the way he treated her. The visits from the police, the disappearing for days on end, the stealing and the dope, she had deserved better from her only son. At the time, he hadn't cared though. This was his life and she was just another 'old' getting in his way of living it. Therefore, when word was out of some sort of riot happening on the other side of town, Leon joined his crew with scarves pulled up over their faces for a bit of good old fashioned 'shopping'. The scenes of bloody mayhem that met them soon put thoughts of a free plasma TV out of their minds. This was clearly no ordinary riot. All the 'badass' attitude in the world wasn't going to save them from the horrors happening around them and one by one, his crew fell, pulled down and torn open by blood soaked maniacs. Sooner than he thought possible, their number was reduced to just himself and his lifelong friend, Joshua, the J-man as they called him. As they ran, with the screams of their dying friends haunting each step, he had but one thought, Mum! However, this time Leon's mother wasn't there to make things alright. This time he would have to deal with things on his own.

When he and J-Man finally reached home, he found his mother on all fours, feasting on the dripping innards of a neighbour. Stopping mid-chew to look up at him, he saw only hunger in those film covered eyes and he knew his mother was gone. Before she could reach him, Leon slammed the door to his mum's flat closed for the last time. Knowing there was nothing left for him there anymore, and with the sound of the thing that had been his mother banging on the door, Leon and J-Man crept into the night to seek refuge from the hungry Dead. Luckily, for the pair they were picked up a few weeks later, hungry and humbled, by one of the bedraggled army convoys. Collecting the few civilians left alive as they travelled, the army gave them a modicum of safety for a while, but they soon learnt there was no real protection from the Dead. Their number was just simply too vast. Sure enough, when they were finally over-run by the Dead, Leon and J-Man had barely escaped with their lives or sanity intact. Forced to move from place to place, the two friends tried to find their place among the other survivors. They were soon forced to put behind them their pointless posturing and childish attitudes. This was a world where Leon and Joshua needed these people more than they were needed themselves. So, as the old world ended their new lives began. Leon soon discovered he had a talent for throwing things at the Dead with some accuracy. What began with fist-sized rocks cracking Dead skulls from metres away, soon ended with an array of knives that wedged into slots up and down the chest of his modified jacket. In total, he now carried sixteen throwing knives and used his skill to clear the bulk of the Dead before others could leave the safety of the cart.

'Earth to Leon,' Patrick said, breaking Leon from his memories.

'What? Oh, sorry, Man, I was miles away. What did you say?' Leon replied, pushing his damp gloves into his pockets.

'I said we're almost there and from the looks of it, we're going to need your knives,' said Patrick, nodding to six Dead people lumbering on the lane leading to the gate in the Sub-station fence.

Moving so he could look through the view slit over Patrick's shoulder, Leon could see the six animated corpses, each more disgusting and pathetic than the last.

'Okay, get a bit closer and I'll do what I can to even up the odds,' Leon said, pulling two sharp knives from his vest; flipping one of them over in his hand to reassure himself of its weight and balance.

'You alright to do this, big man?' Leon continued, nudging Ryan's leg with his boot.

'Just get on with it, hot shot. I thought you wanted to get home,' Ryan replied, barely giving Leon a glance.

Patrick pulled the mare to a stop and turned to look at the two men behind him. Glancing from one to the other, he tried to gauge if the antagonism that had risen between them was going to be a problem. With lives on the line, he had to know his small team would work together effectively. Out here, you needed a friendly pair of eyes watching your back at all times. With one hand already on the bolt of the top hatch, Leon flicked his eyes to Ryan and shrugged his shoulders.

'Ready?' Patrick finally said, reaching for his heavy club, still unable to tell what was going on in Ryan's head.

'Yep,' Leon said, and taking a quick deep breath, he threw the top hatch open.

At the sound of the hatch hitting the roof of the cart, one of the Dead slowly turned in their direction. The thing that had once been a woman in her mid-forties had certainly seen better days. What was left of her hair was matted with filth and plastered to the side of her grey tinged skull. Missing most of the flesh from one of her arms and with a large gaping wound in the side of her mottled face, she turned her hungry gaze upon the figure of Leon now in view. Raising her only working arm in desperate recognition of the living flesh now before her, the Dead woman let forth her low moan through broken and blackened teeth. Her call, filled with so much pitiful need, was cut short as one of Leon's knives flew fast and true. Hitting his chosen target, Leon's knife lodged deeply into her forehead. For an instant, she stood frozen in place and then as her brain finally gave in to the nature of a true death, she collapsed to the floor. However, her call to arms had not gone unheeded. One by one, the five remaining Dead turned to face Leon and the cart. The next to fall had once been a teenage boy. With much of the skin stripped from his neck and the lower part of his face, his blackened tongue moved sickeningly behind his torn and ruined mouth. Raising cracked and broken hands beseechingly towards Leon, he took a slow shaky step in his direction. Leon drew back his arm to take aim and once the boy was in his sights, the knife flew soundlessly from his grasp. With a dull 'thud', the boy stopped, never reaching the living flesh he so compulsively wanted. As before, Leon's knife found purchase, lodged deep in the skull just above the boy's film covered left eye. As a trickle of dark, long dead blood ran from the hilt of the knife, the boy fell to the side, forever still. Two of his Dead companions, unable to recognise the obstacle now lying in their path, stumbled over the body of the boy, falling comically to the road surface. With their withered arms, they struggled to right themselves, never taking their eyes from the sight of Leon.

'Their arms are moving too much,' Leon called to Patrick, 'I don't want to risk a knife ending up in an arm when there are easier targets.'

'Okay,' Patrick replied, 'we'll get those two later. Can you get the other two?'

'Sure thing,' Leon said under his breath, more to himself than to Patrick, and looked toward the next walking corpse.

This time, Leon paused briefly, sickened by the abomination he was forced to confront. The creature that Leon thought might have been a man had a sagging mouldy bare chest, its ruined flesh writhing with maggots. Even as it took a shambling step towards the cart, its wriggling offspring dropped from rotten wounds to the floor.

'Jesus,' Leon whispered, as he pulled the third knife free of its sheath.

The maggot-ridden cadaver was now only a few meters away and even for the Dead, this one was ripe. Even their mare, which was used to the Dead pushing past her to get to the living within the cart, began to snort and swing her head in annoyance at the smell., Covering his mouth and nose with his arm to block out some of the fetid odour, with his eyes beginning to water, Leon threw his knife.

'Crap,' he said, as the knife in flight only sliced off an ear covered in green mould. His aim had been too low and far too much to the right.

'I've got it, Hot-shot,' came Ryan's annoyed voice, loudly kicking open the side hatch.

'Ryan!' Patrick shouted, as he scrambled from his front seat after his idiot friend.

Ignoring Patrick, Ryan walked calmly up to the Dead thing to slam the blunt end of his pipe square in its chest. With the sound of decaying bones breaking and rancid flesh tearing, the creature stumbled backwards with something approaching surprise on its face. Then with a sucking sound, Ryan pulled his pipe free of the cadaver's chest and readied himself for a second blow. With another shower of maggots falling to the floor, the animated corpse, ignoring the now gaping hole in its chest surrounded by shattered bone, lurched forward to grab the living flesh almost within reach. By now, the sixth and final member of this Dead gathering was only a few steps behind the maggot carrier. This final creature must have been verging on seventy when it succumbed to its unnatural existence and as Patrick ran past Ryan to tackle it, he thought it surprising the thing could still manage to stay upright on such skeletal limbs. With his muscular six-foot frame giving power behind his swing, Patrick's club connected with the side of the Dead man's head. With a sickening crunch, his decrepit skull not only shattered but also detached from the spinal column with such force that it tore itself free from the body completely. Briefly following the detached head with his eyes as it came to land in a small slushy puddle at the side of the road, Patrick glanced back to see how Ryan was faring. Ryan had taken a step back from the cadaver to give himself more room and then with a hefty kick to the maggot ridden chest, the animated corpse was thrown back onto the cracked road. Quicker than Patrick thought possible, Ryan then stepped forward, swung and buried his pipe deeply into the creature's forehead. Patrick glared at Ryan, feeling the anger building within him.

'You fucking...' Patrick began, his anger boiling over.

'Heads up guys!' Leon's urgent call came from above, interrupting him.

The two moving cadavers that had fallen finally righted themselves and they were slowly dragging broken limbs and torn dead flesh towards where Ryan and Patrick stood. As the two men turned, they saw another of Leon's knives fly through the air and lodge in a Dead woman's decaying skull. Falling to the road in a crumpled mess of soiled rags and limbs, one final almost relief filled moan escaped her Dead lips, before becoming still forever.

'You, stay here,' Patrick said through clenched teeth, as he prodded Ryan in the chest with his club.

Walking over to the remaining Dead man, Patrick realised the time for diplomacy with Ryan was over. Thanks to his actions, he had been left with no choice, He would have to have it out with him. Realising his mind wasn't focusing on the task at hand, Patrick turned back to the Dead man shambling towards him. Excited by the proximity of Patrick's living flesh, the Dead man reached slowly for him. Compared to his travelling companions, this corpse was in good shape and from the look of him, could not have been one of the Dead for more than a few weeks. Yes, a chunk of flesh might have been torn from his cheek and both his lips ripped away to reveal the yellowing bone beneath, but compared to the others, he looked positively healthy. Patrick looked at the Dead man in front of him. It took him a moment to realise what was wrong with the figure he saw. Both of the man's hands were missing. From the look of the stumps, they didn't appear to have been eaten away but more like removed by some sort of blade, not that his lack of hands made him any less dangerous. Wanting to get it over and done with, Patrick delivered a quick hard kick to the Dead man's kneecap, snapping the leg sideways. With his club raised high, standing over the now prone corpse, Patrick took a deep breath. Letting the club fall with as much power as he could muster, Patrick aimed for the spot just above the bridge of the eyebrow bone. Oblivious to the club that would finally put an end to it un-natural existence, the Dead man's stumps pawed impotently at Patrick's trouser leg, desperate to get to the covered flesh. With the sound of a wet crack, they soon fell lifeless, no longer controlled by a brain that didn't know its body should be still. Wiping the worst of the gore of off his club on a part of the Dead man's jacket, Patrick tentatively lifted the now lifeless stump to take a closer look. Yes, they had definitely been amputated rather than eaten, he decided. What worried him though was the thin wire wrapped tightly around each wrist, so tight that it dug into the flesh.

'*This has been used as a type of tourniquet,*' he thought to himself. '*These hands were removed while he was still alive and someone had wanted him to stay that way, for a while at least.*'

Storing the information to think about later, Patrick knew that first, he had to deal with more pressing matters; namely Ryan. As he walked back to cart, he watched Ryan cleaning bits of bone and flesh from his trusty length of pipe.

'So, what the fuck was that all about Ryan?' He asked, trying to keep his anger in check.

'What?' Ryan replied, a bored tone creeping into his voice. 'Knife boy here, missed, so I dealt with it, no...'

'Dealt with it,' Patrick interrupted. 'You put us all in danger. You know the rule. We never leave the cart until we outnumber the Dead!'

'But...' Ryan tried to continue.

'No fucking buts, you screwed up, Ryan. You screwed up. Oh, just get in the cart, Ryan,' Patrick said, his anger evaporating leaving a tired sadness. The others had been right all along. Ryan was becoming a liability.

Travelling in silence along the cracked and overgrown lane, the fence that promised relief from the Dead soon came into view. They had survived another trip amongst the death and decay to return to the people they loved and cared for. They had returned to the one place left to them they could call home.

'Well, at least there are no Dead at the gate,' Leon observed absentmindedly as he peered through the front view slit over Patrick's shoulder.

'Do we need to raise the flag or can you see anyone in the open?' he continued.

Should everyone be up on the pylon when a foraging party returned home, Duncan had constructed a hand-operated winch situated on the outside of the fence that would raise a flag within the grounds to alert those within of their presence.

Pulling Shadow to a halt, Patrick leant forward to get a better look.

'Erm… yes, there's Gabe over by the stable,' he said. 'Give him a shout will you.'

Flipping open the top hatch, Leon stood and with his loud high whistle breaking the silence, he managed to get Gabe to look in their direction. Recognising Shadow and the cart she pulled, Gabe waved enthusiastically at the returning group.

'They're back! Patrick and the others are back!' he cried to the unseen people on the pylon above him, before jogging to one of the small concrete block buildings to retrieve the padlock key.

'They're back, Sarah,' he said with a beaming smile, running past the older woman as she came out of the livestock building, a basket of fresh eggs under her arm.

'I heard you, Gabe. I heard you,' she smiled, as she watched the eager teenager disappear inside the next building.

Gabe was a bit of a mystery to the rest of the survivors at the Substation. He was found wandering their fields eight months ago, alone and half starved. Unsure of even his real age, Gabe had been unable to tell them much of his past. He had probably only been six or seven when the Dead came to claim the earth as their own. His young mind, unable to process the many horrors he was unable to escape, had blocked out whole years of running and hiding. He sometimes had vague snapshot images of his parents that would rise through the fog of his memory but he knew at some point during those missing years, his parents had been taken from him by bloody hands and gnashing teeth. He remembered the lid of a large blanket box closing down on him, and his mother's concerned face slowly disappearing from sight, as her hand slipped through to touch his cheek one more time. Then as he lay there curled in the darkness, he heard the screams. How he then escaped the Dead that surely had torn into his parents, he had no idea. He also had brief memories of creeping through the darkness foraging for food and even seeing other survivors from time to time. Wary of approaching the strangers, he kept to himself.

Over the years, Gabe developed a remarkable talent for hiding from the Dead. His small malnourished frame was perfect for sleeping away the day in even the smallest of crawlspaces. Cupboards, crates, the trunks of burnt out cars and even under floorboards; all were handy places to hide in. Spending his days hidden from both the living and Dead alike, he would then silently creep from his hiding place to begin his nocturnal scavenging. However, as puberty kicked in and his thin body grew taller, if not wider, he found many of his regular hiding spots were now too small for even his starved gangly limbs. He remembers leaving the urban sprawl that had become his night-time world when a large wave of the Dead descended upon the area. Even taking into account their poor night vision, he knew it would be stupid trying to stay. He had pushed his luck to the limits, nightly dodging their outstretched arms as they sensed his living body run past them, but now those arms were just too great in number and it was time to leave. Gabe was unable to recall completely how he left the city or how he ended up in the turned fields outside the Substation but he certainly remembered the constant hunger pains that never left him. When Patrick came upon him eating raw potatoes from the mud, he had simply been too weak to flee. Collapsed in Patrick's arms, dirty and starving, he was carried to a new life, a new life of friends and safety behind the Substation's high fences.

With the clucking of startled chickens, their evening doze interrupted, Gabe came rushing out of the cement block building with the padlock key clutched in his hand. Following at a more leisurely pace was J-Man.

'He makes me feel old,' he said to Sarah, nodding towards Gabe as he ran like an excited child to the gate.

'Sweetheart, how do you think he makes me feel?' Sarah replied with a chuckle.

'Come on, old timer, let's see what they managed to find for us,' she continued, putting down the basket of eggs on a large plastic barrel and slipping her arm through J-Man's. 'Perhaps we'll have something special for dinner tonight?'

The last seven years had not been kind to Sarah, not only robbing her of family and those that she loved but they also had stolen her looks. Bit by bit, the hard living had taken its toll until she appeared a good fifteen years older than she actually was. Even though Sarah realised it was utterly ridiculous even to think about such things when she was lucky to be alive at all, it still bothered her slightly. Although she had never been what was described as classically attractive, she had always been particular about her appearance, making the best of what she had been given. She had always one of the first in line for the next beauty miracle promising to keep the wrinkles at bay. At forty-five and as an executive for an exclusive brand of Health-spar products, it was just expected she should look a certain way. Of course, the Dead had changed all that. Her hair once cut, highlighted and styled to perfection was now a drab grey mess. Her skin once bathed in every conceivable mix of potion and lotion was now weather worn and wrinkled. So when one of the survivors brought back a half empty bottle of one of the old products she used to sell, it brought back a flood of bitter sweet memories. After the initial grieving for a way of life that no longer existed, she was surprised to notice that the happy memories had ridden piggyback with the bad. Small details came flooding back to her, everyday joyful things she had forgotten until triggered by the simple plastic bottle of conditioner she held in her hands. From that moment on she made it her mission to pass on this secret joy held by the mundane objects of their past. Anytime a group were going outside the fence, she would ask them to collect small random objects, knowing each one was a potential window to the past for someone. Bottles, packaging, old magazines or catalogues, she wanted them all. Her cabin on the Pylon was a celebration of what had been. People would often stop outside her door, peering at the walls covered in another life's flotsam. Sometimes they would cry for a bit. Sometimes they would smile but always they would remember and that was the important thing for Sarah. They would remember a time before the Dead came to taint everything with their fetid corruption. They would remember their loved ones alive and happy, and if this memory could replace the scenes of horror that haunted their dreams just for a moment, it was worth it.

With the padlock sitting at his feet, Gabe was just removing the heavy chain that kept the gates secure when Sarah and J-Man arrived beside him. Normally, they would wait until those in the cart had removed any threat of the hungry Dead before opening the gate, but as there were none in sight, Gabe and J-Man each took one of the wide gates and pulled them open. Once Shadow had pulled the cart all the way in and the gate closed behind them, Gabe began to rewrap the heavy chain back through the metal supports of the gate methodically. Giving the gates a rattle and the locked padlock a final tug to make sure everything was secure again, Gabe ran back to the animal shed to replace the key. It was one of the rules of the Substation; the key was always replaced immediately on its hook, no exceptions.

Flipping open one of the side hatches, Leon's smiling face appeared.

'Hey, Sarah, you corrupting my J-Man there?' He asked, nodding to her arm in his, 'He's an innocent, Lady. He don't know shit about what to do with a real woman like you. You want to get yourself some Leon, he'll treat you right,' he continued, waggling his eyebrows and giving her a wink.

Squeezing his cheeks together with her fingers, Sarah lent in close to his now protruding lips.

'I'd break you, honey,' she said, giving him a friendly slap on the cheek, as behind her J-man burst into laughter.

'She got you there man,' J-Man said, stepping forwards to knock knuckles with his friend.

'Yeah, yeah,' Leon said, joining Sarah and J-Man on the ground. 'You're a wicked woman, Sarah.'

'But that's why you love me,' she replied, pulling the young man into a friendly hug. 'I'm glad you came home safely. Any trouble?'

'Well,' Leon began but stopped himself as Ryan jumped from the cart and walked past the group and over to the ramp leading up onto the Pylon.

'Oh dear,' said Sarah, her eyes following the troubled figure of Ryan as he disappeared into his cabin on the first platform of the pylon.

'Is anyone going to help unload all this stuff?' Patrick asked, pulling the first sack of potatoes from the cart with a grunt.

'Sorry, Man,' J-man said, taking the sack from Patrick. 'You go get reacquainted with Helen and Jasmine. I'll get some of the others to unload all this. You too, Leon, we've got this.'

'Thanks,' Patrick and Leon replied in unison.

'Welcome home, man,' J-Man said, slapping Patrick's shoulder as he walked past rubbing the sore muscles of his neck.

Being such a tall man had its disadvantages when it came to travelling in the cart. Hunched over for hours at a time so he could see clearly through the front view slit, he always ended trips with a terrible stiff neck, which only Helen's soothing touch could relieve.

'Make sure you rub Shadow down well and give her a good feed,' Patrick called over to Gabe who was unhitching the black mare.

With a wave, Gabe led Shadow slowly to the stable building, patting and stroking her muzzle as he talked softly to the trusted beast placed in his care.

Seeing the arrival of the cart some of the other members of the Substation community began to jog down the ramp, eager to help move the much-needed food into the storage building. Each saying their 'hellos' and 'welcome homes' as they passed Patrick, the return of the cart meant they could all eat well again for the next few weeks. The smiles he got from the passing faces almost made the three days away from Helen and his daughter worth it. Well, almost.

They had gone to the former Penhaligan place to collect some of their stored fruit and vegetables. The manor house with its large vegetable garden, fruit orchard and more importantly a cool, dry cellar had been a welcome addition to their resources. Like Charlie of the Lanherne community, the Penhaligan family had fallen victim to the blade wielded by a religious fanatic six months ago. Only their youngest son, Alex, had survived and only then by virtue of his age alone. He now lived with the rest of the rescued children, safe behind the high walls of the Lanherne convent. Leon, Ryan and Patrick had spent much of their time at the Penhaligan digging up potatoes and harvesting cabbages. It had proven to be back breaking work, but if they wanted to eat, it was a necessary evil. They also brought with them two sacks of apples they had been storing in the dry cellar. The orchard had given them a bumper harvest and after carefully wrapping each apple in old dry newspaper, they easily had enough to last them for the next few months.

Reaching the base of the pylon, Patrick absentmindedly patted one of the support struts. Whether it was to reassure himself everything was as it should be, the completion of a subconscious lucky ritual or a simple 'hello' to the object that had become a home for them all, he didn't really know, but every time he returned to the Substation, he would find himself giving the pylon a friendly pat.

'Hey hot stuff,' a woman's voice high came from above him.

Looking up, he could see Helen's smiling face leaning over the railing. Helen was even more beautiful to him now than the day he met her. With her dark rich coffee coloured skin and her eyes always full of mischief, he was hard pressed to resist her. Patrick had fought and killed for Helen's right to say 'No' and won her heart in the process, but at a slight cost. Although Patrick thought the large angry scar that ran down the side of his face had ruined his looks, it was a small price to pay for the love of the woman that had become the centre of his world. In fact, Helen herself could only see the scar as a symbol to the world of how much he loved her and each time she saw the scar, she realised she loved him even more for it.

'Hey,' he called back, waving to her with his free hand, his smile broadening as Helen lifted Jasmine up for him to see.

Waving up to his infant daughter, Patrick realised there was a slight tingle coming from the fingertips of his left hand. Glancing down at the hand resting on the pylon strut, he noticed that, one by one, the hairs on the back of his hand began to rise. Yes, he could definitely hear a low hum just at the edge of his range. As time seemed to slow, the realisation of what was wrong took form.

'My God, no… It can't be,' Patrick said to himself, his words escaping him in barely a whisper.

Feeling as if he was moving through treacle, Patrick turned his head to look back up at his wife and daughter. The moment their eyes met, Helen knew something had changed; she could see the terror in his eyes. The smile fell from her lips and knowing something was wrong, she took a painfully slow step towards the ramp. With a loud popping noise, something in the stable building sparked. Patrick subconsciously registered the flash of light sparking in the corner of his eye. With the pounding of his heart deafening in his ears, he removed his hand from the Pylon. Even now, he could almost sense something building in the air. The hum that had begun as a barely audible background sound was now quite obvious. With each thud of his heart, the hum increased in depth and Helen took another slow step towards the ramp. Then in a blink, time sped up again.

'RUN!' screamed Patrick, his panic and fear adding something horrific and desperate to the word.

In an instant, heads with scared questioning looks began to appear over the many pylon platform rails.

'Get off the pylon! Get off the pylon! Run!' Patrick shouted, as even more long forgotten circuits popped and sparked in the stable.

Knowing he was helpless to save his woman and child, all he could do was watch. With Helen's eyes widening in terror, she caught his gaze once more before she clutched Jasmine to her, turned and ran. The hum had now drowned out all other sounds in Patrick's mind. His whole world consisted of Helen's frantic flee to safety and the building buzz that promised only death for all those on the pylon. Helen was two steps from the top of the ramp when the rowboats hanging from the electric cables high above her exploded in a shower of sparks and flame. One step from the ramp and the world above her erupted in a storm of fire and debris. Clutching the side of his head in despair, Patrick could do nothing but watch as the cabins on the platforms exploded, raining wreckage burning down upon him. She wasn't going to make it, he knew it, there was no way she could get down the metal ramp before she was electrocuted. As a large section of one of the cabin walls hurtled down towards him un-noticed, Patrick was unable to tear his gaze from the figure of Helen clutching Jasmine tightly to her. In that instant, he prayed to every god that had ever existed. With one whispered word, he beseeched them all to spare her.

'Please!' Then with a flash of pain, the wreckage hit him, knocking him to the floor.

Helen had a fraction of a second left but she knew she wasn't going to make it, so placing her foot on the edge of the ramp, she pushed hard, throwing herself and Jasmine off into space. The word, 'Please!' escaped her lips.

***

In the refectory at Lanherne convent, two heavily pregnant women and a Carmelite Sister stared in disbelief at the small glowing bulb on the wall sconce, which had flared back to life only moments before.

'What does it mean?' Alice asked, voicing the question they all wanted to ask.

'I don't know,' replied Liz, her hand moving in large circles over her stomach, comforting the unborn child, 'but I hope it means things are going to change for the better.'

Suddenly, the bulb brightness increased and then with a pop, shards of thin glass were suddenly falling to the floor.

'Oh,' was all Sister Rebecca could say, unable to keep the disappointment from her voice.

Before Sister Rebecca could bend down to collect the bits of broken light bulb from the floor, Imran appeared in the doorway, panting, out of breath and with an excited look on his face.

'You'll never guess what happened on the way to the courtyard,' he panted.

'We know,' Liz said, nodding towards the broken bulb. She felt a bit of a spoilsport, watching the excitement drain from the face of the man she loved. 'Sorry,' she continued, shrugging her shoulders and giving him a smile.

'Oh,' Imran continued.

With the wind suddenly taken from his sails and with no more amazing news to pass on, he took a few moments to catch his breath. Pulling off his cream Kufie cap, Imran ran his fingers absentmindedly through his hair. Despite being a Carmelite convent, the remaining Sisters of Lanherne had proven to be very welcoming and accepting to all who sought refuge behind their walls. Imran only wished previous communities had been as tolerant of his Muslim faith. Most of his family had fallen victim to bigots looking for someone to blame for the horrors forced upon them. He and his now dead twin brother, Mohammed, had only just escaped that time with their lives. It seemed like a lifetime ago that they had stumbled upon Charlie's convoy of survivors and he gave thanks to the heavens they had. Not only had he found a second father in Charlie but also Liz, the woman he loved, had been among their number.

'Anyway, it can only be good news, can't it?' He asked, his breathing now back to normal. 'Someone somewhere is trying to get the electricity back on, and that's good, yes?'

'I don't know?' answered Liz, a concerned look on her face. 'I think we should call a meeting about this.'

Alice, who had been silently thinking things over, stopped nervously chewing her lip.

'I agree with Liz,' she said. 'This could be anything. Good or bad, we should come up with some sort of contingency plans, just in case. We have too many children here to think about.'

Mirroring Liz's subconscious actions, Alice also began to stroke her own distended stomach. Unlike Liz, the father of her baby would never see his child's first steps or hear their first words. Charlie, Alice's love, had been taken from her by the Dead six months ago at the cavern home of a religious cult. At times, she was still angry at Charlie for not being here but she knew even if he had known the rescue mission was going to be a one way trip he still would have gone. She knew he had loved Liz and her little sister, Anne, as daughters and nothing in the world could have stopped him from saving her. As it turned out, they had actually rescued five other small children at the same time as Anne, so she knew his death had certainly not been in vain. As if thinking of them conjured them up, two little faces appeared around the doorway to the refectory. Catching her eye, the two five year olds giggled and disappeared from sight.

'I saw you, you wicked children,' Sister Rebecca called after them, her laugh softening the words. 'Jimmy and Samantha, you've escaped your lessons again, haven't you. You just wait till I catch you.'

'I'll let everyone know about the meeting, once I get these two scamps back to Nadine and Lars,' Sister Rebecca said, turning to the others before running after the two escaping toddlers.

Within seconds, squeals of childish laughter could be heard from down the corridor as the old nun caught up with her fleeing truants.

Jimmy and Samantha had both been lucky to survive the deadly test sent them by the twisted religious group. As brother and sister, they at least still had each other for comfort. The three other children had not been so lucky, not by a long shot. They knew that little Alex had witnessed the cult leaders murdering both his parents and older sister, all because they had decided that only children under the age of seven were pure. Of Bailey, they knew very little, apart from his name and that he was six, but they could only assume what had become of his family. Of their last foundling child, they knew nothing at all. At only three, the poor little boy was unable to tell them anything, not even his name, so they called him Danny. Nadine thought the child might even have a hearing problem, as even now, despite that he was settled and safe, he could still be found staring off into the air, lost in a world of his own, completely unaware that someone was talking to him. However, the people of Lanherne had grown used to this type of behaviour a long time ago. After all, they had had to deal with Penny.

Penny had been just a teenager when she saw her classmates torn apart by the Dead. If it hadn't been for Lars, her geography teacher, pulling her over the side of a bridge into the river below, she surely would have suffered the same fate. However, unable to deal with what she had witnessed, Penny retreated into the child-like world inside her head and it had seemed she would stay there for ever. It wasn't until Lars himself was fighting for his life with one of the Dead that she managed to force herself through this foggy dream world, back to reality and back to save him. Since then, Penny had become the confident, intelligent young woman she was always meant to be. When she wasn't tinkering with some homemade device with Duncan, their resident engineer, she could be found looking after the community's horses. She once shared this work with Lars but now the arthritis in his hands had gotten to a point that he was unable to even buckle or unbuckle any of the tack without causing himself great pain. So still wanting to be a useful member of the community, he had fallen back on his former career as a teacher. Joining forces with Nadine, their local bookworm, they had formed a school of sorts, for the seven children now living among them.

'You two might as well take the weight off those ankles while we wait,' Imran said, trying to lead Liz back to a seat.

'Oh, stop fussing, Imran,' Liz said, regretting the tone of her words as soon as she said them.

Although she couldn't wait to hold her baby in her arms, pregnancy itself was not at all enjoyable. She tried not to take her irritation out on the man she loved but sometimes it just slipped out.

'Sorry,' she quickly added, as she gave into his concerned pestering.

Once Liz and Alice had managed to manoeuvre their increasingly awkward bodies back down into the chairs, they both let out a sigh of relief.

'Right, that's it. I'm not moving again until I go to bed,' Alice said looking down her bulge. 'In fact, just throw a blanket over me and I'll stay here till this one pops.'

'I might just join you,' Liz said, sharing in her friend's irritation.

'Oh, for God's sake,' Alice said, throwing her hands up in exasperation. 'I need a wee now. Help me back up, will you, Imran.'

With a smile, Imran helped Alice hoist herself back up from the seat. Once she was upright, Alice slowly began the walk to the bathroom. As she left the refectory, she passed Nicki and her husband Richard.

'Sister Rebecca said there was a meeting,' Richard said, sitting down at one of the long wooden tables. 'What's up?'

'They'll fill you in,' Alice said, cocking her thumb in Imran and Liz's direction. 'Back in a mo, I'm busting.'

'Do you need any help?' Nicki called after Alice.

Nicki had been a mother herself before the Dead came, so she knew how difficult getting up and down off the toilet could be so late in the pregnancy. As she watched Alice disappear down the corridor, she thought of her own son taken from her so long ago. Even now, all these years later, to think of him was like a knife twisting in her heart. The fact that she had not been with him when he needed her most just added bitter salt to her emotional wound. At least Richard's brother, Barry, had not allowed him to return as one of those abominations; that would have been more than she could bear. At the time and for years afterwards, she blamed Barry for her loss and hated him for it. It hadn't been until Barry had sacrificed himself to ensure the safety of Justin, her adopted foundling, that she could really understand what he had done for her all those years ago.

'Nicki,' Richard called to her, snapping her from her painful memories.

He could see from the look in her eyes what thoughts had been running through her mind. So, as she came to sit next to him, he gently took her hand and kissed it. He was about to say something when Justin appeared through the doorway leading almost all of the other members of their little community. He immediately gave his new parents a beaming smile before running over to them to tell them something hysterical that had happened with Stinky, the pig he had been given charge over. As always, wherever Justin went, the old Golden retriever plodded behind him. Reaching down to give the old beast a welcoming pat, Richard pretended to look engrossed in Justin's report. Pulling all the appropriate facial expressions in all the right places, Richard let Justin complete his tale before sitting him down next to Nicki. He knew she needed the contact of the young boy she loved to prevent the spectres of the past overwhelming her and as he suspected, she immediately put her arm protectively around the boy.

'Nadine's going to stay with the young ones,' reported Lars, taking a seat next to Richard. 'Bryon or I will fill her in later. Oh, and we've left Cam and William on wall duty, just in case.'

'So what's this about?' Bryon asked, looking from one face to the next as he walked awkwardly to one of the seats at the end of the table.

Bryon had broken his leg a few years back and despite doing the best she could, Nadine had been unable to reset the bones properly, resulting in the limp Bryon was forced to endure.

As Liz glanced about the room, mentally checking everybody off the list, she realised that apart from Nadine, Cam and William, everyone else was now there. Damien and Sally were sitting apart, obviously midway through another argument. Since the children had arrived at Lanherne, Sally had changed. Not only had she taken to the role of foster mother to Alex wonderfully but also she had realised she could prove her worth to the community on her own. She no longer needed a man, namely Damien, or his attentions as her back up plan.

When Phil caught Liz's gaze, he gave her a sly wink. He knew that, even though the community was a democracy now that Charlie was gone, she was the lynch pin that held them all together. Imran, Alice and her sister, Anne, followed her without question, as did Nadine and Lars and so by association did Bryon, Duncan and Penny. He didn't think even Richard and Nicki would really question her judgement, though he could tell Richard felt a little emasculated being told what to do by an eighteen year old girl. As for him, he knew she had a wise head on those young shoulders. He had entrusted the blade of her sword with his own life on countless occasions. She wouldn't guide them wrong now.

'Yes, what's the matter?' Sister Josephine asked, concern on the mother superior's kind face.

'We're not sure,' Liz said, glancing up at Imran for re-assurance. 'A few minutes ago, some of the light bulbs flared up. It was only for a few seconds but the electricity definitely came on.'

For a second there was stunned silence as people processed what she was saying. Then as one, people began talking, excited as to what this might mean. As she waited for the furore to subside, she noticed Duncan quietly walking over to the large detailed map of Cornwall they had put on one wall. Slowly, his fingers danced from one area on the map to another, a look of concentration on his face as he fought to resolve some inner conundrum.

'Duncan? Duncan!' called Liz, almost having to shout so she could hear her over the talking of the group.

One by one, people fell silent and turned toward Duncan, his finger tapping against his chin as he intently studied the map in front of him.

'Duncan, what are you thinking?' Alice asked, unable to wait for him to speak as she lowered herself slowly back down into her seat.

Only realising he was the centre of attention when he turned back to the group to answer Alice, Duncan's face did not mirror the joy felt by the rest of the group.

'What is it?' Liz said, knowing something bad was about to be said.

With a cough, Duncan cleared his throat and pointed to a point on the far south west point of the Cornwall peninsula.

'There's a hydro-electric power station here that would have fed into our grid system,' he said. 'It is feasible that if someone had enough man power to clear all the Dead in that area, they could have gotten it up and running, assuming of course they had someone with them who knew what they were doing.'

'So why did it go off again?' Sally asked.

'My guess is it must have been in such bad repair after all these years that the capacitors burnt themselves out almost instantly,' Duncan replied. 'Which is why the bulbs flared brightly before the brief surge totally fried the system.'

Liz knew there was more to come; she could see it in his eyes.

'And?' she said, dreading what he was about to say.

Looking Liz directly in the eye, Duncan sighed. Then turning back at the map, he simply let his finger follow a dark wriggling line until it stopped at another point, forty or so miles away from Lanherne. Liz knew that spot, because she had been there, many of them had.

'The Substation,' Liz whispered, a million scenarios running through her mind, none of them ending happily for her friends at the Pylon.

'If anyone had been on the Pylon when the electricity surged...,' said Duncan, slowly shaking his head, not needing to finish the sentence.

'Fuck,' said Imran. 'We've got to see if anyone's still alive.'

'Are you crazy?' Damien said, his chair squeaking across the floorboards as he stood, looking from one worried face to the next. 'They're gone. Either they've been fried or their own Dead have already got them. By the time we could get there, it'll be all over. I'm sorry but you know I'm right.'

'That's not the point,' Imran replied, 'There are good people there... people who don't deserve to be so easily abandoned or written off as corpses... Patrick would come for us if he knew we were in trouble, you know he would.'

Silence descended on the group. Nicky held Justin tightly as she looked into Richard's eyes, willing him not to volunteer to go.

'We have to try,' Imran said, then kneeling down and cupping Liz's face in his hand. 'I have to try.'

Liz knew he was right and simply nodded, leaning into his hand for comfort.

'I'll go too,' said Phil, his hand wiping back and forth over the bristles of his shaved head.

As much as he didn't really want to put himself in danger, he knew he was the only other choice if Nicky wasn't going to let Richard volunteer.

'Right, so Imran brings the accuracy, I bring the muscle, so we just need the expertise,' Phil continued, turning his gaze slowly towards Duncan.

'Yes, I should come,' Duncan nodded. 'I might be able to do something with the transformers at the Substation to make sure this doesn't happen again.'

'That's hoping there's still someone there to live on the pylon,' Richard mumbled, finally tearing his gaze away from Nicky.

'That's settled then,' Liz said, looking from one group member to the next. 'So, when do you leave?'

'You've only got another four or five hours of daylight left,' Lars said, looking out the window to the cloudy grey sky beyond. 'You'll never get there before nightfall and even with your skill with the bow, Imran, you still need to be able to see the Dead to hit them.'

'We could make it as far as the Penhaligan place though, couldn't we?' he responded. 'What do you think, Phil?'

'Yeah, and then go on to the Pylon at first light. Sounds like a plan,' said Phil, nodding as he toyed with the hairs of his thick beard.

'Right then, let's get busy people,' Imran said, clapping his hands and taking charge. 'Sister Rebecca, Mother Josephine, we'll need food and water for the trip. Sister Claire, Penny, can you get Delilah ready? Oh, and put some extra reins and rope in the cart in case we need to lead their livestock back here with us. We'll just have to leave their chickens. We're not hanging around trying to catch them if there are Dead about.'

'I'll put some of the extra weapons in the cart too, just in case,' Richard added, wanting to be useful.

'Thanks,' Imran said, trying to think if there was anything else.

'Sally, could you go and relieve Nadine with the children, fill her in on what's happened and ask her to sort out some medical supplies for them to take,' Liz added.

'Will do,' Sally replied, jumping up to join the exodus of people with jobs to do, leaving the refectory.

'I need to go sort out my arrows,' Imran said, mentally calculating how many he had ready to take with him, 'back in a minute.'

With most of the group leaving to do what they could to help prepare for the unexpected trip, Phil walked over to Liz as she watched Imran walk through the door. Kneeling down, he took her hand in his. His large fists made hers seem delicate by comparison.

'Don't you worry, Lizzy, I'll bring him back safe and sound,' he said giving her hand a small squeeze.

Tearing her eyes away from the now empty doorway, she was unable to hide the worry from her friend.

'I know you will, Phil,' she said, managing to force a small smile, 'and anyway, you don't fool me, Philip, you only want to go to see if

Patrick and Helen have any male visitors who happen to be fond of bald men with beards.'

'Busted,' he said, giving her a wink.

Leaning forward, Liz pulled the bear of a man into a tight a hug as her bulging stomach would allow.

'You be careful too,' Alice added, touching the man's arm with concern. 'Don't forget you promised to do all the nappy changing for this one.'

'I did, didn't I?' Phil said, gently patting Alice's belly. 'Don't you pop before I'm back, promise?'

'Promise, Mum,' Alice replied, rolling her eyes comically.

Alice had grown close to Philip since Charlie's death. He had offered her the proverbial shoulder to cry on, and as a gay man, she knew there was no hidden agenda behind his friendship.

'Right, I'd better go sort myself out,' said Phil, ruffling Anne's curly blonde hair as he stood up, 'and you be good for your sister, scamp.'

'Don't forget your good pants, in case you pull,' Alice called after him, as he walked out of the room.

Suddenly, a large fist appeared back around the doorframe giving her the finger before disappearing again with a deep chuckle.

**

With a prayer on her lips, Helen threw herself from the pylon ramp. She knew if she had hesitated for even a fraction of a second longer, both Jasmine and herself would surely now be dead. She had placed her life and that of her daughter in the will of the gods. Only they would decide if either of them survived the seven metre plummet to the ground beneath them. Again, time seemed to slow down and as she fell, every detail shouted out to her for recognition. She watched as a buckled section of one of the cabins flew past her and knocked Patrick from her sight. Then a second section, broken and aflame, banged heavily against her shoulder, knocking into her mid-air. With the force of the passing debris, she was twisted round so she now fell towards the earth backwards. Mercifully denied the sight of the ground rushing up to her meet her, all she could see was the place they had made their home above her, burning and broken. She knew the impact would shatter many of the bones in her body but at least Jasmine had been given a chance of survival. Somewhere the Gods were looking favourable upon Helen and her child, for the piece of corrugated iron that had knocked into her landed at an angle to the section that had hit Patrick. So as she came into contact with it, the force of the impact was only a fraction of what it could have been. Still feeling the jarring impact in every bone, the wind was painfully knocked from her lungs as Helen rolled uncontrollably off the crumpled corrugated iron that had broken her fall. In the rolling confusion, her head banged heavily against something and as she came to a stop with Jasmine screaming but unharmed in her arms and with the blackness threatening to close in on her, Helen glanced up at the ruined pylon to see a torn and damaged figure pulling itself free of the twisted wreckage.

'No...' she managed to whisper and then the darkness claimed her.

Leon, Sarah, J-Man and three others of the community that had luckily left the pylon to help unload the cart, all watched with shocked expressions as out of the blue, their world fell apart. For a second, they all just stood there unable to comprehend what had happened. Slowly, Leon took a shocked step forward and then another, until he was running to where he had seen Patrick hit.

'Help me!' He shouted to some of the still stunned survivors.

One by one, they snapped into action. With J-Man's help, Leon managed to lift the wall section off of Patrick, who despite a cut to his forehead was already coming round.

'H...Helen?' Patrick stammered, as he slowly pushed himself up on his elbow. He tentatively reached his other hand up to his forehead and finding it coming away wet and red, he winced and looked up at Leon and J-man.

'She didn't make it. Helen, she didn't make it...,' he continued, heavy tears welling up in his eyes.

'Man,' was all Leon could say, his own tears beginning to mirror Patrick's.

'No, wait!' J-Man said, running over to the crumpled form partially covered by a ruined piece of corrugated iron a few metres away. 'She's here! She's here!'

Pulling the debris frantically off her, he could now hear the wailing sound of a baby.

'Jasmine's here too and she sounds okay to me,' he continued, turning to wipe away the tears that had moments ago threatened to fall.

By now, Sarah had reached them and she fell quickly to her knees at Helen's side.

'She's alive,' she said, feeling for a pulse. 'She's unconscious but alive.'

Looking around her for a safe place, Sarah caught sight of movement on the pylon. At first, her hopes flared that there would be other survivors but when she saw what was moving about up there, her hopes faded fast.

'Patrick, we've got to move,' she called, not taking her eyes from the reanimating Dead above them. 'Now, Patrick!'

Even as she spoke, a Dead man, who up until moments ago had been one of their friends, threw himself from one of the platforms ten metres above them. With self-preservation an alien concept to the Dead, the corpse happily plummeted down to the living flesh below him. With a sickening thud, his body impacted with the hard earth. Bones broke and skin tore but this did nothing to deter him. Pulling himself along by his arms, the Dead man now dragged shattered and broken limbs behind him with only one need compelling him to move. It had to reach the living, warm, bloody flesh. It must feed this unquenchable hunger that burned inside him.

'Shit!' Leon said, as he turned to stamp on the crawling cadaver.

As he raised his boot, a moaning call to arms was sounded on the pylon above him.

'There's no time!' Patrick shouted, as he rose shakily to his feet and looking around for a safe haven. 'Get everyone to the stable.'

Lying among the broken beanpoles and winter vegetables, where the explosion had thrown him, Ryan's burnt body twitched. Something new within the burnt shell he had once been was taking control. As seared eyelids opened, milky eyes saw their new world for the first time and Ryan was no more. No longer able to register pain, Ryan's Dead eyes barely spared a glance at the piece of smoking wood embedded through its ribcage, part of some bloody ripped organ dripping from its end. The only thing that mattered was the hunger, the hunger that burned and consumed his whole being. Turning its head to the sound of panicked voices, it knew it should seek out its source. It knew those sounds promised release from this need. It knew those were the sounds of the living, the sounds of life itself and it would not be denied its share. Pushing itself upright, the thing that had been Ryan began to stalk the darkness, intent on ripping into something bloody and warm.

'They're coming back!' A young woman wept, her life having been spared by pure chance.

As she backed away from the pylon, the moans of their Dead companions already drifting down to them, she did not see Ryan's charred and ruined body running towards her from the shadows of the tall plants. The Dead man had found its prize and he would not be deterred. Slamming into the woman's warm flesh, he brought her violently down. With a shriek, the shard of wood pierced her body, pinning the two together like macabre lovers. The Dead man wasted no time and began to tear into her flesh with a ferocious abandon. No sooner had she screamed from the shock and pain of the wood ripping into her lungs, than the doomed woman began to drown in her own blood. It did not take long for that spark of something indefinable to leave the woman's shell and instantly, it was no longer of interest to the Dead Ryan. With a wet ripping sound, he pulled himself and the piece of wood free of the woman's savaged body.

With Jasmine held in one arm and his head still spinning, Patrick relied heavily on Leon for support, as they made their way to the stable building. Following them closely behind, J-Man and Sarah dragged Helen's unconscious form.

'They're coming down the ramp!' J-man shouted, glancing up as the burnt bodies of their friends appeared at the top of the ramp. 'We've got to hurry, man!'

Patrick turned his head. Leon was right. They didn't have much time.

'Help J-Man with Helen!' Patrick cried, pushing himself away from Leon. 'I'm okay. Just get Helen to the stable.'

Even as Leon dashed back to Sarah and J-Man, a wave of dizziness hit Patrick and he had to steady himself briefly against a water barrel. As he waited for the spinning to pass, he saw Ryan appear. With a gasp, he took in Ryan's burnt and bloody form and realised his friend was now one of the Dead. Even as he watched, he saw Ryan lock his predator's gaze on J-Man.

'J-man!' Patrick shouted, 'Behind you!'

Before J-Man could turn his head, a pair of Dead hands fell upon his shoulders. He barely had time to drop Helen's feet before he was pulled violently backwards towards a pair of snapping jaws with nothing to promise but death in their bite.

'No!' screamed Leon, terrified at what he may be forced to witness.

Still holding Helen under her arms, Leon knew that even if he dropped her, he would be too late to save his friend. Helplessly watching Ryan lean in to take a bite from J-Man's neck, Leon did not notice Sarah swiftly grab from the ground a short section of scaffolding pipe that been thrown from the pylon. With a fraction of a second to spare and with Sarah screaming with the effort, the pipe flew passed the back of J-man's head to smash Ryan full in the face. It gave J-Man the smallest of opportunities to save himself and he took it. Twisting in the Dead man's grip, J-Man turned and kicked at him hard. Ryan's Dead body that had been knocked back just enough to give J-Man a fighting chance stumbled slightly before reaching in again for the flesh it so desired. J-Man wasn't to go down without putting up a fight and before he felt Dead hands upon him again, he quickly reached for the pipe Sarah had thrown. Holding onto it with only one hand, there wasn't enough power in his backhanded swing to do any real damage, but as the pipe connected with the side of Ryan's head shattering the bone beneath, burnt Dead flesh ripped free.

'Down!' shouted a familiar voice behind him and trusting his friend's instincts, J-man did just that.

With a wet 'thud', one of Leon's knives appeared in the Dead man's skull. For the briefest of moments, Ryan's body stood motionless before falling to the ground, its unnatural existence ended.

'Move it!' Sarah screamed sprinting to the stable, as a dozen of the reanimated Dead began to stampede down the ramp towards them.

As the wave of death descended upon them, they knew their time running out. With Leon and J-Man lifting Helen's unconscious body again, they followed Sarah as fast as they could.

Needing to ensure Jasmine was safe first, Patrick had managed to force his unstable feet to get him to the stable. Reaching the safety the metal doors promised at the same time as Sarah, he kicked open one of the doors. Even as she ran past him, she plucked the screaming infant from his arms and ran inside. Standing in the doorway with one hand ready to slam it closed should the Dead attack, Patrick watched as the running corpses drew closer to Leon and J-Man. They weren't going to make it. He could tell and even as the thought demanded recognition, he saw the Dead splinter into groups. One group of four instantly took down and tore into one of the other fleeing survivors. Even from where he stood, he could hear the growls and grunts of the Dead as they ripped apart the screaming terrified man. Elsewhere, two badly burnt Dead men and a woman were chasing a screaming petrified girl fleeing for her life

'Shit! Shit! Shit!' Leon was shouting, as he saw the Dead were now only metres behind them.

Turning his head briefly towards the stable still ten metres away, he knew even if they dropped Helen, there was no chance of getting to safety before they were taken down by the Dead hoard on their heels. Then, like a saviour from the Middle Ages, Gabe charged past, riding Shadow.

'Come on, you fuckers!' shouted Gabe, the black mare rearing up to knock two of the Dead off their feet with her front hooves.

It was just the distraction they needed and fighting though his dizziness, Patrick ran forward to help Leon and J-Man save Helen.

'Get back!' Patrick yelled, lifting Helen up onto his strong shoulders.

Not waiting to be told twice, they ran the short distance to the stable door and after the briefest of stumbles, as Patrick fought of a wave of spinning that threatened to unbalance him, he joined them.

'Take her,' he said, dropping Helen into Leon's arms.

Turning, he saw Gabe charge after the group chasing the terrified young woman, Shadow's hooves running down two of the Dead in her path in the process. However, four of the Dead had almost reached the stable and although Patrick hated himself for it, he slammed the heavy doors closed, leaving Gabe and the girl to their fate.

'What about Gabe?' J-Man asked, panting as he tried to force oxygen into his shocked body. 'We can't just leave him...'

Patrick just looked at him not knowing what to say, his silence speaking volumes. They all knew if they wanted to survive, there was nothing they could do for Gabe. Their own situation was hopeless enough as it was and they knew it. Already Dead hands had begun to bang on the steel double doors.

Outside, Gabe charged past a Dead woman, kicking her head hard to knock her down, if only temporarily. That left just one Dead man who was now almost within arm's reach of the screaming woman.

'Yah!' Gabe yelled, turning Shadow a fraction to the left so the man was directly in her thunderous path.

The Dead man paid no heed to the sounds behind him. The living flesh was almost in his grasp enrapturing him totally. So as Shadow's hooves rained down upon him, breaking bone and tearing flesh in her wake, his decaying mind could not comprehend why he had been robbed of his bloody prize. Even now, with his body trampled into the earth, he tried to reach with shattered limbs for the warm bodies that demanded his sole attention.

'Get up!' Gabe shouted, reaching his arm out to the petrified woman, called Chloe.

'Chloe!' he shouted, breaking through her hysteria, 'Hurry!'

Seeing more of the Dead focusing their bloody attention on them, Chloe reached up to take his arm. Straining what muscles he had, Gabe managed to pull her up onto Shadow's back.

'Now what?' She cried, wrapping her arms tightly around Gabe's waist, as she looked at the approaching Dead.

Scanning the scene before them, Gabe knew their options were limited. With the main gate still locked, there was to be no easy escape from the Dead for them but they could definitely wait them out until they slowed down a bit, this he knew for sure. With a kick of his heels, he urged Shadow into a gallop to the perimeter fence. As he suspected, the Dead followed, desperate to taste their flesh, but they had no chance in keeping up with Shadow's pace. Within thirty seconds, Shadow had followed the fence round to the section closest to the stable. Breaking off, Gabe steered Shadow towards the single story, flat roofed, concrete building.

'Get ready!' He shouted over his shoulder to Chloe.

Pulling Shadow to an abrupt halt next to the wall, he turned to help Chloe stand. Gripping tightly to the lip of the roof, she frantically pulled herself up.

'Hurry!' She screamed, glancing at the fast approaching Dead.

With a brief look over his shoulder, Gabe threw his arms up to reach for Chloe's hands reaching down for him. Screaming with effort, Chloe pulled Gabe high enough so he could grasp the edge of the roof himself. Even now, the Dead were reaching around Shadow, their arms aloft, desperate to get hold of the flesh being denied them.

'Gabe!' Chloe screamed, as one of the Dead grabbed his ankle.

Kicking his legs wildly, Gabe managed to shake off the Dead man's unholy grasp and with an effort born of terror, pulled himself up onto the roof to collapse, panting, in Chloe's arms.

'That was... close,' he managed to say between gulping breaths.

Bursting into tears, Chloe pulled him close to her, only able to say two words over and over between her sobbing.

'Thank you...'

***

'We haven't forgotten anything, have we?' asked Duncan, checking the supplies they brought with them for what seemed like the tenth time.

'Hey, we got all we need,' Phil said looking over at the anxious man. 'Just calm down. There'll be plenty of time to freak out later when we get there, okay?'

Unlike Imran and Phil, Duncan didn't go on foraging trips into the world beyond the safety of convent's walls. He spent most of his time contributing by making gadgets and gizmos that would make their lives easier within them, so to be out among the Dead again was making him a bit nervous. Despite knowing they were perfectly safe inside the box-covered cart, hidden away from the Dead roaming the countryside, he couldn't help himself. Although he could of course defend himself should the need arise, he would've been dead a long time ago if he couldn't. He just didn't have a hope of matching Imran for skill or Phil for pure brute strength.

'Sorry,' he said, nervously sitting back down.

For a moment, he didn't know what to do with his twitching hands. Therefore, after trying to rest them in various positions, he gave up and just sat on them to keep them still. Giving Phil a weak smile when he noticed the big man watching him, he shrugged his shoulders and said, 'Devil makes light work for idle hands.'

'If you say so, Duncan,' replied Phil, smiling as he made a show of sitting on his own hands.

'Yes, that's right. Laugh at the jittery fool,' Duncan said, laughing.

'Hey, jittery is fine by me. At least, it means you know what's possible out here,' Phil continued, leaning forward to give Duncan's leg a friendly tap. 'It's the cocky ones that think they know it all. They're the ones that end up getting someone killed. I've seen it too many times before, believe me.'

For a moment, Phil was transported to other communities he had stayed with. To other trips like this one, where some alpha-male who took one risk too many, just to prove some point about being a real man, only to end up one of the Dead himself. Phil knew hungry teeth that appearing without warning, didn't care who you chose to sleep with. Then there were the kids, too young and too stupid to realise the Dead didn't give a shit that their lives had barely started. He had seen it countless times. They thought they knew it all. They thought they had the Dead licked. What did they need to be cautious for? The Dead were slow, the Dead were stupid. What they always forgot, and what always got them killed, was the Dead had them impossibly outnumbered and more importantly, the Dead could wait for-ever.

'Hope for the best but plan for the worst?' Duncan said, understanding what Phil was saying.

'Exactly,' Phil replied, giving Duncan a sad smile, the long forgotten faces of so many wasted lives fighting for his attention.

For a while, the three travelled in silence, each lost in their own thoughts. They had barely reached the end of the tree-lined lane leading away from the convent and already Imran was missing the feel of Liz in his arms. He tried to concentrate on steering Delilah through the maze of cracks and potholes that had made the lane a minefield of late. It had been bad enough in the summer but the constant frost and thaw of the winter was making it a lot worse. In years to come, the roads might become nothing more than obscured lines criss-crossing the countryside greenery; their presence only made known by the shards of cracked and broken asphalt hidden deep among the foliage. Despite this concentration, his input wasn't really needed yet. Delilah travelled this lane countless times and she knew automatically when to veer to the left or right to avoid the worst of the potholes. It wouldn't be until they reached the end of the lane and passed through the battered open wooden gate, that Imran would really be needed at all.

Sure enough, when they arrived at gate, drooping on its long rusted hinges, Delilah came to a stop. It used to be that she would always be told to go left but since the group had cleared the large fallen tree blocking the direct route to the village, she now had a choice of going right too. With a click of his tongue and a slight pull on the reins, Imran urged her to go right.

'Liz asked us to just check in on Jackson before we start out for the Penhaligan's,' Imran called to Duncan and Phil over his shoulder. 'Just to make sure he's okay. If his lights came on too, it might have shaken him a bit.'

Phil made grumbling noises behind him but didn't say anything. Jackson had been a bone of contention for quite a few people when it was discovered what he had locked in one of the store cupboards of the small school he had made his home. Like many, he had been unable to come to terms with the loss of his wife to the Dead and adamant that no one would take from him what little of her he had left. He had effectively kept her living corpse trapped with him in the school for the last seven years. After many hours of arguing and promises from Jackson, he had given Charlie the only key to the door of her prison, ensuring that the Dead woman would never be able to escape the cupboard that was to be her tomb for-ever. Each day, Jackson would sit next to the door and chat to his Dead wife's decaying corpse. Sometimes he would even look through the tiny re-enforced glass panel but more often than not, just to know she was close to him was enough to help through another day of loneliness. Those at Lanherne had offered him safety behind their walls on more than one occasion but there would be a price to pay. He would have to leave his wife behind and that was a price he simply couldn't comprehend paying, so he stayed.

It didn't take long before they began passing the first few dilapidated cottages of St Mawgan village; their ruined shells collapsing in on themselves and overgrown, as nature reclaimed what was hers.

'It's lucky that whoever decided to try to turn on the electricity did so during the winter,' mused Duncan, peering through one of spy holes at the passing wreckage of an old world.

'Why?' asked Phil, subconsciously stroking his beard, while he kept watch through a hole on the opposite side.

'Well, think about it. A sudden surge causing sparks from every fused or exposed electrical point. If it had happened during the hot summer, where everything was tinder dry already, we could be looking at a firestorm right now. It would soon spread from house to house and round here, the foliage is so dense there would be no stopping it. We would've lost the crops, everything,' Duncan replied, turning away from the spy hole to look at Phil.

'Well, I guess we're just lucky then,' said Phil, smiling as he gave him a sarcastic 'thumbs up'.

'Don't be a smart arse…' Duncan began to say.

'Uh-oh?' Imran's voice came from the front of the cart. 'Looks like we've got a problem here.'

'What?' Duncan and Phil asked in unison, as they moved forward to look over Imran's shoulders.

To someone who didn't know better, the scene before them looked much like the rest of the forsaken village. However, as the cart drew along the lane, cracked and spotted with large tufts of overgrown weeds, those in the cart knew something was terribly wrong. The school that Jackson had made his home stood before them at the next crossroads. As usual, the weather worn doors that had been taken from every home in the village, still stood bolted to the iron railings but the gate was open, creaking slightly in the winter breeze. The large heavy bucket, usually filled with brightly coloured plastic balls, no longer sitting sentry by the gate, awaiting visitors to announce their presence, but had been kicked over spilling its contents over the ground.

'Well, this doesn't look good,' said Phil.

'No, it doesn't,' added Imran, as he assessed the possibilities of what could have happened. 'Duncan, swap places with me and take Delilah over to the gate, will you? Phil, pass me my bow.'

Within a few minutes, Delilah had pulled the cart level with the open gate and with the top hatch now open, Imran could look into the dug up school playground. Instantly, he could hear the frantic barking of the puppy Jackson had found in the woods six months ago, coming from somewhere inside the school. Whatever was going on inside, the poor mutt wasn't happy about it. Then as if to confirm the worst, a creature so decayed it was impossible to determine what sex it had once been, shuffled into view.

'We've got Dead inside,' Imran called down to his companions below. 'At least one so far.'

At the sound of his voice, the Dead thing turned its putrid face in his direction. Its skin, mouldy and maggot ridden, hung so heavy on its skull that it pulled its lower eyelids down to expose the grey Dead flesh of its cheeks. Even from his position, Imran could see the maggots writhing under the loose skin on its neck, taking sustenance from their rotting host. Imran had seen enough and drawing his arrow back, he took the creature in his sights. With the slightest intake of breath, Imran steadied himself and then exhaled slowly as he let the bowstring slip from his fingers. As always, his arrow flew with precision, burying deeply in the creatures forehead. With the softest of sighs, one last fetid breath escaped its torn lips before the creature fell to floor.

'I can't see any more of the Dead from here,' Imran said, climbing back into the cart.

'Right, we'll have to go in. Duncan, you stay in the cart and keep watch. Imran, I'll be on point. Your bow's not too hot in tight corridors, so we'll rely on this,' Phil said, lifting a length of metal tubing with long twisted nails hammered through one end,

'And this,' he continued, strapping an object onto his wrist that looked like a glove with two long metal spikes bolted to a plate covering the back of the hand.

He had got the idea from Charlie. Charlie had lost a hand during one of the desert wars long before the Dead came and realising he would need as much weaponry as he could carry, he had modified his artificial limb to hold a large hunting knife.

'One of yours?' Imran said to Duncan, nodding at the spiked glove.

'I aim to please,' Duncan said, bobbing his head.

'Right, come on, ladies. Let's get to business,' said Phil, kicking open the side hatch.

By the time Imran had followed him out of the cart, Phil had already taken position by the gate. With his bow in his hand and a full quiver of arrows on his back, Imran gave Phil the nod and they began walking into the playground slowly. Phil glanced briefly down at the Dead thing Imran had dispatched. Even now, the maggots carried on their harvest of the Dead flesh, their lives oblivious to the change in state of their host. Putting his booted foot on the creature's head, Phil yanked Imran's arrow free and silently passed it back to him. Walking down the small path Jackson had made between the rows of vegetable beds towards to school entrance, they could still hear Toby's frantic barking coming from within the building. When he first took over the school, Jackson had sensibly boarded up the lower two thirds of the large classroom windows, just in case the Dead should ever breach his perimeter. What had been a positive for Jackson was now a hindrance for Phil and Imran because they had no idea what they could be walking into. What they could see through the top third of the glass didn't bode well though. A multitude of well-fed flies made tapping noises as they continually ricocheted off the smeared glass. In Phil's experience where you found flies this fat, you could bet your arse there were rotting corpses too. Pausing as they got to the door, Phil motioned to Imran he would open it on the count of three. Counting down on his fingers, one by one, Phil took a breath and slowly pushed the door inward with his foot. Instantly, the smell hit them. This was not the dry almost sickly sweet smell of old death but the rotting stench of death in its first bouts of decay. Phil hacked phlegm into his mouth and spat, desperate to clear his mouth. Even after just a few breaths, the foul odour almost felt like a coating on his tongue, because it was so strong.

Walking down the dimly lit corridor, which would have once teamed with the carefree jostling and laughter of young children, they knew they would only find death and the Dead awaiting them here. Checking each small classroom as they passed it, the detritus of Jackson's life littered every available space, Phil and Imran could see Jackson had lived a life of lonely sad regret. Whether a regret that his wife had died or that he had survived, they could only guess, but the words scribbled over walls and blackboards showed Jackson's unstable mind could not forgive himself for this imagined slight. The words 'sorry' and 'forgive me' were scrawled in shaky handwriting over many of the available surfaces, which clearly showed a man who had tortured his own soul beyond reason. With one last classroom to check, they knew they had reached their goal. Coming from the room was the sound of the tell-tale moaning of one the Dead and Toby's anxious barking.

'Ready?' Phil whispered.

With the smallest of nods from Imran, Phil pushed open the last classroom door, readying himself for whatever may be inside.

'Oh, crap,' Phil said, lowering his weapon.

There, with his arms outstretched desperately reaching for a frightened Toby and his legs kicking back and forth trying to gain purchase was Jackson. He had tied a rope to one of the thick heating pipes that ran along the top of the wall, and by climbing up on a chair for some height, had hung himself. He must have done it almost a week ago, judging from the rancid smell coming from his corpse.

'Here, Toby, come on, boy,' Imran called to the distressed dog.

With one last worried look at its master, Toby reluctantly walked over to Imran to lie down at his feet.

'Well, at least he tied the knot right, so it broke his neck instantly rather than strangling him,' mumbled Phil, stepping close to look at the kicking Dead man.

'Not much consolation,' Imran said quietly, reaching down to pat Toby's head. 'Does he have any bite marks?'

'Hang on, I'll check,' replied Phil, swinging his pipe in an arc so the tip connected with the top of Jackson's head.

With a wet cracking sound, Jackson's body suddenly went limp.

'Well, I couldn't check while he was moving.'

After Phil had cut down Jackson's body and checked for any obvious bites, he looked up at Imran.

'Nothing,' he said, 'Must've topped himself.'

'Shit!' Imran replied. 'We should have kept a closer eye on him, the poor bastard.'

'But why now?' asked Phil, looking down at the Jackson's still form. 'It's not as if his wife died recently. He's lived with her decaying corpse for almost eight years... I wonder what tipped him over the edge?'

'I think I know,' said Imran, gesturing to the pair of dead feet sticking out from behind an over turned table.

The body of Jackson's long dead wife had been propped up against the opposite wall. It would have been the last thing the poor man saw as he left this world. Phil walked over to the body and crouching down, examined the still corpse.

'Well, no prize for what sent him over the edge,' Phil said, yanking a wickedly sharp serrated knife from her skull.

The woman's skull had been shattered with such force that even part of the blade guard had punctured through into her cranial cavity.

'The question is who finished off the old lady? Certainly wasn't Jackson, here.'

'No,' Imran agreed, his brow creasing with concern, 'Not only did he simply not have the strength to inflict a blow like that, I doubt he could've brought himself to do it even if she'd been attacking him.'

'And this is new, barely been used,' said Phil, holding up the knife covered in thick dark blood. 'Whoever left this behind was either stupid or had enough to spare.'

'Look, let's deal with one problem at a time shall we?' Imran said, realising there was nothing more they could do here. 'If raiders are in the area, the Convent is well protected. They won't have a hope of getting in, and I think we should get going to the Penhaligan's if we want any chance of getting there before nightfall, don't you?'

'Hmmm,' was all Phil could say, as he stood to follow Imran out of the classroom, still examining the strangely new knife in his hand.

'Well, come on then, Toby,' Imran said, tapping the side of his leg, 'Can't just leave you behind, boy.'

Instantly, the dog jumped to his feet and with his tail wagging furiously, the three of them left behind the two corpses of Mr and Mrs Jackson, who were finally brought together again in death.

'Well?' Duncan asked them, as they climbed back into the cart. 'Oh,' he continued as Toby jumped in after them.

Duncan knew the old man had loved the foundling puppy, so the worst must have happened for him to be coming with them now.

'Someone finally took matters into their own hands and offed Mrs Jackson,' Phil replied.

'What about Jackson?' Duncan asked, already knowing the answer.

'Either they did Jackson as well or his wife finally being taken from him was more than he could cope with, so he hung himself,' Imran added, pulling out a small amount of cooked chicken meat for Toby from one of the supply sacks.

'So what now?' asked Duncan.

'Now, we continue with the plan,' said Imran. 'We go to the Penhaligan place and hope there's someone left at the Substation alive when we get there tomorrow afternoon.'

Duncan didn't need to be told twice. He didn't relish being on the road at night, so the sooner they got to their next stop, the better as far as he was concerned. So, with a gentle flick of the reins, he urged Delilah into motion; leaving behind them just another home in this world of the Dead where death had paid an unwelcome visit.

***

'She's coming round,' Sarah said looking over at a worried looking Patrick holding Jasmine in his arms.

As the darkness slowly released its hold on Helen, she forced her consciousness upwards towards the pounding in her head and the muffled voices around her. With relief, she grasped onto the pain that threatened to send her tumbling back into oblivion. The pain told her she was alive and if she was alive, then she had somehow managed to survive the fall from the pylon. With a painful intake of breath, Helen finally opened her eyes. Looking around the dimly lit stable, past J-Man, Sarah and Leon, her eyes fell on a concerned Patrick with Jasmine.

'We made it?' the whisper barely escaping her lips.

Still fighting his own dizziness, Patrick crawled over to Helen, tears brimming in his eyes.

'We made it,' he said, as he leant forward.

Kissing Helen gently on the forehead, his tears of relief fell freely. Trying to push herself up to take Jasmine, Helen winced with pain as her cracked ribs made themselves known.

'Shit!' she winced through gritted teeth, 'I think I've busted some ribs.'

'Rest back down,' Sarah said, gently easing her shoulders back down. 'We're safe for now, so rest while you can.'

'Are we the only ones that made it?' Helen asked, her eyes drifting to the steel door rattling, the Dead on the other side pounding against it.

'I'm afraid so,' replied Leon, the faces of so many missing friends running through his head, 'and if we don't come up with some sort of plan to get out of here, we're in big trouble.'

'What's happening outside, J-Man?' Patrick asked.

Pushing past one of the Substation's pigs, J-Man jumped up onto a feed box so he could look through the high horizontal window that ran three quarters of the width of the wall. Outside, most of the Dead had congregated in front of the stable doors, their burnt and broken hands clawing relentlessly at the impervious steel; desperate to get to the living flesh denied them.

'There's more than a dozen of the Dead at the doors, so we're out numbered,' J-Man said. 'By the time they wind down, it'll be pitch black out there, man.'

'We won't stand a chance fighting even the slow ones in the dark,' Patrick said, knowing that because the doors had to open inward, they would be swamped by the animated corpses as soon as they tried to escape.

It didn't help that only J-Man, Leon and him would be able to fight with any effectiveness.

'I think we should wait until morning,' he continued. 'At least that'll give us a fighting chance.'

'The door will hold that long, wont it?' Sarah asked, as the Dead continued their attack.

'It has to,' Leon muttered, knowing their lives depended on it.

Unknown to Patrick and the others, above them on the roof, Gabe held Chloe in his arms, shivering. The heavy grey clouds, that had threatened snowfall all day had begun to release their burden slowly.

'Just what we need,' Gabe grumbled to himself, looking up at the silently falling white flakes.

Already, the snow had started to settle around them quickly. It was going to be a cold night for them both, but Gabe was determined they would survive. After fighting and winning against the Dead for so many years, he would be damned if hyperthermia took him from this world. Pulling Chloe up, they began to walk back and forth along the roof.

'We need to keep moving, Chloe,' he said, glancing down as the Dead continued their wild assault on the stable door.

He knew he and Chloe didn't stand a hope in hell against the hungry Dead below them at the moment. It would be hours before their frenzied attack would wind down, making the Dead slower and giving them perhaps their only chance to outrun them.

'We've just got to wait until morning,' Gabe said, rubbing her arms to keep her warm. 'We just got to hold on till then, okay?'

'And then what?' Chloe asked, needing Gabe to say something, anything, to give her the hope she needed.

'Then… then we get out of here,' was all Gabe could think of to say.

It wasn't much, but Chloe held onto Gabe's brief words and their promise of survival. Her story would not end this way. With Gabe's help, she would get out of this. She would survive.

***

Blowing onto his hands, the young man tried to get some warm blood flowing to his freezing fingers. The snow started to come down with gusto over an hour ago and already it was settling around him. Every so often, he would shake his shoulders, dislodging the flakes that threatened to settle even there. Not for the first time that night, he cursed his bad luck at pulling 'watch' on a night like this.

'Well?' a familiar gruff voice came from behind him, his tone indicating only good news was welcome or there would be trouble.

'The cart hasn't come back yet, Sir, sorry,' the young man replied, desperate to keep his voice from shaking.

'I don't want your apologies, Blackmore. I want reliable Intel on what we can expect down there,' he replied, lifting up a pair of night vision binoculars.

Looking through the lenses, the gauges electronically adjusting to focus on their target, the man knew that with this one, they could possibly fill their quota.

'And how many of the Dead?' He continued, not taking his eyes off then next target.

'Just six so far. They seem to have been keeping the area pretty clear,' Private Blackmore replied, looking up at the man stood next to him.' Permission to ask a question, Sir?'

'What is it, Blackmore?' The man asked, an aggravated tone dripping into his voice, as if the concerns of those in his charge were beneath him.

'Will we be engaging the civilians tonight?' He asked, hoping it would mean he wouldn't be spending most of the night lying face down on the freezing earth.

'No, we need as many as we can get,' the man replied, 'We'll wait until first light and move in. Perhaps the cart will be back by then, as long as that meets with your approval of course, Private Blackmore.'

'Yes, Sir, sorry Sir,' was all Stephen Blackmore could think of to say.

His commanding officer was a harsh man, unnecessarily strict and didn't give a monkey's ass about the grunts under his command. Getting the job done was always the prime objective. If any of the squadron fell during the process, so be it. Like everyone in the squadron, Steve hated the man as much as he feared him. He threw the lives of his men away like chess pieces, sacrificing the pawns to ensure the completion of the mission. If it wasn't for the Special-Ops goons that backed up his commands, Steve knew the squadron would have taken control long ago. It didn't matter that the man was his father. Steve Blackmore had seen enough of 'Dad' in action to know he was a bastard, unstable and unfit for command.

With a 'tut' of disgust for his son's lack of backbone, Staff Sargent Graham Blackmore, decided to continue on his rounds of the men on watch.

As the binoculars were dropped next to him and the heavy retreating footsteps of his commanding officer left him alone in the darkness, Private Steven Blackmore of the Queens Dragoon Guards third squadron gave his cold fingers one last warming breath before returning his attention to his rifle sight. Looking at the large stone building, he realised that whoever had chosen the old Convent for a home had certainly chosen wisely. It looked as if they had a pretty good thing going here. Much better than him and his fellow squaddies were used to, that was for sure. Well, that was all going to end for them come morning. They would move in, process the civilians and that would be that, another mission, another empty building left behind. The civilians would be rescued from their lives among the Dead.

'God help them…' Steve said quietly to himself.

DAY 2

Imran could hear them in the house. The Dead were in here somewhere, he was sure of it. He could not only hear their dry moans but also the reeking stench of decay hung heavy in the air making it difficult to breathe. Standing in a window of early morning light at the top of the large winding staircase, Imran looked down at the entrance hall of the Penhaligan home. The once grand hallway, with its checkerboard style marble floor and exquisitely carved mouldings, was now covered in years of dust and debris. A world of spiders lived out their whole existence catching well-fed flies in the webs that now claimed as their own the large central hanging chandelier. However, this decay was not what caught Imran's attention. There, scuffing their path through the thick layer of dust, were two sets of bloody footprints. As Imran placed a foot on the first stair to descend the staircase, a wave of moaning rose from below to greet him.

With his heart beating heavily in his ears, Imran fought to fill his lungs with air. With each sharp intake, he became more and more convinced the fetid odour all about him was coating his mouth and tongue with a putrid layer of death. Taking another two steps down, again, Imran fought to catch his breath. It seemed that the further he descended the less breathable air there was. Death had somehow removed the life giving oxygen from this house and replaced it with little more than vapours from an open grave.

Reaching for the banister to steady himself, Imran gulped for air uncontrollably. Somewhere in the back of his mind, Imran knew he should fight to slow his breathing. If he hyperventilated and passed out, he would plunge blindly down the staircase to the dead that surely waited for him below. Managing to calm himself slightly, Imran reached behind him for his bow. In shock, his hand grasped nothing but air and came back empty. With his bow inexplicably gone, Imran could feel the panic rising again, threatening to overwhelm him completely this time. Then, as if to show his own body that he was its master, he clenched his fists tightly until his fingernails began to dig sharply into his palms. He concentrated on this pain to block out all else that his body was forcing upon itself. He willed his breathing to slow and the panic began to subside.

Once he was calm again, he reached down and pulled a large knife from the sheath tied about his ankle. At least now, he wasn't defenceless. Step by step, he forced his feet to move, each pace taking him closer to the Dead somewhere below him. After what seemed like an eternity, his foot finally touched upon one of the dusty marble tiles sending a multitude of spiders and other insects scurrying into the shadows. Now that he was on the ground floor, the moaning of the Dead was louder and interspersed with a strange knocking sound. Hoping that, perhaps the Dead were somehow trapped, Imran scanned the large hallway for danger. With nothing here but the dusty remnants of a world long gone, he knew he would have to follow the trail of bloody footprints to reach his quarry and readied himself for the inevitable attack that was to come. Placing one foot in front of the other, he cautiously mirrored the path the Dead had taken. As the stairs began to rise up to the first landing on this right, the bloody trail led to the archway created beneath them. Imran suddenly stopped, not understanding what he was seeing. The footprints of the two Dead corpses that had been a clear path to follow seemed to stop abruptly, midway through the arch.

'What?' He managed to whisper, not understanding how the Dead could simply manage to disappear.

It was then that a frantic knocking sound demanded his attention. Slowly he looked upwards to the source of the sound. There, banging furiously against the wall supporting the grand staircase's ascent, were two sets of bloody and cracked feet. Reluctant to draw his gaze away from the dark smears each foot was leaving behind with each jerking movement, Imran knew he had to look upwards at the two Dead men hanging above him. Slowly, bloody feet became gore encrusted trousers, then the torn and ripped flesh of torso's came into view, until finally the two gaunt but recognisable Dead faces were looking down to meet his gaze.

'No...,' Imran said, taking the smallest of steps backward, as the shock made stars dance at the corners of his vision.

There, with nooses about each of their necks were Phil and Duncan. Someone had strung up their Dead corpses. The hangman's ropes had been tied to the bannister high above them but even now, Imran could hear the splintering of wood as it strained to support their weight. Excited by Imran's living presence they began to reach desperately down to the flesh they so craved to consume. With the frenzy now upon them, the two Dead men kicked wildly to release themselves; each movement straining and cracking the wood that held them in place. Then, as Imran looked up at the two Dead men that had been his friends, they seemed to go strangely still and in unison, their Dead mouths slowly opened but instead of the usual moan escaping their bloody lips, just one hissed cold word drifted down to Imran.

'Ssssorry!'

Then with a loud snap, the banister holding them broke and the two Dead men plummeted down towards him, snapping and snarling for the Imran's flesh.

'No!' Imran screamed, his hands flying up to protect himself, but instead of being seconds from death, he found himself sitting upright on the floor of the room they had chosen to spend the night.

Opposite him was sitting Phil, a startled expression on his face.

'Jesus! You made me jump!' said Phil, 'Bad dream by any chance?'

'Ermm, what? Yeah, sorry,' Imran managed to say, his heart still racing wildly in his chest, as he reached down to calm a furiously barking Toby.

Imran rubbed his face to clear the last images of his dream from his mind.

'Where's Duncan?' Imran asked, untangling himself from his blanket.

'Gone for a piss,' Phil replied, as he took Imran's blanket from him, neatly folded it and placed it with the others.

'Could use one, myself…,' Imran began to say but at that moment, the door was knocked forcibly open.

'What? What is it?' Duncan said, hobbling into the room, swinging a length of pipe in front of him, while his trousers and underwear hovered just above his knees.

'Look, I like you just as a friend, Duncan, okay?' chuckled Phil, laughing as he glanced at the half naked man.

'Fuck! I thought you were getting eaten in here,' said Duncan, putting the pipe down so he could pull up his clothes, 'I heard Imran shout and came running.'

'Sorry,' Imran said, smiling, as the flustered and slightly embarrassed Duncan finally tucked in his shirt, 'Bad dream, that's all, but thanks anyway.'

Late last evening, just as the falling snow had decided to do its best to become a blizzard, they had arrived at the manor house the Penhaligans had once made their home. As the Penhaligans had never had a horse, there was no stable or shed large enough that could offer protection from the elements for Delilah. So, after drawing the cart within a metre of the wall of the house, Phil had used some lengths of wood and a tarpaulin, to rig a cover for the poor beast. Imran had hoped there would be survivors from the Substation there to greet them, but as they searched room after empty room of the Penhaligan home, he soon realised either survivors had not made it this far yet or they were trapped somewhere in the Substation compound, awaiting rescue. Of course, there was always the third option. That nothing but the Dead awaited them at the pylon.

'How deep is the snow outside?' Imran asked, taking a chunk of grainy bread from the supply sack.

The light coming through the window told him the snow had settled last night without him even having to look and they could probably expect more that day. The weak morning sun reflecting up off the blanket of snow had a certain un-definable quality to it, somehow flat and harsh, yet still holding a hidden beauty within it.

'Like the flash from a polished blade,' Imran thought to himself, as he pushed aside the dusty old curtains.

The exposed pane of glass that met him was covered in a thin sheet of ice, swirling in amazing patterns across its surface. Leaning forward, Imran breathed warm air onto a patch and began to rub away the ice with his hand. Outside, he could already see the first few flakes drifting slowly down from the heavy-laden clouds above. The coverage, at only ten or so centimetres, wasn't as deep as he had first feared. Their journey to the Substation would be slow but manageable. Roads could be difficult enough to travel at the best of times now and a deep snowfall would make it almost impossible to manoeuvre through the myriad of hidden obstacles.

'Oh, it doesn't look too bad out there,' Imran said, turning back to his travelling companions, 'Give me a few minutes for a leak and we'll pack up.'

'Okay,' said Phil, throwing the supply sack over his shoulder, 'I'll go give Delilah a bit of a walk around to warm her muscles up. I've already given her some warm mash so she's got something warm inside her.'

'There's a bucket in the bathroom three doors down,' Duncan called after Imran, as he disappeared down the hallway. 'Oh, there's an old telephone directory someone's left hidden down the side of the bath in case you need more than a piss,' he called after him.

'Thanks.' Imran waved back, entering the room that had once been a proper bathroom.

Now the bath, toilet and sink shaped blocks of porcelain only hinted at a once practical use. Unlike Lanherne, the Penhaligans hadn't had the luxury of a nearby stream or Duncan's expertise to ensure a constant water supply so these items had become little more than defunct shapes taking up room. What passed for the actual bathroom now was little more than just the commode bucket and a barrel of water.

'*Oh, and the hidden directory for toilet paper,*' Imran thought, smiling as he reached gleefully for the thin printed pages. What he wouldn't give for a proper roll of toilet paper, but as least this was the next best thing.

Five minutes later, Imran was climbing down the rope ladder from the first floor window to join Duncan and Phil outside.

'Just a few more minutes and she'll be set to go,' Phil said, patting Delilah's neck as she snorted large plumes of fogging breath from her nostrils.

'Well, I've checked things out back and from the look of things someone's been here recently doing a bit of harvesting,' said Duncan, putting the last of the blankets into the cart. 'So you never know. Some of them might have not been there when the electricity shot through.'

'Hmm, well let's hope so,' Phil added, buckling Delilah into her tack.

As Imran stood up on the side plate to get into the cart he looked up at the big house that had been their haven for the night. Even in the summer, he thought this would still be a cold and lonely place. An abandoned shell devoid of both life and hope, it would now be forever haunted by the ghosts of its past. It had become little more than a testament as to how fragile life now was. One day, a loving family had lived and blossomed here, the next, their lives taken away in the blink of an eye by the insanity of man, who would then ultimately bring death and loss the corridors of Lanherne. He hoped when they got to the Substation they didn't find a similar situation there.

'Come on then, let's get this party started. Toby! In!' Phil called to the puppy who had been snuffling playfully around in the small snowdrifts.

'We should be there in a few hours, if we're lucky,' he continued, pushing Delilah's reins back through the front slit into the cart.

'Yes, but who or what will we find?' Imran thought to himself, pulling closed the side hatch and taking up Delilah's reins again.

With a flick and a clicking sound from Imran, Delilah began to walk slowly forward along the winding driveway, away from the building the Penhaligans had once called home and on towards the unknown.

***

With the clear cold light of morning coming through the small high window, Liz pushed aside her heavy blankets with a weary sigh. What with missing Imran's comforting presence beside her and a combination of the cold and the baby kicking for much of the night, she had not had much of a refreshing night's sleep. Pulling her big baggy jumper down over her hands for warmth, Liz swung her thickly socked feet off the bed and down onto the worn rug that covered the otherwise cold stone floor. Like everyone in the Convent, Liz slept fully clothed, it was simply far too cold not to. Of course, it didn't help that it was snowing again outside. Lanherne might well have proven to be an impenetrable home in which they could live their lives in relative comfort and safety, but it was damn cold.

Even though it was early, she could already hear her sister talking in the next cell. From the muffled rise and fall of her voice, Liz could tell she was reading a story to Jimmy and Samantha with whom she now shared a room. Anne had fallen into the role of 'big sister' to the two rescued siblings and was relishing her new role of responsibility. Like everyone, Anne had been forced to grow up fast. Childish dependency was simply a thing of the past. Even the youngest of the children would be expected to pull their weight and do whatever they could to help keep their community alive. No matter how small their help, a contribution was expected. Anne had made some of their chores into games for her younger charges. Collecting eggs each morning was transformed into a fun egg hunt, while helping Bryon in the poly-tunnel became a competition as to who could find the most weeds or caterpillars. Liz hated the fact that the Dead had robbed Anne of a proper childhood. Even though she was only eight, she had seen too much death and suffering in her short life. It seemed no sooner had she made room in her small heart for someone, than they were snatched from her by the hands of the Dead. She had lost people she considered friends to the Dead but none of her small 'family' until Charlie, that is. It had taken Anne a long time to let go of Charlie finally and even now, Liz would catch her having a quiet cry when she thought no one was looking. Charlie had been the only father figure Anne had ever really known and with Liz and Imran with her, she had been spared the loss that each and every survivor had been forced to endure. However, that had changed and Liz knew Anne now understood the terrible pain that hid behind the eyes of all those she met.

With her stomach growling for attention, Liz put on her boots. Unable to reach down to tie up her laces, she left them loose, pushed herself slowly up from the bed and wrapped a shawl about her shoulders. As she passed Anne's room, she gave the door a quick knock.

'Jimmy, Samantha, Anne,' she whispered, not wanting to wake anyone else that might be asleep. 'Are you coming down for breakfast?'

With the sound of the bolt sliding across the frame, the door creaked open a crack.

'We'll be down in a minute, Aunty Liz,' Jimmy answered, peeping through the gap. 'Anne is telling us a story.'

'Oh, okay,' Liz said, smiling down at the child, 'Don't forget to wrap up warm, because it'll be cold out today.'

'We will,' came the trio of children's voice from inside, the door abruptly closing in front of Liz.

Within seconds, Anne resumed her story, gaining squeals of delight and giggles from her enraptured younger audience. Knowing there would be warm porridge awaiting them in the kitchen, Liz assumed the story would suddenly become a condensed version. Anne had lived too much of her life on a near starvation diet to pass up the opportunity of a full warm belly for long.

Liz left the children to their story, trusting Anne not to dawdle for too long. There were chores to be done after all. Making her way down to the kitchen and the warmth it promised, her breath lightly fogged in the chill of the stone corridors. Passing one of the tall thin windows by the staircase, Liz looked out over their snow covered home. She could see on the walkway the thickly bundled up figures of Sally and Damian. Damian, as always, found other things to do rather than the watch duty that was meant to be occupying his time. Flapping his arms about and stamping his feet through the layer of snow along the walkway, the one place Damian wasn't looking was over the wall. At least Sally wasn't shirking her responsibilities and ignoring the antics of her 'on again, off again lover'. She seemed to be watching something at the far end of the lane. Motherhood had stripped Sally of her pointless vanity and her attentions were no longer something she used as a commodity to gain favour with men. Now Alex was the centre of her world and just like the wildcat protecting its kittens, she would do anything to make sure he was safe. Truth be told, before Alex, Liz had found Sally to be a bit of a sad person. Sally had been a woman who used her body to ingratiate herself with the men around her so she could gain power by association. Not that she blamed her for that, you had to get by how you could now and Lanherne was certainly an exception rather than the rule when it came to how women were treated in this new world.

Taking care not to trip on her bootlaces as she walked, Liz decided she had to ignore the protests of her stomach for a few minutes more, because her bladder simply would not wait. Entering the bathroom that had been put aside for the women, she was pleasantly surprised to see someone, probably one of the sisters, had lit a small fire in the grate to take the chill of the room. Dipping a bucket into a large barrel of water,

Liz waddled with it into one of the stalls. Imran would be mad if he saw her doing this on her own.

'*needs must*', she thought to herself, placing one foot after another up onto the small steps by the side of the toilet bowl.

Slowly, she began to lift the bucket up over her head so she could fill the cistern. They had been lucky at Lanherne; she doubted there were many places left that still had working drains. Thanks to Duncan's monthly trips down into the old Victorian sewers, they had been able to maintain this last bastion of the old civilised world, though Duncan had warned them it might not last much longer. Liz certainly wasn't looking forward to that day. She had lived in places with open cesspits before and they were far from fun. As the last of the water fell from her bucket, she heard the door opening behind her.

'Busted!' came Alice's voice. 'Just what would Imran say if he heard you've been climbing ladders?'

'Ladder?' Liz asked, smiling as she looked over her shoulder. 'It's two steps, Alice.'

'Yes, well, I'll have to think what you can do for me to buy my silence,' Alice replied, giving Liz a grin and a wink, as she filled a bucket of her own. 'Don't tell Phil.'

After the two pregnant women had finished, they replaced the now empty buckets on their hooks and left for the porridge that awaited them. They would have a wash later when they had collected some of the warmed water that was perpetually sitting on the range, heating. Walking though the kitchen door, they were met by a wall of warmth. Nicky was helping Sister Rebecca and Sister Claire with the breakfast while Justin helped his father put out the bowls and cutlery. During the cold weather, they always ate in here rather than the roomy refectory. Despite there being a few too many residents at Lanherne to sit comfortably around the large kitchen table, the warmth from the range made up for a bit of squashing. At first, Liz didn't even notice William slumped in a chair in the corner, dozing. He had been unlucky enough to be on night watch last night and had to cocoon himself in multiple layers of coats and jumpers to keep out the chill night air. Looking now more like a pile of rumpled coats than a man, William began to snore softly.

'Should I wake him, do you think?' Sister Rebecca asked, looking over from the large pot she was stirring. 'He'll only get a sore neck sleeping like that.'

'Bill,' Richard said, softly shaking the man awake, 'You have something to eat and get yourself to bed, man. You're dead on your feet.'

With a large yawn and a stretch, William stirred himself from his slumber.

'Sorry… was I snoring?' He asked looking around the room, while he rubbed eyes, 'I must've walked for miles around that walkway last night just to keep warm. Well, at least there was no sign of any of the Dead, so that's something.'

'And we thank you for your diligence, William,' Sister Claire said, thrusting a steaming bowl with a spoon into his hands. 'Now, eat.'

He didn't need to be told twice and gratefully began to spoon down the warm meal.

'Got any of that for me?' Cam asked, walking into the kitchen, combing through his damp hair.

'You know the rules,' Sister Rebecca said, nodding to the large empty pan on the floor.

Cam had just used some of the warmed water for a brisk shower so now it was time for him to pump the replacement water for heating. Dropping his comb in his back pocket, Cam moved to the pump that Duncan had rigged up for them at the sink. Via a series of pipes and hosing, they would collect water from the nearby stream without leaving the Convent. Of course, they would double boil the collected water first to kill off any of the bacteria that might be present. Only after it had been boiled twice was it then poured into the large barrel in the corner for storage.

'Looks like we might have a bit of a problem here,' Cam said, being rewarded with just a thin trickle of water after three pumps of the handle. 'Perhaps the stream or the pipes are frozen.'

'Well, looks like we'll be melting snow for water until Duncan comes back and checks it out,' Sister Rebecca said, looking at the pump as if it was somehow to blame. 'If you could just refill the pan for now, Cam, that'll be fine.'

With a nod, Cam took an empty pan over to the barrel and turning the small spigot tap, began filling the pan with the already boiled twice water for heating.

'We've got enough to last us today and tomorrow at least,' said Cam, pulling aside the barrel cover to check the water level inside.

'Well, if you want, Richard and I can collect snow this morning. It shouldn't take long to fill the reserve barrel,' said Nicky to Sister Rebecca.

'Thanks,' replied the Sister. 'I was going to say, it would be better if the children didn't get involved with this. We want clean snow with as little of it that has come in contact with the ground as possible.'

'Skimming off the top layers,' Richard said, 'no problem. Justin and Anne can move some of the woodpile into the store after they've dealt with the animals instead.'

Cam lifted the heavy pan over to the large range for heating and received a bowl of thick warm porridge for his efforts.

'Thanks,' he said, taking the bowl and reaching for a jar of deep golden honey.

With a flurry of activity, Sister Josephine and Penny came into the kitchen with all of the children of Lanherne in tow. Penny was holding Danny in one arm, waving a bright blue ball to get the child's wandering attention. She was trying to coax the silent child to say 'ball' but was having little success.

'Good morning, everyone,' Sister Josephine said, raising her voice over the chatter of the four talkative children.

Justin paused in his animated conversation to go over to Nicky quickly, giving her a quick peck on the cheek, as Richard affectionately ruffled his hair.

As Sister Josephine looked around the now crowded kitchen, she smiled to herself. She knew now that this was why she had been called to serve God all those years ago. His plan had been convoluted and the path had been troubled, but He had seen fit to spare these souls and send them to her door. It warmed her heart that life could still flourish in this world of the Dead and if her only service to Him were to offer sanctuary to those that needed it then she would do so gladly until her days ended and she was called to Him.

'Where's Alex?' Liz asked Sister Josephine, noticing the little boy was missing from the gaggle of children.

'Sally has already fed him and dropped him in with Nadine before she relieved Cam and William,' Sister Josephine replied.

'Oh, right, very efficient,' Liz said, raising her eyebrows, 'Motherhood suits somebody alright. Hope I'm going to be that organised when this one comes.'

'Now don't you worry, you'll be fine,' said Nicky. 'You'll be a mess, question everything you do and cry a lot, but I'm sure you'll be fine.'

'Thanks,' Liz said, taken aback a bit.

'No, what I mean is that's how it is for every mother with a baby, and don't worry, we'll all be here to judge your mothering skills and talk about you behind your back,' Nicky added jokingly. 'Sally's just been lucky. She's skipped the screaming, poo-ing, not sleeping baby stage and gone straight to fun little boy stage.'

'Oh, that's alright then,' said Liz.

'Does Bryon need any help in the Poly tunnels today?' Liz asked, feeling that her current physical state made her somewhat of a burden on the group.

'No, you and Alice need to take it easy,' Nicky said, passing the two women their porridge. 'We can't have you falling over on the frozen mud. It's not worth the risk.'

'We're pregnant, not invalids,' said Alice.

'No, Nicky's right,' added Sister Josephine. 'We'll just have to find you something inside to occupy your time.'

'Well, one of you can help me with preparing dinner for tonight and there's bread to make too,' Sister Rebecca said, ticking through the short list of things she felt comfortable asking the pregnant women to do.

'Oh, I'll help you with that, Sister,' Alice quickly said, knowing it was this or trying her hand at knitting again and she knew she had neither the skill nor the patience to tackle it with any enthusiasm.

'Traitor,' whispered Liz, under her breath to her friend.

'I know, why don't you make an inventory of the clothes store,' Sister Rebecca continued, 'It's been a while since it was last done and you never know you might find some jumpers to unravel or even some baby clothes.'

An uneasy silence fell upon the kitchen. The clothing store was one of the attic rooms where they kept all of the clothing they had scavenged on their trips. Coats, dresses, trousers, tee shirts, shoes, anything they could find that had been left abandoned in long forgotten wardrobes or drawers. They took every scrap of it. Any clothing they had was going to have to last them a long time, manufacturing fabric without the help of sheep was an impossible task even Duncan couldn't overcome. Mention of the baby clothes was what set everyone thinking. They would be the clothes of a long dead child, snatched from their mothers and torn apart by Dead hands. By their very presence in the attic, the garments indicated what fate had befallen their brief owners.

'Okay,' Liz finally said, pouring herself a large mug of rosehip tea. 'What I'll do is separate all the children's clothes from the piles and arrange them in sizes. At least then as the kids grow, we'll know what we've got available for them to grow into.'

'Good idea,' said Sister Josephine, ruffling the silent Danny's hair sitting on Penny's lap. 'The little ones will be growing fast.'

Ten minutes later, leaving the noisy warm kitchen behind her with a clip board, paper and a pencil tucked under her arm, Liz made her way up to the attic room they had put aside for the clothing store. With the sound of her boots echoing off the cold stone walls, she annoyingly readjusted the strap to her sword for what seemed like the hundredth time. The strap that had once fit snugly over her small taut frame had to be lengthened considerably since pregnancy had changed her body beyond what she thought possible. By the time she had managed to place the strap so that it didn't rub uncomfortably or dig into her, she had already gotten to the small door that would lead up to the attic.

'Damn,' she said to herself, pushing on the door handle.

With a forceful shove or two, the warped door finally jolted open inwards. In a building as old as Lanherne, it was to be expected but what concerned Liz was that this area definitely had the distinct smell of damp hanging in the air. She would have to tell Sister Rebecca they needed to find another place to store the clothing if they wanted to keep it for any length of time. They simply couldn't afford to lose their precious fabric to mould.

Leaving the door ajar to let some fresh airflow through, Liz took a deep breath and began to climb the small winding staircase up into the attic. After cursing her body for having to rely half way up on the banister for support, she finally reached the top of the staircase a little out of breath.

'Right,' Liz said, taking in the mounds of boxes jammed into the small dark room.

Outside, the cold wind buffeted against the old roof tiles creating a constant whistle and low moan as it sought to find a way in. She realised the promise of a warming fire in the tiny fireplace was quite out of the question. The room was simply too full to risk a stray ember.

'*Well*,' Liz thought to herself, '*I might not be able to have heat but I don't see why I have to work in this half light.*'

With barely enough room for her to guide her protruding belly around the boxes, Liz quickly began squeezing herself through to get to the single window set into the roof eaves. After much huffing and puffing and a particularly undignified clamber across the top of a large box, she finally managed to get to her goal. Using the back of her sleeve, she wiped away months of dust and cobwebs from the small planes of leaded glass sending a few startled spiders scurrying off into the shadows in the process. When she had finally removed as much of the grime that would come off, the small window filled the room with a soft cold light. Liz hoped cleaning the window would help lift the sad atmosphere of the musty smelling room but with the overcast sky outside doing its best release more of the snow they had had during the night, it didn't have much effect.

Liz looked out of the small leaded window, down to the courtyard far below her. Smiling, she could see Justin and Anne taking charge of the other children, showing them which logs from the pile they could carry inside. Glancing over to the walkway, the smile fell from her lips as Liz's dark eyebrows creased together in concern. There, on the walkway, running towards the gate section was Sally. She was shouting something and waving her arms at Damian, who was positioned by the gate.

'No, No, No...' Liz found herself saying, her heart beginning to pound in her chest.

Even from here, Liz could tell the outer gate was already open and for some insane reason, Damian was also opening the inner gate. The whole point of their two gates was to prevent the convent from being openly exposed to the Dead forever at the walls. Once that inner gate was open, those in the courtyard would be in danger. Scenes of the terrified children below her being torn to pieces before anyone could save them, flashed in her mind. Frantically, she began to bang at the small handle locking the window closed.

'Come on, come on,' she said, with increasing urgency, as she banged her palm painfully against the latch to release it. 'Come on! Fuck!'

With a snap and a low 'thud', the latch slipped downwards, opening the window.

Frantically pushing open the window, Liz took a sharp intake of breath, readying herself to scream down to Anne and the other children. However, what she saw rolling through the gate stopped any sound that she was going to make abruptly in her throat. There, arriving in a convoy of noise, hard metal, camouflage paintwork and exhaust fumes, where four heavily armoured large army vehicles. Tearing her gaze from these metal monsters from another time, Liz glanced down at the children in the courtyard. The stunned children had already begun to draw close to Justin and Anne slowly, scared of the strange machines before them. As she watched, Sally practically threw herself down from the walkway ladder and ran over to the scared group of children, putting her between whatever Damian had let into their home and them.

Even as she watched, Sally raised her club in defence of the children behind her. Side doors on two of the armoured vehicles slid open and soldiers in combat gear poured out, positioning themselves in an arc with their rifles cocked and aimed.

'Shit!' Liz said, the howling wind stealing the word from her lips, as it whipped her short hair across her face.

She had seen enough and she knew she needed to get down there as soon as possible. Turning away from her position in front of the window, she realised her mistake almost immediately. She had now given the wind what it wanted, a way in. With a slam, the door at the bottom of the staircase was blown shut.

'Fuck!' Liz snapped, pushing herself back across the boxes to the door that she prayed she would be able to open again.

Then, as a single shot rang out from the courtyard below, Liz froze. After what seemed like an eternity, she collapsed onto a pile of old coats, her hands instinctively moving to cover her unborn child. She knew even if she did get the door open, everything had changed. The world they had created behind the safe walls of Lanherne was gone and it scared the hell out of her.

***

Patrick looked down at the woman he held lightly in his arms as she slept fitfully. Nameless horrors had stalked her dreams much of the night causing her to call out his name as she fought against the terrors that danced behind her eyelids. Each time she said his name, Patrick would stroke her face, hoping his love would somehow break through her dreams and bring her back to him. At first, they tried to keep Helen awake for as long as possible, afraid her head wound was worse than they feared, but thankfully simple natural exhaustion had eventually taken its toll on her late into the night and she finally drifted off into a fitful but natural sleep.

Touching her cheek again, Patrick glanced up from the face of the woman he loved and then over to see Sarah holding in her arms the other girl in his life that he would die for, Jasmine. It had been cold in the stable that night and each of them had made the best of the limited resources they could find. Horse blankets, sacks and even an old tarpaulin had been used to trap their precious body heat. The remaining mare, Flo, and the one sow with her four piglets, which had luckily been inside when the disaster struck, had added their body warmth to the stable but even so, it had been a far from comfortable night.

'How is she?' Sarah whispered through the dimly light stable, as she nodded towards Helen.

'She's fine, apart from the splitting headache,' came Helen's voice, as she slowly raised her hand to touch the back of her head.

'Welcome back,' Patrick said, relief flooding his voice, 'Thought we'd lost you then.'

'It'll take a bit more than almost being electrocuted and falling fifteen metres to get rid of me,' Helen mumbled, her brittle smile cracking when she tried to sit upright. 'Ouch'

'Hey, just take it easy,' Patrick said, gently trying to push her back down to stop her from moving too fast.

'Easy is not going to get us out of this,' Helen replied, easing away Patrick's concern to force herself slowly into an upright position.

'She's right,' came J-Man's voice from the other end of the stable.

He and Leon were standing on some crates, straining to look through the long high window at the Dead just outside the door. Their hungry jailers had wound down in their ferocity during the night, but still, they pounded relentlessly against the door to get to the living flesh they knew was being denied them.

'We've got to come up with a plan to get out of here,' he continued.

'We need to somehow draw some of them off to give us a chance when we open the doors,' Leon mused, biting on his thumbnail to help him think.

'Hmm… any ideas?' Patrick asked.

One by one, he was met with blank expressions. Ideas, it seemed, were thin on the ground today. With the window too thin for anyone to fit through, they knew their only option was the main door but with so many of the Dead eager to get in, they would be swamped before any of them had a chance to get out.

'Bollocks!' Patrick growled, realising their only option was really no option at all.

***

Above them, Gabe and Chloe sat huddled down with their heads together in one corner of the flat roof. A dusting of snow rested on their still heads and shoulders. If it wasn't for the soft plumes of their fogging breath rising slowly above them, they could easily be mistaken for statues, they were so motionless. They had walked back and forth across the roof for hours, trying to keep warm but the biting wind, whipping across the exposed roof stole any heat they could generate. They had finally decided to wedge themselves in one of the corners. At least there, the high lip that ran the perimeter of the roof would offer them some relief from the wind.

'We need to move, Chloe,' Gabe whispered to the cold face, so close to his own, 'If we sit here much longer, we'll freeze to death.'

When he got no reply, he gave her a gentle nudge and prayed to God, she hadn't fallen asleep. If she had, hypothermia might have taken her from him and he would have to get rid of her before she came back.

'Chloe?' He repeated, his apprehension creeping into the word.

'It's… it's alright, G…Gabe,' she finally replied, trying to form the words through her numb cold lips and chattering teeth, 'I… I don't want to d…die here, Gabe.'

'Right then, get up,' Gabe said, pulling her stiff body up from the roof.

Grabbing hold of her hands, he began to pull her arms up and down in front of her.

'Now, jump,' he continued, showing her what he wanted her to do.

Now that the biting wind had died down and the sun was adding its appreciated, if weak warmth to the sky, their frantic jerky movements soon managed to generate a little warmth in their stiff, cold muscles.

'Ring, a ring, a roses, a pocket full of posies,' Gabe sang out loudly, as he and Chloe did star jumps together to get warm.

Chloe began to laugh at the absurdity of it all. There they were singing nursery rhymes and jumping about like idiots, while a couple of metres away, the Dead pawed the walls for their very flesh. Her laugh was infectious and soon, Gabe too was laughing, as he clapped his hands over his head in time to the tune.

'Gabe!' shouted a voice from nowhere.

Immediately, the pair stopped. With their panting breath pluming in the cold early morning air and their cheeks flushed, they looked at each other. Each hoped they hadn't imagined it.

'Gabe!' Shouted the voice again. This time, they could tell it came from beneath them. 'Gabe, are you there?'

'Leon?' Gabe cautiously said into the air.

'Oh, thank God,' Leon replied, 'Thank God you're okay... and who's with you?'

'Chloe,' Chloe added, rushing to the side of the roof, 'It's Chloe. Leon, is anyone with you? Did anyone else make it?'

They could hear Leon mumbling to someone else in the stable, so Gabe and Chloe knew he wasn't alone.

'Yes, there's me, J-Man, Sarah, Helen and the baby too,' came Patrick's voice replacing Leon's through the narrow window beneath them.

Chloe and Gabe looked at each other, hope blooming in their eyes. Patrick had looked after them, he would save them now; they were sure of it.

'Gabe, we need a diversion to get some of the Dead away from the door,' said Patrick. 'It's a lot to ask, son... Gabe?'

Gabe silently peered over the lip of the roof to the Dead below, waiting for their opportunity to feed. Then, standing, he gazed over at the fence where at least a dozen the Dead had arrived, drawn by the hungry moans of their Dead brothers and sisters. He then slowly walked a complete circuit of the stable roof, looking over the edge on each side. Bit by bit, a plan was taking form in his mind.

'It'll be tricky,' Gabe finally called down to Patrick.

Chloe looked into Gabe's eyes, slowly shaking her head, guessing what he was planning to do.

'No, Gabe, you can't,' Chloe said flatly.

She knew before the words were even said that Gabe had made up his mind.

'I have to, Chloe,' Gabe said, taking her cold hands in his own. 'We don't stand a chance without the others, even if we do get off of here, you know that.'

Chloe snapped her hands angrily away from his, tears pricking at the corners of her eyes.

'You don't have to,' she said quietly, though as she said it, she knew there was no truth behind the words.

Their options were limited and she knew it.

'Just don't get yourself killed, okay,' she finally said, looking back up into Gabe's face.

'They won't get the chance,' Gabe said, forcing a smile.

'Patrick!' Gabe called down. Now that he had the plan sorted in his head, he just wanted to get it over with, 'I'm going to lower myself down off the roof, run like crazy to get to the fence and climb it. Chloe can then give you the heads up, when enough of them have moved away to follow me. How's that for a plan?'

After some more mumbled talking from within, it was agreed that this was their best chance.

'Ready?' Gabe said to Chloe.

With a sad nod, Chloe began to shout and holler, as she waved her arms over the edge of the roof. They were well out of reach of the Dead hands below, but it distracted and enticed them long enough for Gabe to begin lowering himself down one of the other sides without getting his legs chewed on. Hanging from his fingertips, Gabe panted as the adrenalin coursed through his small body. Glancing down, he knew he should be able to make the last two metre drop easily. Then out of the corner of his eye, he caught movement. One of the more badly burnt Dead had been slow to react to Chloe's calls from above and had been rewarded with Gabe for its diligence. Fixing its Dead gaze upon the living meat lowering itself into view, the burnt corpse began to shuffle towards its prize.

'Shit!' said Gabe, his fingers slipping from the roof edge, dropping him to the ground below.

As he landed, his right foot twisted and collapsed beneath him, a blast of pain shooting up his leg.

'Fuck!' shouted Gabe, reaching for his ankle and praying that it wasn't broken.

Broken or not, he knew he had to get moving. Already some of the other Dead had noticed their burnt brother's moans and had begun turning in his direction.

'Fuck!' said Gabe, using the wall to pull himself upright as he tested a fraction of his weight on his ankle.

Again, pain shot up his leg but he knew he would have to ignore it if he wanted to live. With a thrust, he pushed himself away from the wall. Already the burnt cadaver was reaching for him, its blackened crispy skin cracking with each movement revealing its dark bloody flesh beneath. Hobbling away from the wall at a lot slower pace than he would have liked, Gabe ducked under the waving burnt arms only to be confronted by a Dead woman less than a metre in front of him.

'Shit,' he said to himself, quickly changing his direction as she reached her blood covered hands towards him.

With a brief glance up to the roof, he could see Chloe still shouting to distract the Dead but his very presence meant more and more of them were beginning to ignore her. One by one, the Dead had turned away from the stable and focused their cannibalistic hunger upon Gabe. Ducking out of reach of another of the Dead, Gabe began to hobble painfully slowly to the fence. With each step, excruciating pain would blossom in his ankle causing his breath to falter but it was by far the lesser of two evils. If the Dead caught up with him, he would soon know pain beyond belief.

Chloe watched from above as Gabe began to make his way to the fence. He was limping terribly and already the Dead were only a few paces behind him. Tearing her eyes away from him to check the door of the stable, she could see there were still four of the creatures lingering, perhaps the memory of the escaping flesh hiding within too strong for them to give up on. A sudden cry from Gabe tore her attention back away from the door; he was on the ground. Chloe screamed.

'Patrick! NOW!' she yelled, panic making her dig her fingers into the concrete of the roof lip so hard three of her finger nails split and bent backwards.

Unaware of the blood pouring from her fingers, Chloe watched in horror as two of the Dead stood over Gabe, their arms and bodies already covered in last night's congealed stolen blood. Below her, J-Man, Leon and Patrick charged out through the metal stable door and immediately began to hack and club at the hungry cadavers in their path. One by one, the Dead fell under their swift powerful blows but Chloe knew they would never reach Gabe in time to save him. She watched as Gabe kicked desperately at the Dead man looming over him, knocking him backwards slightly only for the second corpse to reach forwards to take its place.

Gabe looked up at the creature above him and screamed. The spasm of pain that had caused him to slip in the icy mud would be miniscule in comparison to what he was about to experience. He prayed he would leave this dead world before he was forced to watch his organs being ripped out, handful-by-handful to be stuffed into the hungry mouths around him. At that moment, the animated corpse threw itself down onto Gabe, a frenzy taking hold of it now that living flesh was so near. Instinctively, Gabe raised his arms to keep some life-saving distance between himself and the snapping jaws so keen to rip into his flesh. However, his hands could find no purchase on the gore covered cadaver and they slipped about the beast's shoulders and chest. Eventually, born more of luck than skill, one of Gabe's hands slipped upwards and grabbing his only chance, Gabe gripped the Dead man just under the chin. But even this action was ultimately pointless because over the struggling and snapping creature's shoulder Gabe could see another of the Dead almost within reach and behind that, another three. His time had come to an end. Instantly, his focus returned to the burnt and torn face, merely centimetres from his own. He looked past the snapping and snarling mouth that housed filthy and broken blood covered teeth, past the torn cavity, where the nose should have been and up into the milky, blind eyes of this Dead thing that would end his life. He wondered if this thing, that up until yesterday had been a friend, knew that he would be an instrument of his death or was the outcome purely incidental. This thing's teeth would soon become his father and his mother and just like his real birth, he would enter his death and new un-life terrified, screaming and bloody.

Then, almost instantly, the Dead man on top of him stopped, inexplicably frozen in his frenzy. It wasn't until Gabe could tear his eyes away from the strangely still face that he could see the long arrow lodged deep in the Dead man's head. With an effort, he managed to push the cadaver off of him just in time to see another arrow fly past his shoulder and strike the next Dead thing that had been reaching for him. Stunned, Gabe could only watch as the thing crumpled to its knees and then finally toppled face down into the cold mud. He was then snapped back to the now by the loud warrior roar coming from a huge man running past him, swinging a lethal looking club left and right as he went. The Dead fell quickly under his blows. Leaving only torn skin and shattered bone in his wake, such was Phil's skill in terminating them permanently.

'Get up, Gabe!' Came a voice from above him.

Looking up, Gabe could see Imran's calm face taking in every detail of the battle with his bow taut and ready to fire.

'Are you bitten?' Imran said, glancing briefly down at the boy in the mud.

'What?' Gabe managed to ask, a little stunned that the group from Lanherne had appeared from nowhere to come to his rescue.

'Are you bitten?' Imran repeated, raising his bow to take aim on the approaching shambling figure of a burnt Dead woman.

'No, no, I'm not bitten,' Gabe whispered, not believing his luck.

Imran let his arrow fly and within the blink of an eye, it appeared lodged in the woman's temple, killing her.

'Good,' Imran said, smoothly reaching for another arrow from the quiver on his back. 'So are you going to lie in the mud all day?'

Imran gave Gabe his hand and pulled him upright.

'Thanks,' Gabe said, resting some of his weight on Imran's shoulder.

As the last of the animated corpses fell to Phil's onslaught, the only sound drifting across the Substation compound was the heavy panting of the fighters trying to catch their breath as their bodies combated the effects of the surge of adrenalin that had been pumped through them.

'Thanks, big man,' Leon said to Phil, hacking up some phlegm to clear the taste of death from his mouth, 'God, do we owe you…'

'No problem, Leon,' Phil replied, tapping some fleshy remnants from the end of his club 'Don't tell me it's just you three left?'

'No, Helen, Jasmine and Sarah also made it. They're in the stable,' Patrick said, walking over to Phil and slapping his shoulder in thanks, 'Oh, and Chloe too, on the roof.'

Looking over to the roof, they could see a still distraught Chloe, her hands tightly gripping the lip of the roof. Where her fingers curled onto the concrete streams of blood from her split fingernails had run down, staining the grey wall.

'Better get her down from there,' J-Man said, walking over to the stable.

'No,' Patrick and Phil said in unison.

'First, we check the rest of the compound,' Patrick said with a nod at Phil, knowing that was what he was going to suggest too.

'Absolutely,' Phil added, smiling, 'But if I were you, I might let the Mrs in there know you're okay.'

'Good idea,' Patrick smiled, running over to the closed stable door and giving it a knock.

'So how did you know?' J-Man asked the new arrivals, plonking himself down on an over turned water barrel.

'The lights flared for a few seconds at Lanherne,' Imran said, helping Gabe, hop by hop, over to join the group, 'and Duncan figured you were on a direct path from the hydro-electric plant near the coast.'

'He figures that's the most likely candidate,' Phil added, using a knife to remove a particularly wedged on scrap of scalp from between the nails on his club.

After Imran sat Gabe down by the stable, the small group began their search of the compound for any more of the Dead. They eventually found one more sorry creature pulling itself slowly along the ground, trailing its shattered limbs behind it. Its back had been crushed under the hooves of Shadow the previous evening and only the massive damage that had been inflicted upon its body had prevented it from joining its Dead brethren at the stable. Once this corpse was finally put to rest, Patrick looked up at the pylon. It had been their home for so long and it pained him that it had ultimately been the implement of their destruction.

'We're not checking up there,' Patrick said, gesturing to the pylon, 'We're not risking any more lives. We don't know if the electricity is off for good again or what? If there are any of the Dead trapped up there… tough.'

He got no arguments from the rest and as they walked over to the stable to alert Helen and Sarah, it was all over, Patrick looked up at the pylon one last time.

'You want it as a tomb then it's all yours,' he whispered.

***

Earlier that morning, Private Steven Blackmore, dressed in full combat gear, was sitting in the canteen tent with a few of his platoon, forcing himself to eat yet another unappetising MRE pack. He knew it was meant to be some sort of pasta in a rehydrated tomato sauce but as always, there was the background metallic tang of something artificial about it. It didn't help that most of the packs they had left were well past their prime and the truth was that only those packs whose contents had been freeze dried all those years ago were even edible at all now. As usual, the men kept their heads down and put up with it. They had learnt hard and fast that those mouthing off to those in charge were usually given the worst detail and in a world of the walking Dead, 'worse detail' could get you killed.

'Man, I can't wait to get back to base,' said the man sitting next to Steve, unenthusiastically with a plastic fork poking at his own MRE packet.

'Tell me about it,' Steve said turning to his friend, Private Matthew Jennings. 'Never thought I'd be looking forward to the slop we get there but this pasta tastes like shit.'

Like himself, Matthew Jennings had become a solider by situation rather than desire. Matt's mother had been one of the original doctors sequestered at the base during the initial outbreak and like all those who had been pressed into service; she took her immediate family with her; namely Matt and his sister Karen. His mother's speciality in molecular biology had seen her whisked away from her work in the pharmaceuticals lab and taken under escort to collect Matt and his sister. Apparently, Mum had had a few secrets she had been keeping from her children, namely that she had also worked for the government on some hush-hush projects; a few of them quite suspect. So when Matt's mother had turned up at his school with his sister holding her hand and armed soldiers on either side of her, he had been more than a little surprised. Scared and a little confused, Matt had left midway through his history class to follow his mother out of the classroom and out of the school, not realising that he would never see any of his classmates alive again. Within the space of an hour, a sixteen year old Matt had found himself boarding a jet with a mixed group of doctors, scientists and army personnel, and on his way to an island government base that officially didn't exist.

Like Steve, Matt and all the other children of the chosen few, soon found out their childhood was to be a brief affair and any thoughts of life returning to normal any time soon were brutally put straight by Professor Farrell and Major Carden. They were told in no uncertain terms that this was to be their life for the foreseeable future and anyone who didn't pull the line was invited to swim to shore and take their chances there. To ram the point home, they were then shown INTEL footage that was shot from a chopper, which had just flown over from the mainland. As gasps of horror filled the auditorium, the children and lucky spouses of the chosen, watched the Dead rampaging through a small town, tearing into any of the living unlucky to fall in their path. No matter how bad life was to be for them now, they would put up with it, because the alternative was beyond contemplation.

Technically, the base started out under Farrell's CDC command, but after a few mishaps involving some active Dead specimens, Major Carden had taken control with an iron fist. Using the loyal muscle of the squadrons under his command, one of which was led by Stephen's father and the three SAS men that had arrived just before all hell had broken loose, Carden had soon put Farrell in his place. From that point onward, he decreed that any children or non-essential personnel above the age of fourteen were also to be conscripted into Carden's forces. Major Carden was no simple power mad idiot though. He knew he ultimately needed Farrell and the skill of his team of scientists to find a cure or vaccine and he made it his job to make sure Farrell came up with the goods. He pushed Farrell day and night for results and he pushed him hard. As months became years and still no effective vaccine had been produced, Carden went so far as to force Farrell to push the boundaries of acceptable scientific practices. It was from that point on that something dark and savage descended upon the base. Troublemakers, the weak and anyone who rocked the boat would disappear and when strict orders were given that no unauthorised non-medical personnel were to enter the labs, it didn't take a genius to put two and two together. By the sixth year, the suicides began. They were not only restricted to the number of mentally frayed soldiers, living in fear for their lives but also among the scientific staff who could no longer cope with the things they were being forced to do in the name of research. One consolation was that, at least on the base, weapons were easy to get hold of and those who killed themselves, stayed dead. Not that Matt and his sister found much consolation in that fact, when one breezy May afternoon, one of the science team came to break the news that their mother had shot herself in the head. It was only when their numbers dwindled noticeably that Carden and Farrell decided to make the 'rescue' missions to the mainland.

For the last few rescue missions, Farrell's team had been looking for something specific among the small groups of survivors they came across. There had been hushed conversations and much consulting of scribbled notes whenever they found somewhere new. However, just what they were looking for, Steve and the rest of the squadron were kept none the wiser. Apparently, the scientists had made some sort of breakthrough and needed to test their theory. They had heard all this from them time and time again over the last seven years and still the Dead tried to eat them, so Private Steven Blackmore wasn't holding out much hope.

Suddenly with a 'beeping' sound, each of the soldiers began to receive orders through their earpieces, telling them the Convent was a 'go' situation in five minutes and they were to make last minute weapons checks prior to rescue mission Alpha-Nine commencement.

'Copy,' each of them said in turn, as they relayed receipt of their orders.

With a clattering of boots, gear and weapons, the soldiers made their way smoothly out of the canteen tent to join the rest of their squadron by the three Jackal armoured vehicles. At that moment, Farrell's right hand man, Dr Frank Morris, came scurrying out of Staff Sergeant Blackmore's tent and over to the mobile med-lab. With sheets of crumpled paper held firmly under one arm, he frantically typed data into his hand-held console. The window for their only satellite connection back to base was due shortly and Frank needed to keep Farrell up to date with any developments his field team had come up with. As the door closed behind Dr Morris, Steve caught a glimpse of the survivor they had rescued yesterday. There had originally been two of them but the man she had been travelling with had turned out not to be suitable for rescue, so now only she was to join the other seven rescued civilians in the holding truck for her journey to a new home. She was having blood samples taken by one of the doctors at the moment while another checked some figures on a computer screen. Even in the split second that their eyes locked, Steve could see the hate and sense of betrayal the woman was feeling. The man obviously must have meant something to her.

'Fuck,' Steve said to himself. 'This isn't right.'

'Shh!' Matt said in harsh whisper, his eyes flicking to the med-lab and instantly knowing what Stephen was thinking. 'You want to get yourself killed... or worse?'

'We all know what going on here, so why are we bullshitting ourselves into thinking it's something it's not,' Steve replied, checking his weapon.

'Look, I don't like it any more than you do, but what choice do we have? You want to end up like Jones?' Matt whispered, checking the magazine of his SA80 assault weapon was fully loaded.

At the mention of the name, Steve froze. What his father had done to Jones had earned him a seat in hell as far as Steven was concerned, let alone all the other bastard things he had done since.

Unlike Matt and himself, Jones had not been one of the conscripted. He had already been a soldier for a few years prior to the arrival of the Dead. He had been a professional soldier. It had been his career and that had made what he had done appear even worse in his father's eyes. Jones had been caught by Dan Hills, one of the SAS Commandos, trying to desert the squadron two weeks before with nothing but his assault rifle, some ammo and a bag of supplies to take him into a new life. He had simply had enough and he knew he had to leave or he would end up, like so many of his comrades, putting a bullet in his own head. Putting yourself before your duty was the most heinous of crimes as far as Staff Sergeant Blackmore was concerned and he meted out Jones' punishment with self-righteous justification.

'Some good old fashioned justice,' he told the men, as Jones knelt in front of the assembled squadron. 'Lance Corporal Jones should be shot for his desertion but I will give him a chance to live the life outside of the army, he was so desperate to have.'

Jones had looked up at Blackmore, even then knowing any hope he had that the man would let him go was misplaced.

'But,' Blackmore continued, and Jones in that moment knew he was doomed, 'we cannot take the incident of theft so lightly, I'm afraid. Lance Corporal Jones, you have been found guilty of stealing one SA80 Assault weapon, 60 rounds of ammunition and multiple food stuffs from our already depleted stores.'

With a flick of his fingers, Hills eagerly moved in with Streiber, one of the other SAS men, and began to wind wire tightly about Jones' wrists.

Steven still remembered seeing the wire pulled so tightly that Jones' hands were soon slick with his own blood.

'Hold him,' was all his father had said, as he stepped forward, drawing his long sharp bayonet from its sheath.

By the time Staff Sergeant Blackmore had moved onto the second hand, Jones' screams had become unbearable to hear. So when the job was finally completed, his throat raw and bloody, Lance Corporal Jones was unable to plead for his life when the two Commandos took him from the camp. Leaving behind the two severed hands and a pool of drying blood as a warning to the rest, Blackmore had seen the whole affair as a good exercise in discipline. In fact, he was quite glad that Jones had been so stupid to get caught. No one else would think of leaving, because he had drawn the line and now they all knew the consequences of crossing that line.

'Right, I want this to go by the numbers,' came Staff Sergeant Blackmore's commanding tone, gaining the immediate attention of the group assembled soldiers in the makeshift compound. 'The Convent might be more fortified than we're used to but I don't foresee getting any more trouble than we're used to. I want smooth tactical formations when we get in, a full sweep of all buildings room by room and all civilians gathered together ready for Dr Farrell's team to process by zero-nine-hundred hours. Any questions?'

As always, no one dared voice any doubts they might be harbouring. To do so would bring Blackmore's disapproving gaze upon them and that could be dangerous. Blackmore had no use for a man who questioned his orders. They were here to do as they were told not think for themselves.

'Right, let's get this over with,' Blackmore said, instantly dismissing the men from his thoughts.

With practiced drilled movements, each man silently took up their positions in their assigned Jackal armoured vehicle and as the engine roared into life, each of them prayed to their gods for forgiveness for what they were about to do.

The Jackals in which they rode, had originally been designed as rapid assault support vehicles and had been built to protect personnel against roadside explosions and mine attacks. With just an addition of a few extra sheets of metal to the already armoured structure, they had been transformed into something that resembled a small tank and had proven their weight in gold in the war against the Dead. Each vehicle could carry three personnel, two of which would be manning the formidable machine guns and as Steve stood, slowly pivoting the large weapon he held, he made a three-sixty sweep of the terrain. Behind him, he could see the third Jackal, the Med lab and then the civilian holding truck came up the rear. Unlike the Jackals and the Med lab, the holding truck didn't have the luxury of air-bag suspension and was bouncing about quite dramatically as its large wheels dipped in and out of the large potholes dotting the road. Catching movement in the corner of his eye, Steve swung the machine gun round on its pivoting gun ring just as a decrepit looking Dead woman stepped out from the roadside hedgerow and onto the road. As always, the noise of their convoy attracted the Dead as effectively as a dinner gong but as long as they only appeared in their ones and two, firepower would not be wasted on them. Sure enough, as his vehicle sped past her decayed reaching arms, she was clipped by the Jackal behind him and pulled under its large heavy wheels.

'Contact imminent,' came his father's flat voice through his earpiece.

'Copy that, Jackal one. Over,' Stephen replied, while ahead of him, the vehicle carrying Staff Sergeant Blackmore pulled up to the large external gate of the Convent.

One by one, the convoy came to a stop behind the lead Jackal, waiting for the living within the Convent to make their move. Surprisingly, the gate had already started to open slowly.

'Idiots,' Steve said sadly to himself, as he watched a man frantically winding a winch to open the gate for them, unaware of what he was letting into his home.

Once the internal gate had also been opened by their welcoming host, the three armoured Jackals pulled into a practiced formation within the convent's grounds.

'No, Damian!' Came a woman's hysterical cry from along a walkway that ran the perimeter of the high wall.

Looking up at the middle-aged woman, he could see her waving her arms at the man as she ran towards a ladder.

'Perhaps they're not all idiots after all,' Steve thought to himself. 'This one knows trouble when she sees it.'

'Take up positions,' came their order through the earpiece.

Like a choreographed dance troop, the soldiers disembarked their vehicles and smoothly going down on one knee, their assault rifles cocked and aimed, formed a tactical wide arc.

'No!' screamed the woman from the walkway, as she threw herself down from the ladder and ran over to a group of small children, desperate to protect them.

Behind him, Steve could hear his father removing his helmet. Showing the locals a human face behind the armoured façade was a proven way to gain trust and Staff Sergeant Blackmore was always one to use all weapons at his disposal.

'Now there's no need to worry, Miss,' he began, the sincerity dripping from every word.

Steve briefly glanced to his left, catching Matt's eye. They both knew there was every need for all those living here to worry but they could do nothing about it. Their fates were sealed, one way or another.

'I'm Staff Sergeant Blackmore, and my men and I are here to help you. You have nothing to fear from us,' he continued. 'We're here to rescue you.'

However, his words did little to put the woman at ease. Steve could see it in her eyes; she didn't trust this man offering her salvation from the Dead.

'Stand down,' his father said and slowly each of the men rose to stand in a purposefully relaxed looking stance; their rifles now aimed safely to the ground.

Suddenly a second woman burst from a doorway and ran to stand by the woman with the children, putting herself noticeably in front of one of the boys in particular. She was quickly followed by two men, one of whom ran with a pronounced limp.

'What do you want?' the second woman asked, fear and apprehension shaking her words.

'Look,' his father began, 'perhaps you should gather everyone together and I'll explain. We're here to help and ...'

'Look out!' the first woman shouted, interrupting him as she pointed behind them.

Turning quickly, Steve could see the Dead woman from the road had clung on to the underside of one of vehicles and was now dragging her shattered and broken body towards the living she knew were so close. Reaching for the leg of the nearest soldier with her bloody broken fingers, a low hungry moan echoed through the courtyard. Then with a loud bang, a shot was fired from behind him, fragments of the Dead woman's skull and brain spraying across the ground.

'Thank you,' said Staff Sergeant Blackmore, forcing a cold smile while he slowly replaced his pistol into its holster. 'Now is there someone in charge here, a leader?'

'At the moment that would be me,' came the soft voice from the aged looking nun who had appeared standing in the doorway stoically. 'I am Sister Josephine, the Mother Superior of Lanherne Convent and you and your men are welcome here. But may I suggest you let us close those gates before we're over run by the Dead.'

'Of course, Mother Superior,' Blackmore said, nodding to the old woman. 'We'll just position one of our vehicles outside and bring in our Med lab in its place... with your permission of course.'

'Of course,' she replied, her own forced smile mirroring Blackmore's.

'*This woman knows the score*,' Steve realised.

She had clearly assessed the situation and quickly realised it was better to invite them in rather than risk any bloodshed. Her group were powerless against such a group of armed men and she knew it.

'Nicky, Sally, take the children to the refectory will you, please,' she said calmly, not taking her gaze from the soldier in front of her, 'Bryon, William, would you please round everybody else up. I think the Sergeant will want to fill us in on what's been happening in the outside world.'

***

The small group of survivors had spent most of the day digging graves to bury their dead friends. They had known and loved these people and as a group had agreed, they would not leave their corpses just to rot. They might have met their ends in violence, but they would be put to rest with respect and dignity. They owed them that much. So, with their breath pluming in the still chilly morning air, they had begun to dig the thirteen graves for their lost friends. Shifting the near frozen earth had been hard going, but they endured their aching muscles in silence.

'Sorry, old friend,' Patrick whispered, as he and Phil lowered Ryan's large corpse into his shallow grave.

The three from Lanherne could say nothing. They knew, all too well, no words of comfort would be adequate to ease this grief. These Dead, who to them had been nothing more than the animated corpses they dealt with every day, had lived, fought, laughed and been loved by Patrick's small group of survivors, for them only to be then snatched away by the random hand of fate.

As a group, they reluctantly decided that the Substation could no longer be a home for them. This place would hold too many ghosts for them now and they simply had to move on. So once the graves had been dug and their lost put to rest, they set about the task of salvaging what they could to take with them.

Duncan had immediately gone to work with his tool set salvaging what he could from one of the Substation's carts that had been damaged beyond repair by flying debris.

'We'll take the three intact wheels,' he had said, examining the wreckage. 'They can be strapped to the other cart.'

'Do you want us to bring these?' Sarah asked Imran, pointing to a collection of spades, forks and hoes.

'I think we should fill up with more essential stuff first and then if we have room, we can take them,' he replied, glancing at one of the carts already nearly full. 'We can always get them on another trip if we decide we need them.'

'But this, we can take with us now,' he continued, picking up a small, wicked looking scythe from the pile and swinging it through the air. 'Nice.'

'Yeah okay, Captain Hook,' Sarah said, taking the scythe carefully from Imran. 'You'll have someone's eye out, waving it about like that.'

'Sorry,' Imran said, feeling like a scolded child.

They decided to take as much as they could with them this time, but with limited space in the two available carts and with ten adults and a baby to house, there would still be many useful odds and ends left behind for a second trip. The livestock was proving tricky though, to not only catch but also the logistics of their actual transport. The Substation had lost their stud boar and one of the sows to the Dead, as well as four of their almost adult piglets. Luckily, one of the breeding sows had been in the stable with her new litter when disaster had struck; otherwise, they might have lost the lot. The chickens, as scrawny as they were, would also be a welcome addition to the flock at Lanherne, but they seemed reluctant to being caught and even as Imran and Sarah spoke, Gabe and J-Man were comically chasing them round the compound.

'Open the hatch, will you,' J-Man said to Gabe, the squawking hen he was holding by her feet flapping her wings frantically in his face. 'Wish we could just leave these behind.'

'You'll be grateful we took them with us when you want a bit of meat, believe me,' Phil called over. 'They might not look like much now but Sister Rebecca can work wonders with any scrawny old carcass.'

'Well, she'll have her work cut out with this mangy lot,' Gabe said quietly, pulling his hand quickly away from the pecking beaks of the already collected birds.

By the early afternoon, the group had packed the two carts with as much as they were physically able. With the assortment of useful odds and ends, food stores, a crate of chickens and the sow with her piglets, the ten human passengers were certainly not going to have a lot of room on their journey but it wasn't as if they had much choice. The group had debated back and forth, whether the sow should simply be towed along behind one of the carts, like Flo, the extra mare, but in the end, they knew it was better to spend a little time squashed up against the beast, rather than risk losing her to hungry Dead hands.

'It's not going to be the most comfortable of rides,' Phil said to Patrick, as he pulled the last rope tightly around the blanket covered crate that contained the four piglets, 'but at least we'll be back at the Penhaligan place before it gets dark.'

'Look,' Patrick said, staring up at the large man who had helped save his family, 'are you sure we're going to be welcome at Lanherne? I mean, you just came to see if we were alright and thank God that you did, but now you've ended up with seven more mouths to feed. We could always just take over the Penhaligan place.'

'Are you crazy?' Phil replied, jumping down from the cart roof. 'There'd be hell to pay if I didn't come back with you. To be honest, since that business with the Reverend, we're a bit thin on the ground and what with all the children, the number of fighters to dependants is way too low. I hate to admit it but we may need you more than you need us.'

'Thought I'd better check,' Patrick said, slapping Phil on the back, 'didn't want to put anyone's nose out of joint by just turning up, uninvited, you know?'

'You'll be welcome with open arms, believe me,' Phil continued, as the two men walked over to the stable. 'In fact,' he continued after a pause, 'I wouldn't be surprised if Liz eventually suggested you take over Charlie's role.'

'What?' said Patrick, stopping.

'We need a real leader, Patrick,' Phil said, turning to face the man who was obviously born to the job. 'It hit everyone real hard, losing Charlie like that. He was the tough son of a bitch glue that held us all together. Imran and Liz are great and he taught them really well, don't get me wrong, but they're still not much more than kids themselves. I can see it in their eyes whenever the group defers to them to lead the way. They're both terrified by the responsibility of having so many people's lives in their hands.'

'But they've done a good job so far?' Patrick asked.

'Absolutely,' Phil replied, nervously scratching his beard, 'but you can't be thinking about not upsetting people when there's a job to do.'

'What about you, Phil? You seem to know the score. Why don't you step up instead?' Patrick asked.

'What, a big old Nancy boy like me?' asked Phil, smiling. 'No, I'm just the muscle that gets the job done. I'll leave the tough decision making to those with the brains.'

Patrick thought Phil was selling himself short but didn't say anything. Like oil on water, a true leader would always rise to the surface whenever a group was really threatened. He knew Phil, Liz and Imran had inadvertently formed a formidable council of leaders between them without even knowing they were doing it. He hoped Liz would leave it a while before broaching the issue of him taking a more leading role in Lanherne, if only for the sake of the existing members of Lanherne. He had only met most of them a few times and if they were to look to him in any sort of leadership role, he would have to win their trust and respect first. The last thing he wanted was to cause unrest or bad feelings.

'Well, let's just see how it goes,' Patrick said, pushing open the stable door.

Inside, Helen was bundling up Jasmine in one of the horse's blankets while Sarah did her best to assure Chloe her bloody broken fingernails actually looked worse than they were.

'Right, ladies,' Phil began, 'are we ready for the off?'

'Yep, I think we've got all we can carry on this trip,' Helen replied, picking up her sleeping child, while the other two women nodded.

'Thanks again,' she continued, reaching up to gently kissed Phil on the cheek, 'I owe you and Imran more than you can possibly know.'

Looking down at the baby that Helen held protectively in her arms, Phil could make a pretty wild guess.

'Just get in the cart, I am immune to your womanly charms, wench.' Phil laughed, thumbing towards the Substation cart hitched up with Shadow.

'Damn.' Helen laughed and playfully slapped Phil's arse as she walked past him.

It had been decided that Gabe and Chloe were to travel with Duncan, Phil and Imran in the Lanherne cart, while Patrick, Helen, J-Man, Leon and Sarah would follow behind in the cart being pulled by Shadow. They had played 'rock, paper, scissors' as to who would have to take the adult sow in their already full cart. Lanherne had lost, much to the enjoyment of Patrick.

Gabe snaked his arm across the cramped cart and stroked the irritated beast's ear to calm her down.

'Shh, it's alright, everything's alright now… Shh,' he cooed to the distressed sow that silently flopped down to take a nap.

'You've got the knack there,' Imran said, nodding down at the big sow already calm enough to be drifting off to sleep.

'Right, this is it,' Phil called from the front seat as he watched Leon un-padlock the gate and swinging it open. 'Time to say goodbye.'

As soon as the gate had opened fully, Leon ran back to his cart, clambering quickly into the back. With a flick of Delilah's reins, Phil guided the cart smoothly through the open gate. Swearing as it then bumped over a few of the scattered corpses, Phil soon let Delilah's powerful strides fall naturally into their own steady rhythm. Their short journey to the Penhaligan home had begun and only time would tell what new life awaited them all.

Gabe moved one of the spy-hole covers aside so he could watch their departure from the Substation. The pylon that had been more than a haven for him over the last eight months, through it and the group that had made it their home, he had been brought back to humanity and given a chance to live. When he pushed one aside for Chloe, the girl silently shook her head. This place was dead to her now. It had become another shell, full of disappointment and death, just like everywhere else in this Dead world. Even though she knew the Lanherne community lived in safety behind their high stone walls, what had happened on the Pylon had proven to her that nowhere was really safe anymore. The Dead would always find a way in, one way or another.

***

Sitting in the Refectory, the adults of Lanherne had subconsciously positioned themselves to form a barrier between the children and the soldiers who stood at one end of the room. The four armed soldiers stood to attention, motionless. Only their eyes scanned continually back and forth across the gathered survivors, looking for trouble.

'Well, you certainly have things set up well, Mother Superior,' Blackmore said, as he entered the room with Sister Josephine.

'We had no choice if we wanted to survive,' she answered, her tone measured and calm.

She knew she had to tread carefully with the man if she wanted all of them to come out of this alive. He had assured her that they had come to Lanherne purely as part of an on-going civilian rescue program, but something about this man told her he was not to be trusted.

'Ah, I see your little flock has been gathered,' he continued, nodding to the assembled group. 'Is this everyone who lives here?'

Sister Josephine looked at the group that she had come to think of as her family. Apart from Imran, Phil and Duncan, everyone was there. It was then that she noticed that Liz was missing from their number.

'S*tay hidden, Liz*,' she thought to herself. '*There's a fox in the hen house.*'

'Yes, we all seem to be here,' she said, moving over to sit next to Richard who stood protectively in front of Nicky and Jason. 'Now, I believe you were going to tell us, Sergeant Blackmore, where you have been and what's happening in the big outside world?'

Staff Sergeant Blackmore looked blankly at the old woman who had just lied to his face. Of course, she wasn't to know he had watched the cart leave yesterday and knew some of their group were absent.

'Right, for those of you who haven't heard, my name is Staff Sergeant Blackmore and I am here with my squadron and a group of medical personnel, seeking out the small communities who have managed to thrive in these difficult times.'

'Where the fuck have you been?' Damien interrupted, 'In case you haven't noticed, we've been dying out here.'

Everyone turned their attention briefly to Damien, murmuring their agreement with his sentiment. Alice was the only one who had kept her eyes on the Sergeant and what she saw flash across his eyes when Damien spoke, froze the blood in her veins. Clearly, this man led his men through fear and intimidation and was not used to being spoken to like that. In that briefest of moments, Alice could see he wanted to teach Damien a very painful, if not fatal lesson.

'Damien, let the Sergeant speak,' Alice quickly added, hoping to diffuse the situation before Damien ended up in a pool of his own blood.

Sergeant Blackmore's eyes flicked in her direction as she spoke and the rage was replaced by something else. Something, Alice found somehow equally disturbing but could not identify.

'My men and I have been stationed on an island military facility since the initial days of the outbreak,' he began. 'There, with a collection of some of the most eminent scientists and doctors available to the Centre for Disease Control, our prime objective was to find a cure to what has been classified as the Death-walker plague.'

'And have you?' Sister Josephine asked, calmly.

'A cure?' the Sergeant said, looking at the expectant faces in the room. 'Although Dr Farrell and his team have had a lot of breakthroughs in determining the properties of the Death-walker virus, its chemical and molecular make up and even how it works, they have been unable, as of yet, to develop any vaccine or anti-virus to counter-act the Death-walker effects.'

The fleeting sense of hope some of the group had been feeling, evaporated with the Sergeant's words. Many had given up on someone ever finding a way of eradicating the Dead completely from their lives, but to be told that, even after all this time the top brains were still fumbling blindly for answers, was still deflating to hear.

'So, we might not have come to you with a cure,' Sergeant Blackmore continued, 'but we have come to offer you sanctuary. We have eradicated all the active Dead on the island and have even devised a way to ensure that we never have to deal with corpses reanimated by the Death-walker virus.'

Once again, hope bloomed for the group.

'But I thought you said your scientist hadn't found a way of stopping it?' Sally asked, little Alex sitting quietly in her lap.

'Private Fisher,' Sergeant Blackmore said, clicking his fingers, 'show them.'

Without saying a word, one of the soldiers who had been standing at the front of the room, stepped forward and began to unbutton his collar. Pulling the collar down to expose his muscular neck, the soldier turned so his back was facing them. Secured about his neck by a black band, was a small silver oblong box.

'This,' Sergeant Blackmore began, pointing to the box, 'is how we ensure no one comes back. Attached to the back of the neck, the device monitors the wearer's heartbeat via the electrical impulses conducted through the skin. Should, for any reason, the device cease to register any impulses for a period longer than two minutes, a micro charge housed within it will fire a single metal bolt upwards, through the base of the skull and into the brain, incapacitating the subject before the Dearth-walker virus can take full effect.'

'So you walk around with basically a loaded gun at your head all the time?' Richard asked.

'The alternative is not acceptable,' the Sergeant said matter-of-factly, 'and I must tell you, there is no negotiation in this matter. Once you are on the island, you will wear one like everybody else, twenty-four-seven. Everyone is subject to this rule. There are no exceptions. Anyone caught breaking this rule will be dealt with appropriately.'

Alice didn't like the sound of that 'appropriately' and wondered what sort of place this island sanctuary had turned into.

'What about the children?' Lars asked. 'Many of them are too young to understand such a rule, surely?'

Sergeant Blackmore looked from the man who had spoken to the young children dotted among the group of Lanherne survivors.

'Any child unable to comprehend the rule is given a similar device that fits about the wrist. This is linked to a partnered device given to a designated adult. Should the child's device be removed or it fails to measure the heartbeat from the child, an alarm will sound on the adult's wrist. The adult with then have the two minutes to reset the child's wrist alarm or deal with the situation.'

'What happens if the adult fails to do that?' Lars continued, not really wanting to hear the answer.

Sergeant Blackmore looked directly at Lars, his eyes devoid of emotion.

'As these wrist bands are only used by the very young, they have been installed with a larger explosive to eradicate the problem, totally, should it arise,' he replied.

'Jesus!' Richard said under his breath.

Sally instinctively pulled Alex a little closer, subconsciously needing to protect the child.

'But what if…' Nicky began to say but was cut short by the Sergeant.

'I assure you that after a while, you forget it's even there. It becomes just part of your everyday life and it's a very small price to pay for life of security, free from the Dead.' Sergeant Blackmore continued brushing aside any further discussion on the subject. 'Now, Sister Josephine has given us permission to stay here tonight before we leave tomorrow morning. While we are here, you will be put in the capable hands of Dr Morris and his team. He will be giving each of you a full health check and will want to find out a little more about you to help us determine how you are to fit into our little community. Please be frank and honest with him when he asks you for your details. We only have your interests and wellbeing in mind.'

With that, Sergeant Blackmore turned and began to walk out of the Refectory, the civilians already dismissed from his mind. As he reached the door, he was met by his son who had a printed report in his hand.

'Yes, Private?' He asked in the tone he used for all those he thought beneath him.

'Message from HQ, Sir,' Private Stephen Blackmore replied, saluting. 'They require an immediate response and we only have a few minutes of the satellite window left, Sir.'

'Very well,' Sergeant Blackmore said, snatching the report from the Private's hand.

As Sergeant Blackmore disappeared down the corridor, scanning his print out, Steve looked into the room to the collection of men, woman and children who unknowingly, had just been co-opted into Major Carden's army. As his gaze moved from one worried expression to the next, he realised that despite there being a lot more young children here, this group was much like any other they found. Granted, these seemed a little better fed and were certainly cleaner but something was always in the eyes of those who had been forced to find a way to survive among the Dead that set them apart from the likes of himself and the men of his squadron. As his glance moved about the room, it fell upon the face of an attractive young woman with short blonde hair and the most amazing eyes. She was sitting next to a man whose hands that even from the doorway, Steve could tell were crippled by arthritis. Something about the mismatched pair itched at the back of his mind. He found something vaguely familiar about them both. It was then that the man turned his head toward Steve, returning his gaze. The man's eyes slowly scanned Steve's face questioningly, as if he was searching for something un-definable hidden among Steve's stubble and cold weather blushed skin. Suddenly, the man's eyes widened in realisation.

'Steven Blackmore!' The man shouted, standing up to point at Steve.

Steve's jaw fell open in shock. He instantly recognised that voice, that pointing finger and that childhood fear that crept slowly up his spine.

'It is Steven Blackmore, isn't it?' the man asked, smiling as he made a move forward.

Beside him, the pretty woman who had also risen to her feet, placed her hand on the man's arm trying to pull him back down.

'Lars?' She asked, looking back and forth between the two men, unsure of what was happening.

'Mr Sorenson,' Steve managed to say with a chuckle, 'I'm afraid I never finished that Geography project you set... something came up.'

Stunned, Penny let go of Lars' arm as he rushed forward to shake Steve's hand. Penny watched the soldier greet Lars with wide smiles and the enthusiasm of a long lost friend. All the while, his eyes kept flicking from Lars over to herself.

'And do you remember Penny?' Lars asked, excitedly leading Steve over to her. 'No, of course you don't. Penny was in the year above you, wasn't she?'

'Yes, yes of course, I remember Penny,' Steve said, his eyes seeming to Penny to drink in every detail of her face.

'You don't have to humour him,' Penny said, nodding to Lars. 'He's not as dotty as he looks.'

'I'm not...' was all Steve could say, as he gazed intently at her.

Lars, looking from one ex-pupil to the next, was more than a little perplexed but then encountering someone you thought sure to be long dead would do that to you.

'So, I take it Staff Sergeant Blackmore is your father then,' Penny said, needing to escape Steven's gaze but not really wanting to.

There was something enthralling but also a little unnerving about the way his eyes moved across her face, as if they savoured the experience; hungry for something only she could give. Penny was not used to men looking at her like that, especially not adult men. Sure, she had boyfriends all those years ago before the Dead came, but even then, they did not look upon her with the obvious fascination and want, that Steve did. This was not the teenage lust she had seen in the eyes of her boyfriends as they fumbled with her cardigan buttons in those brief teenage moments. She could tell Steve needed to touch her and even now, as she glanced down at his strong hands, he clenched his fists to stop them from reaching for her. It was only when she thought of his hands slowly moving forward, that she realised her own fists had clenched tightly, mirroring his restrained desire.

'Sorry?' Steve said, his voice sounding distant to himself.

'Sergeant Blackmore, he's your dad, right?' Penny said softly, wondering to herself what it would be like to feel his strong arms about her, his lips on hers.

'Oh, yes... yes he is,' Steve replied, his smile dropping slightly. 'Lucky old Staff Sergeant Blackmore was on the list and so by proxy, Mum and I got dragged along, like so much luggage to the base, with him.'

For the briefest of moments, Penny was sure she saw something akin to regret or shame hidden beneath his beautiful facade. Perhaps he felt guilty that he had been spared the horrors of the Dead.

'That was lucky for you too?' remarked Lars, shaking his head. 'People have done some terrible things to each other out here, just to survive... terrible things.'

'What? Yes, I suppose it was luck, sorry, I didn't mean to sound like a brat. I know it must've been hell for you all out here,' Steve replied.

Suddenly remembering there were other people in the room apart from Penny, Steve looked at the others nearby who had been watching their exchange and he blushed slightly.

'Well, you're here now, my boy,' Lars chuckled, as he slapped Steve's shoulder. 'Better late than never.'

'Believe me, we thought it would be never,' said the smiling pregnant woman sitting next to a small girl. 'I'm Alice, by the way,' she continued, awkwardly turning her large body so she could reach her hand out for him to shake.

'Pleased to meet you,' Steve replied, taking her small hand in his own. 'When's it due?' he continued nodding to her belly.

'Oh, not for another month or so yet,' Alice smiled, her hand subconsciously stroking her unborn baby, 'and now that you're here, at least I'll have a proper doctor to bring it into the world.'

Even though Alice, like everyone else, was wary of the new arrivals, she had to admit she also felt a sense of relief that her baby would be brought safely into the world with the aid of doctors and perhaps more importantly, pain killers.

'Well, Doctor Morris will be...' his words were cut short by the sound of rapid gunfire coming from outside .

'What the fuck are they doing out there?' Richard asked, standing up to walk over to one of the tall windows that overlooked the courtyard. 'Don't those idiots know they'll attract the Dead for miles around with that racket?'

'I think that's the problem,' Steve said. 'We've had a steady flow of them drawn to the noise of our vehicles ever since we got on the mainland. Normally we just lose them at a turning but sounds like a large group have managed to follow us here.'

With a 'beep' from his earpiece, Steven Blackmore and the other four soldiers in the refectory were relayed orders.

'Sorry, got to go,' he said, jogging to the door.

Turning briefly at the doorway, Steve stole one last look at Penny and then throwing caution to the wind, he gave her a quick wink, before disappearing from view.

'Shit!' Richard said, while he watched the soldiers outside firing at the Dead from the Convent walkway, 'We've survived here for over a year and a half and we finally get over-run thanks to the trigger happy noisy goons.'

'But the gate's still closed?' Nicky nervously said, pulling Justin a little closer to her.

'Yeah, at least they got that right,' Richard finally said, moving away from the window. He had seen enough. 'I don't know about you lot, but I don't feel any safer with the army here. I don't know if we can trust them.'

'They certainly are an unknown factor that we haven't had to deal with so far,' Lars began, 'and I know we should be cautious, but if they can guarantee a life free of the Dead, surely we should take them up on their offer, even if it's just for sake of the children.'

Outside, the shooting stopped as quickly as it had begun and a silence blanketed the room.

'Where's Lizzy, Sister Josephine?' Anne whispered, a concerned look on her young face.

'I thought it best if she stayed where she was… just in case,' she replied cupping the small girl's face in her hand.

'So you don't trust them either?' Nadine asked, worrying her lip, as she began to pace back and forth.

'There is something about Sergeant Blackmore that I don't like. I can't put my finger on it, but no, I don't trust the man. So, until we really know the lay of the land, I suggest Liz stays in the attic and off their radar. We don't want to show all our hands in one go,' Sister Josephine replied, looking to the adults for assurance. 'It's just a pity they saw all the children, otherwise we could have hidden them too.'

'Well, we'll just have…' Bryon began, but his words died on his lips, as a fidgety man in glasses busted into the refectory. He was followed closely on his heels by a group of men and woman. The armbands they wore over their army fatigues indicated they were part of the medical team.

'Good morning, everyone,' he began, his eyes flitting from one survivor to the next, instantly breaking them down into analytical groups of data to be processed. All the while, he never truly met any of their returned stares. 'My name is Doctor Morris and I hope you'll bear with us as my team and I spend the next few hours getting to know you.'

Doctor Morris was quite a short man in his late forties with thinning grey hair and ill-fitting glasses, which seemed to be forever trying to escape their perch on his nose. At the moment his slight frame was comically exaggerated by the baggy army fatigue inform he was forced to wear. Obviously, whoever requisitioned supplies for the base hadn't taken into account they would have to cater to people whose proportions were not that of the usual solider. As Alice watched the Doctor walk briskly about the room, dispatching various members of his staff to different members of the Lanherne community, she could tell he wasn't comfortable wearing the uniform. Not only did it not fit him at all but also his hand nervously kept returning to a pocket that wasn't here; the ghost of the lab coat he was used to wearing, she presumed. As he came to a stop in front of her, she noticed that he also had the habit of rapidly touching each of his fingers on his left hand in turn to his thumb. Although probably just a subconscious movement, it did little to instil a confident bedside manner.

'Hello... and you are?' Dr Morris, asked looking from Alice to Anne and then back to Alice again.

'I'm Alice and this is Anne,' she replied, her hand slowly moving to hold Anne in place.

'Chambers,' he called over to one of the female doctors who were checking over the other children, 'would you take Anne for a moment please?'

'I'm not a baby,' Anne said, 'you can just tell me to go to her, you know.'

Dr Morris raised his eyebrows, startled by the young girl's forwardness.

'Come along, Anne,' Dr Chambers said smiling, as she held out her hand and led her over to the other children who had each already been paired off with a member of the medical team.

'Start general checks,' he called over to his colleague, Anne's presence already dismissed. 'Then I want blood work and initial psych reports by the morning. You know the drill.'

'Yes, Doctor Morris,' Chambers replied with a nod.

'Now,' Dr Morris said, going down on one knee, as he fiddled to put his stethoscope in his ears, 'looks like we came just at the right time for you, Alice.'

Placing one hand gently on her stomach, he slowly laid the circular disk against her to listen to her baby's heartbeat. After a few seconds of counting, he looked up at Alice.

'Nice and healthy rhythm,' he said, smiling.

***

'Well?' Sergeant Graham Blackmore asked, looking up from skimming through Dr Morris' initial breakdown of the civilians.

Sister Josephine had offered him the use of her old office and sparse as it was, at least he was out of the drizzling sleet that had persisted for most of the day. Outside, what little sun light there had been that day, began to dip over the horizon, turning the Convent in a maze of shadow.

'Four of the men and two of the woman are viable. There are possibly two more of the women, if you feel we need the manpower. One's above our ideal age bracket but she's verging on savant with regards to memory and the other is a bit younger but sterile,' Dr Morris began, flicking through his notes, 'erm…all the children are good, apart from the one they call Danny. He appears to be quite high on the autism scale but that could just be trauma.'

'Worth the risk?' Blackmore asked, leaning back in his chair, as he studied the pitiful and jittery excuse for a man in front of him.

'No, we don't want to have to deal with that sort of thing later down the line,' Dr Morris replied, trying to politely phrase what he was about to say. 'It may cause bad feeling later should the child have to be… removed.'

'Hmm,' Blackmore agreed.

The last thing Major Carden wanted on the base was a bunch of new arrivals kicking off even more than normal.

'Then of course, there's the pregnant woman,' said the Doctor, checking his notes again for her name. 'Alice. Simply finding her has made the mission worthwhile and she seems in remarkably good health, if a little underweight but that shouldn't pose any real hindrance.'

'I take it you've informed Dr Farrell of her condition?' Sergeant Blackmore enquired.

'Yes, I managed to get the message out before we lost our satellite window,' Dr Morris replied, 'I'll have his agreement first thing to proceed, I shouldn't wonder.'

'Good.'

***

In the small cupboard next to her office, Sister Josephine sat quietly on a stool, listening to the two men talking through the small grate set high in the connecting wall. What she heard disturbed her and confirmed she had been right not to trust the Sergeant. Not needing to hear any more, Sister Josephine left the two men talking and silently slipped out of the cupboard. With no one else in the corridor to see her, she began walking quickly towards the staircase that would lead to the attic and to Liz's council.

After their extensive questioning that day, Lanherne had been abuzz with pent up excitement but Sister Josephine had sensed it was tinged with a justifiable apprehension for what was to come. They had all grown so used to their life safe behind the Convent walls that for an opportunity of salvation to arise suddenly was more than a little unsettling. Walking through the dark, echoing corridors, Sister Josephine didn't need to see to know when each turn was coming up. This had been her home for most of her adult life and each brick, crack and doorway had burned itself into her subconscious. One way or another, she knew she would not be leaving the Convent with the Sergeant and his men. Lanherne would be her home until the day she died. She just hoped that day would not come with the rising of the sun tomorrow.

Shaking herself from her thoughts, she realised she had reached the door that led to the attic. Placing her hand on the handle, she went to push it open. Nothing happened. She tried again, to no avail. Apparently, it was wedged tight.

'Can I help you, Sister?' came a voice from the darkness.

Startled, Sister Josephine turned abruptly round to face a young soldier appearing from the darkness.

'My, you scared me, young man,' she said, afraid he would be suspicious.

Once he was close enough, she could tell he was the soldier that had recognised Lars and Penny.

'It's Steven, isn't it? You went to school with Penny,' she continued, hoping to distract him from the door, 'Quite miraculous indeed, you finding not one but two faces hidden away from the world after all these years.'

'Yes,' he replied, smiling, 'I certainly wasn't expecting it.'

As he said this, his smile seemed to falter, as if he somehow regretted finding them at all.

'Here, let me,' he said, changing the subject to ease in front of Sister Josephine before she could protest.

Holding on to the door handle, he levelled a sharp kick to the base of the door.

'There you go,' he said, regret still haunting his smile.

'Oh, thank you,' Sister Josephine said, placing herself slightly in the doorway to block his view, 'Err... you see, we have a cat who's due to have her kittens and she sometimes likes to wander around up here.'

'Do you need any help looking for her, Sister?' Steven asked.

'No, no, I'm quite alright. I'm sure you've got other things to do.' she replied, hoping he wouldn't try to follow her up into the attic.

'Oh, okay Sister,' he said, staring intently at Sister Josephine face, as if he was trying to read something hidden there.

Supressing a sigh of relief, Sister Josephine watched as Steven Blackmore, finally nodded, turned and began to walk down the hall. He had barely gone a few steps when he turned back to face her.

'I'd tell that cat to stay hidden if I were you, especially with kittens due,' he said calmly. 'Oh, and best that she stays away from the window too, because someone might see her... Goodnight, Sister Josephine.'

'Goodnight,' she replied, the words barely a whisper.

Shocked and more than a little puzzled by what he was plainly implying, Sister Josephine watched Steven finally disappear back into the shadows down the corridor. He had obviously seen Liz from outside and he had just warned her to keep her hidden. Perhaps those that left with the soldiers tomorrow would find an ally in Steven if things turned sour, she certainly hoped so.

'*Dear God, what have we let into our home?*' Sister Josephine thought to herself, as she quietly ascended the staircase to fill Liz in on the day's events.

DAY 3

Patrick could feel the rise and fall of Helen's breathing as she lay sleeping next to him. Slowly, he opened his eyes, taking a minute to register where he was. The sad dusty room was hidden in shadow, except for a single beam of light breaking through a chink in the drawn curtains. As he watched, a million dust motes caught in an unfelt air current danced in the beam of light, flowing upwards only to merrily swirl and fall again. Patrick thought the falling snow must have turned to sleet or rain during the night because he could hear the tell-tale drips coming from near the window. Savouring the warmth of his bed for a few moments longer before he would have to brace the chill of the room, Patrick listened to the rhythmic sound of the dripping of water. Laying there listening, he realised it wasn't coming from the window at all but the dark shadowy corner by an old antique looking wardrobe. Surprised that the roof on the old but well-built building had sprung a leak, he shifted his weight up onto one elbow to discern the extent of the damage. What he saw made his breath catch in is throat and his heart hammer wildly in his chest. There, standing motionless, hidden in the deep shadows was the figure of a man.

'Who's there?' He asked, his hand slipping silently from the covers to the club he had placed by the bedside table. 'What do you want?'

If the figure heard him, it gave no indication. No sound escaped the shadows that enveloped him, save for the 'drip, drip, drip' of water hitting the dusty wooden floorboards. Patrick's hand slowly reached the spot where his club should have been and found it gone. In fear for Helen and Jasmine, Patrick, inch by inch, began to move one of his feet out from under the covers and down onto the floor. The moment his foot came into contact, his sock became drenched, obviously the water had been leaking through for some time and had formed a large puddle.

'Look, mate, we don't want any trouble,' said Patrick, holding up his empty palms. 'I'm just going to get out of the bed, nice and slow. No reason for anyone to get jumpy.'

Swinging his other foot slowly from the bed, so he was now in a sitting position, Patrick noticed the beam of light that moments ago had been a source of beauty, now did nothing but highlight a horror. There, where the shaft of light hit the floorboards, he could see a spreading pool of glistening red.

'Blood!' the word shouted in Patrick's mind.

As soon as the word demanded recognition, he noticed the heavy coppery smell that filled the room.

'Helen!' He urgently whispered, as he rocked her sleeping body, his eyes never leaving the still form in the corner.

As he said her name, the figure took a stumbling step forwards, the sound of its boots scraping across the blood covered floor making Patrick spring to his feet. Standing unarmed in a dimly lit room, in wet socks on a blood covered floor, was not the best way to take on an unknown attacker, but Patrick had little choice if he was to protect Helen and Jasmine.

'I said I don't want any trouble,' he repeated, as the man took another painfully slow step towards him.

With a step, the man was struck by the thin beam of light coming through the curtains. With a gasp of shock, Patrick took an involuntary step backwards, knocking into the bedside table behind him. There, standing just as he had last seen him, burnt, torn and bloody, his organs ripped from his body by the wooden post that still pierced his chest, was Ryan. Patrick shook his head in disbelief. This could not be happening, he told himself. This abomination had been left safe in its grave. It had no right being here. Stunned, Patrick could do nothing but watch the slow, steady trickle of blood running along the post. As its ragged tip the blood collected and then fell in heavy drops to the floor. Ryan's corpse made a strangled gurgling sound as if his ruined body was trying to form unspoken words. At this, Patrick tore his eyes up to Ryan's charred face only to be met with the milky film covered eyes of the Dead. Looking into the eyes of this man who he had called his friend, Patrick could see nothing but an endless hunger and pain.

'Oh, Ryan,' Patrick managed to whisper, regret and guilt filling the two simple words.

Ryan stared back at Patrick, his brow creasing in concentration as his damaged brain desperately sought to access the memory of speech. Then his blood splattered lips opened a fraction, the dark viscous spittle that gummed them together, stretching. There was movement in Ryan's throat, as air was sucked into long dead lungs, now clogged with earth. His mouth, now opening wider to allow a dry rasping flow of air over his withered vocal cords, began to shape a word.

'D..A..M..S ...N,' the animated corpse slurred, drawing out each sound painfully. 'D.D.D....AAAMS...NNN,' it repeated.

Then in a motion full of purpose, Ryan nodded his blistered and charred head in the direction of Patrick's left. Suddenly realising what word the Dead man was trying to form, Patrick reluctantly turned to look at his daughter. In that fraction of a second, Patrick's world ended. There, in a bloody mess of torn limbs and savaged flesh, were the remains of what had been Jasmine. Patrick screamed. Anger, horror, grief and despair filled him in equal measures and all demanded their share of his pain.

Suddenly, he was awake, a tangle of blankets wrapped about him but still the screaming filled the room.

'Jesus!' Helen cried, jumping from the bed and running to the window.

'My God, Patrick!' She said, turning back to face him. 'The horses!'

With the adrenalin still pumping through him, Patrick leapt from the bed, as Helen pulled open the sash window frantically.

'It's a pack!' She cried, turning to Patrick, the fear clear to see in her eyes.

If the feral dogs killed their horses, they would be effectively stranded in the building and travelling across a countryside riddled with hungry animated corpses by foot would be suicide.

Below them, the three tethered hoses were under attack from at least a dozen dogs. Just like a pack of wolves, the dogs had fallen back onto the hunting tactics hidden deep in their genetic memory to take down the horses. As some of the dogs circled to dart in to snap and worry the beast's legs, the larger pack members went in for the kill. The horse from Lanherne reared up, its hooves kicking wildly, braying in pure panic. One of their horses, Flo, was already down, her blood flowing freely while two large Alsatians savaged her flanks and a third animal tore at the flesh of her belly. It was Flo, who in her death throws, was giving out the almost painfully human screams. Watching, stunned by the terrible scene before them, Patrick was relieved when with a yelp, an arrow appeared in one of the Alsatian's side, knocking it loose from Flo's back. Out the corner of his eye, he could see Imran leaning out of the adjacent bedroom window, his bow already poised to let fly another arrow. Leon had also joined in the defence of the horses, one of his knives flashing through the air, to land deep in the neck of a large mongrel that had its jaws clamped onto Shadow's neck. With a sharp whine, the canine fell to the ground, lifeless. More arrows and knives soon rained down upon the pack members, taking them out one by one. Eventually, knowing they were beaten, the remaining stragglers, turned tail and fled, leaving their dying pack brothers to bleed out onto the compacted earth behind them.

'You're not serious?' Gabe asked, watching Phil retrieve a large knife and an axe from one of the carts.

'Meat is meat, Gabe,' he replied. 'We can't afford to just leave it. Pity we haven't the room for the offal but the muscle will make good eating in a stew.'

When it was clear what was left of the pack had finally gone, the group descended the rope ladder to tend to Delilah and Shadow's wounds. Phil knew Flo had been more than an animal of burden to Gabe but he was damned if he was going to leave the valuable meat to rot when there would be stomachs grateful for the flesh back at Lanherne.

'He's right,' Added Patrick, placing his hand on the boys shoulder. 'I'm sorry, Gabe, but we just can't waste the meat.'

'It's not meat... it's Flo,' Gabe said quietly, giving her muzzle one final stroke of farewell before he stood and hobbled over to sit in the cart.

'Right, I'll do this as quickly as I can,' Phil said, laying out an old tarpaulin to wrap the meat in. 'J-Man, Sarah, can you collect the larger of the dog's carcasses? We'll just tie them to the roof for now. I'll skin and butcher then when we get back.'

'Will do,' said Sarah, sharply turning her back on Phil as he began to cut into the muscle of Flo's right flank.

Within half an hour, Phil was stripped to waist and he was washing the last of the horse's blood from his arms in a bucket of freezing cold water. There was a surprising amount of blood in a horse and even now, the gore was still spreading in an increasing pool from what was left of Flo's body, colouring the frozen earth a deep red.

'Is he going to be alright?' Phil asked Helen, nodding over at Gabe who sat with a sullen face staring at the corpse of Flo.

'I know it seems stupid to feel remorse for one dead horse when we've just seen so many of our friends killed,' she began, 'but for Gabe, Flo was a friend too.'

'And friends are hard to come by these days,' Phil said, standing to dry the last pink tinged water from his hands. 'Is that what you're saying?'

'Yeah, something like that,' she said, shrugging her shoulders.

'So, we ready for the off soon?' Patrick interrupted, walking up to Phil and Helen, Jasmine held tightly in his arms.

'Yep,' Phil replied, pulling his jumper down over his bulky muscular torso. 'Barring any more incidents, in about five hours we'll be back at Lanherne and you'll have a safe new home.'

'*Safe?*' Patrick thought to himself, looking down at Jasmine sleeping in his arms and wondering if anywhere would ever be truly safe again.

***

'It's crazy, man,' Matt said to Steve, as they sat cleaning their weapons, 'to meet up after all these years, in the middle of nowhere, what are the odds? She's quite easy on the eye and nice arse too.'

'Yeah,' Steve replied, only half listening to his friend.

Daydreaming as they worked, Penny was his sole distraction. Even now, as he automatically jammed the cleaning cloth through one of the chambers of his gun, he could picture the shape of her neck, the soft curve of her jaw, the way she tucked a stray bang of hair delicately behind her ear with her fingers. All these minute details that seemed to have shouted out to him in their brief re-acquaintance last night, came back to him now. He remembered how his hands had itched to reach for her, to feel her skin under his fingertips and to feel her body next to his but he knew it was nothing but a hopeless fantasy. He knew that any thoughts of being with Penny were nothing but pipe dreams. Especially not after what he would be part of later that morning, she would hate him for it.

'Damn!' he said, throwing the cloth to the floor.

He knew anything he could have possibly had with Penny had already been trampled by this mission. It was over before it had begun. She would never forgive him and after today, would only look at him with hate and resentment. He had seen it time and time again. Most did not look back fondly upon their rescue. To them, this was not a benevolent act by their army heroes but rather, for many, a time when they were forced to leave those un-chosen behind.

'I don't think I can do this anymore, Matt,' Steven quietly whispered, looking down at the snow dusted ground so only his friend could hear him. 'What's the point in surrounding ourselves with people who hate us? What sort of brave new world does Carden think he's going to be able to build on that foundation. It's doomed from the get-go… nobody wants to play this crazy game.'

Steven looked up, meeting his friends gaze.

'I know I don't, not anymore,' he continued, shaking his head, his words barely a whisper.

'You know what you're risking, Stevie-boy?' Matt asked, calmly returning his attention to his weapon, as if Steven hadn't just spoken of desertion, 'You can't save her, you know that, don't you. She's fit, healthy and is of an age to make nice fat happy babies. She'll be on the list to be rescued. They'll not let her or you just slip away.'

'I know,' Steven replied, looking up at the small attic window. He had a plan forming and whoever was hiding up there, might just be his unaccounted for ace in the hole.

'And what about you, Matt,' said Steve, trying to gauge what was going on in his friends mind. 'Do you think what we're doing is right?'

Matt put his rifle aside and with a sigh, looked over to Steve.

'I agree with you, something has definitely gotten turned around at the base... something bad. What was supposed to be a place of hope that we'd beat this thing, has turned on the very people it set out to save,' he began, quickly scanning the other members of the squadron to see if any were within earshot, 'but I can't go with you, you know that.'

Steve felt the hope that he wouldn't have to do this alone, deflate within him. He and Matt had been part of this right from the beginning and to contemplate going it alone was terrifying.

'Shit, if it was just me, then I'd be with you like a shot. You know that, don't you?' Matt added, 'but I've got Karen to think about. She's all I've got left of my family. I can't just leave her back on the base, you do understand.'

The sad thing was that Steve did understand. It was selfish of him to think Matt would come with him without his sister and he knew if the tables had been reversed, he would do the same.

'Sorry, mate,' Steve said, 'I didn't mean to put you on the spot. Yeah, of course you need to think about Karen. I just hoped...'

'Hey, look, I might not be able join you but I'll be damned if I'm not going to help you get out of this shit hole army. I've got your back, Stevie-boy, always.'

'Thanks, man,' Steve said, relieved that he could rely on Matt to help him get away, hopefully with Penny at his side.

'Just be sure you've thought this through,' Matt added, a tone of warning creeping into his voice. 'You get it wrong, Steve, and that bastard Dad of yours will nail your arse to the wall. You know that there'll be no second chances, so make sure you know this is what you want to do and do it right.'

Steve looked at Matt, knowing he was right. His father would offer no reprieve to any man he caught deserting, not even his own son.

'Look, at this precise moment, I know this is what I have to do and who knows, I might live to regret it. I might not, but either way, I promise you I'll think it though properly before I act, okay,' said Steve, his voice dropping to a whisper again as he saw his father walking towards him across the courtyard. 'Heads up, 'Best Dad' nominee on his way over.'

The two soldiers immediately stood at attention and saluted, as Staff Sergeant Blackmore stopped in front of them.

'I want all civilians gathered in the refectory in half an hour,' he said, to the gathered men scattered about the convent courtyard, barely sparing a glance at his son. 'We're moving out at 0900 hours and I don't want any hold ups. If the any of them kick up a fuss, I want them dealt with swiftly. I will not have some bleeding heart civilian jeopardizing the completion of my orders, understand!'

'Sir!' the gathered men said in unison.

They all knew which they would rather piss off. Between the civilians and the Sergeant, the Sergeant won hands down. Knowing his orders would be carried out without question, Sergeant Blackmore turned and left the men to their duties.

'Shit!' Steve said, once his father was out of hearing range, 'I'm going to try to give Penny the heads up and try to explain before it gets too crazy up there. You know what it can be like.'

'Just be careful, Stevie-boy,' Matt called after him, as Steve bolted for the convent doorway.

Plunging in to the shadowy corridor, Steve hoped he could get Penny to understand before the shit really hit the fan in the refectory. If he couldn't, she would forever only see him as one of the uniformed monsters that came into their home and tore their lives apart. Despite barely sharing a dozen words with the young woman, Steve already knew he could no sooner stop breathing than live without her in his life. By some divine force or bizarre twist of universal fate, he had met again, all these years later, the girl from his childhood who had entranced his every waking moment. Of course, the beautiful girl in the grade above him hadn't even known he had existed but even now, he remembered how he had treasured every glimpse of her walking through the school corridors or the sight of her sitting in the assembly hall. She was his first love, unrequited definitely but he had loved her nonetheless.

'*Penny has to understand*,' he thought to himself, as he walked briskly down the corridor. '*I've got to make her understand that it's not my fault.*'

***

'Liz will find you and bring you back,' Sister Josephine said, kneeling down to cup Anne's small scared face in her hands. 'She says you must believe her, no matter how long it takes, she'll get you back.'

Anne's large blue eyes, already full with tears could hold them back no longer. She had been stolen away from her sister before. With a knife at her throat, and death all about her, Liz, Imran and Charlie had turned up without a second to spare, to rescue her and it certainly wasn't something she would want to go through again. Liz had been the only constant in her young life. More than a sister, Liz had been filling the roles of mother and father for as long as she could remember. Nevertheless, if Liz said she would come for her, Anne knew nothing in the world would stop her from doing just that.

'She said to stick close to Alice if you can, or Richard and Nicky. They'll look after you until she comes for you,' Sister Josephine continued.

'But why can't she just come with us?' Anne asked, her tears spilling freely down her cheeks.

'Oh, Anne,' Sister Josephine replied, wiping away her tears. 'Liz said it's easier to break in somewhere than break out... We'll just have to put out faith in her that she knows what she's doing. She's never steered us wrong so far.'

'Everything alright, Sister?' came a male voice from behind her.

Abruptly, Sister Josephine stood, worried about how much the man had heard of her reassurances to Anne.

'You seem to make a habit of sneaking up on me, Steven Blackmore,' Sister Josephine said, relieved it was the solider she had encountered last night outside the attic door, 'Anne here is just a little upset about leaving her cat behind, that's all.'

Steve looked down at Anne's tear streaked face and he knew the time had definitely come to make a stand against his father and the missions Major Carden and Dr Farrell sent them out on. Who were they to decide who would be given sanctuary? Who were they the skim off the most able and useful to take back to the island, leaving behind the old and weak to fend for themselves, unprotected. What gave his father the right to act like a callous tyrant to the men under his command, ruling with fear and effectively condemning those who tried to leave to the most hideous of deaths? No, his father had certainly crossed a line with Corporal Jones, sending him to his death, bound and bleeding among the Dead. It had been clear to him at that point that this army had a monstrous cancer flourishing through it, a cancer of desperation, fear and selfish intimidation, and he could stand it no more. Sadly, it was too late to hide the little girl as he would Penny. She had already been approved for rescue and would be missed, but he may be able to help her down the line, especially with a little assistance from Sister Josephine's hidden attic friend.

'Well,' he began, knowing the next sentence would ultimately commit himself to desertion and hopefully if everything went to plan, a new life somewhere free of his father, 'perhaps, her cat could follow us at a distance, Sister? Tell her to be ready for her chance. She'll know when.'

The unspoken pact was confirmed by the smallest of nods from a now hopeful Sister Josephine.

'I'm afraid everyone has to gather in the refectory in half an hour, Sister. Can you spread the word?' Steve said with a sigh, guilt and regret dripping from every word.

With that, Private Steven Blackmore, turned and walked silently down the corridor. As he walked through the shadowy hallway, the sound of his boots falling on the stone floor echoing around him, he wondered what he was getting himself into and would he even survive his plan long enough to regret setting this first foot on the path to his liberty.

Checking each room for Penny as he went, Steve went over in his mind how he would explain to her what was about to happen without her being horrified he had been part of this for so long. He needed her to understand what life was really like at the base. How, when his father had described this supposed Utopia, he had left out the constant cloud of fear and mistrust that they were all forced to live under. How people who didn't follow the rules or showed any form of insubordination could be made to disappear and how everyone was too scared to ask questions for fear they too would suddenly be taken from their bed in the dark of night.

Steve finally found Penny working in the kitchen with some of the other members of the Lanherne community.

'Private Blackmore,' Lars said, smiling as he looked up at the young soldier walking into the kitchen.

'Sir,' Steve said with a nod, his eyes automatically finding Penny's face in the room full of people.

When Penny eyes met his, something bloomed within him and the words of warning fled him. Now that she was in front of him, he didn't know what words could shed a true light on the soldiers and their supposed rescue without her hating him for it.

'Steve?' Penny said, seeing something in his gaze that wavered on apprehension.

'Erm…Penny I must speak to you,' he managed to force himself to say. 'It's important.'

Her brow creasing in concern, Penny didn't see the looks exchanged between Lars and Sally. They had seen the way the two looked at each other last night and now understandably assumed the Private was making his move. Penny pushed her chair back from the table and plopped the potato she had been peeling into a large bowl of water.

'What's the matter?' she asked wiping her hand on the tea towel tied at her waist, 'Steve, what is it?'

She was standing in front of him now, waiting for him to speak. She was so close that Steve could see the soft rise and fall of her chest and even now, he wanted to reach out to her and hold her, telling her everything would be alright. However, he knew that would be nothing but a lie, nothing but words of promise, easily said and easily broken. For some of those that Penny loved at Lanherne, nothing would be the same again after this morning. They were to be abandoned by the very people they thought had come to save them and he knew Penny would be devastated by this betrayal.

'Penny…' he began, finally building the courage to reach out and take her delicate hand in his.

'Private?' Came a cold voice from behind him, a voice that filled his veins with ice. 'What's going on here?'

No sooner had his fingers brushed Penny's, than he snapped his hand back, hoping his father hadn't seen the gesture.

'Nothing, Sir,' Steve said, turning to face the man that was his father in name only, rather than deed. 'I was letting the civilians know they needed to assemble in the refectory.'

Staff Sergeant Blackmore looked from his son to the young woman standing close to him.

'Well, if you wouldn't mind, ladies and gentleman, we have an announcement to make, so if you could do as the Private requested, we get can started,' Sergeant Blackmore said, indicating with his hand for them to leave the kitchen.

One by one, those in the kitchen filed past the Sergeant, knowing from his tone and stance that this was more than a request. One of the last to leave was Penny and as she moved past Steve, she was caught briefly by his sad expression.

'I'm sorry,' he managed to say as she passed him and she saw something in his eyes that scared her. Whatever he was apologising for he meant it with his whole being.

*****

'Right, listen up people,' Sergeant Blackmore began, addressing the gathered members of Lanherne. 'When instructed, you will stand and go over to Dr Morris and his team.'

Nicky pulled Justin close to her, not liking the way the soldiers stood poised with their assault rifles. Whatever was going on here, it didn't look good for the Lanherne group, if the heavy fire presence was anything to go by.

'You three… and you,' Sergeant Blackmore said pointing to Richard, Nicky, Justin and Anne.

Richard looked at his wife, seeing his own apprehension mirrored in her eyes. He didn't like the tension that was building in the room, but knew if he was to keep his family safe, it was best not to rock the boat.

'Nicky,' he gently said, taking her hand to lead her and Justin over to the doctor.

Slowly, Nicky rose to her feet and with a glance over to Alice and Sister Josephine, allowed herself be taken across the refectory floor to stand with Dr Morris's medical team.

'It's alright, Anne,' Sister Josephine said, kissing the young girl's hand. 'Go stand with Nicky and Richard.'

'But,' Anne began, tears already filling the corners of her large blue eyes.

'No buts now. Come on and do as I say,' Sister Josephine said, pulling Anne briefly into a tight hug so she could whisper, 'Remember, she'll come for you.'

'Miss,' the Sergeant said nodding towards Alice.

Instantly, by unspoken command, two of the medical team, bolted forward to help Alice up from her seat and across the room.

'You, you and you,' Sergeant Blackmore continued, indicating William, Damian, Cam and Penny, 'over here.'

Penny looked at Steve, and after briefly meeting her gaze, his eyes fell to the floor in shame. Instantly, the pieces fell into place, this was not to be a rescue for all.

'What's going on here?' Penny demanded, not moving from her seat.

'Miss, that was not as request, so move,' Sergeant Blackmore said, his eyes narrowing as he turned his steely glare upon the young woman daring to question him.

'I said what's going on here? Why are we being separated?' Penny repeated.

With the smallest of movements from the Sergeant, one of the soldiers stepped forward, his rifle raised in Penny's direction.

'Penny! Please,' Steve said, taking an involuntary step forward, panic rising in his throat.

Sergeant Blackmore's head snapped to glare at the soldier who dared speak out of turn.

'Private,' he spat, his harsh tone promising punishment.

Looking from Penny to his father, Steve stepped reluctantly back into line.

'Miss,' Sergeant Blackmore said, the cold word challenging her to disobey him.

Looking from the rifle to the Sergeant's hard stare, Penny knew just like everyone else at Lanherne that she was not being given a choice. Her fate had been decided for her and to rail against it was pointless and would simply get her killed.

'And bring that child,' the Sergeant continued, pointing to Alex held tightly in Sally's arms.

'No!' Sally said, instantly pulling Alex tighter to her.

'What?' Penny asked, looking from Sally's panic-stricken face back to the cold emotionless facade of the Sergeant.

'I will not tell you again, young lady,' he replied.

Penny stood motionless, her refusal to act a challenge to the Sergeant's authority. Steve could see the anger building in his father. Penny had no idea what she was dealing with. This man, who would gladly sacrifice a man in order to maintain his control over his squadron was not to be trifled with. Steve knew Penny had but a few seconds to do as his father said and her time was almost up. Stepping forward, Steve would have to risk showing his hand if he wanted to save Penny from his father's anger. Slinging his rifle quickly over his shoulder, Steve walked over to Sally and began to pry the small boy from her arms. Instantly, the room erupted with cries of protest, as Alex began to scream.

Penny dashed forward to help Sally, only to be grabbed by Matt, pulling her back.

'He's saving your life,' Matt said, turning her sharply to face him.

Struggling against Matt's firm hold, Penny was forcibly dragged across the room away from Sally.

'You bastard!' Penny shouted to the Sergeant when she was finally pulled past him to join the others.

With a crack, the Sergeant's hand snapped out to strike Penny hard across the face. Stunned, Penny could do nothing but let Matt pull her past the man who held her life in his hands.

'No!' Sally screamed, as Steve finally pried a struggling and screaming Alex from her arms.

Unable to bear the hate and betrayal that would be in Penny's eyes, Steve kept his gaze to the floor, as he pushed Sally away roughly from him and turned to take Alex to the group of the chosen. However, Sally would not give up her adopted foundling so easily. With the power of a threatened lioness protecting her cub, she threw herself at Steve's back. Suddenly, a single shot rang out and Sally was thrown backwards, landing heavily with a 'grunt' against one of the long wooden tables. With a collective shocked intake of breath, the room was silenced and stilled.

'Sergeant Blackmore!' Sister Josephine snapped, standing to meet the soldier's cold stare, the fired gun still in his hand.

'Oh, my God,' said Nadine quietly, turning Sally's prone body over. 'She's dead. You killed her!'

As if the news meant nothing to him, Sergeant Blackmore walked calmly over to Sally's corpse and looked down at her. The single shot had cleanly entered her chest, the bullet tearing though ribcage and heart, continuing its deadly journey out her back.

'This is the result of not following orders,' he said matter-of-factly, levelling his gun with Sally's head. 'From now on, you will all do as I command. Any insubordination will be met with accordingly, understand!'

With a second shot, the Sergeant made sure Sally's corpse was confined to its oblivion.

'Here, take him,' Steve said sadly, pushing a stunned Alex onto Richard.

Richard held the silently weeping boy in his arms, gently turning his head away from the bloody scene before them. The members of Lanherne were in a state of shock. Their home and community that so recently had been flourishing, now lay in tatters with one of their number taken from them forever by the very people supposedly sent to help them.

'Take them too,' Sergeant Black said to two of the medical team, indicating Jimmy, Samantha and Bailey. 'Leave the retard though, we don't need the burden.'

'And is that what the rest of us are?' Nadine asked, 'a burden?'

Sergeant Blackmore turned towards the mousey woman who had spoken.

'You of all people should understand,' he began, 'I'm sure you've read in one of your books about survival of the fittest. We can only take with us those who will be of use if we are to rebuild society, which are the women of childbearing age and the able-bodied men. Anyone else would simply be a drain on our already limited resources.'

'What sort of society are you building, where the old and weak are cast aside?' Sister Josephine asked.

'One that will survive,' the Sergeant replied flatly.

'Then may God have mercy on your souls,' Sister Josephine said, sitting down with a sigh, 'You are already doomed to fail.'

***

Liz nervously watched the soldiers below her, as they led her friends at gunpoint to a waiting holding truck. As each member appeared through the Convent doorway, she breathed a sigh of relief, mentally crossing them off her list. When Sister Josephine had come to her last night telling her she had been seen by one of the soldiers, Liz considered revealing herself to be with Anne, but after some reassurances from the Sister that the Private had advised her to stay hidden, she reluctantly agreed. Despite this, she had still almost bolted from her hiding place when she first heard the two gunshots, desperate to make sure Anne was okay and it had taken all her resolve to stop herself, knowing she would be of no use to any of them if she gave herself away now.

She watched as Richard appeared with a weeping Alex in his arms and a terrified looking Nicky, Justin and Anne by his side. Thankfully, Nicky held both of the children close to her as she anxiously made her way past the armed soldiers to the truck. From her viewpoint high above them, Liz could see there were other unknown scared survivors, huddled together deep in the shadows of the truck. These too had obviously fallen victim to the Sergeant and his men with their rescue that was no rescue at all. At that moment, as if somehow Anne had known her sister was watching her, Anne turned a tear streaked face up to look at the small attic window. Seeing the look in Anne's eyes, Liz subconsciously placed her hand against the small pane of glass, silently vowing nothing would stop her from getting her back. For the briefest of moments, their gazes locked, and Liz, willing her sister to be strong, forced her mouth into a sad reassuring smile. Nicky, noticing where Anne was looking quickly turned her forward, knowing that if any of them were to have any chance of a return to Lanherne Liz's presence must remain unknown to the soldiers.

Liz then saw William, Cam, Damian, and an angry looking Penny being reluctantly led to the truck. Three of the medical personnel were close on their heels with the remaining children carried in their arms. Sister Josephine told her last night that poor silent Danny was considered nothing but a troublesome burden by the Sergeant and his team, so he would be left behind. Because of this, his absence from those being stolen away from Lanherne didn't trouble her too much, but she still prayed that even the Sergeant wouldn't be callous enough to kill a small child when he could just as easily be left behind. After what seemed like an eternity to Liz, Alice finally emerged through the doorway. The medical personnel were on either side of her helping her across the courtyard. Unlike the others, Alice was taken directly to the mobile med-lab to be left in the charge of the excited looking doctors standing in the doorway.

Liz watched as one of the soldiers climbed up onto the walkway and began to wind the winches that would open the two gates, while the rest his squadron clambered silently into their armoured vehicles. Once the gates were fully opened, the first of the vehicles already starting to leave, the soldier on the walkway turned and looked directly at Liz. Her breath catching in her throat, Liz stared back at the man, terrified that her only chance to follow the convoy had just been dashed. Nevertheless, with the smallest of nods to her, the man climbed back down from the walkway, ran over to his vehicle and jumped in.

'Thank you, Private Steven Blackmore, I owe you,' Liz said to herself, knowing he must be the man Sister Josephine had told her about.

Finally, only one vehicle remained with the single figure of the Sergeant standing in front of it, watching those chosen to be left behind gathering forlornly on the doorway.

'Shit, no…' Liz said, noticing Sally was absent from the group. 'Oh, Sally.'

It was clear to her now that the shots she heard earlier had taken Sally from them. The woman who had found a new way to live through being a mother to Alex had paid the ultimate sacrifice to protect her rescued child and for this, Liz vowed not only to get Anne back but each and every one of them, even those nameless hidden strangers. The Sergeant would pay for what he had done today. One way or another, she would see to it. With hate bubbling up inside her, she watched as the man who had torn their world apart addressed the gathering of those he thought unworthy. Just what he was saying, she could not hear but when he walked across the snow-dusted courtyard to their remaining cart and began to hack into one of the wheels with an axe from the woodpile, his intention was clear. They were not to follow.

Realising the time had come to put her plan into action, Liz pushed herself away from the window with the scene of the Sergeant already turning his back on the group dismissed from his concern and left the attic room that had been her self-imposed prison for the night. She knew she didn't have much time and had to play this out carefully. Leave too soon and the convoy would see her, leave too late and she ran the risk of losing them.

'Get one set of those gates closed before we're over run by the Dead, will you, Nadine?' Liz said appearing beside the group, as the Sergeant's armoured vehicle pulled out of the courtyard.

'Oh, Liz… Sally,' Sister Josephine said, turning towards her, tears in her eyes.

It seemed to Liz that the frail woman had aged in the last hour. The toll of the last seven and half years had suddenly caught up with her.

'I know,' was all Liz could say, knowing no words were enough to console the woman before her, 'but we need to get those gates closed, Sister, now.'

'On it,' Nadine said, running over to the ladder.

'Lars, I need you to get Samson ready,' Liz continued.

'But Liz, the cart?' Lars replied, looking over to the ruined wheel, 'It'll take days to fix it, even if Duncan was here.'

'Well then, I guess I'm going to go without it,' Liz interrupted, 'and yes I know what that means, but what choice have we got? I have to go after them.'

As much as they hated to admit it, even in her heavily pregnant state, Liz was still the most skilled at killing the Dead among those left at the Convent and to argue with her was not only pointless but would also waste valuable time that they did not have.

'Did you do as I asked?' Liz asked, turning back to Sister Josephine.

'What... erm, yes, I'll go get them now,' she replied, disappearing back into the Convent.

The previous night, Liz and Sister Josephine had come up with the plan that Liz would follow the soldiers when they left, leaving behind her a trail of rags tied at various points. These would allow Imran and Phil, when they returned, to follow her and know they were heading in the right direction.

When Sister Josephine returned, she carried with her a battered looking holdall stuffed full of torn strips of cloth and Liz's sword.

'Here, I've also put some bread, boiled eggs and a bottle of water in there,' said Sister Josephine, handing Liz the holdall, 'I pray you're not out there too long before Imran and Phil catch up with you, but this should keep hunger at bay for a little while.'

'Thanks,' Liz replied, slipping the strap of her sword over shoulder.

'Liz,' Nadine called from the walkway, 'the Sergeant's vehicle has almost reached the gate at the end of the lane. You better be making your move or you'll lose them.'

Liz looked anxiously from Nadine to the group around her. These people had effectively been left to die by the Sergeant and as much as leaving the Convent without the protection of the cart terrified her, she knew it was the only option left open to her if she wanted to get Anne, Alice and the others back.

'May God go with you, child,' said Sister Josephine tearfully, taking her hands in hers.

'Right, let's get this started,' Liz said, trying to hide the fear from her voice as she took Samson's reins from Lars.

'Good luck, Liz,' said Lars, hooking the holdall over Samson's saddle. 'We'll send the others after you as soon as they get back.'

Bryon had brought her a box to stand on, and with a little push, Liz managed a very ungraceful mount. When she finally settled herself on Samson's back, she gave the smallest of flicks on the reins, urging him towards the gate. With one last look at those she was leaving behind, she waited nervously for Nadine to re-open the gate.

***

Steve watched the Convent slowly disappear behind him, hoping the unknown woman in the attic wouldn't leave it too late to follow. If he were to escape with Penny, he would need this woman's help as much as she needed his. Already in the lane behind them, some of the Dead, attracted by the noise of their armoured vehicles had started to clamber through the tree line to follow.

'It wasn't your fault, mate,' said Joe, the fellow soldier assigned to drive the armoured Jackal he and Matt travelled in. 'You weren't to know Sarge would take her out.'

Steve turned to look up at Matt, who was manning the machine gun on its pivotal gun ring. Only Matt knew what the death of the woman who had refused to give up the small boy really meant to Steve. He had seen the look Penny had given Steve as she had been led past him. Her hate and sense of betrayal was clearly evident. Steve knew that to earn Penny's trust and forgiveness, he might have to take extreme measures. His father, Major Carden and Dr Farrell had set the rules of how they lived and how they treated the survivors, they came across. It sickened Steve that he had gone along with it for so long, but enough was enough. For Steve, it was time to fight back. He would play the game their way if he had to and if he had to kill to make things right, then so be it.

***

'Shit,' Liz mumbled to herself, as ahead of her three more of the Dead stumbled through the hedgerow and into her path to join their scattered brethren.

Her journey had barely begun and already she was confronted by a dozen of the Dead. Luckily, they had been attracted by the noisy convoy and were facing away from her at the moment. They mindlessly followed their quarry but Liz knew if one were to turn her way, they would be on her. With movement learnt from years of wielding her sword, Liz reached behind her to release her blade from its sheath silently. The smooth flow and practiced motion was somewhat spoilt by her pregnant condition, causing her to rather ungracefully reposition herself in the saddle again afterwards. Thankfully, the Dead eyes had remained fixed on their prize that disappeared into the distance and her ungainly moves had gone unnoticed. Liz braced herself, for what she knew would be just the first of many encounters with the Dead over the next few days.

In her mind, Charlie's words came to her.

'Mark your targets calmly,' he told her. 'Never attack without planning your moves first, that's one quick way to get over powered by the Dead, girl. You rush into things and the Dead will get the jump on you. You can't focus on their numbers and positions if you're hacking at them like a wild thing out of control.'

So, taking his long given advice, Liz slowly took a steadying breath and calculated her path through the meandering Dead ahead of her. She knew her pace would be a paramount factor in following the soldiers, if she were to survive. Too fast and she might get too close and be seen. Too slow and she would spend the whole time dealing with a multitude of the Dead attracted to sounds of the vehicles. She needed to travel in that small window where the road in front of her was still relatively clear and her path through the Dead manoeuvrable. It was always better to avoid conflict with the Dead altogether if you could. So, if she could manage to pass them before they became too numerous, she might be able to follow without having to deal with the dead at all. With luck, she would be beyond their grasp before their decaying brains even had chance to register or react to her passing. However, this time she knew a simple avoidance was not an option open to her. She would have to deal with at least a few of the Dead ahead of her to clear a safe passage. With the muscles in her legs tensing, Liz flicked her gaze briefly to the cracked road surface and traced her route again. No point dodging the Dead, only for Samson to lose his footing on a sheet of ice or in a deep pothole and throw her.

Realising that she was risking her life with each second she hesitated, Liz finally gave Samson a sharp kick with her heels and urged him forward. As Samson broke into a gallop, she came alongside the first of the Dead. Alerted by the thundering hooves behind it, a cadaverous head, its grey skin mottled with a bloom of green mould, turned to face her. No sooner had the animated corpse fixed its milky stare upon her, than her blade had started its deadly swing. For a spilt second, Liz would have sworn she saw a look of something akin to surprise flash behind those hungry eyes and then as the decapitated head flew free of its withered body, the threat instantly dismissed from her thoughts. Her focus had shifted smoothly to the next Dead thing in her path.

With the might of Samson charging down upon them, one by one, the Dead turned to meet this new approaching feast almost within their grasp. Faster than she thought possible, the corpses fell to the swing of her blade and the crash of Samson's hooves. A small Dead child, its emaciated arms reaching for her beseechingly, was thrown aside as Samson barrelled past; its small body crushed underfoot. However, Liz could spare no thought for these poor souls who had been forced to stalk the living by a sick twist of nature. To break through the approaching Dead was all that consumed her mind. Once she was past the clambering hands and the moans of desperate need that seemed to surround her, only then would she be able to process the horror of what she was forced to do.

Purely by chance, a Dead man, his blackened and ripped lungs visible through his torn chest cavity, had managed to hook a claw-like hand onto her foot as she sped past. Hating herself for the scream that escaped her lips, Liz knew she would be unable to slash at the man without risk of hitting Samson's flank. Therefore, with a tight hold on Samson's reins, Liz leaned over and began to pound at the brittle finger bones clasped about her ankle with the hilt of her sword. To his credit, Samson ignored the flapping collection of skin and bone he dragged alongside him and kept his course true. Liz winced. Not only was her ankle gripped in a vice-like hold born of the agonising need of the Dead, but she was also only managing to hit his hand with every other jab. Her ankle would soon be black and blue with bruises from this self-inflicted beating. With the Dead man's weight hanging precariously from one hand, the skin about his wrist could withstand the onslaught for only so long. Within a few moments, it began to split, exposing bone and fetid flesh beneath. Glancing away from the Dead man's hand to make sure she wasn't about to be knocked off completely by another corpse, Liz quickly slid her sword back into its sheath, waiting the barest of a second for the click that indicated it was secure. Then, leaning precariously out of the saddle, Liz reached down to the exposed wrist joint. Already the tear in the puss coloured skin had increased, now stretching along much of the Dead man's arm. With as much force as she could muster, Liz thrust her fingers under the skin just above the wrist. With a yank, she began to rip away at the greying muscle ribboned with dark clotted veins and yellowing tendons, hoping to get to the bones beneath. With a snap, she felt the first of the small bones breaking, instantly increasing the stress on the already ruined wrist and arm. Then, almost as surprisingly as he had latched on to her, he was gone. With nothing but a ruined detached hand and a flap of rotten skin dangling from her boot, Liz pulled herself back upright into the saddle. After a few flicks of her aching foot, the hand fell to the snow dusted ground below her with a sickening slap, rolled and was lost behind her as she continued onwards.

By now, Samson had managed to take her the entire length of the lane that led from Lanherne to the main road, leaving the Dead shattered in their wake. Slowing him down to a trot, Liz guided Samson through the wide rusty gate. She needed to find out which direction the soldiers had taken, because to lose them was simply not an option. Standing up in the stirrups for a better look, Liz could just about see the tell-tale rise of exhaust plumes disappearing off to her right.

'*So, they're following the road back to the village,*' she thought, as she reached awkwardly behind her to pull free one of the fabric strips Sister Josephine had prepared the night before. Leaning over slightly, she finally managed to tie it to the top of the right hand gatepost.

'*The first marker for Imran,*' she thought to herself, praying he wouldn't be too far behind her.

Then, looking back the way she had come one last time, Liz stared up at high stone walls of Lanherne in the distance.

'Say a prayer for me, Sister J,' she said aloud. With a click of her tongue, Liz guided Samson towards to the village and the convoy of soldiers who had violated their home.

***

'Now, this may feel a little cold on your skin,' the female doctor said, as she applied the clear gel over Alice's stomach.

When Alice had first been led into the Med-lab, she was in a state of shock. Everything she had come to rely on was now gone, stolen from her. She still could not work out how it had all gone wrong so quickly. One minute, they had hopeful anticipation of the long awaited rescue and return to a normal life, which was almost within their grasp and next, there was screaming and blood with poor Sally's body slumping to the floor.

The doctors fussed over her as soon the lab started to pull away from Lanherne and for the last few hours, they had done nothing but give her a full medical examination. There didn't seem to be a part of her body or a fluid inside it that had not been probed and examined. Of course, on some level, she was grateful for their concerned attention, but with each set of questions or vial of blood taken from her, the hate bubbled within her, threatening to erupt. These people, no matter how grand their motives were could not be excused for their share of the blame for what had happened. What shocked her most was that no one from either the medical team or soldiers thought to voice any protest when the Sergeant murdered Sally. It was if they were too scared or that perhaps this was simply an usual occurrence. At the moment, she did not know which caused her the most concern, the possibility that these people could have such little regard for human life or that the man in charge of them was an out of control monster. However, as the image of Alex's terrified face flared in her mind, she realised it didn't matter. As far as she was concerned, they all had blood on their hands. Their actions or rather the lack of them, made them all complicit in Sally's death and one way or another they would pay.

'Foetus is a little smaller than we'd expect in the third trimester,' the female doctor said aloud, looking over at a small screen to Alice's left, 'but that can be put down to mother's borderline malnutrition. I'm getting a steady heart beat though and there are no obvious abnormalities present with regards to physical development.'

'Good, good,' Dr Morris said, absentmindedly pushing his glasses up onto his forehead to look at the screen.

The Med-lab looked to all intents and purposes like a cross between a science lab and a medically refitted, but heavily armoured caravan. The only windows were long, thin and set high along one wall, near the ceiling. Everything seemed to gleam with a cleanliness that seemed alien to Alice after all these years. Above her, tubes lightly bathed the room in a harsh light and the constant high-pitched buzz they produced seemed to exist just outside her hearing range. At one time, it wouldn't even have registered to Alice, but now the light and sound only came across as something cold and unnatural. Along one wall, were a row of four beds, and next to each, various monitors and electrical gizmos had been built into the wall. To monitor what, Alice could only guess.

Alice lay without moving while the Dr Chambers swept the ultrasound reader back and forth over her stomach, electronically seeing her baby hidden within. The woman, who looked to be in her early fifties, appeared to be well fed. Unlike Alice and everyone else at Lanherne, her face had a round quality to it. Not that she was fat by any stretch of the word, more that her face had none of angular feel that came from living one meal away from starvation. Apart from Dr Morris and the woman, there was also one other Doctor with her in the Med-lab and he seemed to keep himself busy darting between checking her blood under a microscope and inputting data from various machines into a computer. Well, Alice assumed he was a doctor. It was not as if he or the other two were dressed in the traditional white coats to indicate their profession. Like the solders, they wore camouflage army fatigues with a bulletproof vest over the top. The only nod to any form of medical identification on any of them was a small embroidered 'medic' patch sewn onto one sleeve.

'Placenta looks healthy and the amniotic fluid appears to be decreasing at an appropriate rate,' Chambers continued, looking back at Dr Morris, 'As good a candidate as we're going to find, Dr Morris.'

'Well, I'll discuss the matter with Dr Farrell when the next satellite window comes round,' he replied, moving forward to peer intently at the monitor image

As much as she hated to ask anything of the doctors, Alice was tantalised by the flickering reflections of light she could see bouncing off Dr Morris's glasses.

'Can… can I see my baby?' Alice asked, berating her herself for the emotion creeping into her voice, making it quiver.

Alice looked from one face to the next. The look of mild surprise that briefly flitted across the faces of all three doctors in the room was almost comical. Their attention had been so focused on the ultrasound monitor that it was as if they had forgotten that she was actually there at all. Dr Chambers' eyes flicked from Alice to the Dr Morris, waiting for his approval.

'Yes, of course,' he replied after a pause, slowly pivoting the monitor towards Alice.

Alice stared in wonder at the dancing pixels in front of her. The overwhelming emotion that seemed to flood into her was alien and indescribable to Alice. An all-encompassing love seemed to bloom suddenly within her, pushing itself to the very limits of her physical form. In that instant, she knew that she would love, or rather, she already loved this chid with every atom of her being. This child would be her world, totally. Without conscious thought, her hand moved towards the image of her developing child.

'That's his head there,' the female doctor said, tracing a section of the screen, 'and that's his heart…'

'His?' Alice whispered, her fingers delicately meeting the screen, 'I'm having a boy?'

'Yes, a boy,' said Dr Morris, 'but now you should rest.'

Standing, he abruptly repositioned the monitor, leaving Alice's hand mournfully hovering in space.

As Alice's hand slowly fell back to rest on her belly, something that had been said nagged at the back of her mind. Something made her feel both protective and uneasy at the same time.

'Candidate for what?' she asked.

'Sorry?' Dr Morris replied, slipping his glasses back down onto the bridge of his nose as he looked at a printed tape coming from one of the machines.

'She said my son was a good candidate,' Alice continued. 'Candidate for what, exactly?'

Dr Morris shot his colleague a quick harsh look before taking a deep breath.

'Alice, your child could be…could be the saviour of Mankind,' he began, a serious look on his face. 'Now don't get me wrong, I don't mean in the form of a religious Messiah but rather his very existence at this moment in time could be just what we've been looking for to end all this… this madness.'

'What do you mean?' Alice asked, pushing herself up on one elbow.

'Erm... where to begin...' he continued, removing his glasses, folding them and using them to tap against his chin, 'well, after a lot of trial and error, we've finally isolated the virus responsible for the Death-walker plague. Put simply, it's a manmade air-born pathogen, deceptively simple in its structure but with a highly complex DNA structure. Whoever manufactured the original viral components certainly did some heavy-duty gene manipulation to make sure it was going to be virtually impossible to pin down. For some reason, known only to its maker, its protective coat of protein molecules mutate as it reproduces but only after it is host bound. This makes it appear quite alien in appearance to its original air-born form. That's why it took so us long, you see. Each time we thought we had it licked, it would up and change again. What the original objective of the virus was, we'll never know, but I'm guessing they hadn't counted on it being partial to burying itself deeply in the synaptic junctions of nerve tissue. Even less likely that it liked to keep them firing even after the host had expired. Anyway, Alice, with each breath we take, we continually infect ourselves. There's not a soul on the plant who doesn't already have the Death-walker buried deep in their nervous system, waiting to take over its host.'

'I still don't understand, Doctor, sorry,' Alice said, not knowing where this was going.

'Well, we've finally managed to develop our own host based anti-virus which contains a specific protein inhibitor gene. Our virus also congregates at these same synaptic junctions and when it comes into contact with the Death-walker virus, it locks its current mutation in place and then uses this as a template to actively seek out and destroy the original invading virus. The major drawback being that to test it, it needs to be introduced to a host uninfected by the Death-walker virus. If we can do this and everything works as we think it should, we can then use the subsequent generations of our antivirus to produce a vaccine or even better an air born version and combat it globally rather than patient by patient.'

The realisation suddenly began to dawn on Alice. She knew the way this conversation was going and she didn't like it one bit.

'And let me guess,' she said, 'this uninfected host you want to test this theory on... is my baby?'

'It's perfectly safe, I assure you,' Dr Morris butted in.

'But surely if I'm infected, my baby is too?' She continued, ignoring the doctor's assurances.

'Not at all,' he replied. 'Like with HIV, the foetus would carry your antibodies, yes, but may not actually be infected itself.'

'No, I'm not going to allow you to experiment on my baby,' Alice said, feeling her maternal panic rising. 'You have no idea what this new virus could do to him... not really. It's all been in theory so far, hasn't it?'

'I think you misunderstand me,' said Dr Morris, shaking his head wearily.

'Oh, I understand you alright and the answer is, no!' Alice shouted, as she began to push herself up from the bed.

'No, Alice,' he continued, 'what I mean is that you seem to be under the misapprehension that we're asking your permission.'

It was only then that Alice noticed that Dr Chambers had moved around her and was drawing a clear liquid from a small vial into a hypodermic.

'You get that thing the fuck away from me!' she shouted, trying to push at Dr Morris as he gripped her shoulders tightly. For a small man, he was surprisingly strong.

'Now, Alice, there's no point in struggling. You'll only cause yourself an injury,' he said, trying to push her back down onto the bed.

'No!' she screamed and with a strength born of pure maternal fear, she managed to wrench one of her arms free long enough to slam her palm into Dr Morris' nose.

With a yelp, he immediately let go of her, his hands automatically rising to his face to staunch the blood flowing freely from his nose. However, from the stabbing sharp pain that was in her other arm, Alice already knew it was too late.

'No, please,' she said softly, turning to the woman withdrawing the needle.

If she had hoped to find anything maternal or compassionate in the woman's face, Alice was to be sorely disappointed. The woman stared blankly at Alice for a few seconds.

'It's just something to calm you down,' she said matter-of-factly, replacing the plastic cap over the needle.

Then, as if Alice was nothing but a test subject, her humanity suddenly ignored, she reached out to Alice's face. With her surgical glove covered fingers, the doctor then pulled up one of Alice's eyelids, wanting to observe her pupil dilation as the anaesthetic took effect.

'Please,' Alice said, trying to pull her face away from the woman's grasp. Already a heavy feeling seemed to be smothering her arms and legs. 'Please, my baby... please.'

With each breath, a blooming darkness crept across her whole body, threatening to pull her down into a dreamless oblivion.

'Her malnourished state seems to have speeded up the reaction time to the Propofol. It's to be expected though,' Dr Chambers said to Dr Morris, as she observed Alice's pointless fight against the drug to stay conscious. 'She'll be out any second.'

With the darkness quickly closing in on her, Alice could fight no more. Three spoken words drifted to Alice through the fog of her mind, demanding attention, but before the last word faded from thought, she was unconscious, their meaning lost to her.

'Strap her down,' said Dr Morris.

***

'I thought the Lanherne group kept on top of the Dead?' Leon whispered, turning from the spy hole. 'We seem to be running into a lot more than I expected.'

'Yes, I know,' Patrick replied over his shoulder. 'Phil said they usually just had to deal with a dozen or so a day, but we're only just reaching the village and we've killed three times that many at least. I don't like it.'

It had taken longer than expected for the two carts with their heavy loads of livestock and survivors to make it as far as St Mawgan village. The snowfall hadn't helped with their progress. More than once, one of the carts had lurched alarmingly to one side as a wheel sank deep into an unseen pothole. Thankfully, they had been travelling at a slow enough pace that the sudden jolt hadn't caused the wheels any damage. To try to repair them on the road would have been a Herculean task at the best of times, never mind the freezing wind and intermittent snowfall that they had to deal with at the moment. It was when they began to pass the first of the dilapidated cottages on the outskirts of the village that they encountered their first large group of the Dead. Phil had made it clear before they left the Penhaligan home that even though it would slow them down, they would deal with any of the Dead they came across rather than simply leaving them to wander. It had been one of Charlie's rules and Lanherne had abided by it religiously, even though he was no longer with them. You never knew when a problem would proverbially come back to bite you on the arse, so to deal with the Dead when they were still a manageable number, just made common sense. You waited too long to cull them and you could find yourself quickly overrun.

'But what's attracting them?' Helen quietly said, nervously pulling a sleeping Jasmine closer to her. 'From what Phil said, this certainly isn't the norm for around here, so something's got them riled up, big time.'

Ahead of them, Delilah pulled the Lanherne cart to a stop. As he watched, a group of more than a dozen Dead in various states of decay milled aimlessly about them, blocking the narrow country lane in the process. Patrick pulled Shadow to a halt, waiting for a sign from Imran.

'Come on,' Patrick said to himself under his breath, urging Imran into action.

On either side of their cart, the Dead stumbled past them. Patrick worried the crush of the Dead might make Shadow bolt if their numbers increased much more. Already the usually steady mare rocked her head back and forth, uncomfortable in the presence of so much Dead flesh. Then a decrepitly decayed woman, her mouldy skin puckering where shards of broken glass had been embedded deeply in her rotting flesh, stumbled and lost her footing. She fell from sight alongside Shadow's flank. As she went down, one of the pieces of glass in her shoulder brushed sharply against the mare's skin, startling her. With a start, Shadow made her displeasure evident and strained against her harness, jolting the cart behind her and those within it violently. With this sudden movement, Jasmine was shaken awake. As expected with an infant brought abruptly from a comfortable nap, Jasmine began to scream in the loud high-pitched tone that only a startled baby could produce. Immediately, the constant rustle of Dead footsteps ceased. One by one, Dead eyes turned towards the cart that up until that moment had held no more interest in them than a rock or tree.

'Shit!' Patrick said, turning to look at Helen, their screaming daughter in her arms.

Then the pounding started. First, one withered fist slammed hard against cart's wooden cover and then another and another. Soon there was a constant drumming and scraping of fists and fingers, desperate to get to the living flesh now known to be hidden from view. Realising that the cart wouldn't be able to withstand this continual onslaught forever, Patrick was relieved when, through the front view slit, he saw the roof hatch of the Lanherne cart open and Imran appeared, already pulling back the string of his bow.

'Leon, J-Man,' Patrick said, 'Get some of these Dead bastards off us before they smash their way in.'

'On it,' Leon replied, while pulling two of his throwing knives free as J-man flipped open the roof hatch.

Steadying himself on the roof, J-man pulled Leon up. After a little too much creaking for comfort from the wooden panels that made up the roof, the two edged themselves over to look down on the attacking Dead.

'Here,' Sarah called from the hatch, handing J-man a long club with wicked looking spikes driven through its end.

'Thanks,' he replied, taking it from her.

In the time it took to retrieve the weapon, two of the Dead had already fallen to Leon's knives and he was smoothly pulling another two blades from their sheath covers. As J-man cautiously moved back to the edge of the cart's roof, he noticed beneath the moans and sounds of Dead clambering hands on the side of the cart, the unmistakable low thud of sharp points rupturing skulls. As if to prove his assumption correct, an arrow suddenly appeared in the temple of a Dead woman below him. Instantly, her jaw went slack as her head was snapped to one side by the force of the impact. If it hadn't been for the press of her Dead brethren about her, she surely would have slumped to the ground, her animated corpse once more claimed by death.

'Right,' said J-man to himself, quickly picking a target from the Dead throng.

A bloated grey corpse, utterly sexless in its advanced decayed state, soon noticed the living flesh of J-man, hovering above it just beyond its grasp. Reaching up, arms sagging under the weight of its maggot-ridden skin, the creature fixed its gaze upon the flesh it knew would somehow quench this burning need that consumed it.

'Not today, Fatso,' J-man said, ramming the club down forcefully onto the top of its hairless baldhead.

With a crack, the spikes ripped through the mottled skin, cracking the skull plates and rupturing the rancid cranial tissue. Grunting with effort, J-man yanked free his spiked club, pulling away shards of broken skull and brain matter in the process. Ignoring the fate of this creature, J-man swiftly moved his attention to the next cadaver, his club falling again to end an unnatural existence. One by one, the Dead began to fall beneath an onslaught of blows from J-man's club, Leon's knives and Imran's deadly flying arrows.

'I'm out of knives!' called Leon, five minutes later as he stepped away from the edge of the cart.

'It's alright, man, Imran's just got the last two,' J-man said, as the final animated corpses fell to the road, finally motionless forever.

'Jesus, where did they all come from?' Leon asked, wiping his sweating forehead with the back of his sleeve. 'God, I hope it's clear from here on in. I'm knackered already.'

'Beats me,' J-man replied, before jumping down from the roof to check on Shadow.

With the Dead now dealt with, Patrick clambered out of the cart, stepping over the rotting corpses surrounding them to join J-man by Shadow.

'Is she alright?' he asked, worried the mare might have received a serious cut from the glass.

'Looks like just a scrape to me,' J-man replied, gently examining the long but shallow wound on shadows flank. 'I think she was more spooked than anything. I'll wash it out with some garlic water for now and get Gabe to see to her properly when we get to Lanherne.'

'Okay,' said Patrick, with a nod, knowing the antiseptic qualities of the garlic water would help prevent any infection setting in.

'Is everyone okay?' Phil called, jumping down from the back of the Lanherne cart and walking over to J-man and Patrick, as he pulled on a pair of work gloves plainly too small for his large hands.

'Yep, I guess Jasmine was just the dinner gong they were waiting for,' Patrick said, looking around at the collection of corpses littering the road while he gently patted Shadow's neck, expelling the last of her jumpy nerves.

'Well, we'd better shift these to the side of the road,' Phil said, kicking the still form of a Dead man missing much of the flesh from one of his arms. 'We'll collect Imran's arrows and Leon's knives as we go. Do you have any gloves?'

'Always come prepared,' Patrick said with a smile, pulling a similar pair of gloves from his back pocket. 'Do you know how many arrows we're looking for? Don't want to leave any behind, because I know how long Imran takes to make them.'

'Erm,' Phil began to say but was cut short by an urgent shout from J-man.

'Phil! The hatch!' he cried, pointing frantically to the Lanherne cart.

Spinning to look behind him, Phil threw himself into action. There, having silently pulled itself up to the open hatchway was the top half of a Dead child. The pitiful creature had lost its legs and much of the flesh from its pelvis, leaving a gaping hole through which rotting bone and organs trailed. Already its small Dead hands were reaching up to latch onto Duncan's back, desperate to pull itself up to the flesh almost within reach.

'Duncan!' Phil shouted, still six strides away from being of any help.

At the sound of his name, Duncan turned just as the small blackened fingers grasped hold of his jacket, his movement inadvertently pulling the mutilated cadaver closer to him.

'Jesus!' Phil heard Duncan scream, as he fell backwards into the cart, trying to escape the Dead thing pulling itself up his body.

'Move out of the way so I can't get to it!' Came Gabe's shout over Chloe's screams.

By the time Phil reached the cart, Duncan was on his back, struggling to dislodge the snapping creature.

'Oh no, you don't,' Phil growled, grabbing what was left of the child's pelvis.

With one mighty tug, Phil yanked the small decaying body from Duncan, swinging it over his shoulder in an arc and releasing it mid-air. With a crack, the child connected with the snowy road a few meters away. His breath pluming in the chilly morning air, Phil watched the bisected Dead child flip itself over and begin to pull itself along by its cracked and blackened claw like hands. As, hand over hand, the child pulled itself closer to Phil, determined to get to the flesh it craved, he could feel nothing but pity for the tragic thing before him. Phil walked forward to meet the Dead child halfway.

'Sorry, little one,' he said softly under his breath, and then with one stamp, he brought his boot firmly down on the child's head, its skull breaking with an audible snap under the pressure of his weight.

'Seventeen,' he said, turning back to Patrick after a brief pause, as if nothing had happened 'Imran will need back seventeen arrows.'

'Seventeen,' Patrick said with a smile. 'Hear that, people, we need to find seventeen arrows and a dozen of Leon's knives among this crap. The sooner we find them, the sooner we can get home.'

It wasn't until he'd said it that Patrick realised he had already accepted what was left of the Substation group would be absorbed into the Lanherne community, permanently. Together, they would become a newer and stronger group, pooling their skills and resources, benefiting all. These people, who before now had only met a handful of times over the last two years, had risked their lives coming to their rescue and he made a promise to himself that he would repay this debt to them, no matter how long he had to wait.

Twenty minutes later, all but one of Leon's knives had been found, Imran had retrieved his arsenal of arrows, barring two broken beyond repair and the bodies of the Dead had been hauled to the side of the road.

'Patrick, Phil, come look at this,' Imran called as he stood by Delilah, keeping an eye out in case any more of Dead were headed their way.

Swinging the last of the Dead between them, Phil and Patrick let go on the count of three, sending the corpse of what had once been a nurse, over the roadside hedge to join the pile of bodies already there.

'What is it?' Phil asked, hoping they weren't about to be surrounded again.

'Look at the snow,' Imran indicated, pointing to the junction where the road they were currently on joined another that would lead through the village to the Convent. 'Call me crazy but can you see tyre tracks?'

'Shit!' said Phil, jogging to the junction with Patrick close on his heels.

'Not just any tyres,' said Patrick, his head following the marks in the shallow snow, up and down the road, 'but big ones, and from the looks of them, more than one vehicle too.'

'This road leads right to Lanherne,' Phil added, nervously scratching his beard. 'Can't tell if they're going to or coming from, but this spells trouble either way.'

'Trouble?' Patrick asked, 'Why? Perhaps it's some sort of rescue.'

'On the way to get you, we found Jackson's Dead wife with a new looking army knife rammed in her skull. I think it was just too much for the old man to cope with so he hung himself,' Phil replied, turning to walk back to the carts. 'I think we better get moving.'

Patrick agreed. It couldn't be just a coincidence that the electricity was suddenly surging, the evidence of petrol run vehicles and a new army knife, all turning up at the same time. Whatever was going on, they needed to find out before any more innocents died.

Despite their need to get home as soon as they could, progress was still painfully slow through the snow-covered lanes. Phil had already made it clear they could break Charlie's golden rule about dealing with any Dead they came across. They simply couldn't afford to stop. The tracks indicated person or persons unknown had not only found the Convent but also been there, so they needed to assess and deal with the situation there before it was too late. As they travelled through the snowy village Phil prayed to God, whom he doubted was listening anymore, that nothing bad had happened to anyone at Lanherne while he was away. Already, the guilt was eating away at him, twisting his insides.

'We should have gone straight back when we found the knife,' he said under his breath, guiding Delilah past the rusty snow covered wreck of a car. 'Stupid, stupid, stupid... all my fault'

'Hey, we made that decision together, Phil,' said Imran, placing a reassuring hand on the large man's shoulder. 'It's no-one's fault. Let's just see what's happening before we beat ourselves up about it.'

Around them, the snow had started to fall again, lightly at first, a few dancing flurries momentarily swirling about Delilah's head before being whisked away by the cold breeze. However, by the time they passed through the village and reached the wide gate at the mouth of the lane, the weather had taken a dramatic turn for the worse. What had started as a few random wispy snowflakes had developed quickly into a thick heavy snowfall that covered their tracks in mere moments of their passing. Phil, struggling to see more than a metre in front of Delilah, knew he would have to rely on the mare's instincts to get them up the lane and to the gates safely. She had made this trip countless times and knowing a warm stable was almost within her reach, she would not steer them wrong.

'Lucky it's just one long lane,' Duncan said, looking through one of the cart's spy holes at the blizzard of snow being whipped about in the wind. 'At least we won't lose Patrick behind us.'

'Can you see them behind us though?' Phil asked, turning to look at Duncan. 'I don't want them falling too far behind. Our tacks will fill up pretty quickly in this snow and Shadow doesn't know this road like Delilah.'

'Yep, they're right on our tail,' Gabe answered. 'I can just about see her through the snowfall. Patrick's steering her to follow our route exactly.'

'Good,' said Phil quietly to himself, as he peered through the front slit into the swirling snow outside.

Suddenly, through the falling curtain of snow, a large shadow began to emerge and take shape. Fuzzy at first, any definition was lost among the twisting eddies of the falling snow, but then it slowly began to form. With each step, Delilah pulled them closer. The walls of Lanherne loomed larger, a signal their journey among the Dead was almost at an end. When Lanherne finally materialised completely before them, Phil swore at what he could see. There at the base of the high wall were at least twenty of the Dead, all pawing uselessly to get in.

'Right, we'll have to clear the Dead before they'll open the gate,' Phil said, pulling Delilah to a stop just outside the gate. 'Imran, can you fire accurately in this?'

'My aim's not going to be great but I'll do my best,' he replied, already reaching for his quiver of arrows.

'Okay, Gabe, if your ankle's not too bad, I'm going to need you to run back to Patrick and get Leon and J-man while they Dead still haven't noticed us,' Phil continued, turning to hand Delilah's reins to Duncan.

'Right,' Gabe replied, reaching past the sleeping sow to grab a length of heavy pipe hanging from the cart wall.

'Be careful,' said Chloe, her words snatched away by the wind as Gabe quickly closed the hatch behind him.

Pulling a whining Toby up onto her lap, Chloe moved one of the spyhole covers aside to make sure Gabe made it to the other cart safely. Absentmindedly, she stroked the anxious dog's black floppy ears to calm her already thumping heartbeat while she watched Gabe hobbling his way through the blizzard back to Patrick. Thankfully, Patrick saw his approach and was already jumping down from the cart, with Leon and J-man close on his heels, their weapons ready for action. She watched as Gabe shouted something in Patrick's ear, gesturing back to the wall to make his point clear. With a nod, Patrick said something briefly to Sarah and Helen in the cart before closing the hatches on them. The four men then braced themselves against the freezing wind to make their way to join Phil and Imran.

Standing in a defensive line behind the gathered oblivious Dead, the five other men waited for Phil's signal. Phil pointed to Imran and Leon to begin. It made sense that the archer and the knife thrower should take down as many as they could before the Dead became aware of their presence. Only then would the others join in with hand-to-hand combat. Imran's initial arrow, blown off course by the wind, finally found purchase deep in the shoulder of a large Dead man. Luckily, with his heavier knives, Leon was having better luck. Already two corpses slumped lifelessly in the snow, a knife lodged deep in each of their skulls, as Leon reached for a third knife. Imran had better luck with his next shot. Aiming slightly higher than his target to compensate for the wind and falling snow, Imran let the arrow fly. With a thud, another unnatural existence ended, the large Dead man finally falling to ground to join his already felled companions. It was at that point that a Dead teenager, his mottled skin tinged green with a creeping mould, turned his head slightly and caught sight of the living behind him. With a low hungry moan, he reached a broken hand beseechingly towards them before stumbling away from the wall towards the flesh he so craved.

'Now!' Phil shouted, rushing forward before any more of the Dead became aware of them.

Like a barbarian, Phil charged forward, smashing the skulls of two of the Dead with a double swing of his club, following the movement through with a hefty kick at the legs of a third. Even over the roaring wind, the buckling legs gave way with an audible snap of brittle kneecaps. Turning, Phil then stamped down hard on the Dead woman at his feet, her skull cracking under his foot. With her head now horribly misshapen and putrid fluid oozing across her face, the Dead woman still tried to claw up along Phil's leg. Knocking her back to the floor, Phil swiftly delivered a second stamp to her head. This time, her already weakened skull was no match for the force being applied to it and with a crunch, Phil's boot sent her brain splashing across the trampled down snow. Without so much as a pause for breath, Phil turned his attention to another of the Dead reaching for him and began his onslaught again.

Gabe and J-man were working smoothly as a team, taking down the Dead quickly with minimal contact. Despite his ankle, Gabe darted under outstretched arms, his pipe swinging, to smash at emaciated ankles and kneecaps left and right. With nothing to support them, the animated cadavers, toppled comically to the ground only to meet the full force of J-mans spiked club when they tried to right themselves.

Patrick, fighting alongside Phil, matched him in his the ferocity of his attack. To give himself room, Patrick kicked violently out at the chest what had once been a young black man, knocking him back against the Convent walls. His once rich ebony skin, now the pallid colour of death, had been torn from much of his weathered body in strips. A few misshapen tattoos on what was left of his forearms still stood out in contrast against his ashen skin. With a powerful overhead swing, Patrick aimed to bring his length of pipe down on the man's skull. However, at that moment, the Dead man jerked forward, causing Patrick to miss his killing mark completely. Instead, as the pipe connected with the Dead man's head, it sloughed decaying skin and flesh from the cadavers face. Rancid tendons attaching the jaw to the skull tore free under this attack, leaving the Dead man's lower jaw to hang uselessly to one side. Oblivious to the fact that he would never bite anything ever again, the Dead man continued to reach for Patrick desperate to fill his mouth with warm bloody flesh. Swearing at himself for his mistake, Patrick used the momentum of his failed swing to bring the pipe back up in a looping arc. This time the pipe smashed into the Dead man's temple with a loud crack. For a spilt second, the Dead man was still. Then as he was shoved aside by one of his hungry brothers in death, his corpse crumpled to the ground, never to rise again.

One by one, the animated bodies fell beneath their blows until the last, a withered thing that may have been an old woman in life, departed this earth with one of Leon's knives lodged in the back of her head.

'Shit, man,' said J-man, leaning over to catch his breath, 'must be getting old.'

Phil reached for the bell to alert those inside of their presence but before his hand could reach the cord, he could hear the cranking of the winch mechanism within.

'Right, inside,' Phil began, waving the men in as the gate began to open. 'Duncan will bring our cart in. We check for any Dead hanging on underneath before the inner gate opens, then we repeat the process with the second cart. Gabe, go give Sarah the heads up, will you?'

With a nod, Gabe ran back outside to let Sarah know what was happening. Phil turned to check out who was on watch duty. Whoever was working the winch was bundled up in multiple layers of coats and scarves, fighting to keep out the cold, so he was unable to tell whom it was. It wasn't until the figure jogged back along the walkway to the second winch, that Phil recognised Bryon's tell-tale limp.

'Shit,' Phil said to himself.

Not only was it a bad sign that Bryon was on watch but in his urgency to get them inside he was already opening the inner gate without the normal checks being done first.

'Imran,' Phil called, 'check the cart as Duncan rolls it in... I think the shit's about to hit the fan.'

Leaving Imran to do the safety check, Phil pushed himself through the already opening inner gate to find a frail looking Sister Josephine there to meet him.

'Oh, Phil, thank God!' Sister Josephine wept as she threw herself into his arms. 'They took them... they took them all!'

***

With little success, Liz tried again to find a comfortable position on Samson's back. She had been riding for hours and the baby was letting her know of its discomfort with a series of sharp kicks.

'Come on,' she said quietly to her bump, 'give Mummy a break. I'm trying to get back your auntie Anne, okay?'

Reaching up with one hand, she grabbed a low hanging tree branch and pulled another strip of cloth from her bag with the other. She had been repeating this at every road junction, leaving behind her a Hansel and Gretel breadcrumb trail for Imran and the others to follow. The going would have been relatively easy, despite the discomfort, if it weren't for the fact that at every turn, she was met by two or three of the Dead stumbling through the snowy hedgerows, attracted by the sound of the passing convoy. Each time she had to stop to deal with them, the convoy got further and further ahead of her, but she knew she couldn't leave the Dead to follow on her tail. She would have to stop at some point to allow Samson to rest and certainly didn't want a hoard of hungry Dead corpses coming up behind her while she waited for Imran to arrive. Best to deal with them when they were still in a manageable number, even if it did mean letting the convoy get further away from her. Luckily, the previous night's snowfall allowed her to follow them at a distance, their tell-tale tyre tracks were clear to see.

Letting the branch go, the blue strip of cloth now fluttering in the wind, Liz looked up at the heavy clouds above her and wondered if she was in for another snowfall. Then, as if the universe had read her mind, she watched as the first flurry of dusty snowflakes spiralled down towards her. Behind her, the scrap of fabric suddenly snapped loudly back and forth as the breeze increased in strength.

'Oh, great,' she said to herself, as she gave Samson the nudge with her heel for him to move again.

Slowly, at first, these initial dancing flakes merely increased the speed of their merry pirouettes as they fell, but before long, the lacy specks were replaced by larger heavier cousins, which barrelled their way through buffeting winds from the clouds above. As the falling snow developed into a full-blown blizzard, a bloom of panic began to grow within Liz. She knew if the convoy's tracks were filled by the falling snow, the chance of losing them became almost a certainty. She needed to shorten the gap that had developed between her and the convoy if she was to stand a chance of staying on their tail. So with another kick of her heels, Samson broke into a canter. Pushing Samson to increase his speed on unknown roads like this was a fine line she dared to walk. Left with only her judgement and a fair amount of guesswork, she guided him around the worst of the potholes and prayed he didn't lose his footing and throw her. She now raced past the Dead, shambling alone or in small groups, knowing she would just have to take the risk and leave them in her wake. Now was not the time to deal with them. With the weather against her, her time was running out.

For an hour, the snow fell and with each buffeting gale that swallowed her briefly in its freezing curtain of snow, she knew the chance of losing her sister increased.

'Fuck!' Liz swore to herself, as the road she was on abruptly bisected another.

Frantically looking back and forth along the cross road, Liz was at a loss as to which turning the convoy had taken. The falling snow had beaten her. She had lost them. She had let Anne and the others down and as the hopelessness of the situation settled like a weight in her chest, her tears fell unashamedly. Sitting back in her saddle, defeated, with her plumes of breath joining Samson's in the cold air, she tilted her head, closed her eyes and cried to the heavens. For a briefest of moments, the heavens seemed to hear her. The wind ceased in its constant howling rage to allow the snow to fall silently about her, bathing the land of the Death with its purifying shroud of white.

'I was afraid we'd lost you,' a man's voice came, making her jump.

Liz snapped her head forwards, her hand automatically pulling free her sword from its sheath. There, standing a few meters in front of Samson was one of the soldiers. Or rather it was 'the' soldier, the one Sister Josephine had told her about, the one that had seen her at the attic window, the one who was going to help her get Anne back.

'Jesus, you made me jump,' she said, still a little wary of the stranger. 'Where did you come from?'

'We've made camp about three quarters of a mile down the right hand turning,' he began. 'You'd better get out of this weather, because it's not going to get any better and we're not going anywhere until the morning now anyway. You've got to find somewhere secure for the night or you'll freeze.'

'Where's my sister?' Liz said, ignoring his show of concern.

'She's fine, believe me. They never hurt the children,' he began, looking nervously back over his shoulder. 'Look, I've got to go back before anyone notices.'

'I thought you were going to help me? Don't you think we need some sort of plan?' she asked. 'There'll be more of my friends following me, perhaps if we work together?'

'Just be ready for me tomorrow,' he replied, already backing away from her. 'I'll get as many out as I can, okay.'

The soldier then turned and began to jog down the lane away from her.

'Be ready for me,' he called, disappearing into the falling snow. 'You'll know when.'

A little stunned that, the soldier should appear out of the blue just when she thought all hope was lost. Liz wiped away her tears with the back of her gloved hand, and took a breath to calm herself. He had been certainly right about one important thing, she needed to find somewhere safe to wait out the blizzard and soon. With a pull on Samson's reins, Liz turned him around to return the way they had come. About five minutes earlier, she had sped past the dilapidated ruin of a cottage, set just off from the road and with the snow continuing to fall at such a steady pace, it looked like it was going to be her only option for a night's shelter.

When she arrived back in front of the cottage, she could tell the fleeting glance she had received as she sped by had been somewhat misleading. The cottage itself was little more than a burnt out shell topped with the remnants of a caved in roof. The garage, attached to one side, seemed to be promising until Liz noticed the door was only loosely attached to its frame by a single hinge. This made the structure useless to her if the Dead decided to attack but it would certainly do as a make shift stable for Samson for the night. Liz was about to give up on the cottage completely when she noticed the bulky shape of a vehicle covered by a tarpaulin at the back of the garage. With a 'grunt' Liz swung her leg over Samson's back and dropped slowly, if a little ungracefully, to the ground.

Clicking her blade free, Liz walked gingerly to the back of the garage, her senses on edge in case the building harboured any of the Dead. Grateful to find the only moving things in the garage were she, Samson and the odd spider. Liz pulled back the mouldy tarpaulin to uncover the vehicle hidden beneath. Brightly painted faces of happy children and dancing cartoon ice-lollies suddenly stared back at her as the ice-cream van was revealed. Once someone's livelihood, the van had seemingly sat untouched for the last eight years, waiting for its owner to return. With its windows high off the ground, it would certainly do for the night and Liz reached up to open the back door.

'Please,' Liz said under her breath, as her hand hovered briefly over the latch.

Gripping the handle tightly, Liz slowly pulled down, praying it would open. With a satisfying 'click', the lock released and the door swung open slightly. Knowing sometimes it wasn't just shelter you found behind a locked door, she placed her feet apart in a defensive stance and held her blade high, as she reached forward with her free hand to slowly pull the door fully open. With a sigh of relief, Liz lowered her blade. It was empty. Just inside the door was a small concertina stepladder and pulling it into its down position, Liz climbed up into the van's small galley. The inside of the van smelt of old dry mould and knowing better than to open the long forgotten freezers, Liz gave the overhead cupboards a quick once over before deciding, despite the smell, it would do for the night.

After she had made sure Samson was sheltered from the wind, she draped the van's tarpaulin over his body, apologising as she did so, that she couldn't offer him anything warmer.

'It's just one night, boy,' she said, stroking his muzzle before returning to the ice-cream van to settle down for the night.

Once she had pulled up the small ladder and closed the door, shutting out the worst of the drafts, Liz hunkered down on the floor of the van and listened to the mournful howling winds that buffeted outside the garage, waiting for sleep to come for her.

***

Outside, Dead eyes caught movement, movement too fluid and lithe to be that of their Dead comrades. Although this was the reasoning for their interest, they could not process the thoughts as such. They only knew something had caught their attention, something that promised blood, flesh and perhaps some relief from the burning need that consumed them. So, slowly they dragged their torn and shattered limbs through the snow to the place they knew held this relief, and as they moved, their hungry moans joined those of the wind to fill the sky. They would have their flesh this night. They would feed.

***

'Where did you disappear to?' one of his fellow soldiers asked Steve when he appeared out of the blizzard.

'Thought I saw something,' Steve replied, breathing onto his cold fingers and stamping his feet. 'Better safe than sorry.'

'Thought some Dead head had got your arse between his teeth,' the soldier replied. 'You could've warned me.'

'I did...' Steve began. 'What? Didn't hear me tell you I was checking it out? My ear-mic connection must be a bit jippy.'

Steve starting tapping the earpiece for effect, counting numbers into the mike for a sound check.

'No. Better get that sorted, mate. Anyway, did you see that blonde piece we got at the Convent?' the soldier asked, whistling. 'Nice tits, that one. Certainly wouldn't say no to a bit of that.'

Steve stopped pretending to test his ear-mic, his hand frozen mid-movement. He knew the man was referring to Penny, his Penny, and a wave of hot anger suddenly swept over him.

'Don't let Sarge hear you talking like that on duty,' he replied, his voice as cold as steel, as he fought to keep the anger within him.

Immediately, a look of fear flashed behind the soldiers eyes. He knew all too well, what happened to people who stepped out of line in this army. People who caught Sergeant Blackmore's attention for the wrong reasons had a nasty habit of getting a beating from the three SAS goons, or worse, they went missing entirely.

'Hey, I didn't mean anything by it,' the soldier added, the panic creeping into his voice.

'Look, forget it,' Steve began, cutting the man's apology short as he turned to start walking into the makeshift camp. 'I'm done here. It's your turn to freeze your balls off for the next four hours.'

Leaving behind the soldier nervously chewing his lip, Steve walked past the Jackal vehicle positioned as their rear guard against the Dead, shouldering his rifle as he went. The two cold looking soldiers sitting inside were hunched down behind their machine guns, trying to keep out of the worst of the wintery blizzard. One briefly nodded to him as he passed, while the other, who was clearly having a bad time of it being off the island was unable to take his eyes from the hedgerows lining the lane. From his tense expression, it was clear he expected a hoard of the Dead to descend on him at any moment.

An hour ago, the convoy had made camp at what had once been a small car park. At one time, families out on day trips would have parked there to enjoy a merry picnic as they overlooked the natural beauty of the Cornish countryside but now, overgrown and littered with the rusting remnants of lives lost, Sergeant Blackmore had made it the convoy's home for the evening.

With one of each of the Jackals positioned to supply covering fire, the Med-lab, the trailer carrying the civilians and the dozen or so army tents, had all found themselves nestled down for the night within this ring of protection.

Steve made his way over to one of the tents, the need for something warm to eat almost causing him miss the solider struggling to unlock the civilian lorry, while juggling an armful of MRE packs.

'Need a hand, Dave?' Steve asked, already taking a half dozen of the packs from the man before he could protest.

'What? Oh thanks, Steve,' the solider replied, finally able to release the lock. 'Don't know which is worse, rescuing them or feeding them this crap, poor bastards.'

Steve forced a smile but it did little to cover his apprehension. He knew Penny would surely hate him for what had happened and he was about to confront her for the first time. He had already prepared the note he would try to slip her unnoticed and hoped it would start the process of winning back her trust.

'Grub up, people,' Dave called, as the door opened.

The door had barely released from its latch when Richard came barrelling through it, his head and shoulders down, rugby style, knocking Dave to the ground.

'Wait!' Steve called, but Richard was already sprinting away from the lorry, Nicky, Justin and Anne close on his heels.

It was then that two of the SAS Commandos stepped out from one of the tents and with lightning speed took in the situation. As Richard and his family sped past them, Hills lunged for Nicky, bringing her to the ground in a tumble of limbs.

'Richard!' she screamed, as the soldier sat across her chest, drew back his hand to give her a fierce back handed slap.

Instantly, Richard skidded to a stop in the snow and turned, the two scared children stepping behind him for protection.

'Fucking get off her, you bastard!' he growled, taking an angry step forward.

'Don't even think about it, shit-for-brains,' Hills said, turning the muzzle of his rifle to face Nicky.

Richard froze mid-step. He was so focused on Nicky, he wasn't even aware of Bill Clarkes, the second Commando, until it was too late. With a harsh jab to his kidneys, Richard fell to the ground as terrible pain exploded across his back. But Clarkes wasn't satisfied Richard had learnt his lesson and without giving it a second thought, he began to kick viciously at the man who was already curled up in pain at his feet. With a scream, Justin valiantly threw himself at the soldier, landing on his back. Of course, Justin's small frame was no match for the brute strength the soldier harboured and no sooner had Justin begun his barrage of ineffectual punches on the man, than he was being thrown to the snow covered ground. Clarkes, with lightning reflexes, drew up his rifle and took aim on Justin, the small boy's eye widening with terror.

'No!' screamed Nicky, panic flooding her voice.

'Soldier!' came a cold voice, from the left. 'Stand down!'

All heads and eyes turned instantly to Sergeant Blackmore standing by the communications tent, his steely gaze taking in every detail of the scene. Silently, Clarkes lowered his rifle away from Justin.

'Get these civilians inside,' he continued, glancing down at Richard, his blood turning a growing patch of snow crimson.

With no more to be said on the matter and knowing this order would be followed to the letter, Sergeant Blackmore, turned on his heels and disappeared back into the tent; the beaten family already forgotten.

'Up!' Clarkes said, tapping Richard's hip with his toe of his boot.

Richard slowly pushed himself up onto one elbow, wincing as pain shot through him. He painfully hacked up a mouthful of bloody phlegm and then bracing himself against the pain that was to come, hugged his ribs with one arm as he tried to push himself up into a sitting position.

'Come on,' the soldier continued, reaching down to roughly pull Richard upright. 'I haven't got all night'

Richard cried out in pain and without thinking, Steve rushed forward to help him, momentarily locking eyes with Nicky as he passed her.

'It's alright, Dave and I can take it from here,' he said, gently slipping Richard's arm over his shoulder.

'Assholes,' the soldier said, already dismissing the group as beneath his concern.

'Well, I know the MREs are bad but they're not worth a beating believe me,' Steve said jokingly, as he helped the beaten and bloody man back to the trailer.

Steve glanced over to Dave who was leading Nicky and the two children back inside, their arms already full of the dropped MRE meals. Once he was sure Dave wouldn't hear, Steve spoke seriously to Richard.

'If you'd waited five minutes you could have spared yourself a kicking,' he said, dropping his voice down to barely a whisper.

Richard looked up at Steve, questioningly.

'You're not the only one who doesn't want to play this sick game,' Steve said, pausing briefly to reposition Richard's arm, 'but you've just got to wait a while, I promise. Please, give Penny this note and tell her... tell her I'm sorry.'

Richard looked into the young man's eyes, trying to work out if this was nothing but a sick trap or if he could he really place his hope in this man. There was something there, though. Something honest and apologetic filled his sad eyes, particularly when he said Penny's name. With a nod, Richard decided he would have to trust him and slipped the folded scrap of paper in his blood splattered trouser pocket.

'Oh, and tell Penny, her sword wielding friend is following us,' Steve added quietly as Dave appeared at the trailer doorway.

Richard glanced at Steve, and in that instant, he knew he had been right to trust him. If he knew about Liz and hadn't done anything about her, he must be truly on their side.

***

'We've got to after her! Right now!' said Imran, as he paced back and forth in the refectory, a mix of panic and anger fighting for dominance within him. 'She'll freeze to death in this weather, unless she finds somewhere to wait out the night.'

For what seemed like the hundredth time, his eyes flicked back to the large pink stain on the wall. Despite Sister Rebecca's best efforts to wash away the splash of Sally's blood that had arched up the wall, the large pink tinged area was just another reminder of what they were dealing with.

'Now be sensible,' Phil began. 'In this weather we're likely to miss one of her flags and then we'll never find her. We've got to wait till morning.'

'We can't just sit here!' Imran shouted, turning on his friend, 'and what the fuck did she think she was doing putting herself and the baby in danger like that? Leaving without the cart… it's just suicide.'

'Hey!' Phil said, grabbing Imran's shoulders to force him focus on him, 'Imran! Listen to me… listen! She did what she had to do. You know that. You'd have done exactly the same if you'd been in her shoes and you know it. She had to go after them and there simply wasn't time to wait for us to come back with the cart.'

'But Phil,' Imran said, the worry and fear for Liz finally smothering his anger as he slumped down onto a bench, his head in his hands, 'I just want her back. I've got to get her back.'

'I know, son, I know,' said Phil, placing his hand affectionately on Imran's shoulder, 'Remember, Liz is one tough young lady. If anyone can make it out there just on horseback, it's her. We'll get her back safe and sound, don't you worry. We'll get them all back.'

'Right, we need to empty the carts now so we're prepared to leave at first light,' Patrick said, standing purposefully to address everyone who had gathered in the refectory. 'J-man, Gabe, I think you two should stay here to keep the numbers of the Dead down.'

'No problem,' J-man replied with a nod.

'Leon, I know it's a lot to ask but I think you should come with us? We could really use your knives out there,' Patrick said, turning to Leon hopefully.

'Patrick, Leon... you don't have to,' Phil butted in but Patrick's simply raised hand stopped him mid-sentence.

'Yes, yes we do. You came for us when we needed you, so now it's time to return the favour and besides, this is out fight too. We're part of Lanherne now, for the good and the bad times. Just happens we came along at a particularly shitty time, that's all,' Patrick said, shrugging his shoulders with a smile.

Phil looked at the man who had already naturally taken charge. With Liz and Imran backing him up, he would be a good leader for Lanherne; that is if any of them survived what was to come.

'Well, those carts aren't going to empty themselves,' said Helen abruptly, standing to give her unspoken support to Patrick's statement. 'Chloe, Sarah, you go with Sister Claire and help her move the new livestock into the stables, and Gabe, you help Lars with the horses. They'll need a good rest and feed before going out again tomorrow. Oh, and see to that cut in Shadow's flank, cause we don't want an infection setting in. J-man, Leon, you're with me. There's a lot to get off those carts, so the sooner we get it done, the sooner we can get in out of the cold. Sister Josephine, if you could just take Jasmine for a while, we'll make a start.'

Handing the gurgling child over to the stunned Mother Superior, Helen looked about at the group of unmoving sad and worry worn faces.

'Come on then, chop, chop,' she continued, with a clap of her hands to spur people into action. 'Arses and elbows, people! Let's get moving!'

'She always like this?' Phil asked, leaving the Refectory with Patrick at his side.

'Pretty much,' he replied, with a chuckle.

'Damn, you poor bastard,' said Phil, laughing as he slapped Patrick on the back.

***

Dr Daniel Morris dropped his glasses down onto the desk in front of him and once again tried to rub the tiredness from his eyes. His eyesight had deteriorated over the last eight years and he could tell from the reoccurring headaches that the prescription of his glasses was now becoming more and more inadequate. He kicked himself that he hadn't taken the opportunity to ditch the glasses altogether with laser eye surgery when he had the chance but he always been funny about his eyes. Unable even to contemplate the use of contact lenses, the thought of lying there while someone zapped his corneas was quite out of the question. Of course, now that the possibility was likely to be denied from him forever, it was easy to wish for something in hindsight.

'Damn,' he said quietly to himself, his fingers gingerly touching his bruised and swollen nose where Alice had hit him.

With only the flickering lights from the various monitors and computer screens in the Med lab for illumination, Dr Morris looked over at the prone form of Alice as she lay shrouded half in shadow. Even with his bad eyesight, he could tell from where he sat that her heart rate and all vital functions were normal for someone in a chemically induced sleep. The procedure on her unborn foetus had all gone smoothly and now within her womb she held the only person on the planet who would hopefully be immune to the Death-walker virus. Of course, this was purely based on hypothesis, examined and extrapolated data and a fair amount of guesswork on their part. Years of their work on the island had culminated into this one moment, this one moment that could bring humanity back from the brink.

The island base had been built primarily as a safeguard for humanity's survival against the use of chemical or biological warfare. Housing state of the art equipment, it had been kept up to date with all innovations in both medical and electrical advances since its conception over thirty years ago. As with all Governments though, their motives had not been totally altruistic. It was also to be a tool through which the British Empire could rise again as a major global player, should the worst ever happen. But even the far seeing 'powers that be' that had hidden billions of pounds worth of funding in various budgets over the past decades, could not have guessed or been prepared for what the base would finally end up fighting against.

Since the outbreak, Dr Morris and his team, despite each being experts in their own field had fumbled blindly in the dark for a solution to this plague that had swept across the globe. Years of getting their hopes raised only for them to be dashed had taken its toll on the overworked and stressed scientists. Suicides had been prevalent among those too weak to do what was needed to study the Death-walker plague in its entirety. To take that step into the abyss, beyond old world practices and ethics was more than some could bear. Nevertheless, those made of sterner stuff carried on; knowing to give up was never an option. To simply relinquish man's superiority and ultimately allow humanity to become nothing but a side note in the evolutionary process was unthinkable. Finally, by chance rather than by design, they had cracked this Chinese puzzle box of a virus, laying bare its genetic contents for them to plunder, mould and manipulate. Through trial and error, they too had engineered their own microscopic deadly assassin. The tide was about to turn in this global battle and Alice's child was to be the first of its many battlegrounds. So, to be so close to seeing all their work come to fruition should have filled Daniel with elation. He knew he should be excited, anxious or even wary of what was to come but he felt none of these emotions sitting there looking at Alice, with the printout of Dr Farrell's orders in his hand.

Pushing himself away from his desk, he threw the printout down and walked slowly over to check on Alice and her unborn child. Watching the small trace line of the foetus's heartbeat on the monitor, Daniel realised there was one small emotion in the back of his head fighting to be heard over his clinical, logical thoughts. It has been so long since he had allowed himself to acknowledge these thoughts that for a split second he was unable to recognise the feeling at all. Then, as Alice stirred slightly in her sleep, he recognised it for what it was… remorse.

DAY 4

Liz slowly moved her neck from left to right, then up and down. Sleeping curled up on the floor of the ice-cream van had not been the most comfortable of experiences, especially now that she was trying to move again. Her muscles protested against the sudden movement, causing Liz to wince as a spasm of pain shot across her shoulders. Rubbing the back of her neck with her hand, Liz sat up.

During the night, her breath has not only fogged up the van's windows but the below zero temperature had frozen the water vapour into swirling patterns of wafer thin ice across the glass. For a few minutes, as she tried to bring warmth to her aching muscles, her eyes followed the intricate ebb and flow of the formed ice. Blooming from the bottom of the windows, it had crept steadily upwards during the night until only a small section at the top was now free of this frozen lace. From what little light that managed to penetrate deep into the garage and through the sheets of ice that enclosed her, she could tell it was early morning. Beyond the confines of the van, she could hear Samson stamping his hooves and snorting.

'*Either hungry or eager to get moving to warm up his muscles... me too, Samson... me too,*' she thought to herself, using the side of a long defunct freezer to pull herself up off the floor.

Standing upright, she was just about the right height to see through the section of the windows free from ice. Through this small clear section, she could see out onto the snow-covered driveway outside, the morning sun reflecting off a thousand diamonds of ice.

'*Better get going before they get too far ahead again,*' she thought to herself, taking one last stretch to loosen her muscles.

Reaching for the handle on the back door, Liz suddenly froze, her hand hovering millimetres from the metal bar. Looking down at her slightly shaking fingers, she knew something was wrong. She knew this as a certainty. Yet what exactly was wrong seemed to dance just out of her reach. Something unknown was shouting out to her, demanding that she recognise the warning it held. Then, in a flash, the thought came to her, solid and terrifying.

'*The garage door!*'

She had made sure it was pulled to last night so Samson would be out of the wind. It now hung open. Slowly she withdrew her hand away from the handle, her eyes flicking back up to the ice-covered glass once more. Outside the van, Samson snorted again, not with eagerness to go, she now realised, but an eagerness to get away. The difference was obvious now that she knew something was amiss. With her heart pounding in her chest and the surge of adrenalin coursing through her, Liz reached up to place her hand against the thin sheet of ice that had formed on the window of the door. Feeling the cold ice beneath the warmth of her palm, Liz watched as the heat from her body radiated out to melt the thin ice quickly. A single droplet of water formed and began to run down the icy pane of glass, a clear path left in its wake. Not wanting to but knowing she must, Liz pulled her hand tentatively away from the glass. With a 'thud', a hand instantly rose to fill the clear void she had left.

'No!' Liz whispered, quickly stepping back to stare at the blackened and rotting hand that had appeared the other side of her handprint.

Shortly the hand disappeared from view, only to abruptly appear again with a second slap against the window.

'Shit!' Liz said, knowing now there was at least one of the Dead outside, if not more.

As the word fell from her lips, another sickening thud came from her right making her jump. This time, the window that would have been the serving hatch, shuddered slightly under the impact from outside. Then another bang came from behind her, as a third set of Dead hands connected with the painted glass. The thing at the door pounded again, determined to gain entrance, determined to get to the live flesh it knew was inside. Already more and more Dead hands were reaching up to join in their assault on the van walls and windows, and soon what had begun with the slap of one hand had become the constant drumming of many. They had also begun to sing their chilling dead chorus, as one by one they let forth their pitiful moans. The van began rocking slightly from the barrage of blows and Liz knew she had to see what she was up against. Taking a breath to calm herself, she stepped closer to the serving hatch and began to use her sleeve to slough away a large section of the ice.

'Fuck!' she said, her arm stopping mid movement.

There, focusing their blind filmy stare on her movements at the window, were at least ten of the hungry Dead, all jostling with their brethren to get closer to the van. The Dead, now rewarded with the sight of her living flesh, renewed their attack with a frenzied gusto. They reached up their withered decaying limbs to her, beseeching her to relinquish the warm blood and flesh they forever craved. Liz angled her head against the cold glass so she could peer down the side of the van. She could see that the crowd continued to the rear by the door, where another dozen of the animated corpses clambered against one another to gain entrance. Thankfully, the door opened outwards, so at least the press of their bodies worked in her favour. Their Dead brains could not process the actions of simply stepping back so the door could open and she was grateful for it. Turning her head to look in the other direction, Liz counted another eight of the Dead at the front of the van and from the hammering also from the side opposite the serving window, she realised she was surrounded.

'Shit, Shit, Shit,' Liz said to herself, nervously rubbing her belly as she tried to come up with a plan that didn't end up with her and her baby getting eaten alive.

Liz paced back and forth within the tiny confines of the van, hoping desperately an escape route would suddenly make itself known to her or an inspired plan come to mind. However, neither appeared and Liz knew she was in real trouble this time. For as good as she was with her blade, even she knew she wouldn't stand a chance in hell against so many of the Dead. Even if she hadn't been pregnant, she simply wouldn't have been able to attack fast enough before they were on her. With this amount of Dead, it didn't matter how slow they were, their strength was in their sheer numbers. Liz knew this was a fight she had no hope of winning.

Looking up, she contemplated the small hatch in the roof. It would be a tight squeeze for her to get through in her current condition and ultimately it would only allow her to be trapped on the roof of the van rather than inside it, but she could use it as a backup plan if things really got bad.

With the sound of splintering glass, Liz snapped her head to the right, instantly fearing the worst. Sure enough, only able to take the bombardment for so long, one of the windows now had an ominous looking crack rising from the base of its frame. With each Dead fist that connected with it, the crack fractured just a little bit more, until within moments, it was branching out across the pane like a terrifying lightning bolt. Finally, when the window could withstand no more of this abuse,, it shattered with a violent crash, sending large shards of glass skittering across the counter to smash down on the floor below. Reaching automatically for her blade, Liz tried to take a defensive stance in the small galley. However, with the low ceiling and no room for a good swing, she knew she would have to resort to a simple stabbing motion to keep these Dead at bay and so she adjusted the hold on the blade accordingly. Her only consolation now was that with all the windows at shoulder height, the Dead wouldn't be able to simply clamber in to get her.

With the glass no longer there to dampen their moans, the cries of the Dead hit her like a wall of fear, washing over her to fill her very soul to the brim. Below her, the Dead jostled and pushed against their cadaverous brothers in their need to push their arms through the broken window. As sure as night followed day, they needed to act out this compulsion, to reach this flesh that promised to quench the burn that filled their very existence. Trying frantically to reach for her, the Dead were oblivious to the wickedly sharp shards ripping and slicing into their decaying flesh. Nothing registered in their rotting brains but the image of the life before them; the life they needed to rip, tear and taste.

Suddenly, a Dead man, who must have been uncommonly tall in life, managed to get a grip on the lip of the counter with one of his hands and with strength born of his cannibalistic mania, he began to pull his himself up slowly. When he head was level with the window Liz saw her opportunity and thrust her blade forward to rip through a puss-covered eye and into the cranial cavity beyond. Over the moans of the gathered Dead, the crunch of her sword shattering bone was barely audible, but through the metal of her blade, Liz could feel the scrape of bone breaking and brain matter tearing. After a flick of her wrist, she pulled her sword free. With the press of the gathered Dead about him, the tall man's corpse was briefly held in place. Then, slowly he succumbed to their shoves and jostling and was pushed aside to slump to the ground at their feet. It was then that Liz realised her terrible mistake. Unknowingly, she had provided the Dead with something to stand on and given them that bit more height they needed to be able to hook their filth covered hands on the lip of the counter.

'Fuck,' Liz said to herself, knowing things were going to get very bad very fast.

Already two more of the Dead had gained the leverage they needed to pull themselves level with the window and as they pushed against each other to get their heads through the ruined window, Liz knew it was time to act. With only the hatch in the roof offering her a temporary respite, she pulled herself onto the waist high freezer sitting opposite the shattered window. Steadying herself on an overhead cabinet, Liz pulled herself to a standing position and began banging against small hatch in the roof. The continued attack on the van from the Dead caused it to un-expectantly and violently rock to one side, jolting Liz and almost making her lose her balance. Hooking her fingers onto the small lip that ran along the base of the cabinet, Liz only just managed to steady herself in time to see the animated corpse of a man pull himself in as far as his shoulders. Already, he clawed frantically to touch Liz's feet, which were just barely out of reach, while behind him, others tried to use his back to climb in. The Dead man only had to pull himself in a fraction further to be within touching distance and Liz could feel the panic rising within her. Using this panic to fuel to her attack on the hatch, Liz screamed in rage.

'Come on! Come on!' she screamed, smashing away at the hatch that hadn't been opened in at least eight years.

Glancing down, the Dead man had now pulled most of his upper torso through the broken window and was pawing at her foot with putrid maggot ridden fingers. With a cry, she yanked her foot away from his rancid touch and stamped down hard on his hand. The satisfying crack of his finger bones was lost among the moans of the Dead and her own cries of rage and she returned her attention to the wedged shut hatchway. Suddenly with a bang, the hatch flew open, landing on the outside of the van roof. Reaching up, she frantically latched her fingers onto the rim of the opening and with a kick, launched herself towards her only chance to survive. Straining the muscles in her arms and screaming with determination, she pulled herself up towards the opening and hooked an arm out on to the roof. Hearing a thump from below that was surely one of the Dead falling into the van, she kicked her legs wildly for momentum so she could wriggle her head and shoulders through the hatch. Not daring to look down at the Dead that had now advanced their way into the van, she screamed again, desperate to pull herself up onto the roof. Then something cold and un-natural grabbed hold of one of her ankles and with a yank tried to pull her down back to the hungry mouth and horrific death that awaited her and her baby.

'No!' screamed Liz, kicking her legs, desperate to shake the Dead hand loose. 'Dear God, no!'

***

Rubbing the sleep from his eyes, Steve looked over at Matt. He was fast asleep with his mouth open, and he was snoring loudly as a result. Steve wished he had his friend's ability to give into his exhaustion, but despite his sleeping bag, Steve had only been able to get a few hours restless sleep during the cold snowy night. The small tent he shared with Matt had done little to protect them from the sub-zero temperatures and its canvas sides had whipped back and forth in the wind noisily, denying him the rest he so needed. As he had lain awake in the freezing darkness, listening to the howling wind outside, he hoped the brave sword-wielding woman on horseback had found some adequate shelter. As ineffectual as the tent was, he didn't envy the woman if she was still out in freezing weather like this. He had spent his time awake, trying to formulate a plan where he would be able to spirit away Penny and the others from the holding truck without getting himself or them gunned down in the process. After an hour or so, he realised the only way he would stand any chance of pulling this off was with Matt's help. Steve knew Matt intended to return to base for his sister, Karen, so he would have to make it look like Matt had been an unwilling participant in the daring escape, which would be more than be tricky. His father had little time for those who failed at their duties and Steve worried the man might take his anger out on Matt. His father's anger could be deadly in the extreme, so unless he made it look convincing, Matt would be risking his own life to help him.

'Hey,' Steve said, nudging Matt's sleeping bag with his boot. 'Sleeping beauty, get your arse out of bed.'

Instantly, the snoring stopped, and with a yawn, Matt slowly sat up but refused to wake up properly.

'I need a piss,' was all Matt mumbled, not even opening his eyes.

'Well, that'll just have to wait for a moment, cause I need to talk to you,' Steve began, hoping he could rely on Matt's cooperation. 'Today's the day, man.'

Matt opened his eyes to look at his friend, with a serious expression on his face.

'Fuck, are you sure, Stevie-boy?' he asked, pushing his arms out of the sleeping bag to rub some drool from his face. 'There'll be no going back once you've started. You do know that, don't you?'

'Yes, I do. I can't stay here anymore. This is no way to live, not really. The way we're treating people is just not right and we all know it. I simply can't do this for even one more day, Matt. I just don't have it in me, and I'm taking Penny and her friends with me,' Steve replied, pausing to think how to phrase what he had to say next. 'The thing is, even though I get why you can't come with me, I'm going to need your help to get away.'

'Christ, Steve. Man, your dad will feed my arse to the corpses if he thinks I helped you and the civvies go AWOL,' Matt began, knowing even before he had finished his protest that he would still do as Steve asked.

'All you'll need to do is turn your back for a few minutes while we're on duty and the civilians and I will disappear into the countryside... gone,' Steve added quickly, nervously chewing his lip.

'Just turn my back, eh?' Matt asked, realising there was more to come.

'Yeah, I will have to knock you out though,' Steve said sheepishly. 'Just so Sarge doesn't think you were involved.'

'Great,' replied Matt resting his chin on his hands, 'can't wait'

'So you'll do it?' Steve said with relief.

Matt looked at Steve, raising his eyebrows. The two men had been friends for so long that they were more like brothers now. They had grown up together on the base, become soldiers together and ultimately because of each other, they became the men they were meant to be. They had stood side by side with the Dead before them and they knew the other would die for them; such was their friendship. Even though he would miss him, there was no way he was going to turn his back on his friend's chance of a life away from the base.

'What's a bit of concussion between friends,' said Matt, his mouth cracking into a smile. 'So what's the plan?'

Ten minutes later, Steve and Matt were once again braving the snow and freezing wind on duty manning one of the Jackals. They were watching the convoy's flank and knowing this would be the direction from which his secret sword-wielding ally would be approaching, Steve had made sure they took this watch position. If he were to make his escape with Penny and the others, this would be the only direction they had a hope of fleeing undetected. While Matt kept an eye on the road ahead of them for any approaching Dead, it was the holding truck that held Steve's attention. He knew he had to time it just right even to have a chance of pulling off the breakout successfully and when he saw Dave approaching the trailer with an armful of meals again, he knew the time had come.

'Right, wish me luck,' Steve said, tapping Matt's shoulder.

'You'll need more than luck, mate,' Matt replied, looking back at Steve. 'Hey, look just look after yourself, man, and have a good life, okay.'

'And you,' said Steve, glancing back to the trailer to gauge how much time he had left with his friend. 'I'm going to miss you, mate, and thanks, thanks for everything.'

'Yeah, okay don't go all queer on me, just get on with it,' Matt butted in, knowing he didn't really want to say goodbye to his friend either.

'Okay, bye, mate,' Steve said with a sad smile, as he swung the butt of his rifle towards Matt's head.

With a 'crack' the butt connected with Matt's skull. For the briefest of moments, Matt's eyes seemed to go out of focus as he swayed slightly in his seat. Then, as the trauma took its toll, Matt fell forward onto the Jackals steering wheel, unconscious. Pulling Matt's prone form back into a seating position, Steve checked once more for any of the Dead on the road and with a final pat goodbye on Matt's shoulder, he turned and jogged over to Dave by the trailer.

'Need a hand with the door again?' Steve said with a smile.

'What? Oh cheers, Steve,' Dave replied, nodding towards the door as he juggled to hold the food packs for the civilians.

Once Steve had unlocked the door, he held it open for Dave to walk through. With one quick glance around the compound, he followed him in.

'Right, grub up, people,' Dave said to the gathered group inside. 'Sorry it's just...'

Dave's apology for the bad food was cut short, as once again, Steve's rifle butt connected with a skull, knocking the man to the floor.

'Time to go people,' Steve began, stepping over Dave's unconscious body, his eyes instantly meeting Penny's. 'We're getting out of here and I need you to be quick, quiet and to follow me, no questions.'

It was only when he looked at the others in the trailer that he realised this wasn't going to be the big escape he had hoped for. Sometime during the night, the group had not only been given their neck pulse detectors, but the men of the group had been handcuffed to one of the interior walls to prevent a repeat of Richard's escape attempt.

'Shit!' Steve said, looking back to Penny.

'Unless you got the keys on you, we're not going anywhere,' Richard said, lifting his bruised and swollen face to look up at Steve. 'But please, you've got to get the women and children away from here.'

'No, I'm staying with you,' Nicky said, reaching for her husband.

'Nicky...' Richard began.

'We haven't got time for this,' Steve interjected. 'We've got to go now, but I promise I'll come back for the rest of you, somehow.'

'How do we know we can trust you?' the woman they had picked up prior to arriving at Lanherne said defiantly, standing to look at the man that had already tricked and betrayed her once.

'Look, nothing I can say can change what happened, but I'm trying to make it right,' Steve replied, 'and this may be our only chance to get away. We've got to go now.'

'You're wasting time,' Cam said to the four women free of the handcuffs that held the men in place. 'Every second you stand around thinking about it, the less chance you have to get away. Just go, go while you can.'

Slowly, Penny stood, pulling her eyes away from Steve's gaze.

'Anne, Justin, look after Alex and stay close to me. We're going to have to move fast, okay,' she said calmly, reaching down to pick up Jimmy.

'You'll have to carry him, if you're coming,' she continued, dumping the small boy in the woman's arms as she picked up his sister, Samantha.

The two women looked at each other, each silently challenging the other. Two strangers brought together by a bad situation, each having to trust the other with their lives. Then something in the woman's eyes changed. She knew the soldier had been right. This may be their only chance of escape and she would have to take it if she could.

'My name's Jennifer,' she said quietly to Jimmy, repositioning him onto her hip, 'but everyone just calls me Jen, okay, little man.'

With the quickest of smiles to the woman who had joined them, Penny turned back to Steve.

'I'm staying too,' said the other woman, holding tightly to the hand of the man sitting next to her.

The two had been picked up together over a week ago and as they had both been selected to be rescued, they hadn't seen just how brutal this rescue mission really was. For them, the base offered a life free of the Dead and they would take it, no matter how strict the regime in charge turned out to be.

'Justin, do as Penny says and we'll be together again real soon. I promise,' Nicky said, pulling the small boy into a fierce hug and praying her words wouldn't prove to be a hopeful lie.

Justin began to cry silently, hugging his adoptive mother back tightly.

'I'm sorry, but we've got to go,' Steve said, anxious not to stay any longer.

'Take care of them,' Nicky said, looking up at Steve, her tears falling freely as she pushed Justin reluctantly away from her. 'Take care of them all.'

'I will,' Steve said, as he nodded seriously to the weeping woman who had entrusted the care of her son to him.

Looking over at the small group now in his charge, he noticed the woman called Jen, struggling to keep hold of the small boy she held in her arms. Unlike those from Lanherne, this woman had lived too long on the brink of starvation and simply carrying the boy's extra weight was obviously a struggle for her weakened body.

'Here, give the boy to me,' he said to her, pulling Jimmy from her arms. 'We'll be able to move faster if I carry him.'

'Thanks,' she replied, steadying herself briefly.

'Right, let's do this,' said Steve, moving to the door.

Opening the door slightly, Steve scanned the makeshift compound for activity. Luck seemed to be with the small escaping group at that moment, with the only sounds of activity coming from the communications tent and with most of the soldiers not on watch duty still in their tents trying to keep warm, they might just have a chance. If Steve could get them across the small open space outside the holding truck and to the tents, they should be able to get to the Jackal and freedom, undetected.

'Stay low, keep quiet and follow me,' he whispered back to Penny, Jen and the children.

Taking a deep breath, Steve darted silently across the stamped down area of snow, over to the row of small tents. Penny, close on his heels, clutched a scared Samantha close to her chest, while Alex ran alongside her holding tightly to her jacket. Behind her, with her heart pounding in her chest, Jen ran with Anne and Justin, trying to keep up. Steve had made it past the first couple of tents and already he could see the back of the Jackal, tantalisingly close.

'*We're going to make it,*' he thought to himself.

It was then that behind him, Jen caught a glimpse of two soldiers about to step out from behind a tent right into Steve's path. Skidding to a halt, she silently grabbed Anne and Justin, pulling them into the small gap between two of the tents, praying they hadn't been noticed. Raising her finger to her lips, the two children looked at her with fear in their eyes.

'Well, what have we here? Going somewhere?' Jen heard one of the soldiers say, followed by the ominous sound of a rifle being cocked.

Jen, cursing the heavens for their bad luck, knew that while the soldier's attention was otherwise diverted, the two children and she might still have a chance to escape. Taking a small hand in each of hers, Jen crouched low and led the two children along the side of the tent. With adrenalin pumping through her as she peeked around the front of the tent, Jen could see the soldiers forcing Steve to his knees, while Alex clung terrified to Penny's leg.

'No!' came Penny's cry, as one of the soldiers began a vicious attack on Steve, while the other had his gun pointed menacingly towards her and the three children to stop her from darting forward.

Jen knew it was now or never. With Penny's screams for the soldier to stop alerting the rest of the camp, her window of escape was closing fast.

'Ready?' she whispered back to the boy and girl crouched next to her.

Not waiting for a reply, Jen pulled the two children forward and darted across the open space behind the backs of the soldiers engrossed in their beating.

'*Please, please, please,*' she silently prayed, desperately hoping neither of the soldiers would turn and notice her escape.

Some unknown deity must have heard her prayer, because she had made it to the back of a large vehicle that sat on the perimeter of the camp, undetected. Pulling the two children down by one of the large wheels out of sight, Jen stole a peek at the man sitting in the driver's seat. With his eyes closed and a small trickle of blood running down his forehead, Steve had planned this escape route for them to take all along.

'We'll make a break for the hedgerows,' she whispered to her two new charges.

With one last glance back at the camp and the sounds of Penny's pleading for the attack on Steve to stop fading behind her, Jen broke their cover from behind the vehicle and ran with Anne and Justin to the nearest patch of hedgerow cover that grew by the side of the road.

'Stop, you bastards, stop! You're killing him,' Penny screamed, as Streiber began to kick at Steve's already bloody body curled up at his feet.

'Streiber,' came the hard voice of Sergeant Blackmore. 'Explain!'

'Caught this one trying to desert with the woman and children, Sir,' the soldier replied, giving Steve one last kick in the ribs.

Sergeant Blackmore walked over to the man on the ground and using his boot, roughly rolled him over onto his back. Seeing it was his son, Steven, he was neither surprised nor disappointed. The boy, just like his worthless mother, had always been weak and he had come to expect nothing better from him. When he thought of all the good men or rather good soldiers that had died at the hands of the infected, Sergeant Blackmore was disgusted at the actions of his own son.

'Take this man to Dr Morris. I want him conscious and aware at his court marshal,' he said to the SAS Commando who had mercilessly beaten his son, 'and get these civilians back to the holding truck.'

'Sir!' the soldier replied with a swift salute.

Without a second glance at his son's unconscious body, Sergeant Blackmore turned and walked past the silent soldiers of his squadron who had come out of their tents to see what was happening. Some of them exchanged discrete looks of concern but all knew better than to voice an opinion on what had happened to Private Blackmore. 'Better him than me,' was a thought that came to most of them and already many had turned away from the sight of the Private's beaten body.

'Start breaking down your tents,' Sergeant Blackmore said coldly, his tone challenging any of his men to question his actions. 'We bug out in twenty minutes, but thanks to Private Blackmore, we'll have to deal with some business first.'

All of the men knew what that meant. Private Steven Blackmore's torment had only just begun.

***

In the Med lab, Alice fought her way back to consciousness. Through the heavy fog that threatened to drag her back to oblivion, she grasped the sound of spoken voices around her, and like a tether, she pulled herself back to reality.

'Well, they certainly gave you a good working over,' Dr Morris's unconcerned voice came, as Alice's eyes fluttered open.

Afraid that the doctors would drug her again, Alice laid still with only her eyes moving to take in the scene. Dr Morris was wiping the blood from the chin of the solider who had known Penny and Lars. The man had been beaten severely and as he sat at a desk, clutching his ribs obviously in pain, Dr Morris administered what could only be called half-hearted care.

'I wouldn't be surprised if you've broken a few of your ribs and your split lip could really use a few stitches,' Dr Morris said to the soldier, as he dropped his latex gloves down onto the tray of surgical equipment. 'But I think you'll agree it would be a little pointless really to fix them... Look, I could give you some pain killers, but we both know your what Sergeant Blackmore has in mind for you.'

'Anything you can give me, Doc, would be great,' Steve said, wincing from the pain.

Doctor Morris looked at the beaten man before him, knowing he really shouldn't waste their valuable medication on a condemned man, but something inside him shouted to be heard, shouted for him to act. Some long forgotten need to help his fellow man in practice rather than just in theory and formulae called out to him, reminding him to treat this man with compassion in what would likely be his last few hours.

'Okay,' Dr Morris said with a sigh, turning to retrieve some medication from a cupboard.

As the doctor rummaged through the cupboard looking for a specific medication that was less likely to be missed, Steve looked down at the stack of papers piled next to him on the desk. Skimming over the printout to take his mind off the waves of pain that rippled through him with each breath, one phrase suddenly stood out and horrified him. Looking up, he caught the gaze of the pregnant woman strapped to the bed. He knew he had but a few seconds to act while the doctor still had his back to him, so silently, he reached forward to the tray of surgical implements. With one last quick glance back to Dr Morris, Steve grabbed one of the small paper wrapped scalpel blades and tossed it to the woman. As the wrapped blade landed by her hip, she looked back at him, her confusion obvious. Steve made an obvious glance down to the printout and then nodded back to her, silently trying to tell her what he had read. Whether she understood or not, Steve had no idea, but as she stretched her fingers to manoeuvre the blade into her palm slowly, he knew at least he had done what he could for her. He had given her a chance to save herself and her baby, and perhaps, if luck was on her side, the line he had read saying, 'terminate inoculated foetus to record anti-virus viability' might never be put into practice.

***

'Fuck! Where are they all coming from?' whispered Leon, turning to face Imran.

'From what Sister Josephine said, the idiots aren't shy about using their guns to put down the Dead,' Imran replied, his whisper mirroring Leon's, 'and looks like they're thundering through the countryside like bulls in a china shop, riling up all the Dead as they go. Of course, as far as they're concerned, they've got what they want from this area now, so what do they care if all the Dead that are able to, suddenly take to the roads to follow?'

When the group had set out from Lanherne early that morning, the first rays of sun had only just begun their struggle to break into the icy darkness of the winter night's sky. The weak rays had done little to dispel the stillness that seemed to have settled over the convent and to Imran, with the children and more importantly Liz now gone, the life of the building itself had been taken with them leaving it as cold and empty as the snow covered countryside about it. He knew he was not the only one to feel this way. In the faces of all those who had braved the chill of the dawn light to see them off, the ache of loss was obvious. Lars, who had taken care of Penny since those first days, was plainly feeling her absence deeply. He had silently struggled through the pain of his arthritic hands to prepare Delilah for the trip and even when Gabe had offered to help, he had refused, preferring to work though his pain. He was determined to prove wrong the Sergeant who had written him off as a nothing burden.

'He would be of use, he would not be a burden,' he had told himself over and over again to blot out the pain.

If this was all he could do to help those given the task of rescuing the stolen members of his extended family, then so be it, he would do it gladly. For that is how he felt about this group of people who found refuge and built a life behind the high walls of Lanherne. They become a family and just like any family, they would fight any way they could for each other.

'Bring them back to us and may God go with you,' Sister Josephine said to the four men clambering into the cart about to set off.

'We will,' Imran said, turning back to look at the woman who had opened her Convent doors to them and made had for them all a life worth living.

As Sister Josephine's hand rose to encircle the Rosary beads about her neck, she gave Imran a simple nod. She could see it clearly in his expression that these words were not merely empty reassurances. He meant it as a statement of fact. His mind was unable to contemplate any other option. He would return with Liz, Anne and the others and woe betide any who stood in his way.

Just as Sister Josephine had said, Liz had left for them a trail to follow. For hours, they had been met at each turning or crossroads, by a rag fluttering mournfully in the chill wind, guiding their way. Even without Liz's tell-tale markers, they could clearly see the route she had taken in pursuit of the convoy. Everywhere, the broken and downed Dead littered the roads, a testament to the passing of Liz's blade and Samson's thundering hooves. From the spacing of the fallen Dead, Imran could tell she had thankfully only encountered the walking corpses in their ones and twos as they had pushed their way through hedgerows and onto the road to follow the noisy convoy of vehicles. However, the longer they were on the road following the trail, the more worried Imran became. More than once, a group of dozen shattered Dead, their now finally still bodies dusted with a thick layer of snow, had shown just how close to being overpowered Liz had been.

'More Dead up ahead, quite a lot of them,' Phil said, looking through the front view slit at the road ahead. 'From the looks of it they must've got onto the road after Liz had already past.'

'Any way we can just get past them?' Patrick asked, knowing every second counted if they wanted to catch up with Liz, let alone the convoy.

'There's about forty of them blocking the lane,' Phil replied, scratching at his stubbly chin 'I don't want to risk barrelling through them, not in this snow. We could break a wheel and then we'd really be up shit creek.'

'Well, we can't afford to stop and deal with them all, we haven't got time,' Imran added, his frustration making him snap at his friends.

Phil turned to look at Imran. He could see the worry consuming the young man. The woman he loved and his unborn child were out there somewhere, alone and unprotected. He needed to get to them.

'Look, if we just clear a path through them, they'll be following us up behind,' Phil began.

'But we can outpace them,' Imran interrupted. 'We might lose them at a turning.'

'And we might not,' Phil added calmly.

'We've got to try. We've got to take that chance, please,' said Imran, looking from Phil to Patrick to Leon.

'Hey, I'm cool with whatever,' Leon said to Imran, holding his hands up.

'That 'whatever' can get you killed, Leon,' Phil remarked under his breath, turning back to follow the movement of the Dead crowd in front of them.

'Leon and I would already be dead by now if it you hadn't taken a chance when you didn't have to,' Patrick added. 'I say we chance it now. We just can't afford to fall too far behind. If that convoy gets to the coast...'

Turning his attention back to his three travelling companions, Phil knew he was beaten. As much as he didn't like leaving behind a large group of the Dead to follow them in their wake, he understood Imran's urgency. Patrick had been right, if the soldiers did manage to get to the coast, their rescue would be over before it began.

'Well, looks like you're up then,' Phil said to Imran, turning back to concentrate on the Dead that shambled along the snow covered road ahead of them. 'Just take out as many as you can that are walking close together. With a bit of luck, you'll only need to get about a dozen of them to clear a space wide enough for us to pass.'

'I suggest you take them out in pairs and then duck back down out of sight. The longer you're visible, the more chance one of them will notice you and start the dinner call,' Patrick added, grabbing Imran's arm as he was about to flip open the roof hatch, 'if that happens and they swamp us, we'll have a real fight on our hands. I doubt the cart or Delilah could cope with such an onslaught.'

'Right, good thinking,' Imran said after a pause, silently kicking himself for almost endangering them all with his reckless haste.

'Right, we're clear sides and back, so unless any of them turn round, this should be like shooting dead fish in a barrel,' Leon said, once he had checked through some of the cart's spy holes.

'Here goes,' Imran whispered, silently opening the roof hatch.

Holding onto the hatch's internal bolt, Imran left it to the last second before releasing his grasp, allowing the hatch to be lowered soundlessly onto the outside of the cart's roof. With a sharp intake of breath to steady himself, Imran slowly stood up through the gap to take his targets. With his feet resting on the wooden benches that ran on either side inside of the cart, Imran's upper torso, arms and head were now exposed for all the Dead to see. With only the barest of creaks from his bow to compete with the soundless shuffling Dead, Imran pulled back the string. Sighting down the arrow, he marked his first target. Whatever it had once been, the creature had much of the flesh torn from its back by the Dead when it was alive and one of its arms ended abruptly mid-bicep among a tattering of moulding skin and bone. What hair it had left on its head, hanging thin and lank, was matted to the pallid and cracking skin that stretched across its skull.

With a barely audible thud, Imran's arrow lodged itself deeply in the back of the Dead thing's head, knocking the creature forward to fall face down in the trampled down snow. Without a second thought, Imran sighted his aim smoothly to the next walking corpse. This time it had been a woman, her once curvaceous half-naked figure was now tinged a sickly grey and traced with a dark spider web of long dead veins. Imran could see a large chunk of flesh that at some point had been ripped from her thigh. Whether by the attacking Dead or by a pack of wild hungry dogs, he would never know, but the wound was deep enough to expose the yellowing bone beneath as it disappeared into the dark rotting flesh of her leg. Again, an unnatural existence was abruptly ended with Imran's arrow perfectly hitting its mark. Following Patrick's advice, Imran quickly ducked back down below the lip of the hatch.

'Any of them turning?' he whispered to Phil, already reaching behind to pull another arrow from his quiver.

'No, you're fine. Try to clear a path for us through the middle. Those brambles along the side might be covering ditches and I don't want to risk the wheels,' he replied, concentrating on the Dead ahead of them.

'Will do,' said Imran, popping up through the hatch to take aim again.

For the next ten minutes, Imran would spring up like a silent jack-in-a-box with arrows flying from his bow to put down the Dead in their path. Only once did one of them turn to catch sight of the living flesh he craved, standing unnoticed behind him. His travelling companion in death had knocked into him as she fell to one of Imran's arrows, spinning him round and alerting him to the presence of the thing he most desired, flesh warm and alive. Imran was just about to pop down from sight when he caught the hungry gaze of the Dead man staring back at him. As if in slow motion, Imran watched the man's arm rise to reach beseechingly towards him, while a ragged mouth slowly opened, preparing to expel fetid breath over withered vocal cords. Knowing the unearthly sound the Dead man was about to make would act like a dinner call to all his unnatural brethren, Imran knew he had to be stopped. Even as Imran reached swiftly behind, pulling another arrow from his quiver, the Dead man's film covered eyes bulged in excitement at his presence. It would be close call as to which would be released first, Imran's arrow or the Dead man's call of desperation. Thankfully, the Dead man's moan died in his throat before it could alert any other of the Dead, as Imran's arrow ripped deeply through a putrid eye socket, to rupture the decaying brain within.

'That was close, man,' Leon said when Imran dropped back down into the cart.

'Tell me about it!' Imran replied, breathing a sigh of relief. 'How many more to clear, Phil?'

'Actually, we should be able to get through now without too much trouble,' he replied, his voice still only just a whisper, 'most of what's left of the main group can be bumped out of the way and further on they're spaced out enough to not really be any trouble.'

'Suits me,' said Imran, eager to be on the move again.

With a quick flick of Delilah's reins, the cart lurched forward and Delilah began to slowly push her way through the now thinned out crowd ahead of them. Every so often, the cart would jolt to one side as one of the wheels went over one of the many bodies now littering the lane. Inside, the sickening crunch of breaking bones and rupturing putrid intestines could clearly be heard over the softened clip clop of Delilah's hooves on the stamped down snow.

When they had cleared the bulk of what was left of the Dead crowd without incident, they could clearly see there were only a dozen or so scattered over the next thirty meters, after which, the lane joined another road.

'Anyone see Liz's flag?' Phil asked quietly, as he scanned the roadside bushes and trees.

'There,' Patrick whispered, pointing over Phil's shoulder to a fluttering piece of white cloth tied to an overhanging tree branch. 'Looks like we're meant to take the right turn.'

An hour later, they were still religiously following Liz's trail winding through the Cornish countryside. At each corner they turned, all in the cart hoped there would be some indication from Liz that they were nearing their goal but each time they were only met with more of the shambling Dead drawn to the road by a noisy convoy that promised to sate their need to feed on the flesh of the living. Steering Delilah round a particularly large pothole that even the covering of snow could not disguise, Phil pulled the cart to a stop.

'What's up?' Leon asked, pushing himself forward to look at the road ahead.

'There's another large group of the Dead up ahead,' Phil replied, looking back at the other three men. 'Luckily, the road's a bit wider here, so we can pass them without stopping this time but keep quiet, okay.'

The three men nodded silently their understanding and Phil turned to urged Delilah back into motion. Looking through one of the spy holes, Imran idly watched the Dead as Delilah pulled the cart along the road. One sorry case after another stumbled into view and then they were lost again as Delilah pulled them onward further down the road. Imran saw small children and teenagers, their lives brutally ripped away from them by Dead hands and teeth, and men and women who had fought valiantly only to succumb later to the unnatural appetite of their fellow man. Finally, there were those so badly damaged that not only were it difficult to tell which sex they had once been, but for many in their current state, their very species was barely recognisable.

They were just pulling through a section of the road where the Dead group were at their most concentrated and something puzzling caught Imran's attention. For some reason, the Dead here were jostling and pushing against each other to move up a small driveway that led to a dilapidated cottage and even from the cart, Imran could faintly hear their excited moaning. Imran 'tutted' to himself as one of the Dead briefly walked in front of the spy hole, blocking his view. Something wasn't right here. Something had the Dead riled up and there was only one thing Imran knew that could catch their interest like this. Reaching forward, Imran silently placed his hand on Phil's shoulder. Puzzled, Phil slowly turned to look at him and in the instant that their eyes locked, they heard a familiar voice screaming in rage and horror.

'Oh God, no!'

'Liz!' Imran said. His voice was a shocked whisper filled with despair, as an icy fear froze his blood.

'Imran, no!' Phil said, making a grab for the young man's hand.

However, Imran was already moving, kicking open one of the side hatches, his need to save Liz blinding him to the danger that awaited him.

'No, there's too many... Imran!' Patrick called, trying to reach for Imran's fleeing body.

Outside the safety of the cart, his life hung in the balance and Imran knew it, but the danger wouldn't stop him from acting. All that consumed his thoughts was to save Liz from the Dead. No matter what happened, he had to save her. One of the Dead that had been close to the cart turned to face the living flesh that had suddenly appeared beside it. Excited by the possibility of feasting on something warm, it reached pathetically for Imran with its emaciated claw like hands. Giving the Dead thing a shove, Imran ran forward towards the driveway. Instantly, more of the Dead began to turn to see the live meal that had unexpectedly arrived among them.

'Hey! Hey!' Imran shouted, waving his arms at the gathered Dead, trying to force their way into the garage. 'Come and get me, you bags of shit! Come on! Come on!'

Even in his panicked state, Imran knew he had to clear some of the Dead from the garage doorway if the others were to stand a chance of saving her. If he had to sacrifice himself for Liz and the baby, so be it. First, he would draw as many of them away as he could. Already a large proportion of the Dead had turned and begun to shuffle their way back down the driveway towards him. The closer proximity of the meal that they could see made them forget the one that caught the attention of those already in the garage.

'I'll lead them down the road!' Imran shouted to the cart, running back down the driveway, dodging the Dead arms that were already reaching for him. 'Save her!'

Inside the garage, Liz screamed again and kicked wildly at the Dead hands that threatened to pull her leg down to the hungry mouths that awaited her. With a crack, she heard cartilage and bone break beneath her, as her boot connecting forcefully with the nose of one of the taller Dead trying to pull her down.

'Save her!' A shout suddenly came from outside.

'Imran!' she said choking back a sob, as tears of shock, fear and exhaustion filled her eyes.

With the sound of his voice, a kernel of hope blossomed within her, somehow giving her the strength she needed. With another hard kick and a twist of her leg, she felt the force pulling on her lessen, as one by one, Dead hands lost their hold of her. With Imran and the others so close, Liz was determined that neither her nor her baby would not fall victim to the corpses below her and with one final frantic kick fuelled by a scream of pure maternal protection, Liz felt the last of the Dead fingers slip from her ankle. Instantly, she pulled her bruised leg up through the skylight. Finally, now out of their reach, Liz collapsed, panting on the roof of the small ice-cream van and allowed her tears of relief to fall freely. To come so close to death wasn't by far a new thing for her. After all, she had survived for eight years, dodging death and the Dead alike, but it was her unborn child that gave her a new perspective on the horror surrounding her. Only now could she really understand just what her mother had been feeling, all those years ago, when she had sacrificed herself to ensure the survival of her two daughters.

Suddenly, coming from just outside the garage door was Phil's familiar war cry. Lifting herself up on one elbow, she turned to the sound that offered her and her child a promise of hope. Already, she could hear the shattering of bone as the Dead fell to Phil's wild attack. Then, without warning, the emaciated body of Dead woman flew through the air, and into the garage. Phil physically picked up her snapping corpse and threw her into the backs of the Dead still gathered around the van, her impact knocking many of them to the ground.

'Liz!' shouted Phil, running into the garage, swinging a spiked club left and right at the Dead, while Patrick and Leon followed close on his heels.

'Up here!' she called, using one of the low rafters to pull herself up into a standing position.

Liz had never been so happy to see Phil's large bulky form smashing his way through the Dead but she could see there were still over a dozen hungry corpses to deal with before she could truly believe she had escaped death so narrowly. Below her, the Dead started to turn away their reaching hands and snapping jaws from the sight of Liz's flesh. Mere moments ago it was the total focus of their desperate hunger but now, closer, easier to reach meat was within their grasp. Unfortunately, for the Dead the knives flew and the clubs crashed mercilessly into skulls and one by one, they fell. The flesh they so desired to be forever denied them.

'There's at least three of them still in the van,' Liz called down to her saviours, as the last of the Dead fell.

'On it,' Patrick said, giving her a reassuring smile. 'Leon, watch our backs.'

With a nod, Leon ran back to the door to stand by Samson, one of his knives held ready in each hand.

'All clear,' he called back to Phil and Patrick, as they cautiously made their way to the ice-cream van's shattered window. 'The rest have followed Imran down the road.'

Inside the van's small galley, three of the Dread jostled and pushed against each other, their focus still on the warm flesh they had seen disappearing through the hole above them.

'Right, I think the easiest way to deal with them is the open to open the back door and let them tumble out. What do you think?' Phil asked, turning to Patrick.

'Sounds like a plan, big man,' Patrick replied, raising his club ready to strike.

On the count of three, Phil gave the door handle at the back of the van a sharp tug and quickly stepped back. The door, now that its lock had been released, could no longer stay closed against the movements of the three Dead inside and as one of them was knocked against it, it slowly swung open.

'Hey, pus bags! Dinner time,' called Phil to the three corpses, who one by one, turned their hungry gaze upon him.

Disposing of them proved to be easier than they had first thought. In their hurry to get to the Patrick and Phil, they tried to push past each other and literally fell through the door to the garage floor in a tangle of rotten limbs and animated dead flesh. Stepping forward, Phil instantly brought his heavy booted foot down hard on the skull of one of the Dead, as it tried to pull itself free of its Dead companions. Before he had pulled his foot free of the now shattered and misshapen skull, Patrick was bringing his club forcefully down to end the unnatural life of another of the Dead. The last of Dead was once a woman and even in her decayed state, Patrick could still see the shadow of her once striking beauty. Her large eyes, presumably doe-like and entrancing in life, now held nothing but her unceasing hunger and as she pushed aside the still corpse of one of the other Dead, she reached towards him with long delicate fingers.

'Not today, sweetheart,' Patrick said, pulling his gaze away from her imploring stare to focus on a patch of her forehead.

With a 'crack' Patrick's club connected forcefully with the Dead woman's head, splitting skin and cracking bone to turn the rancid brain to a useless mass of pulp. As her delicate hand fell, now forever lifeless, to the garage floor, Patrick noticed a small gold chain about her wrist.

'Rest in peace, Katie,' he said sadly, reading the swirling letters of gold hanging on the delicate gold chain.

'Right, let's get you down from there, Missy,' Phil said up to Liz. 'You want to jump into my arms or climb back down?'

'Well, as long as you don't drop me,' Liz began, already swinging her legs over the side of the roof of the van. 'Ready?'

Holding his strong arms aloft, Phil caught hold of Liz's legs and Liz slowly shimmied herself down into his grasp.

'What were you thinking?' Phil said, pulling Liz into a tight hug. 'We could have lost you.'

'I didn't really have much choice,' she replied softly, finally letting go of the large man. 'They took them and it was all I could think of, so I had to follow.'

'Shit!' Leon shouted back to the others in the garage. 'Imran's in trouble! They're surrounding him.'

Before he could stop her, Liz pulled herself free from Phil's embrace and ran to the garage door.

'No,' she said, the word catching in her throat.

Imran's plan to draw the Dead away from the garage had worked a little too well. A hundred meters along the road, Imran could be seen battling for his life. As well as those who had been outside the garage, a crowd of the Dead had also been drawn to his shouts from further down the road, effectively cutting off his escape route. Surrounded on all sides, Imran was spinning wildly and firing arrows at the approaching Dead as fast as he could pull them from his quiver. As manic as his defence was, even from the garage, Liz could see he would run out of arrows long before the Dead were cleared enough for him to get past.

Before she knew what she was doing, Liz was running down the driveway to the cart with only one thought shouting in her mind; she had to save him. The cries from Patrick and Phil for her to stop didn't even register, she was so focused on this need to do something. As she reached the cart, she paused for a split second to look at the route along the road she would need to take. In that briefest of moments, Leon appeared at her side, panting.

'Liz, wait!' he said, reaching for her arm.

With the contact of his hand on her, sanity returned and Liz realised if she sped to Imran's rescue in the cart she would be condemning the others to possible attack.

'Get in!' she shouted, as she clambered into the front seat and gathered up Delilah's reins.

Patrick and Phil, who were already half way down the driveway, put on an extra spurt of speed. Phil knew Liz was showing great restraint as it was, for every second she waited for them was a second Dead teeth could be ripping into the man she loved.

'Come on, come on…' Liz said under her breath, her tight hold on the reins turning her knuckles white.

Patrick and Leon were already inside and with Phil halfway in she knew she could wait no longer.

'Hold tight!' she shouted over her shoulder, causing Patrick to make a grab for Phil whose legs were still hanging out the open hatchway.

With a scream of encouragement, Liz snapped Delilah's reins, sending the cart lurching forward. Immediately, the cart was barrelling down the road towards Imran with Delilah's thundering hooves kicking up snow in their wake. They were some thirty meters away now and Liz could see Imran was not only down to his last couple of arrows but more importantly, the Dead had almost gotten to within grabbing distance. If she didn't get there within the next few seconds, it would be all over for Imran. The Dead would be on him and she would have to watch helplessly while they tore him apart. Suddenly, with a barrage of flying hooves and pluming nostrils, a large shape tore surprisingly past the cart. Shocked by his appearance, Liz swerved the cart abruptly to the left, as Samson, free of the extra weight of the cart and its occupants flew past them and into the Dead crowd. Whether he just didn't want to be left behind or was actually making an attempt to rescue Imran, Liz had no idea, but as the animated corpses were knocked to the ground to be trampled on, she knew Samson had just given Imran the slim chance he needed.

Kicking out hard at a Dead man that had grabbed hold of his jacket, Imran realised there was now, thanks to Samson, a small window of opportunity and he knew it might ultimately be his only chance of survival. Turning quickly to push aside the withered corpse of an emaciated woman that had been reaching for him, Imran threw himself in the sudden gap in the Dead mob that Samson had created. As he did so, Samson reared up to bring his hooves crashing down on more of the Dead and with the sickening sound of breaking bones audible even over their terrible moaning, more of the hungry corpses finally met the oblivion that had been denied them. Even as Imran pushed aside more desperately reaching hands and bodies to get to Samson's side, the Dead refused to give up their claim on him. They had hungered for so long, they could not let this creature, whose living flesh called out to them, escape their putrid bite so easily. A corpse that had once been a young teenage girl, threw herself at Imran's back. Knowing that even the smallest of bites would mean his death, Imran grabbed helplessly behind him to pull her off. However, the struggling girl was just out of his reach and with each second he fought to remove her, more of the Dead shambled towards him. Then suddenly the cart thundered to a halt behind him, crushing more of the Dead in its wake. Two of the closest Dead had been trapped beneath its wheels but even now, they continued to paw the snow-covered road, hoping uselessly to pull their shattered bodies to Imran. With a bang, a side hatch opened and the girl was yanked violently from Imran's back and onto the wickedly serrated blade of a large hunting knife. Without a second thought, Patrick quickly threw the girl's now motionless body to the ground.

'Get in!' he shouted, while more of the Dead pushed their way round the side of the cart, knowing mouthfuls of warm bloody flesh awaited them there.

Imran glanced to the open hatch, Patrick's hand reaching for him to get in and then he turned quickly back to the stamping agitated horse.

'What about Samson?' he called, concerned they would lose the faithful beast that had saved his life.

'He'll follow us. Just get in, you idiot!' Patrick yelled, grabbing for Imran and pulling him to the hatch.

'For Fucks sake, Imran, get in the fucking cart!' Liz screamed, her nerves almost fried by the horrors of the last half an hour.

Knowing from her tone that he had better do as she said, Imran threw himself through opening to land in a heap among the men already inside the cart.

'Go!' Patrick shouted, pulling the hatch closed as soon as Imran was inside.

Immediately, Liz flicked Delilah's reins again, spurring her into action. Bumping over bodies and debris, the cart bolted toward the cross roads that Liz knew lay just up ahead. Once they were finally clear of the Dead and with their deathly moaning fading behind them, Imran was relieved to hear the hammering of Samson's gallop alongside them. Just as he had saved his life, the beast had also chosen to follow them in their flight from the Dead.

Despite the cart, and Imran and Samson putting a lot of the Dead permanently out of action, Liz knew there must still be twenty to thirty of the Dead behind them; each now slowly turning to follow the meal that had so narrowly escaped them. Thankfully, their pursuit would be slow and if she could just put some distance between them, they could catch their breath to come up with a plan. As the crossroads came into view, Liz quickly weighed up her options. It would be risky but she would just have to hope the convoy was far enough down the right hand turn as to not notice as the cart sped across the road junction. Tossing a silent prayer to the heavens, the cart thundered across the open space and carried on for another hundred metres.

'Hey, easy now, Lizzy, easy, easy… We'll break a wheel if we keep up this pace,' Phil calmly said, trying to pry the reins from her tight fists. 'They're a while behind us now, so we can stop…. We can stop.'

It wasn't until Phil managed pull Delilah to a halt and force open her fingers that Liz realised just how fast her heart was hammering in her chest. Phil gently took hold of her face at look into her eyes.

'He's okay, sweetheart. No one's been bitten, he's okay,' he said softly. 'We're all okay.'

'Lizzy,' came Imran's soft voice from behind her.

Liz instantly spun and after less than gently pushing Phil aside, threw herself into his arms, a wave of relief sweeping over both of them. When Liz stopped crying, she pushed herself away from Imran to look into the face of the man she loved beyond words and slapped him hard across the face.

'Don't you ever pull a stupid stunt like that again,' she said. 'If it wasn't for Shadow…'

However, love and relief washed away her anger before she could finish and she pulled him to her in a passionate kiss.

'You're one crazy woman. You do know that, don't you?' Imran mumbled through their crushed lips.

'And don't you forget it,' she said, pulling out of the kiss to give him a more friendly slap on the cheek.

'When you two have quite finished,' Phil said, feeling a bit of a killjoy for breaking up the lover's happy reunion, 'Liz, what have you found out about the convoy? Any ideas how we're going to get everyone back?'

'Well…' she began and told them all about Private Steven Blackmore.

***

'On your feet, solider,' barked Streiber, roughly pulling Steve from his seat in the Med lab while two other soldiers from the squadron carried an unconscious Dave and a groggy Matt over to the narrow bunks that lined one side.

Grabbing Steve's chin, the solider turned his bruised face back and forth. He was obviously inspecting his handiwork and from the look in his eyes, what he saw gave him some sick sense of pleasure.

'You've been a naughty boy, haven't you?' he said pinching Steve's face hard. 'Attacking two of your squadron, attempting desertion and worst of all, trying to escape with that bitch with the hot ass. Very greedy of you, mate… very greedy indeed. Frankly I don't appreciate that at all.'

Steve looked blankly up at the man through a swollen eye. Knowing it was pointless to talk back to the man and just as pointless to try to reason with him, he simply pulled his face from the man's grasp and stepped silently towards the doorway and the Court Marshal that awaited him. However, the man decided he would not be denied his fun so easily.

'Don't fucking ignore me when I'm talking to you, you little shit,' he spat, jabbing Steve hard in his already cracked ribs.

With a grunt of pain, Steve's legs buckled beneath him but the solider held him up, not letting him fall.

'Need a hand?' Hills said, standing just outside the doorway, his rifle resting casually in his arms.

'Nah, this one's no problem,' Streiber replied, pushing Steve through the door, causing him to fall face down to the stamped down snow outside.

Spitting gravel and dirty snow from his mouth, Steve cradled his ribs as he slowly pushed himself up. Looking around, he saw that camp had been dismantled while the doctor had done what little he could for this condemned man. Steve held no illusions that he was nothing but already condemned. He knew for certain his father would show him no mercy. Discipline among his men and being seen to be in control was far more important to his father than any vague paternal considerations. Sure enough, just like with the doomed Private Jones, his father had gathered all of the squadron and the captured civilians to witness just what happened to those who disobeyed the rule of command. Looking over to the sorry looking civilians being held at gunpoint, Steve's eyes automatically found Penny. Seeing his bruised and battered face, Penny's hand rose to cover her mouth in shock while heavy tears began to spill silently over her eyelashes.

'Private Steven Blackmore,' came his father's cold voice, snapping Steve's attention from Penny's distraught gaze to the man in front of him. 'You have been accused of assault, aiding and abetting the escape of civilian detainees and more seriously of desertion and dereliction of duty. Have you anything to say?'

Steve knew this was nothing even remotely resembling a trial and his father was simply going through the motions as a show for those under his command and the new civilians. The sentence had already been chosen for his betrayal and no pleading for mercy would alter the outcome.

'Look at what we've become!' he shouted to the gathered men and woman in uniform, making a point to ignore his father. 'We're meant to be helping these people, but we're treating them like objects to be collected and used!'

'You have been found guilty of all charges,' his father continued, talking loudly over Steve's call for sanity from his fellow soldiers.

'Now they're going to murder that woman's baby just to test a new virus,' Steve shouted, hoping the woman inside the Med lab could hear him and use the blade he had given her wisely.

'And the sentence is death,' Sergeant Blackmore said, Steve's words suddenly falling silent.

'No!' cried Penny, darting forward only to be met with the rifle muzzle being raised towards her.

With a flick of his hand, Hills and Streiber swiftly moved forward and pulled Steve to his feet. Using a zip lock tie they bound his hands together in front of him, pulling it so tightly that it dug painfully into his skin. Then they threaded a thin rope through the makeshift handcuffs to lead him over to a large tree at the side of the road.

'Wait!' said Sergeant Blackmore, his word stopping everyone.

The gaze of all those assembled flicked between the Sergeant and the beaten form of his son, wondering if he was to be given a last minute reprieve. However, Steve knew better than to expect anything other than cold detachment from this man. So when his father stood in front of him and reached up to his neck, it was no surprise to him that after a tug, his father's hand came away clutching Steve's pulse detector.

'You bastard!' Steve spat.

His father, not content with condemning Steve to a slow and painful death, also wanted him to die knowing he would come back as one of the rotting corpses that were cursed to walk the earth and Steve realised he had never hated him more.

'No, you can't do this! This is madness,' cried Penny, as one of the soldiers threw the rope over a thick overhanging tree branch, 'Please, please don't do this.'

With a cry of pain, Steve was slowly pulled into the air. Already the weight on the wrist ties was causing rivulets of blood to run down his arms and with each jolt from the men hoisting him aloft, pain from his cracked ribs would spasm through him making him cry out.

'That'll do,' Sergeant Blackmore said when Steve's feet were hanging chest level to the soldiers.

With one last disapproving glance at his son, Sergeant Blackmore turned to address the gathered crowd.

'Let this be a lesson to you all,' he said, looking from one face to the next. 'Cross me and you will regret it. There will be no second chances and no mercy. Now get those civilians into the truck, we're leaving.'

'No! You fucking bastard, you're a fucking animal!' Penny screamed, as the group from Lanherne were shoved roughly back to the holding trailer by the soldiers.

'No!' Penny screamed again and moved to break from the group. Luckily, Cam grabbed hold of her waist, pulling her sharply back.

'Penny! Penny, they'll shoot you down before you've taken three steps,' Cam said, pulling the hysterical young woman through the door and into the trailer. 'There's nothing we can do for him now. I'm sorry, Penny. I'm sorry.'

'This is insane!' she cried, slumping down onto the padded bench in the trailer. 'Why can't they see it?'

Outside, the vehicles were roaring to life, one by one, filling the small compound with their choking exhaust smoke.

'Sir, do you want us to look for the missing woman and the two children before we bug out?' asked Clarkes. 'They can't have gotten too far.'

'No, orders are to return to base,' he replied, scanning the surrounding trees and hedgerows. 'Dr Farrell wants to examine Morris' data asap, so we're to get to the pick-up point asap.'

'Yes, sir,' the solider snapped, saluting before jogging over to board one of the Jackals.

The Sergeant turned to scan the tree line one more time. As much as it galled him to let the woman and two children escape, orders were orders. Consoling himself that without weapons and in a terrain crawling with walking corpses, they were surely as good as dead already, he pulled himself into the lead Jackal and gave the signal to leave. As his vehicle pulled out of the small picnic area they had made their home for the night, Sergeant Graham Blackmore didn't even look back at the figure of his son he had left hanging within easy reach of the Dead. In his mind, the man was already dead, and quite frankly, he would not grieve for his passing.

***

Jen pulled the two children close to her at the base of a large snow blasted oak. Already exhausted and out of breath, she dusted away much of the shallow snowdrift to find the large gnarled roots beneath to sit on. Holding her finger to her lips for quiet, she listened intently for any indication they were being followed. She knew their trail would be easy to follow through the wild overgrown fields that ran alongside the road. Their tell-tale tracks in the snow gave them away, so it surprised her that they had managed to get so far from the convoy without any sound of pursuit.

'We'll just catch our breath here for a moment,' she whispered to the two children, but it was really for her own benefit that they had stopped.

Despite the children being small, they seemed to be in a much better condition than she was. They obviously had a good life at the convent, certainly better than she and her brother had been forced to endure. They had lived with a constant hunger burning in their stomachs, always finding just enough food to keep them going. After years of living like that, she simple didn't have the reserves of energy to call upon and already she was fighting the stitch in her side that pained her with every step.

'Perhaps if we follow the road we can find our way back to Lanherne,' Anne suggested hopefully.

'I don't think so, sweetie,' Jen replied, placing a comforting hand on Anne's shoulder, as she nervously scanned the tree line for soldiers or any sign of the Dead. 'We turned a lot of corners since we left the convent and any tyre tracks they made would have been covered over by last night's snow, but first we've got bigger problems to think about. Okay, we need to find something to protect ourselves with, so look for something heavy you can fit in your fist like a large rock or something.'

As upset as the two children were, they knew if they couldn't protect themselves, they were as good as dead already.

'How about this?' Anne asked, digging out a large stone from the base of the tree.

'It's a start,' Jen replied, the weight of the rock in her hand making her feel slightly better about being out in the open with two children to look after. 'See if you can find some more.'

Suddenly, the two children froze, their heads snapping to look in the direction from which they had come. In the distance, they could hear the convoy's engines suddenly roaring to life. It was odd to hear such a sound after so many years of its absence and even to Jen, it had become something alien and unnatural. For the children who had few, if any, memories of working cars, the sound was quite unnerving.

'It's alright,' Jen said softly, pulling the children's attention back to the task at hand. 'They're leaving, so we're safe. Well, at least from them.'

As much as she hated to admit it, the soldiers were the lesser of two evils that challenged them at the moment. The Dead, that surely must even now be pulling themselves through the snow-covered hedgerows to follow the departing sounds of life, were by far a greater concern for her.

'Right, let's follow this ridge... it seems to run parallel with the road for a while,' she said stuffing more of their collected rocks in her jacket pockets, 'keep close, keep low and if I tell you to stop, just do it, no questions, okay?'

'Okay,' both children replied in unison, their eyes nervously scanning every shadow about them.

'Oh... and if we do come across any of the Dead,' Jen said turning each child to look at her to know just how serious she was. 'For God's sake don't scream, or we'll be swamped with them.'

Anne and Justin nodded silently that they understood, and once Jen was satisfied that all was clear, the three escapees began their journey through the snow covered high winter grasses and brambles. A journey that the children hoped would eventually take them back to the safe walls of Lanherne.

With the threat of the soldiers catching up with them now gone, Jen decided they could afford to slow their pace down to a simple walk. This also allowed them to move with the necessary stealth that they would need if they hoped to avoid the Dead. Every so often they would hear the snap of wood or an ominous rustle of unseen movement somewhere deep in the thickets and each time, with her heart pumping loudly and a surge of adrenalin flooding through her, Jen would hold up her hand for the children to halt. Jen didn't know if she could take this tension for long, since they had only been walking for ten minutes and already her nerves were frayed. It had been different when she had been travelling with her brother, he could take care of himself and she had always felt safe with him by her side. Now that she had the two children depending on her and with only a few meagre rocks for protection, safe was the last thing she felt.

'We'll stop here for just a minute,' she softly said, resting against a tree.

The effects of the adrenalin pumping through her was taking its toll on her already strained and weaken body and even if was for a short while, she needed to try to calm herself down.

'Are you alright?' asked Anne, crouching down beside Jen.

'I'm just not in very good shape, I'm afraid,' she replied looking across into the young girl's concerned eyes. 'I'll be alright in a minute…'

Suddenly, a tattered shape barrelled into Anne, knocking her to the ground.

'No!' cried Jen, throwing herself at the Dead man that even now was struggling to get to the soft flesh of the small girl's neck.

From somewhere deep within her, Jen found enough hidden reserves of strength to grab hold of the animated corpse to pull him away from Anne but as she did so, her hands slipped on his wet and slime covered clothes, allowing the cadaver to twist in her grasp. The Dead man did not care whose flesh he tore into and as he refocused his attention to Jen, he lunged for her. Catching her off guard, he pushed her back against the tree and darted in with his jaws snapping, eager to bite into the flesh of her face. As his decaying face came perilously close to hers, Jen could not help but cry out. At that moment, time inexplicably seemed to slow down for Jen, allowing her to take in every detail of the mottled and emaciated face rushing towards her own. Somehow frozen in time, she noticed a small metallic green beetle moving within the dead man's matted hair, burrowing into the corpse's thin putrid skin. Then in an instant, time sped up again and she was throwing her arms up to fend off the deadly snapping teeth rushing towards her.

Even as she fought to push away the Dead man, she feared she could not win this fight. Already she could feel the strength draining from her arms, her muscles protesting against what was suddenly demanded of them. Then with a dull thud, the Dead man's head was knocked sideways by a fist-sized rock bouncing off his skull. Over the struggling Dead man's shoulder, Jen could see Anne pounding at his skull with a second rock. However, Jen could tell Anne's efforts, though admirable, would be wasted. The small girl simply didn't have the power to crack the Dead man's skull enough to save her and she prayed the children would have the sense to flee the moment the Dead man bit into her. Nevertheless, she had survived the Dead for almost eight years with her brother and for him alone she would not give up her life so easily. Therefore, with determination she slipped her hands up to lodge under his chin to keep his snapping jaws away from her as long as she could. Her fingers dug deeply into the rotten flesh of his throat and she could feel the cartilage of his trachea crunch beneath her grasp. Tearing her eyes from the Dead man for a split second, she noticed Justin had pulled his pulse detector from his neck and had rushed past Anne to press it against the Dead man's head. Remembering what the soldiers had said would happen if someone died wearing one of the small metal boxes, Justin had obviously had a flash of inspiration and already Jen could see a tiny red light flashing on the small box, the rate of flashes increasing as its counter thankfully ran down. Knowing that now she only had to hold the Dead man at bay for a short while longer, she found within her a hidden compulsion to survive that burned at her very core. As the flashing increased and the seconds passed, Jen held onto this need to live, this need never to give up and then finally the moment came. One moment the small red light was flashing and then it was a constant red glowing dot. Suddenly, there was a small snapping sound and the pressure explosive sent a single metal bolt into the Dead man's skull to end his unnatural existence. With a sob of relief, Jen pushed the now still corpse away from her, allowing it to flop lifelessly to the ground by her side.

'Th...Thanks,' she whispered, her voice still shaky as she pulled the two children to her.

'We should go,' Justin said, releasing Jen to help her to her feet.

***

'So he's going to help get our people back?' Phil said after Liz had told them about Steven Blackmore. 'But can we trust him?'

'Well, he had more than one opportunity to hand me over to his father the Sergeant and perhaps seeing Penny and Lars again after all these years reminded him of how life used to be,' she replied softly, as she checked through one of the spy holes to watch the Dead ambling pass.

After Phil had secured Samson to the back of the cart, they had used a layby to wait for the bulk of the following Dead to pass them by. Now, twenty minutes later, the decaying crowd had thinned down enough for their pursuit of the convoy to begin again. They made their way back to junction and started their slow trek along the road the Private told Liz to follow, when they heard the distant rumble of engines starting up.

'Sounds like they're on the move again,' Patrick whispered. 'I'm surprised they've hung around this long. Would've thought they'd have left at first light.'

'Perhaps, our soldier friend has already done his bit?' Imran said hopefully.

'Well, if he has let's hope he's had the sense to take with him some sort of vehicle,' Phil added. 'All those children out here unprotected...'

He didn't have to finish the sentence, but they all knew what he meant. With the best intentions in the world, if the Dead attacked and you had a group of young children to protect, it was inevitable someone would end up getting killed. You simply couldn't watch your back effectively with a toddler in your arms. They had all seen it before. Parents desperate to keep their children safe in their arms were unable to defend themselves when the Dead inevitably pulled them to the ground and they ultimately sacrificed not only themselves but also their children to the very creatures they had tried to protect them against.

'From what I saw of the sergeant, I don't think he'd just let someone under his command waltz off with one of his prized vehicles without trying to get it back first,' said Liz, turning away from the spyhole. 'Anyway, the Private knew I was in this direction and the convoy is moving away from us, so I'm guessing he either hasn't made his move yet or they're making their way on foot towards us.'

'So we'd better keep an eye out for them then,' Leon said, pulling aside one of the spyhole covers.

'Watch for movement in the hedgerows,' Patrick said, following Leon's example. 'They'll know it'll be too risky for them to walk along the road out in the open, so I'm guessing they moved into the undergrowth for a bit of camouflage.'

***

By sheer luck rather than by design, Jen and her two charges hadn't come across any more of the Dead since the man by the tree, although the presence of the walking copses could clearly be heard as they crashed and stumbled through the thicket to get to the road and the sound of the disappearing convoy. With each snap of a branch or flurry of disturbed starlings, the small group would halt, their hearts pounding as they awaited the appearance of the Dead. So far, someone had been looking down on them favourably but Jen knew this was too good to last and soon enough, they would be battling against Dead hands and teeth desperate to tear into and consume their flesh.

When they suddenly reached a natural break in the thick hedgerows and saplings, Jen pulled the two children down into a crouch to listen for any close movement. The plant cover on this narrow stretch was noticeably thinner than what they were used to and Jen realised it must have once been an access lane leading from the road to what would have been a field behind them. Knowing that if any of the Dead had, by chance, also come across the overgrown lane that they would use it as an easy way to get to the road, Jen wanted to make sure she and the two children could cross the breach undetected. Even as they patiently listened, they could hear something crashing its way somewhere through the hedgerow to begin its slow painful approach to the road. Opposite her and a few metres to her right, Jen could see a Dead woman stumbling into view. As the woman made it fully into the breach, what was left of her rotten jumper snagged on a broken branch causing her to fall face first to the snow covered ground. Jen instinctively pushed her arm in front of the two children, edging them behind her deeper into the shadows, where they would hopefully be unseen. Jen watched as the Dead woman slowly pulled herself to her feet.

Even from a distance, Jen could see the woman had become one of the Dead in a terrible manner, because in the process of righting herself, the Dead woman turned what was left of her face in her direction. Much of the flesh from her nose upwards had been viciously torn away, together with one of her eyes, leaving only a full bottom lip surrounded by shreds of decaying skin and muscle as a testament to the horror this woman had gone through. Luckily, Jen and the children had been unnoticed by the Dead woman and as she stepped further away from the dense thicket, Jen was relieved to see that the fall had inadvertently pulled the caught jumper free of the branch, allowing her to continue on her endless trek. With her back now facing them, Jen edged silently forward on her stomach to see if any other of the Dead had found this path of least resistance. As much as she feared for his safety, Jen felt a small wave of comfort when Justin nudged up alongside her to look also. Thankfully, the snow here was relatively shallow so she brushed some aside to get to the winter grass beneath and as Jen sneaked a peak from her prone position at the retreating Dead woman, she cursed silently under her breath. Another four of the Dead were making their way to the road but at least these too had their backs to them. If they were quiet and moved slowly, they might be able to cross unseen. Reaching behind her for Anne, Jen nodded silently and giving the scared child a smile, took her hand.

When she realised the situation wasn't going to get any better any time soon, Jen decided they would have to take a chance, before any more of the Dead added to this already risky situation. Pointing across the breach to where the thickets grew wildly again and then pressing her fingers to her lips, she silently told the children they would be making the stealthy break to the other side. With one final quick glance at the retreating Dead, Jen edged forwards in a crouch stance, out into the open. The track itself could only have been six or seven metres wide but each exposed step she took felt like it could be her last. It wasn't until they were over half way across that she realised Justin had not only stopped and was standing up but he was peering intently down the track towards the road. Looking back at the boy who was scared for his life, she saw his eyes widen and little mouth open in surprise as something he recognised came into view. Slowly, Justin managed to pull his gaze from the road back to Jen.

'Cart,' he whispered, raising his hand to point.

Jen immediately stood up herself, just in time to see the rear of a cart disappearing from view with a large horse tethered to the back.

'Samson!' Justin continued, 'That was Samson... one of our horses from the Convent.'

Jen could see what was about to happen and made a grab for the two children before they could bolt off.

'Wait!' she whispered urgently. 'If we just run after them without a plan, we'll get killed.'

Justin looked from Jen to Anne, visibly itching run after the cart.

'But that's what I used to do all the time before Mum and Dad found me,' be replied. 'If you just keep moving and don't stop, you can weave in and out of them, no problem. They can't catch you, because they're too slow and too spread out.'

Jen knew every second she thought about it, the cart was getting slowly further and further away, which meant more of the Dead would be between them and a rescue. She looked into Justin's eyes and knew he meant it. This child had survived on his own this way for God only knew how long, and perhaps if he could do it, so could they.

'What about you, Sweetie?' she whispered to Anne, 'do you think we can make it?'

'Yes,' Anne said with a nod.

She might only be eight, but she knew this could be their only real chance if they wanted to live longer than a few days. They simply couldn't survive for long out in the open like this, not without proper weapons. They had been lucky with the Dead man, but their luck could only stretch so far.

'Yes... we've got to,' she added in a tone older than her years.

'We shouldn't clump together,' said Justin. 'It'll be easier to dodge in and out if we're not running in a line.'

'Okay,' Jen said taking a breath to calm herself. 'You're the expert, so we'll follow your lead.'

With that, Justin smiled and began creeping forwards. When he was a few steps behind the first Dead woman, he turned quickly to Jen and Anne to make sure they were ready. Seeing a pair of nervous looking faces staring back at him, he realised they were as ready as they were ever going to be, so he turned, rushed forward and shoved the Dead woman hard in the back, knocking her to the ground.

'Now!' he said, darting forwards like a maniac.

All three of them sprinted effortlessly past the fallen Dead woman and before she had even reacted to landing face down in the snow for a second time, they were already dodging past the first of the other four walking cadavers on the track. It wasn't until they were approaching the second of them, a man with an arm missing, the ragged strips of flesh hanging uselessly from his torn sleeve, that one of the Dead further on turned. His attention was drawn to the sound of movement behind him. Then, it was like a chain reaction that the moaning began filling the air. Reaching for Justin as he darted past, the man swung his remaining arm uselessly, desperate to grab hold of the flesh that was just out of his reach. Anne then made it past him smoothly while his attention was focused on Justin. Jen, feeling brave, kicked out at his knees. With his legs buckling beneath him, he fell to the ground.

'Don't stop to deal with them!' Justin called back to her. 'Just get past them. It doesn't matter if they follow, just keep moving.'

After weaving in and out of the remaining three of the Dead, each of whom were momentarily too dazzled by the choice of so much meat running past them to notice it easily escaping their reach, Jen and the two children swiftly made it to the road.

'Shit!' Jen said, taking in the deadly minefield she and the children would have to manoeuvre.

There between the disappearing cart and themselves were at least forty of the Dead, shambling their way along the road. Already some of them had started to turn, their interest aroused by the call of their Dead brethren behind them.

'Don't think about,' Justin said calmly looking from Anne to Jen. 'Just do it.'

'I must be mad,' Jen said, darting forwards, taking a slightly different route to Justin and Anne.

Justin and Anne seemed to have no difficulty dipping under the outstretched arms as the Dead lumbered towards them. However, for Jen, her very height was making it more of a challenge. More than once, she felt the deathly brush of Dead fingers on her back as she rushed past them, and knew that any minute, one would grab hold of her for good. When it finally happened, she was surprised it came from such a low-level attack. Darting past a putrid decaying fat man, his large body a seemingly unending feast for maggots, Jen failed to notice the cadaver of the child until it was too late. Being not much older than Justin, the Dead child latched onto her jacket as she ran past, causing her to trip. With a scream, she went down hard, taking the Dead child with her.

'No!' she screamed.

Looking back over his shoulder, Justin could see Jen fighting to push away the small animated corpse, while more of the Dead began closing in on her.

'Get to the cart and get help!' he shouted to Anne, as he sped back to help Jen.

Barely breaking her stride, Anne knew it was up to her, but she simply didn't know if she could get to cart in time. It was already quite far down the road and it was about to disappear round a corner.

'Lizzy! Lizzy!' she screamed over and over as loudly as she could.

She was desperate for her saviours to hear her, but she knew with each second, they were getting too far away and Anne's screams soon became choking sobs. She knew she was going to die on this road, because it was simply impossible to outrun the dead forever. However, she would not give up just yet and through her sobs, she screamed for her sister again and again. Then as she dodged past a Dead man that had turned his putrid gaze to her, she saw the cart come to an abrupt halt. Before the wheels had even stopped turning, the top and side hatches had been flung open and three men were piling out. High on cart's roof, Imran stood, his bow already letting fly his life saving arrows, while barrelling towards her was Phil, screaming with rage as he swung his club left and right knocking the Dead to the floor to get to her. Reaching her in mere seconds, he effortlessly scooped her into his arms, knocking away a reaching Dead man with a sharp kick to his hip.

'Thought we'd lost you, Darling,' he said, pulling her tight to his chest.

'Help Justin and the woman!' he shouted as he ran back past Patrick and Leon, each dealing with the Dead in their own brutal way.

Skidding to an abrupt halt, Phil lowered Anne back to the ground.

'I told you to wait in the cart,' he said angrily to Liz, as she pushed him aside to pull her sister into a tight hug.

As the two sister wept in each other's arms, Phil turned back to the job in hand. With a warrior's roar, he leapt back into battle again, smashing skulls or simply removing them from their unnatural shoulders.

Back down the road, Justin was doing his best to dart in and out between the Dead, knocking them down or drawing their attention away from Jen, who still battled with the snapping Dead child on top of her. Then, one moment the child's face was but a breath away from her own and the next it was being yanked violently back away from her and thrown back into the Dead crowd by a young black man.

'Are you alright? Did it get you?' Leon asked, reaching out his hand to help the shocked woman back on her feet.

'No... I'm fine... thanks,' Jen replied, a puzzled expression falling on her face as she watched him pull a knife from a slit on his jacket and seem to take aim on her.

'Duck,' he simply said, only moments before letting the blade fly from his fingers.

'What the fuck?' Jen cried, fearing he hadn't heard her say she hadn't been bitten.

It was only when a decrepit looking Dead woman slumped to the floor by her side that she realise he had saved her yet again.

'I'll have to charge for the next one,' he said with a wink, reaching past her to yank free his knife.

'Err... you could've given me a bit more warning, I thought you were going to kill me,' she said letting go of a tight breath that up until that point she had been unaware she had been holding.

'You're welcome,' Leon replied with a smile.

He knew the woman wasn't being ungrateful on purpose, it was just that almost having your face ripped off could make you forget your manners sometimes. They had all been there, so he didn't take offense. In fact, there was an indefinable something he instantly liked about her and it wasn't just that he quite liked the feisty type either. Of course, she was a far too skinny for him at the moment but beneath the angry glare, angled bones and taut muscle, he could see the makings a strong and beautiful woman.

'Here, take this,' he said thrusting a large hunting knife in her hand, 'and get to the cart.'

'No, I'll help keep them off Justin,' she replied, looking for the small boy that had surely kept the Dead hoard away from her.

'Do as you're told woman, you can barely stand yourself,' Leon butted in, 'we'll deal with the Dead... get to the cart.'

Jen opened her mouth to argue but closed it again. She knew he was right and it galled her. As much as she wanted to help Justin, she would only be a hindrance and in her weakened state, someone could end of dead because of her. Holding her head up and pushing her shoulders back she moved to pass Leon.

'This isn't over Flyboy,' she said, noticing his smirk.

'Whatever you say, Hot-stuff,' Leon replied, unable to help himself from winking at her again.

Jen paused for a fraction of a second mid step. It had been a long time since anyone had referred to her in such a way and it threw her for a second. Frustrated that this cocky young man, so sure of himself, had been able to get under her skin so quickly, Jen turned with a 'humph' and stepped over the fallen Dead to make her way to the cart.

After a brief glance to make sure her path to the cart was clear, Leon turned back to the dozen or so remaining Dead that were still shambling about excitedly on the road. Imran, Patrick and Phil had already dealt with the most able bodied of the walking corpses, so those left were either unable to stand or were so pitifully decrepit that any threat they posed was minimal. Even as Leon stamped down on the skull of a Dead girl, her back broken by one of Phil's mighty club swings, he watched as Justin kicked out at the withered legs of a particularly emaciated looking Dead old man, snapping his brittle bones easily.

As the last of the incapacitated corpses were forever silenced, an eerie quiet descended on the lane. Its once pristine covering of white snow was now littered with broken, twisted bodies and large dark patches of fetid gore.

'We haven't got time to move them,' Phil said, looking around at the corpses. 'We should quickly collect Imran's arrows and then get back in the cart before any more turn up, otherwise we'll be here all day.'

'Come on, Killer,' Patrick said, smiling as he ruffled Justin's hair. 'You did good, your mum and dad will be proud.'

Something sad and far too adult for his young face flashed behind Justin's eyes.

'We've got to get them back first,' he said quietly.

'We'll get them back, don't you worry,' Phil said, picking the small wriggling boy and hugging him. 'Hey, you may be the big bad man now but you're never too old for a hug, Sonny… just glad we found you, Justin.'

'You found us?' Justin said smiling. 'More like we found you.'

'Yeah, whatever,' Phil said, finally releasing Justin and playfully knocking his chin. 'Come on… get in the cart, smartarse.'

After they had darted from one felled corpse to the next collecting Imran's arrows and Leon's knives, the three men and Justin squashed themselves back into the cart with the others. The cart, which had not exactly been roomy with the four men in it, was now positively cramped, thanks to the two women and two children they had collected.

'Looks like we made it just in time,' Phil said quietly, as he saw through the front view slit another three of the Dead already pushing themselves through the hedgerow and onto the road.

'Is Delilah going to be able to pull us all?' Liz asked, worrying that if they didn't catch up with the convoy soon, the trusty mare certainly wouldn't be able to keep pulling the extra weight long term.

'We'll use Samson and Delilah in shifts,' Phil replied, whispering over his shoulder. 'That way, neither of them will bear the burden for too long.'

Nodding, Liz turned to their newest adult addition and noticed she seemed to be staring intently at Leon, with a puzzled expression on her face. It was almost as if she was trying to figure something out. Only when Leon caught her gaze, raising a dark eyebrow in reply, did the woman turned away from him.

'I'm Liz, and Anne is my sister,' Liz began, nodding towards Anne sitting squashed tightly next to her.

'You're very lucky to have each other,' Jen said quietly, images of the soldiers shooting her brother suddenly flooding her mind. 'She was very brave.'

'Yes, yes she was,' Liz continued, realising from the look on her face that the woman had obviously lost some family of her own recently, 'and that's Patrick, Phil, Imran... and you've met Leon.'

'Yes, I've met Leon,' she said, her eyes flicking briefly back to the young black man. 'My name's Jennifer, but you can just call me Jen.'

'I take it Private Blackmore helped you escape, Jen?' Patrick asked. 'What happened to the rest?'

'The men had been shackled during the night,' Jen began between mouthfuls of the cooked chicken that Imran had handed her. 'Apparently the Sergeant didn't think the women and children would try to escape on their own. Anyway, the Private wasn't aware of the shackles so when he made his move, only Penny and I were able to go. Justin's mother and another woman decided to stay with their men. When we got out, the others were seen by some soldiers but I pulled Anne and Justin out of sight just in time behind some tents. We managed to creep away.'

'What about Penny, the Private and the other children?' asked Liz, concerned for her friend and the man who had risked everything to help them.

'I think she'll be okay. They'll want her... for breeding ...' she replied, with her lip curling in disgust. 'I doubt the solider will be quite so lucky though. That Sergeant doesn't look the type to just forgive and forget.'

'No, I don't think he is,' Phil said in an angry tone, pulling Delilah to a stop. 'Look.'

***

As the rumble of engines faded into the distance, the only sounds Steve could hear were his own sharp shallow breathing and the slow creaking of the rope as he swung gently back and forth. With his chin resting on his chest, Steve watched his laboured breath pluming clouds of vapour in the cold air. For a moment, it would billow out from him like tiny summer clouds, only to dissipate into the air seconds later. The rope tied tightly around his chest had pinned his arms to his sides and with each cloud of breath, a spasm of pain shot from his bruised and cracked ribs. Nevertheless, Steve held onto the pain, pulling it to his very core to fuel the hatred burning there for his father. He had certainly underestimated the darkness that he now knew dwelled within the shell of the man who had given him life. It was bad enough that he had left his own son hanging from a tree like some macabre piñata, full of bloody treats for the Dead, but to go out of his way to ensure Steve knew that he would rise from his all too brief oblivion as one of the Dead himself was beyond sadistic. His only hope was that the pregnant woman and her friends would turn up before the Dead found him, but with the noisy convoy attracting all that could walk, he didn't fancy his chances. When the snap of twigs finally came from his left, it was almost with relief that he realised the time had come when his fate would be decided. He would survive the encounter or he wouldn't, it was as simple as that.

Craning his head to the left, he watched as the corpse of a teenage girl stumbled onto the road. Dressed in the tattered remains of a school uniform, the Dead girl steadied herself for a second on the compacted snow covered road before turning her film-covered eyes to Steve. She had been drawn to the road by the sounds of the convoy but she had found in its place a prize of flesh and blood waiting for her. With every burning cell of her body, she knew she must claim this prize. It was hers by right, hers to rip and bite into, hers to gorge upon to quench the fiery hunger that consumed her. Almost instantly, she reached a decaying hand toward him, beseeching Steve to relinquish the life he so selfishly hoarded. As she took a painful step towards him, Steve noticed her hand was missing three of its fingers.

'*There were worse ways to be conscripted into the army of the Dead,*' he thought to himself, pulling his eyes away from the blackened stubs on her hand.

'Like having the fucking flesh stripped from your legs while you're trussed up like a pig,' he said aloud.

At the sound of his voice, she became more excited, and as if to answer him, she let forth a low brittle moan of her own. Step by Step, the Dead girl sang to him her call of death, demanding he pay for her deadly aria with his flesh. Sooner than he hoped, she dragged her decaying corpse across the road to stand directly below him. Panicking that at any moment he would feel the cold press of her blackened lips against his flesh, Steve kicked out hard with one leg aiming for her head. The lightning bolt that suddenly shot through him from the jerky movement of the rope made him cry out in pain and as his vision spun, he feared he would blackout completely. Fighting the oblivion that threatened to swamp him, Steve did his best to ignore the spasms of pain pulsing from his chest and tried to concentrate on the Dead girl already reaching up for his leg. But it appeared Lady Luck was looking favourable down on him for once, because the Dead girl had been short for her age when she was alive and with his feet only coming level with her forehead, there was no way she could reach up to bite him. Of course, that would not stop her fingers ripping into the flesh of his legs if she could get through his combat trousers. Steve knew his kicks, even if he didn't blackout from the pain, simply couldn't muster the force needed to do any real damage to the Dead girl, so with a flash of inspiration, he tried to manoeuvre her under him. Perhaps if he could use the top of her head to take some of his weight, he might be able to relieve the pressure on his ribs just enough to be able to stamp down on her head to crack her skull or break her neck. It was a wild shot, but with no other options open to him, Steve knew he at least had to give it a go. However, when he heard the sound of more snapping of branches over to his right, his heart sank. There, pushing its way through the snow-covered hedgerow was a Dead man and more importantly, he was a tall Dead man. This new arrival, drawn to Steve by the Dead girl's song, could easily reach the flesh of Steve's calves with his mouth and condemn him with a bite.

'Shit! Shit! Shit!' said Steve, focusing all his attention on the newly approaching cadaver.

Already, his low baritone moans had joined those of the girl, weaving their calls together to create a mournful dirge full of hunger and loss. The Dead man must have been in his forties when he was taken and from the looks of him, he must have only died within the last few months. His flesh, though grey and rotten, was still mainly intact and apart from a black creeping mould that appeared from under the collar of his jacket to bloom up his neck and onto one side of his face, he seemed in relatively good condition. How he had died, Steve had no idea. At the moment it was his own demise that concerned him and as the man shambled closer, he knew it was about to happen a lot sooner than he hoped. With each tortured step, Steve's death became more and more of a certainty.

'Fucking hell!' Steve said quietly, tears of frustration and anger filling his eyes, as the Dead man's arms reached towards him.

Suddenly, when the Dead man was but one step away from claiming the flesh he craved, he turned his deathly gaze slowly away from Steve. Something behind Steve had caught the Dead man's attention, something that interested him more than Steve's body hanging there ripe for the slaughter and whatever it was had also caused the girl to abandon her fruitless efforts to get to Steve as well. As if instantly forgotten, her withered hand fell from his boot and she awkwardly turned her stiff body away from him. Whatever was behind him had certainly been considered a better option by the Dead pair; though he had no idea how their decaying brains had been able to make such a choice. How and why they made their choice, it didn't matter, because all Steve knew was that it had given him a few more moments of life to live.

Ignoring the pain from his ribs, Steve began to move his shoulders left and right. Slowly at first, and then increasing in strength, the movement made him spin back and forth. When the momentum had been built up enough for the rope to spin him round, Steve was shocked by what he saw walking calmly down the road towards the two enraptured Dead.

There, walking towards him as if he wasn't about to encounter two walking cadavers hungry for his flesh was a large man. He was shirtless, exposing the muscles of his broad chest and thick arms to not only the winter cold, but also the Dead. Walking with his arms opened wide, as if to welcome their deathly embrace, he was gladly showing the Dead a menu on which his flesh was the only dish pictured and they wanted it all.

'Come on, you pus bags,' Phil said, waving the Dead closer. 'Come get yourself some of what you need.'

Tearing his eyes away from the approaching mad man, Steve noticed that behind him, further down the road, a cart had pulled to a stop. Without warning, a hatch opened silently on the roof of the cart and a young Middle Eastern looking man rose with a bow in his hand. As Steve began to spin back to face his original position, he just caught a glimpse of the bowman taking aim on one of the corpses. With the whistle of an arrow flying through the air, followed swiftly by a crunch and then the sound of something heavy falling to the floor, Steve knew he would live to see another day.

'Sorry, Britney,' he heard the shirtless man say. 'You're just not my type.'

A grunt of effort and then a sickening cracking sound came again and again. Quickly, the cracking sound developed a wet, sucking quality and as Steve began to twist back to face the shirtless man, he was thankful to see that he was repeatedly stamping down hard on the girl's skull. With a snap, the man's boot finally did enough damage to her rotting brain to put her to rest.

'I take it you're Private Blackmore?' Phil asked, smiling up at the battered man as he began to wipe stinking bits of the girl's brain off the sole of his boot.

'Yes,' was all Steve could say. 'You?'

'Phil,' he replied, walking over to place Steve's feet on his shoulders to brace him up. 'Now, let's get you down from there before I freeze my tits off.'

***

Each time the Doctors looked away or were too engrossed reading test results to notice her, Alice would slowly and carefully draw the scalpel blade she held in her fingertips slowly against the strap of her restraints.

She hadn't known why the solider had tossed her the blade but after he had been dragged outside, she had clearly heard his shouts. They wanted her baby or rather, they wanted what he held in his tiny veins but more importantly, they wanted to prove they had been right. Her baby would be forced to pay the ultimate sacrifice to prove these doctors had been correct with their formulae and microscopic engineering. Now that the anti-virus had established itself with her baby, his very blood alone was the stuff of legend. They would grow the cure to the Death walker plague from his blood and her baby would be the saviour of the human race. However, like all Messiahs, first he would have to die so that they could live. If they were right, he would be a Messiah who would never rise from the dead.

When they heard the soldier shout his warning, Dr Morris and Dr Chambers had carried on regardless of his accusations. They did not care if she now knew what they had planned. For them, this was simply what had to be done. It was only when Alice caught the eye of the other younger doctor, who she remembered was called Dr Avery, that she saw any remorse and shame. He instantly dropped his eyes back to his microscope and nervously glanced back and forth at a pile of papers. He hoped she hadn't seen him looking at her but his twitchy movements and the blush of shame rising up the back of his neck, spoke volumes. Even one of the soldiers who had been brought in semi-conscious had tried to push himself up on one elbow when he heard the shouted warning. He had looked at Alice with a sad drowsy look in his eyes, his mouth opening and closing mutely as if he wanted to say something reassuring. However, Alice could see he had been hit pretty hard on the head and even if he was on her side, he was in no state to help her. It was going to up to her to do something and if it meant killing someone so that her baby could live, then so be it.

'Well, the incubation period will be up in an hour or so,' Dr Morris said looking from his watch to his female colleague, as she rubbed the back of her neck with her hand to ease her aching muscles. 'We'll take one final blood sample from the foetus for comparison and then induce labour.'

'Why aren't we doing a C-section,' she asked, giving up on her tight muscles. 'We'll be able to report back to Dr Farrell our findings within a few hours if we do.'

'No, Dr Farrell ordered that the birth be as natural as possible, because any local anaesthesia that would be needed to perform the C-section could interfere with results we get from the foetus,' he replied. 'Also, without the process of birth to jump start the clearing fluid from the lungs, there could be breathing difficulties and that's the last thing we need'

'Okay,' Dr Chambers said, pulling a pair of surgical gloves from a box on the wall and walking over to Alice.

'Now, we're not going to have to put you under again, are we?' she continued, giving Alice a stern look as she pulled the ultrasound monitor back into place. 'It's quite a straight forward procedure, retrieving a blood sample from the foetus. You'll only feel a slight cramping sensation as the needle breaks through the placental wall, that's all.'

Now that she knew what they had planned for her son, Alice needed to be on the lookout for every opportunity that might offer her escape. She could ill afford to spend any of the time her son had left unconscious.

'Just get on with it,' she said sharply, turning away from the woman who was willing to be complicit in the murder of her baby.

In her hand, the scalpel blade itched to not only finish cutting through her restraints but also do some serious damage to these people who had casually planned to take her child from her. However, with the female doctor paying such close attention, she knew she would have to bide her time, keeping it hidden from sight in her clenched fist, until the ideal opportunity presented itself. Only then would she show them what it meant to really live among the Dead for all these years and how it changed a person, making them capable of the unexpected.

After lifting up Alice's gown and squeezing a small amount of lubricant gel on her stomach, Dr Chambers began to move the handheld transducer back and forth to determine the position of the foetus.

'There it is,' she mumbled to herself, as she studied the flickering image on the monitor.

Reaching over to a drawer, she pulled out a device that looked like a long metal tube with two buttons near one end, while at the other end the top of a small glass vial could be seen. Placing the flat end against Alice's stomach, Dr Chambers double checked the foetus position again and when she was satisfied, pressed the first of the buttons.

'This will just pinch for a second,' she said to Alice, never taking her eyes from the monitor. 'Try not to move.'

There was a small mechanical buzzing sound as the thin hypodermic needle was driven into Alice and as it pierced through the placenta and into the amniotic sac, Alice winced from the sharp stab of pain.

'Almost done,' Dr Chambers said, some long forgotten bedside manner slipping into her tone by habit rather than concern.

Alice didn't know if she had expected to feel anything from her baby when the blood sample was taken but as Dr Chambers pressed the second button and the small vial began to turn red, there was no sudden maternal claxon going off inside her. Pressing the first button again, the needle was slowly withdrawn back into the metal tube and with a 'click' she released the already sealed small vial of blood.

'Done,' said Dr Chambers, pushing the monitor back into place and turning to hand the vial to Dr Avery.

Instantly, it was as if Alice, as a person, was forgotten again. Now that the doctors had their precious sample, she was merely the incubator in which their test subject was housed. Already the younger male doctor had placed the glass tube containing her son's blood into another device. What it did or how it did it, Alice had no idea but after a series of internal beeps and clicks, world changing data was already being processed and sent to the computer terminal next to it to be cross checked, analysed and studied.

For the next hour, Alice silently drew the blade back and forth across the restraining strap while the three doctors busied themselves darting between their printouts and their computers. From the excited buzz, Alice could tell their hopeful cure for the Death-walker plague had taken hold within her unborn baby, turning him into a possible hope for humanity. A possible hope that Alice knew they would put to the test by killing him.

'Right,' Dr Morris said solemnly pulling on a pair of surgical gloves, 'let's get this started.'

With a tug Alice could feel the restraint holding her in place was moments away from breaking. She just needed a few more swipes of the blade and her hand would be free, but as Dr Morris walked over to a drawer near her and pulled out a tube of something, she knew her time was running out fast.

'Now this is just a gel that contains a hormone that I apply to your cervix,' he said to her, breaking the seal on the tube. 'It prepares the muscles in the birth canal for stretching.'

'Please don't do this,' she said quietly.

However, Dr Morris carried on as if she hadn't spoken and with a click, he pulled the stirrups into place either side of her bed.

'Please lift your legs up,' he said, nodding towards the stirrups. 'This won't take a minute.'

Alice knew it was pointless to fight him just yet and as she reluctantly lifted each leg into place, she turned her face away from him, shame and anger fighting within her. As Dr Morris began to apply the gel inside her, Alice looked over at the solider who had called out earlier. Their eyes locked and something passed between them, something Alice couldn't pin down, but she could tell from his expression that he knew what was happening here and it troubled him. Whether it troubled him enough to act was another matter. Alice knew she really only had herself to rely on and as Dr Morris' attention was diverted, she gave the restraint another sharp tug.

'So, we'll give that a few minutes,' said Dr Morris to himself rather than to Alice. 'Sometimes the gel itself is enough.'

'I don't think we should wait,' said Dr Chambers looking up from a stack of readouts. 'To be sure, we should give her the Pitocin injection now.'

'Yes, I suppose you're right.' Dr Morris agreed, swivelling in his chair to reach back into the drawer, pick up a vial of clear liquid and draw some into to a hypodermic needle.

Alice had been waiting for this chance. With a flick, the scalpel blade cut through the final thick strands of strapping and after a forceful yank, her hand was free. Immediately, she began to unbuckle her other hand, her fingers frantically pulling at the heavy buckle.

'What the...' Dr Morris began, the small bottle of Pitocin slipping from his grasp to smash to the floor.

With panic threatening to overwhelm her, Alice pulled at the buckle, desperate to be free but already Dr Morris had grabbed hold of her arm and was pulling it back while behind him Dr Chambers and Dr Avery were rising from their seats.

'No!' Alice screamed, swinging her free arm wildly to beat Dr Morris away from her.

Dr Morris gave a sudden gasp and instantly his hands flew from her arm up to his neck. Alice glanced up into the man's wide eyes and saw only shock and terror there. For a split second, all was silent in the Med lab as Dr Morris held tightly to his throat. However, they all knew the damage had been done. In her attempt to keep Dr Morris away from her, Alice's scalpel blade had sliced clean through the flesh of his throat, severing a major artery. Already his blood was pumping forcefully through his fingers spraying across Alice and much of the bed.

'Jesus, no!' cried Dr Chambers, running forward to help apply pressure to his neck.

As she lowered Dr Morris him to the floor, watching him silently open and close his mouth in shock, she knew her efforts would be in vain.

Holding him in her arms, his own panic ridden heart wildly pumping his blood over her, Dr Chambers knew there was nothing she could do for her colleague and as Dr Morris's hand fell slowly from his neck, he gave one last blood filled sigh and was gone.

Dr Chambers lowered the dead man's head gently to the floor and turned to Alice, with a look of pure hatred and anger burning in her glare.

'You stupid fucking bitch!' she spat, rising from the dead body at her feet. 'Do you think this is over? Do you think this ends with him?'

Reaching behind her, she pulled from the back of her blood soaked trousers a small handgun and pointed it at Alice.

'Drop it!' she said. 'Believe me bitch. I can just as easily get that brat out of you if you're dead'

Alice looked at the blood covered woman and knew what she was saying was true. She would happily kill her to get to her unborn son, so with an over-whelming sense of defeat Alice let the scalpel blade drop from her fingers to land in a puddle of the late Dr Morris's blood. Stepping round Dr Morris's body, Dr Chambers moved over to retrieve the full syringe of Pitocin that Dr Morris had left on a cabinet.

'Now, I'm going to give you this injection,' she said, placing the gun back in her waistband. 'It will induce labour and if you struggle, I'll shoot you… you piss me off and I'll shoot you… Do we understand each other?'

Alice just looked at the woman with barely concealed hatred.

'Give me your arm,' said Dr Chambers coldly.

Reluctantly, Alice thrust her arm forward. She had her chance and blown it, and now her baby would die. Dr Chambers stepped forward, roughly grabbing hold of Alice's arm with one hand.

'Wait!' Dr Avery's voice came from the other side of the lab. 'We don't have to do this, Helen. The results from the blood work alone are conclusive… this is just madness.'

With a sneer on her face, Dr Chambers snapped her head round to look at Dr Avery.

'You always were weak!' She spat and turned back to lower the needle to Alice's arm.

'I'd listen to him if I were you,' said Matt, placing the cold muzzle of his gun against the back of her skull. 'Now, drop it!'

Slowly, Dr Chambers held up her hands in surrender and then made a show of placing the hypodermic down on the counter.

'You're making a big mistake, soldier,' she said calmly.

'Yeah, well that seems to be happening a lot lately,' he replied, nudging Dr Chambers over to a seat.

Suddenly, there was a small popping sound, as the timer on the late Dr Morris's pulse detector ran out, sending its bolt up into his brain. Dr Chambers looked down at the forever still form of her colleague and shook her head.

'Such a waste,' she said to herself.

'Yeah, well forgive me if I don't send flowers,' Alice said, finally unbuckling her final restraint so she could ease herself down from the bed.

'So what now?' asked Dr Avery, looking from Alice to the soldier.

'Now we wait until the convoy stops for camp tonight and then think of a way out of here that doesn't involve getting shot or eaten,' replied Matt. 'You two just sit tight and no one will get hurt, okay?'

Dr Avery slumped back in his chair and then with his head in his hands, he looked up at Matt.

'Take me with you,' he asked, his voice full of sadness. 'Please, I don't want to go back to the base....it's... it's like being in hell... all the rumours are true, you know. Cardin gives Farrell the troublemakers for research, he...'

'Avery!' snapped Dr Chambers, glaring at the man who had broken their unholy pact of secrecy.

'It's over, Helen,' Dr Avery said, trying to rub the tiredness from his face. 'What's going on at that base is wrong and we all know it. Just how long did you think we could keep treating people like lab rats. It was bad enough when we used the Dead ones, but what Farrell has made us do is... is horrific.'

'Sacrifices had to be made, Avery,' she replied, with conviction adding strength to her words. 'For the greater good of the human race, some had to be sacrificed.'

Dr Avery looked up and stared back at Dr Chambers, trying to read something in her face.

'You really believe that, don't you?' he said, his voice full of pity and regret. 'Don't you see... we've sacrificed the very humanity we were trying to save.'

However, Dr Chambers simply shook her head and looked back at Dr Avery as if he was a small child unable to understand the conversation of adults. Like any zealot, her truth was the only truth and because of that, she was simply unable to comprehend anything outside the world she had created for herself. In fact, Dr Avery might as well have been speaking Mandarin to her, for all the impact his words made on her. Seeing there was no reaching the woman who had been his colleague and friend for the last eight years, Dr Avery let out a weary sigh and turned back to Alice and the solider.

'So will you take me with you?' he asked. 'Please, I need to make amends for what I've done.'

'If you're planning some sort of double-cross, you'll be sorry,' Matt said coldly.

'No, please. You've got to believe me,' Dr Avery added. 'I can help you. I can buy us some time.'

'How?' asked Alice, discarding the hospital gown and pulling on her own clothes.

'When the convoy stops, Sergeant Blackmore will expect a report from Dr Morris,' he replied. 'I'll go to him saying that Alice has begun labour and he doesn't want to leave her. He knows how important the Foetus... the baby is... so it could buy us a few hours.'

Matt looked at Dr Avery, trying to gauge the sincerity of the man. In just a few exchanged words, Matt was being forced to pass judgement on him in order to measure his worth and reliability, and ultimately, whether he could place Alice's and his own life in his hands. Seconds after Dr Avery had confirmed that the horrific rumours that, they had all heard whispering through the corridors of the base were true a terrible realisation hit him. His sister, Karen was still there and no matter what happened here, he would have to find a way back to her. In that moment, Matt realised he would need the doctor's help if he wanted to get Alice and her baby away from these monsters and he simply had no option but to trust the man and hope his contrition was genuine.

'Okay,' Matt said, with a nod, sealing his fate one way or another.

'But what about her... and him?' Alice asked, gesturing to Dr Chambers and the other still unconscious solider. 'What's to stop her from calling out for help as soon as we stop?'

'Well, he's not a problem,' Dr Avery began, nodding toward the solider. 'He was hit pretty hard. We think he may have already had a minor underlying physical defect. The knock has caused some bleeding on the brain, so I doubt he'll come round for a long time... if at all. As for her, well, I think we'll just have to sedate her.'

'What!' Dr Chambers snapped.

'Come on, Helen, I'll only give you enough to keep you under for a few hours,' said Dr Avery looking from Matt to his irate colleague. 'You'll be perfectly safe.'

'Screw this!' she replied, jumping from her seat.

'I wouldn't if I were you,' Matt said, swiftly grabbing her arm to pushing her back down and pointing his gun at her. 'Up to you which type of shot you'd prefer, lady.'

Looking from Dr Avery to the soldier, Dr Helen Chambers knew she was beaten.

'If you think Blackmore is just going to let you waltz out of here with her, you're crazy,' she said, already rolling up her sleeve. 'He's going to feed you to those walking corpses out there when he catches up with you.'

Dr Avery went to a drawer and pulled out a bottle of clear liquid and a vacuum-sealed new hypodermic.

'If you think you'll get any better treatment, you're as deluded as they are,' she continued, turning to Alice while Dr Avery wiped her forearm with an antiseptic swab. 'Blackmore will catch you and you'll be back on that bunk soon enough. I'll get to rip that thing out of you yet, so you're just delaying the inevitable.'

'Excuse me, Doc,' Alice said, stepping around Dr Avery to land a hefty punch on the woman's jaw, knocking her out cold. 'Some people just don't know when to shut up.'

Dr Avery looked from the unconscious Helen Chambers to Alice and back again.

'Remind me not to piss you off,' he said to himself, as he inserted the needle into Dr Chambers' arm and depressed the plunger.

'I don't suppose that can be taken orally?' Matt asked, after he had helped Dr Avery move the prone form of Dr Chambers over to one of the beds.

'The Propofol? No, why?' Dr Avery replied.

'Well, I thought if I could get enough into the water tank, we could knock out most the squadron when we park up for the night. They're bound to want coffee or at the very least they'll need water to rehydrate the MRE packs.'

Dr Avery thought for a minute before walking over to a cabinet and pulling about a box.

'Thiopentol,' he said with a smile, 'is a handy little barbiturate that, although will take longer to take effect than if it was intravenous, it can be given orally. Not too great if someone has liver problems, but it's all I can think of that we've got enough of.'

'Right, so that's the plan then,' said Matt. 'When we stop for the night, you'll go fob off Blackmore while I dope the water'

'And then what?' Alice asked, easing herself awkwardly down into a chair.

'Then we wait,' Matt replied, 'and just hope enough get knocked out for us to get away.'

***

Now that the rope had been removed from his cracked ribs, Steve was finding it easier to breathe and as he looked at the expectant faces of his rescuers, he knew that they wanted answers.

'What can I say?' he began, taking a gulp of cold water from the bottle passed to him by the pregnant woman who had shadowed the convoy since leaving Lanherne. 'It was meeting Penny and Mr Sorenson... sorry, I mean Lars, again after all these years that made my mind up for me. Coming face to face with someone from the past reminded me that life didn't used to be like this... that it wasn't meant to be like this. They were meant to be doing something good with the base. That was the whole point, but after a while it changed... we changed. Living all those years, not knowing who you could trust or who was going to disappear next was unbearable. We were constantly living on a knife's edge and in the end, you just do what you needed to not be noticed, and not rock the boat... but... but I couldn't do that anymore, not when I found Penny and Lars again.'

'People have died while you didn't rock that boat,' Leon said sternly, thinking of Sally and Jen's brother, knowing there must have been other nameless men and women who had fallen afoul of the soldiers. 'It's not going to be so easy to wipe the slate clean with a few words.'

'Don't know but you might've missed the part where my own father strung me up as a meal for some corpse to chow down on. I almost paid with my life to put things right, so don't fucking give me this 'just words' crap, okay!' Steve said angrily, wincing as he pushed himself up from the cramped floor of the cart.

There was silence in the cart as Steve's words were taken on board, but finally Phil spoke.

'Well, I guess we do owe you the benefit of the doubt,' he began. 'From what Liz told me, you've known she was following from the moment the convoy left the Convent... and you did try to get as many away as you could.'

'Yeah, you do, and I did,' said Steve.

'Even if you did botch it,' Phil continued, shaking his head.

Steve was about to point out he got a good kicking when he was caught when he noticed Phil was chuckling.

'Oh, I see you're the funny man of the group,' said Steve.

'I try,' Phil replied, smiling. 'Now, how are we going to get everybody else back, any ideas?'

With one more body now in the cart, space was non-existent and if they were to collect any more escapees, they would definitely need some other method of transport. They soon decided they would have to try to liberate not only their stolen friends, but also the truck that they were being held captive in. However, getting in and out of the camp without being noticed was not going to be easy and all of them were under no illusion. This was not a simple rescue exercise; this was war. Their weapons, which until that point had only been used on the Dead, could soon be used to take the lives of their foe. They could be responsible for ending the existence of other living beings, beings that were in very short supply these days.

'Until they make camp for the night, we can't make any concrete plans,' said Patrick quietly, 'but I agree with Steve. We'll have to deal with the armoured vehicles first if we want to have a chance of getting away with the holding truck.'

'Last thing we want is one of them firing on us,' Steve added, his volume mirroring Patrick.

He hadn't spent a lot of time on the mainland among the Dead and certainly no time at all traveling the countryside with only the wooden walls of a cart for protection. The whole situation seemed insane to him. Every so often, they would hear the distant moans of the Dead and each time, Steve's hand would subconsciously move to grab a rifle that was no longer there.

'How on earth do you get used to this?' he whispered to Liz, who had the two dozing children wedged on either side of her.

'It's all we've ever known,' she replied, trying to shrug her shoulders but not finding the room to move. 'I was just a child not much older than Anne when they came, so we had to adapt to a new way of life pretty quickly. Luckily, I had someone to look after me who knew how to fight and survive, but most weren't so lucky. Look, it's just a culture shock for you now, that's all. You'll get used to it, you'll see.'

'And what about the Dead?' Steve asked, 'Do you get used to them too?'

'Well, don't get me wrong,' she replied, trying to manoeuvre her bump into a more comfortable position, 'but for the most part they're sort of more of an annoyance really, a deadly annoyance admittedly if things go wrong, but an annoyance none the less. You just have to know what you're dealing with... you know, play by their rules... and once you understand them, they're just like any other problem nowadays. You just deal with it and hope tomorrow's going to be easier.'

'My woman, the philosopher,' Imran whispered to Steve with a wink, as he reached over Anne to stroke the back of Liz's head lovingly.

'Snowing again,' Phil said to himself rather than to anyone in particular, 'should make it easier to follow them.'

'Great, as if it wasn't cold enough in here as it is,' mumbled Jen, pulling her jacket tighter about herself.

'Here,' Leon said, struggling to take off his coat without poking one of his fellow travelling companions in the eye, 'take this. I've got a couple of thick jumpers underneath.'

'No… I didn't mean…' Jen began to protest.

'Honestly, it's fine, so take it,' Leon continued, finally pulling his arm out of the sleeve and handing it over to Jen.

'Thanks,' she replied, pulling the coat over her shoulders.

'Sorry about your brother,' Leon said softly, while Jen slowly pulled the coat's hood up over her head. 'Shit that it happened like that, you know?'

'Yeah, real shitty,' Jen replied quietly. 'Thanks.'

The young black man was a puzzle to Jen. Sure, he had that cocky, self-assuredness, big man attitude that instantly rubbed her up the wrong way, but there was also something else in there, something that broke through all the pointless bravado to show the real man within and it irritated Jen slightly to realise she was starting to like what she saw.

'How far ahead do you think they are?' Imran asked Phil.

'Probably a good few miles,' he began glancing back at Imran, 'but we'll catch up to them this evening when they make camp.'

'Whatever we're going to do, we need to do it tonight,' Steve added solemnly. 'It'll be our only chance, since tomorrow they'll reach the rendezvous point on the coast and if that happens, we'll lose them.'

Imran looked back at Liz, his own worry mirrored there. They all knew some people would have to die tonight if they wanted to get back their friends. It was simply one of those 'us or them' situations and being totally outgunned as they were, it didn't look like it was going to be easy for the Lanherne survivors to pull it off without losing one or more of their own in the process.

'Hey, we've not lost yet,' said Steve, looking from one anxious face to the next, 'and don't forget we've got three aces in the hole.'

'And what are they?' asked Patrick, pushing back one of the spy hole covers.

'Well, firstly, you've got the element of surprise,' Steve began, ticking off the points on his fingers, 'and you know how to get done what needs doing while the Dead are on your heels.'

'And the other?' asked Patrick, not at all assured by these first lifelines.

'Me,' Steve replied matter-of-factly, 'I know what and where the firepower will likely be positioned, how many will be on watch and what the rest of squad will be doing at any given time. With Intel like that on an enemy, the battles are already half won… believe me.'

'Okay,' Patrick said still not convinced.

'Look, have you got anything to write on?' Steve continued, seeing his pep talk hadn't really done the trick. 'I'll draw you a probable layout of the camp. It's pretty much the same each night and we can come up with some rough plans that can flesh out once we actually get there.'

'Here,' said Imran, pulling a scrap of paper from a pocket, 'show us what you've got, and I'll want that paper back afterwards.'

'Thanks, but why?' Steve replied, taking the paper and turning it over to see if it was something important.

'Oh, you'll find out soon enough the next time you need to take a crap,' Phil said chuckling to himself.

Steve looked from one face to the next, trying to work out if Phil was joking. He plainly wasn't.

'Oh, looks like I've got a lot to get used to,' he eventually said, working a stubby pencil from his pocket.

'Tip of the iceberg, man,' Leon said, smiling as he shook his head. 'Tip of the iceberg.'

***

'It's snowing again,' Matt said, looking up at the high oblong window that ran the length of the Med lab.

'Heavy enough for us to stop early?' Alice asked, following Matt's stare.

'No, Blackmore will want us to get as far as we can while there's still light,' Matt replied, turning to look at Alice. 'He'll want to get to the coast before nightfall tomorrow for the pick up.'

'Oh, so I guess we just sit tight then,' she added, wincing slightly.

'Are you alright?' asked Dr Avery, moving from his seat to crouch down in front of her. 'Are you having labour pains?'

'I don't think so,' she replied, shifting uncomfortably in her seat. 'He's just in an awkward   position and I'm a bit hungry.'

'Of course, you weren't given anything to eat, were you?' Dr Avery said, jumping up to go back to his desk.

'It's not much, I'm afraid,' he said, handing her a packet of cheese-flavoured crackers. 'All the food is stored in compartments under the Med lab and holding truck.'

'This is a feast, believe me,' she replied, eagerly ripping open the packet to get to the crackers.

'Sorry,' she said through a mouthful of crumbs, looking from Matt to Dr Avery who was watching her eat. 'Did you want one?'

'No, you're fine,' Mat said smiling. 'You obviously need them more than we do.'

'Well, we might as well kill some time decanting these,' Dr Avery said pulling over the box of Thiopental and an army issue water bottle. 'We'll need to pry off the sealed caps carefully. Try not to spill any, because we'll need every drop.'

For the few hours, Matt tried to make his large fingers do the intricate work of lifting off sections of the sealed lids of the vials.

'You seem better suited to this type of work than me, Doc,' Matt said comparing his pile of empty vials to that sitting in front of Dr Avery.

'Well…' Dr Avery began, his words stopping mid-sentence as the Med lab suddenly came to a halt.

'Looks like it's show time,' said Alice, nervously catching Matt's eye.

'We'll give it half an hour for camp to be set up and people to get where we expect them to be and then it's all system go,' Matt said looking at an anxious Dr Avery. 'You are going to be able to do this, aren't you, Avery?'

'The die is cast, as they say,' Dr Avery replied, his words meeting only a blank look from Matt. 'That means I don't have much choice… so yes, I can do this.'

Twenty five minutes later and with the last of the Thiopental decanted into the flask wedged into one of the large pockets on Matt's combat trousers, the two men stood by the door waiting for the last sounds of movement outside to die down.

'Right, just go straight to the communications tent. Blackmore's bound to be there,' Matt said, trying to calm Dr Avery down. 'He'll want to radio in our location and set up the evac for tomorrow. Give him the message from Dr Morris and get out. Say you've got to get back to help him or something.'

'Will do,' said Avery with a nod, his hand hovering on the door handle.

'Back in a minute,' he said turning back to Alice to give her a not very convincing smile of reassurance.

Alice's brittle smile matched Avery's, but before she could wish him luck, he had taken a deep breath and was already pushing open the door, with Matt fast on his heels.

'Bye,' said Alice quietly to herself, as the Med lab door closed with a bang.

Taking a quick look about, Matt could see that the convoy had stopped in an area much like all the other places they had made camp before. From the faded sign still barely hanging on a post by the side of the road, Matt could see this had once been a miniature golf course. Fun For All the Family said on the sign, but it was in the small car park that Blackmore decided to take refuge for the night. Not that there was much to distinguish the golf course from the car park now, both were overgrown, wild and covered in a thick layer of powdery snow. Only the absence of saplings, yet to work their way through the cracked concrete, made the presence of a car park known at all. Matt could see that two of the Jackals had already taken their watch position near the car park entrance, while the third was out of sight, presumably watching the approach from the old course itself. As always in the centre of this triad of firepower, the Med lab and holding truck had been parked. The Communication and NAAFI tents were close by and were surrounded by the dozen or so small individual sleeping tents of the squadron.

Not looking at Dr Avery, Matt casually pushed aside the flap of the NAAFI tent and went in. Inside there were two soldiers sitting at a fold away table, already tucking into their MRE packs. As if it was the most natural thing in the world, Matt went over to the table piled with the MRE packs, a hot water urn and the large water container and began unscrewing the cap at the top. Standing on tiptoe, Matt could just about peer down into the water barrel, and seeing it was over half full, removed the water bottle from his hip pocket.

'How's your head?' asked one of the soldiers, when he noticed Matt standing behind him.

Matt froze, his hands clutching the water bottle tightly and turned to the man who had spoken.

'Oh, okay... got a banging headache but better than Dave... he's not woken up yet,' he replied, consciously putting the water bottle down to pick up an MRE. 'Doc says I'll be okay for duty tonight.'

'You better fucking well be,' the soldier said gruffly, turning back to his own meal. 'I ain't freezing my arse off covering your watch.'

And that was that, camaraderie was in short supply these days and at that moment, Matt was thankful it was so. Keeping a watchful eye on the two soldiers, Matt finally got the cap of his water bottle off and began to tip two thirds of the contents into the large plastic barrel. The remaining third, he emptied into the hot water urn. With the snow falling softly again outside, he knew the two soldiers who had already made up their MRE's would make a hot drink before they bedded down for the night, so that only left the six men currently on watch in the Jackals to deal with. Matt knew they wouldn't be off watch for at least four or five hours and that was time they simply didn't have to waste. They had to be dealt with at the same time as all the others if they wanted any hope of escaping. Then with a flash of inspiration, Matt refilled his water bottle from the already doctored hot water urn and grabbed a handful of coffee sachets. Mixing up a strong brew and hoping the added Thiopental would go un-noticed, Matt left the tent and began making his rounds of the sentry Jackals, bringing with him the surely welcomed hot coffee for the soldiers on watch.

'Phoenix, this is squadron Alpha-nine. Do you read me? Over. Do you read me, Phoenix? Over,' the communications officer said into the small microphone held near to his mouth.

'Well?' Sergeant Blackmore said, looking at the solider as if it was his fault they were receiving no answer from the island base.

'Nothing yet, Sir,' the man replied, removing his ear-piece. 'The satellite's orbit must be slowly decaying. This was our window yesterday and there's still no contact from Alpha-eight at the power station. I'll keep trying though.'

'Yes, you do that,' Sergeant Blackmore replied, bored of the man's excuses.

'Staff Sergeant Blackmore,' Dr Avery said, standing in the doorway of the tent.

As much as he hated to do it, Dr Avery saluted. He knew the man got off on making the doctors and scientists show him the respect he thought he deserved and Dr Avery knew now was not the time to rub Staff Sergeant Graham Blackmore the wrong way.

'Yes, Dr Avery?' Sergeant Blackmore replied, barely looking up from the printouts he held in his hand. 'What is it?'

Dr Avery was about to speak when Streiber and Hills, the SAS goons, entered the tent. Without even giving Dr Avery a glance, the two men gave sharp salutes to the Sergeant and stood at attention.

'Ah, Hills, Streiber, south watch have spotted a rising smoke trail about a mile south east from here. Check it out,' said Sergeant Blackmore to the two stony faced men. 'We're down on civilians, thanks to Private Blackmore's little stunt, so go see what you can find. Use what force you deem necessary. We don't have time to pussy foot around.'

'Sir,' the two men replied in unison.

As they turned to leave, Dr Avery caught Streiber's eye. The look that flitted across the man's face sent a finger of ice to the pit of Avery's stomach. There was something very wrong with these men, something almost gleefully psychotic and Dr Avery pitied anyone who had the grave misfortune to come across them that night. However, he knew he couldn't think about that now, because he had to make what he was about to say convincing and believable. The last thing he wanted was for the Staff Sergeant to think anything odd was going on. If the Sergeant decided to go to the Med lab, their escape would be over before it began and that would mean a swift, brutal and probably fatal punishment.

'Dr Avery?' the Sergeant asked, wondering why the man still hadn't spoken.

'Dr Morris told me to keep you abreast of the situation regarding the test subject,' he began. 'The woman is now in labour but as it is her first, it might be some time before we can get the definitive results from the foetus.'

'And?' Sergeant Blackmore said, looking up from his papers, not sure, why the doctor was telling him this.

'Dr Morris is concerned there could be complications and prefers to deal with the birth himself, so he won't be able to make his report to Dr Farrell at present.'

'And that's what I tell Dr Farrell, is it?' Sergeant Blackmore said, dropping the papers down onto a small collapsible table.

'I'm sure Dr Farrell will agree,' Dr Avery said, trying to look unfazed by the Sergeant's tone. 'This foetus and the potential it holds is too important to place it under any unnecessary risks, even for a few minutes. The results must be conclusive and absolute.'

Sergeant Blackmore looked at Dr Avery for a few seconds, silently weighing something up in his mind.

'Fine,' he simply said, dismissing Dr Avery from concern as he turned back to his reports.

For a heartbeat, Dr Avery stood motionless, unable to believe it had been that simple. However, knowing to get out while the going was good, he gave the Sergeant a quick salute, turned, and walked back to the Med lab as normally as he could without breaking into a run.

'Well?' asked Alice, nervously biting her finger nails.

'No problem,' Dr Avery replied, letting go of a long breath as he dropped down onto a chair. 'Now we just have to hope Matt's part goes as smoothly.'

The two of them knew Matt had by far the harder task to perform. It would be no easy feat to dope the entire squadron effectively enough for them to escape and it only took one of the soldiers to notice something was wrong and the whole plan would blow up in their faces. But there was nothing they could do but wait and hope the Gods were looking favourably down on them.

'What's your name, Doc,' Alice said quietly. 'I mean your first name. If I'm trusting my life in someone else's hands, I at least like to be on first name terms.'

Dr Avery screwed up his face before speaking.

'Colin,' he said wincing, 'but most people just call me Avery. It sounds less... you know.'

'Less nerdy?' Alice said with a smile, 'Okay, Avery it is then...'

Avery was just smiling back at her when the door to the Med lab opened and Matt walked in.

'Done,' he said placing the empty water bottle down on the desk. 'Now we just wait, I suppose'

'How long?' Alice asked, her hand anxiously rubbing her stomach.

'At least a couple of hours, perhaps three,' Avery replied. 'We want to be sure they're all out.'

'I want to leave them a little less well armed before we leave to even up the score a little,' Matt added, looking up at a clock on the wall. 'So to be on the safe side, let's say midnight, agreed?'

'Agreed,' repeated Alice and Avery, knowing the next few hours would feel the longest in their lives.

***

'How come we're the ones freezing our nuts off checking out a smoke signal?' Hills said, pushing aside a low hanging branch. 'Why didn't he send a couple of those pointless shits back there, they'd be no loss.'

'Oh, quit your bitching,' Streiber replied, scanning the surrounding bushes intently. 'You never know, we might be able to have a bit of fun here.'

The two men exchanged a look, because they both knew what 'fun' Streiber meant and it was usually at someone else's expense. The two men had a knack for the sadistic, and the perverse pleasure they got watching their victims beg and squirm, only added to their enjoyment. Their skill at getting information by not so legal measures from terror suspects had seen them promoted within the SAS and then ultimately side lined for special projects that called out for their unique talents. When the Dead came, they saw a chance to thrive and enjoy this new world order. Ditching their squad and taking with them Clarkes, a man with dark tastes after their own heart, the three men had set themselves upon an unsuspecting civilian population with relish in those first few weeks. Only the chance interception of communication between the base and the mainland on an army frequency alerted them to a new possibility. Realising that they could thrive there with no one to oppose them, they had made their way to the base and a new community for them to enjoy.

Just then, a skeletal looking Dead woman stepped silently into their path, but unfazed, Hills simply smashed the woman in the face with the butt of his rifle, knocking her to the ground. Before she even had the chance to right herself, Hills stepped purposefully forwards and stamped down hard on her skull. With an audible crack, her skull collapsed under the weight of his boot and her blackened hands fell forever lifeless to her sides.

'There'd better be some pussy there fresher than this bitch,' Hills said, giving the still woman's corpse a kick, 'or someone's going to have a really bad day.'

'Yeah, come on, Casanova, sooner we get there, the sooner you can get your pussy,' Streiber said, stepping over the woman's body.

For the next half hour, they slowly crossed the small golf course, dealing silently with any of the hapless Dead who happened to wander their way. Finally reaching the far side of the course, they found the source of the plume of smoke.

'Fuck me,' Streiber said, looking up at the large multi levelled tree house.

Before them, the tree house, once a professionally constructed children's adventure playground, had been transformed into a home well beyond the reach of any Dead hands below. Although all was dark and quiet in the tree bound fortress, smoke was rising from a less professionally attached chimney.

'Hey!' Hills called. 'Anyone alive up there?'

After a few minutes of silence, Hills turned to Streiber shrugging his shoulders.

'Hello,' this time Streiber gave it a shot. 'Hello up there, we're soldiers. There's nothing to fear, we're here to help. Our squadron is camped in the car park on the other side of the golf course. We're here to take you somewhere safe'

Slowly, after much whispering from inside, a wooden shutter opened, revealing a man.

'You're the army?' he asked.

'Yes, Sir,' Hills said in his most polite manner, 'I'm Hills and this is Streiber, someone from our squadron saw your smoke and we were sent to offer assistance.'

'You're the army...the army! Oh Christ, thank God, thank God,' the man replied almost bursting into tears. 'Wait, wait there, I'll let down the ladder.'

Turning, someone unseen said something in an urgent whisper but the man brushed off whatever was said, and went to another hatchway. Streiber and Hills smiled to each other as they watched a rope ladder dropping down from the hatch.

'What's your name, Sir?' asked Streiber, placing his foot on the first rung of the ladder.

'I'm John... John Viney,' the man replied, 'and this is my wife Marie.'

'Pleased to meet you, John,' said Streiber, beginning to climb the ladder. 'Now let's get your things together...'

An hour later, the body of John Viney lay motionless in a pool of his own blood while his wife pulled the tattered remains of her clothes back over her body. The two soldiers had enjoyed their time with the couple.

Each of the Vineys had satisfied one their twisted interests in one form or another. John had clearly come off the worse for meeting the two depraved soldiers. They had broken both of his legs, stamped repeatedly on his back until they heard the vertebrae snap and organs rupture, and then taken great delight in cutting off his fingers one by one, all the while forcing his wife, Marie, to watch. By the time it was her turn, all John could do was follow the brutal rape and beating of his wife with his eyes, while he lay choking on his own blood.

'Time to go, bitch,' Hills snapped, pulling the zipper up on his trousers.

'He said time to go!' Streiber repeated, grabbing the woman by her elbow to pull her up.

However, the woman pulled away from the soldier who had raped and brutalised her body to throw herself over her husband's barely alive form.

'For fuck's sake!' Hills spat, his temper flaring while he grabbed Marie by her hair to pull her up.

As Marie screamed, kicked and struggled to break free, Streiber stepped past her and levelled his gun at John's head.

'Anymore of that and this fucker gets it, okay,' he said coldly.

Instantly, Marie stopped her struggling.

'Now you've got to understand something, we're going back to the camp,' Streiber began, 'you try to run or make a noise and Hills here will be happy to take out your kneecaps... you got me?'

Marie's terrified eyes flicked to Hills. After what he had done to her and her husband, she had no doubt that he would shoot the legs from under her and leave her for the Dead. Marie nodded.

'Sorry. I didn't hear you,' Streiber said, cupping his ear.

'Yes,' Marie managed to sob, 'yes, I understand.'

'Good,' Streiber said, giving Hills a sly grin as he shoved Marie towards the ladder.

As he pushed her, Marie stumbled against a table. Banging her already bruised hip painfully, she cried out.

'Come on,' Streiber said, pulling her upright again, 'follow me down and don't forget Hills has his beady eyes on you.'

When Streiber reached the bottom of the rope ladder, Marie began her own painful descent.

'What about John?' she asked, stopping to look up at Hills still at the top of the ladder, 'I don't think he can walk...'

'No,' Hills said with a sick smile, as he began climbing down the ladder. 'No, he can't.'

'You bastards!' she wept, realising Hills and Streiber had left her husband to die on the floor of her home.

'Just move,' Hills commanded, giving her a shove.

Although the snow had stopped falling earlier, it was still freezing out on the wild overgrown golf course and Marie pulled what was left of her blouse tightly around her with one hand. Her other hand, she thrust firmly into her trouser pocket. There her thumb ran back and forth over the sharp blade of the potato peeler she grabbed when she pretended to bang into the table. Knowing she would only get one chance, she would have to be on the lookout for the perfect opportunity. She would bide her time for now, but these men would pay for what they had done and they would pay in blood. That was a promise.

DAY 5

'I think we should make a move,' said Steve, looking at the glowing hands on his watch. 'By now, they'll be bored to tears and probably even taking turns grabbing a quick nap while the other keeps an eye out for the Dead … and good old Dad of course.'

'What about the rest of the soldiers?' asked Liz.

'Those not on watch duty will be asleep by now,' Steve replied, reaching for a length of pipe on the wall. 'So, are we good to go?'

They knew the time had come and they could stall no longer. Therefore, after giving Justin and Anne a tight hug goodbye, Phil and Imran jumped down from the cart to join Leon and Patrick on the glistening snow covered road. There had been a heated, but whispered, discussion between Imran and Liz concerning whether she should come or not. Of course, Imran got his way in the end when Liz was finally made to see sense. If she went with them, Imran's concern for her safety would override his own sense of self-preservation. He would act without thinking and end up putting his own safety in jeopardy. Liz knew it was true, because on more than one occasion, Imran had acted recklessly when he thought he could save her from danger.

'Be careful,' said Liz, her cold breath pluming in the still, cold air. 'Come back in one piece, because we need you. I need you.'

With a lot less grace than she would have wished, Liz lent forward through one of the cart's side hatches and grabbing hold of Imran's coat collar, pulled him toward her lips. For the briefest of moments, she closed her eyes, wishing the world would stop turning and the passage of time would pause so she would never have to let him go. But the world kept on spinning and time refused to halt its progress and when Imran began to slowly pull away, she opened her eyes. What she saw made her breath catch in her throat. His beautiful dark eyes, normally so full of love and mystery, were but disks of silver light. It wasn't until he blinked that she realised it was simply the reflected full moon from overhead. Instantly, she remembered the name of an old Roman deity that Charlie had once told her about. Diana, Goddess of the hunt and of the moon, normally so aloof in the affairs of mankind, seemed to be looking favourably upon their small band and had surely sent them her blessing. Not only had the snow stopped falling an hour ago and the clouds had cleared to reveal a clear star splashed sky, but her moon seemed to be hanging strangely low in the sky above them. It was as if the goddess herself wished to watch her champions hunt their quarry across the countryside that she now bathed in her radiant light.

'I'll come back,' Imran whispered, reaching out to touch her belly. 'I'll come back for you both, I promise.'

'Sorry, but we need to get moving,' said Steve quietly, as he blew on his fingers. 'We don't know how many of the Dead are between them and us by now. We really don't want to spend our time fighting the Dead just to get to the convoy the moment they speed off, do we.'

Earlier that evening, as the weak winter sun had made its slow transition over the horizon to cover the countryside with the dim smoky light of dusk, the group from Lanherne caught up with the camped army convoy. In fact, they had almost given themselves away and it had only been Phil noticing that the tyre tracks in the snow had abruptly turned into a small car park that prevented Delilah from pulling the cart across the intersection and into view. After silently dealing with a small group of the Dead who had been following the noisy vehicles, Phil managed to turn the cart around unnoticed and take them the hundred or so metres back down the tree lined lane to where the cart now sat hidden in the shadows of some large conifers.

'We need to deal with any of the Dead as quickly as possible,' Patrick whispered. 'They may be at a disadvantage in the dark, but with this bright moonlight, we shouldn't rely on them not being able to see us. We can't let any of them start moaning, of it'll just attract more of them and we'll be swamped.'

'From here on in, we should keep talking to a minimum,' said Steve, his hand instinctively moving up to his ribs, as a shock of pain made him wince. 'Try to use hand signals where you can, okay?'

'Are you going to be okay?' Imran asked, noticing Steve reacting to the pain from his cracked ribs. 'You can always stay here. This isn't your fight now, after all.'

'Yes it is… scores to settle,' Steve replied coldly, as he stepped away from the cart to take the lead.

As the five men began their slow walk back down the lane to the car park, the only sound heard was the soft crunch of the newly fallen snow under foot and the rhythmic in and out of their breathing. As Imran watched the plumed breath of the four men in front of him, rising above them only to be whisked away by a breeze, he stole one last backward glance to the cart behind him. He promised Liz and their unborn child he would return to them and though he meant it with all his heart, even as he said the words, he knew it could be a promise he might not be able to keep. It would be so easy to turn back to the woman he loved, but Charlie had instilled in him a sense of duty. These were his people that the soldiers had stolen. They looked to him and the skill with his bow for protection, and he would not, he could not, let them down.

Imran was snapped from his thoughts by the sight of a figure slowly pulling itself through a large holly bush that spilled out onto the road. The glossy evergreen leaves appeared almost black in the moonlight and as the spiky leaves snagged on the already tattered clothes and flesh of the cadaver, Imran took aim on the pitiful creature. Drawing back his bow, with a slight creak from the taut string alerting the others to his actions, Imran took a calming breath and focused on his target. The Dead thing, which had once been a young man, turned its head back and forth, trying to locate the source of the sound that had somehow reached his Dead eardrums. Still deep in the shadows of the Holly bush, his film covered eyes failed to see the living figure that would have driven him into a wild frenzy and as he flailed impotently trying to free himself from the sharp spiky bush, his unnatural existence was finally ended as Imran let his arrow fly. With a dull 'thud', the arrow was embedded deep in the creature's skull and the Dead man's limbs were at last still.

Hanging in the bush like a marionette with its strings cut, the Dead man would be forever trapped within the branches that had snagged him. His flesh would eventually fall from his bones to feed the soil beneath him and then in turn, the plant that held him would be nourished by his decaying matter. Such was the way of life now, the plants had grown strong and wild fed by the flesh of the Dead, while the fall of man was silently written as a side note of history.

Wading into the snowdrift by the side of the road, Imran reached over to the corpse to retrieve his arrow. He did not know what the night before him held and every arrow he could carry was one more chance he could keep his promise to Liz. With a yank, he pulled the arrow free and after examining it in the moonlight to make sure it was still viable, he slipped it back into his quiver. With a tap on his shoulder from Patrick, telling him they needed to keep moving, Imran and the others continued their slow but stealthy progress along the lane to the camp.

Although the turn to the car park wasn't actually that far, it had taken the cautious raiding party thirty minutes until the break in the hedgerow finally came into view. Each footstep along the lane had been tentative and measured. Every snap of a twig or rustle in the undergrowth had stopped them in their tracks, their weapons held high and ready for an attack. At one point, three of the Dead had loomed un-expectedly towards them from the roadside shadows. But with smooth practiced movements the Lanherne men had stepped in front of Steve, who was less used to hand to hand combat with the Dead, and dispatched all three of them before even one of them could alert their decaying comrades of the presence of the living.

Crouching down, Steve held up his hand signalling the others to stop. Patrick and Phil edged forwards, their hunched over posture mirroring Steve.

'What is it?' Phil whispered, placing a hand on Steve's shoulder.

Silently, Steve pointed to the driveway that led up to the car park. Something was wrong. Even from where they hid, the men could hear the angry moans of the Dead coming from the camp. What worried Steve was that these were not the pitiful cries of the decrepit Dead who had wandered the countryside seeking out the living, but the desperate calls of those newly awoken to their unnatural state. The Dead had attacked the camp and claimed new lives but what confused Steve most was that all in the camp would have been wearing their failsafe pulse detectors, so just who had died only to rise again and why were they not being dealt with by the soldiers.

Out of nowhere, the driveway was flooded with light, making the men shield their eyes from the sudden brightness and with the powerful roar of an engine adding to the hungry moans of the unseen Dead, the men pushed themselves deeper into the shadows in the hope they would not be seen.

'What the fuck's happening?' asked Patrick.

'Trouble,' was all Steve could say, as one of the Jackals thundered down the lane, its wheels spinning slightly on the icy road.

Within seconds, the Jackal was speeding past them, to disappear in a blizzard of snow thrown up by its large tyres.

'What now, man?' Leon whispered, unsure if they should go back or carry on.

'Now we get our people back,' Imran replied, standing to pull an arrow from his quiver.

***

Half an hour earlier, Avery was handing the last of some selected medical supplies over to Matt to put in a holdall.

'That's about all there's room for, Doc,' said Matt, taking a handful of sealed tablets from Avery. 'Everything else we'll just have to make do without.'

'Erm… okay,' Avery replied, looking anxiously at the cupboard containing a variety of medicines they would be forced to leave behind. 'You just know whatever I don't take we're going to need sometime in the future and I'll be kicking myself for leaving them.'

'Let's just get out of here in one piece first, then we can have regrets,' Matt replied, zipping the holdall closed as he looked over to the clock on the wall.

'You think we've waited long enough?' Alice asked, noticing Matt's glance at the clock.

Matt looked back at Alice, shrugging his shoulders.

'What do you think, Doc?' he asked relying on Avery's knowledge of the barbiturate they had used.

Avery glanced at his watch and after weighing what he knew about the drug and with more than a bit of guess work, he looked over to Matt.

'We can't be sure, but I think now is a good a time as any, I suppose,' he replied, knowing their lives depended on what they found outside.

'You don't sound too sure, Doc,' said Matt nervously scratching his head, 'Look, I'll go out, and do a circuit of the camp. If anyone is still conscious at least they'll think I'm just arriving for my watch. If it's all okay, then I'll come back here to get you both and we're out of here.'

'Sounds like a plan,' Alice said with a huff as she stood up in the hope she could convince her baby to get in a more comfortable position.

For a moment, the three people looked at each other. The time had come. Their plan had either worked or it hadn't and there was only one way to find out. Matt slung his rifle over his shoulder and paused in front of the Med lab door.

'Wish me luck,' he said turning back to the two people with whom his life about to take a new path.

'Good luck,' said Avery, stepping forward to shake the soldier's hand.

'Yeah, knock 'em dead, kiddo,' Alice said through clenched teeth.

'Are you okay?' said Matt, concerned at seeing Alice in obvious pain.

'Got a twinge, that's all,' she replied, her brow creasing as she glanced over at Avery.

She knew now was not the time to distract Matt, because he needed to keep his mind on the job at hand. What they were about to do was going to be risky enough without him worrying about her.

'Now get going,' she continued. 'The sooner you go, the sooner we get going.'

Still not convinced, but knowing it was now or never, Matt gave her a reassuring smile, turned and stepped silently out the door.

Outside the Med lab, the camp was silent. Somewhere in the snow-covered countryside, he could hear the distant bark of a dog but apart from that, the usual sounds of life that drifted from the tents or those on watch were absent. It was then that Matt noticed the first of the unconscious soldiers. Walking over to the body that lay face down in the snow, where he had obviously fallen when the drug had finally taken effect, Matt crouched down to turn the man over. It was the SAS man, Clarkes. Gingerly, Matt gave the man a prod and waited for any response. When none came, he lent forward and lifted up one of Clarkes' eyelids. Even with only the full moon to see by, Matt noticed the man's exposed iris slowly contracting.

'One down,' he said quietly to himself, pushing himself back up.

He had taken a step away from Clarkes when he had second thoughts and turned back to kneel back down to the unconscious man.

'This is for Steve, you bastard,' he said, taking a knife from his belt and slicing the black band that held the pulse detector to the man's neck.

Dropping the now flashing pulse detector by the man's side, Matt left him to his fate and went to check out the Jackals. He decided if they wanted a realistic chance of escape, then taking one of the Jackals was going to be their best option. Silently, he walked past the row of tents the off watch soldiers would be sleeping in. Thankful to be met with the sounds of snoring and farting that usually came from the men as they slept, Matt edged his way to the first of the large Jackal assault vehicles.

'Knock, knock,' he said quietly, approaching the front of the vehicle.

Matt smiled to himself when he saw the two men slumped in their seats. Dr Avery's anaesthetic had done the trick; the two soldiers were out cold. Knowing that the position of this vehicle, facing the overgrown golf course as it was, ruled it out as the one he would take, Matt decided to move onto the two other Jackals. He knew they had been parked to guard the road approach and one of these would be the one they would be using to escape. Making his way around to the front of the camp, Matt found a few other men slumped where they had fallen, unable to fight the effects of the barbiturate coursing through their bodies. With his confidence growing that their plan had worked, Matt increased his speed. Running up to the second Jackal, he was met by two more unconscious men again.

'Mind if I take catch a ride, lads?' he asked, grabbing the first man by his collar to pull him from the vehicle.

After a struggle and more than a bit of swearing, Matt finally managed to pull the two men from the vehicle.

'Time to even things up a bit,' Matt said softly to the two prone soldiers, 'nothing personal.'

Pulling aside each of their collars, Matt then cut away their pulse detectors, just like he had done with Clarkes and tossed the flashing devices over into a nearby bush. This time though, he also removed their rifles. Turning, he placed them back into the Jackal. Any firepower they could take with them would be a godsend in the future and any advantage he could take from Blackmore and his men could only be one more thing in their favour in the long run.

Leaving his chosen escape vehicle, Matt then jogged over the last remaining Jackal. Just as before, the soldiers sat slumped in their seats and after a bit of tugging at their prone bodies, Matt relieved them of both their weapons and pulse detectors. It was then that Matt had a flash of inspiration and reaching again into the Jackal past the driver, he pulled a small lever under the dashboard. With a click, the Jackal's bonnet sprung open as the catch was released. Dashing to the front of the vehicle, Matt began to pull at various parts of the engine. It wouldn't hold them for long but every minute he could stall Blackmore was a minute they could get further away.

After dropping the second set of rifles back at the Jackal he was taking, Matt decided to continue his raid on the sleeping soldiers. Moving from tent to tent, weaponry was taken to add to his stash and as he left each tent, a small red light began to flash its count down. He was just dropping off the last of the acquired rifles and ammunition back at the Jackal when Matt heard the scraping sound of approaching footsteps. Turning to locate the source, Matt swore under his breath. There, dragging their decaying corpses into the camp was three of the Dead.

'Time to go,' he mumbled to himself, crouching out of sight.

He had only made it part of the way back to the Med lab when the first wet tearing sounds drifted through the camp. The Dead had found the helpless soldiers and already they were ripping at their flesh and stuffing lumps of stolen flesh greedily into their mouths.

'Shit. Shit. Shit!' Mat whispered as he approached the Med lab.

Behind him, the sounds of gorging continued. They were in real trouble and he knew it.

'Time to go people,' Matt said, bursting through the Med lab door. 'Oh, crap!'

There, clutching her stomach with Dr Avery holding her arm for support was Alice with a pained look on her face. This was more than a simple twinge, Mat could tell. With the large wet patch down the front of her trousers an obvious sign, he dreaded the words Avery was surely about to say.

'Her water has broken,' Avery said, looking up at Matt as he ran through the door.

'No time for that,' Matt said grabbing the bag of medical supplies. 'The Dead are in the camp and they're eating the soldiers, so we've got to go, now.'

'But...' Avery began.

'Alice, can you walk?' Matt interrupted. 'We've got to get to the front of the camp and we've got to go now.'

Alice gritted her teeth through the pain and nodded. She was not going to let her baby die in this place. If she had to crawl on her hands and knees, she would get out of this camp and dead or not, the soldiers would not stop her.

'Let's go,' she said, pushing herself away from Avery.

'Here,' Matt said passing to Alice and Avery each a handgun he had lifted from the more than likely now Dead soldiers. 'Keep close and keep low. It's not far... We'll make it, okay?'

'You're fucking right we will,' Alice said, steadying herself against a table for a moment, before stepping towards Matt. 'Let's do this.'

Matt gave the ballsy woman a smile and looking beyond her to see that Dr Avery was also ready, he turned and stepped back out into the cold death filled night.

Crouching directly outside the Med lab door, Matt lifted his rifle to provide cover for Alice and Dr Avery, ready for the cannibalistic attack that was sure to be only moments away. Matt could see the reflected moonlight flashing off of Avery's gun as it shook in his hands. Just like everyone on the base, Avery had a basic knowledge of firearms, but knowing 'how to' and actually 'doing' were two completely different scenarios. Up until now, the Dead had been something secured to a bench, studied, dissected and under his control. This was an alien world for Avery and the horror of the Dead had now become a terrifying and deadly reality. Matt looked at Avery, his wild eyes darting from one shadow to the next and prayed the doctor could keep it together long enough to get the Jackal. If the man panicked and started shooting, the Dead would be on them like a pack of wolves.

Mat pulled Avery and Alice down to a crouch and pointed out the direction they would need to go. When they both nodded their understanding, Matt began to edge them forward, leaving the safety of the Med lab behind. He had barely gone three paces when there was a crash to his left. Holding his hand up abruptly as a sign, Avery and Alice froze mid-step. In the shadows created by the row of tents, Matt could see movement. Suddenly, standing to his full height, the silhouette of a man could be seen. There was no doubt in Matt's mind that this man was now one of Dead and as it turned its head left and right looking for prey, even the night could not hide the horror of the man's death. The moonlight soon caught the side of his face, or rather what was left of it, throwing the gouged and torn flesh into stark relief. Matt heard a sharp intake of breath from Avery behind him and watched in dread as the Dead man slowly turned his head in their direction. Whether it was the Dead man's film covered eyes unable to see them in the dark or that he simply hadn't noticed them, Matt didn't know, but he watched with bated breath as the Dead man's gaze passed back and forth over them. Then with a sudden jerk, the Dead man threw himself at the tent next to him, tearing at the fabric to get to the unconscious body he knew lay hidden inside. Within seconds, the Dead man had ripped his way through the tent opening and was clawing his way up the prone body to get to the expose flesh of the man's neck and face. Sooner than he had expected, Matt began to hear ripping and slurping sounds coming from the tent. Knowing now was their chance to move, while the Dead man gorged himself on the living flesh that had been so kindly laid out for him, Matt began to edge forwards again. They crept past more of the tents, some already ripped and dripping with spilt blood, while others still housed the drugged soldiers unknowingly awaiting their own deaths. Matt was surprised how quickly the Dead had overrun the camp. Like locust, they moved from body to body, increasing their number with every lump of flesh torn from their victims.

Each growl, stumbling footstep and crash they heard coming from the shadows, promised a bloody death for Matt, Avery and Alice, but with easier meat for the Dead to claim, their luck seemed to be holding out. The rear of the Jackal was tantalisingly close now and with only one more tent to creep by, they hoped their thin run of luck would last them these last few meters to safety. However, when Matt heard movement from the other side of the canvas, he realised they were to be sadly disappointed. Matt briefly closed his eyes and held his breath, praying whoever the creature inside was feasting on would keep them occupied long enough for the three of them to pass undetected. Then, without warning, Alice's hand shot forward to grab his, making him jump. Surprised, Matt turned to look at her and knew immediately what was wrong. Alice's face was contorted with pain and with her eyes screwed tightly closed. She bit down forcefully on her lip. As the pressure from her grip increased, the pain from the growing contraction visibly shot through Alice. Her teeth broke through the skin on her lip as she fought the urge to cry out, knowing it could mean death for all of them and blood began to run down her chin. Matt knew the time for stealth was at an end. They needed to get Alice to the Jackal and away from here. Surely, she could only hold back the pain for so long before crying out and each step they could get closer to the Jackal was one step closer to getting out of there alive. The moment, Matt felt the tension on his hand begin to lessen, he pulled Alice up into a standing position and tugged her forwards.

'Just get to Jackal,' Matt whispered urgently to Alice and Avery. 'Move!'

The moment he spoke, the blood chilling noises from the tent paused.

'Go!' he said, urgently pushing Avery behind him, readying himself to fire on whatever was to pull itself from the tent.

Backing up slowly, step by step, all Matt could hear was the hammering of his heart and the sounds of other feasting Dead around him. With a dull click, the door to the Jackal opened and closed behind him, telling him Alice had made it. Taking another step backwards, Matt froze. A bloody hand, stripped of much of its flesh and a few fingers, pushed aside the tent opening to reveal a vision of death with nothing but hunger in its eyes. Matt had known the soldier the Dead man had once been. A single patch of his gore encrusted hair the only thing that made him identifiable. He might not have considered the man a friend in life but he had not wished such visible butchery of the man in death. With nearly all of the skin ripped from his face and the flesh torn from his cheeks and neck, it had been a mercy he had been unconscious during his attack. With no eyelids left to speak of, the Dead man had a wide penetrating stare and as he locked his eyes onto Matt, a flash of menacing glee flitted across them. Matt took another shaky step backwards, knowing the creature would charge him at any moment, but then a second animated corpse began to push itself out of the tent eager to follow the thing whose teeth had helped it cross over into a world of the hungry Dead.

'Shit!' Matt said realising things had just got twice as bad.

However, the Dead hadn't finished playing their hand just yet and as Matt turned to join Avery to sprint the last few meters to the Jackal, he watched as an unnoticed Dead solider suddenly appeared from his right. With a hungry moan escaping its savaged lips, the Dead man barrelled into Avery, pulling him to the ground. With a cry of basic animalistic terror, Avery began to fight for his life. With his hands slipping on the soldiers blood soaked chest, Avery fought to keep the Dead man's snapping jaw away from him. But even in death, Avery was no match for the large muscular soldier on top of him and he knew his moment had come. When a dribble of blood filled drool began to fall from the tongue that writhed only a hair's breadth from his face, all he could feel was a deep sense of regret. He simply hadn't been given the time to make amends for the horrors he had been forced to participate in and he knew that this stain on his soul would now follow him forever.

'Doc!' Matt cried, jabbing the butt of his rifle at the Dead man's head.

With a crack, the cadaver's head snapped to the left, taking his jaws mercifully further away from Avery's flesh and giving him the slimmest of chances now to save his life. Seeing what might be his only opportunity, Avery thrust his hands up under the soldier's jaw and with a strength fuelled by fear, he yanked the soldier's head further to the side, smashing it hard against the metal bumper of the Jackal.

'Let go, now!' shouted Matt,

Trusting the man who had already saved his life once, Avery did as he was told. For a split second, with its head wedged against the metal frame of the vehicle, the Dead soldier was still. Then, as it began to turn its head back to Dr Avery's living flesh, Matt brought his boot forcefully down on the creature's neck. With an audible snap, the neck vertebrae shattered and cartilage tore. Matt once again pulled his knife quickly from his belt to stab down on the crown of cadaver's skull.

'Get up!' Matt shouted, pulling Avery from under the now still corpse.

The two Dead men that had been pulling themselves out of the tent now fixed their attention solely on the fleeing group, and with a sudden burst of speed gave chase.

'Get in!' cried Matt, throwing open the back door for Avery, while he ran to get in the driver's seat.

Avery didn't need to be told twice and threw himself head first onto the rear seat that would normally have held the man responsible for manning the rear machine gun. With a quick glance to make sure Avery was on board, Matt began to flip switches on the control panel. Almost instantly, the Jackal roared into life and jerked forwards, the sudden movement almost knocking Avery out of the vehicle.

'Hold tight,' Matt shouted, pressing his foot down hard on the accelerator.

From behind him, Avery gave a fearful scream. One of the Dead soldiers from the tent had latched onto his leg just as the vehicle had lurched forwards and even now as the Jackal thundered out of the car park, it tried to claw its way up his leg.

'Avery!' screamed Alice, turning back to see the Dead man trying to pull himself into the Jackal.

'Fuck off!' Avery shouted, kicking out at the corpse's head with his free leg.

With a 'crack' Avery's boot smashed into the Dead soldier's face, rendering his nose a bloody pulp and his teeth mere broken shards. Then as the Jackal jolted over a bump in the driveway, the Dead man rose in the air momentarily only to slam back down again on Avery's leg. Suddenly, out of the blue, the animated corpse was inexplicably ripped from sight. Its legs, that moments ago had been flailing uselessly down the side of the Jackal as it tried to pull himself in, had gotten caught under the Jackal's large tyres and in the split second it took for the wheel to turn, his Dead body was torn from sight.

'Go! Go! Go!' screamed Alice, banging her fist on the dashboard, seeing more of the shadowy Dead running in their direction.

Matt did as he was told, and with a roar, the Jackal left the car park behind. For a second, he thought he was going to lose control when the tyres hit a large patch ice on the snow covered road, but he yanked the steering wheel violently in the opposite direction and control was his again.

'Shit,' Matt finally said, letting go of a deep breath.

'Are you okay, Avery?' said Alice, looking back at the obviously shaken man. 'Did it? Did it bite you, Avery?'

'What?' Avery replied, shifting his attention back to Alice. 'Erm... no, no, I'm fine. It didn't bite me. Is this is how you live your day to day life, Alice? Shit! Blackmore messed with the wrong people this time.'

With his words, a sudden realisation hit Alice.

'Fuck!' she said, 'What about everyone else? My friends in the holding truck... they're still back there.'

'Calm down,' Matt began, swerving the Jackal around the corpse of a woman lying in the road. 'They're safely locked in, probably unconscious thanks to Doc's cocktail and I don't think the Dead have the wherewithal to unbolt the door. we'll find somewhere to hold up for the night and when the Dead have slowed down, we'll go back and get your friends in the morning, okay?'

'Okay,' Alice replied, knowing he was right. 'They'll be okay until...'

However, her words were cut short as another labour pain shook through her.

'Jesus fucking Christ!' she screamed, her hand automatically snapping over to grip Matt's arm.

'God, you've got a grip on you, woman,' Matt said, smarting as the pressure on his arm increased.

Alice just glared at him sideways, panting through the pain.

'You want to swap?' she asked through gritted teeth.

'I think we need to find somewhere as soon as possible,' Avery shouted through to them in the front. 'That baby wants out and if you're having another contraction already, it's not going to wait long.'

'Crap, that's all we need,' Matt said to himself, peering into the darkness looking for a suitable stop.

Almost immediately, the light from the Jackal's headlights flashed briefly across a broken pain of glass.

'There!' said Matt, pulling the Jackal to an abrupt stop and reversing back.

If it hadn't been for the reflection of their headlights, the small house would have gone by quite unnoticed. Set just off the side of the road, the house that must have been a farmer's cottage at one time was a riot of evergreen ivy and large boxwood bushes. Apart from the one broken glass pane in the small front window, the house looked in relatively good condition and more importantly, it still had a front door. So many houses and buildings had been broken into either by hoards of the Dead early on when the plague first struck or by scavengers years later.

'I think we've found our room for the night,' Matt said shutting of the engine.

A stark silence suddenly struck them. Without the comforting rumble of the engine, the countryside was eerily quiet.

'We need to get her inside before we attract any of the Dead,' Avery said, grabbing the bag of medical supplies and one of the rifles.

'Well, let's just hope there's none inside,' Matt replied, helping Alice down from the Jackal and handing her over to Avery.

Despite her best efforts to keep quiet, the pain of her contractions was fast becoming too much for Alice to bear. Her panting had quickly taken on a grunting quality and as she gripped tightly onto Avery's arm, she prayed he had packed something in the bag that could help her.

'Avery,' she managed to say through her clenched teeth as another wave of contractions flowed through her.

'We need to hurry,' Avery said to Matt.

'Hurrying can get you killed,' Matt said to himself, as he pushed aside a waterfall of ivy that covered part of the front door.

Clicking on a small torch sitting mounted on the top of his rifle, Matt angled the beam through a small dusty glass panel set in the door.

'Let's see if anyone's home,' he mumbled, watching the narrow beam of light bouncing of the dusty furniture within.

The fact that the furniture inside was still upright and neatly positioned was a good sign. Often, one of the first things to be moved during an attack of the Dead were the bulky pieces of furniture. Usually sofas, sideboards and tables had been used to blockade windows and doors in the futile attempt to keep the Dead at bay. More often than not this did little except create a temporary prison for those inside, buying them a little time until, by their sheer numbers, Dead eventually broke through anyway. So to see a small faded floral print sofa facing a television gave Matt hope that the Dead might have passed over this home. Satisfied the house wasn't holding any deadly surprises, Matt took a step back and kicked hard at the door. With a brittle snap of decaying wood, the lock gave way and the door swung in half way where it stopped suddenly with a squeak when the bottom of the warped door scraped the tiled floor.

'Stay close,' Matt said, quietly stepping through the door.

The doorway opened directly into a small musty smelling living room, still littered with the pointless everyday knick-knacks of a life long gone. The light from Matt's torch fell on a small coffee table on which a neatly stacked pile of celebrity gossip magazines sat next to a dust covered television and DVD remote controls. Matt's torch then slowly panned up across the fireplace, its mantle dotted with framed photographs and small porcelain figurines.

'I think this place is clear,' Matt said, swinging the beam of light through an open doorway to an equally tidy kitchen. 'Let's get upstairs and find you a bed.'

Turning to the small staircase on his right, Matt began to lead their cautious ascent. With every other step creaking loudly when Matt put his weight down on it, by the time he reached the top step anyone upstairs, living or Dead, would surely have been prepared for his arrival. Thankfully, apart from some mice annoyed by the sudden intrusion, the group found upstairs to be as abandoned as the rest of the rest of the house.

'Bedroom in here, Doc,' Matt said, peeking through the doorway. 'I'll check out the front room.'

Avery led Alice over to the bed, leaving her for a moment as he opened the curtains, filling the room with radiant moonlight and then he pulled off the duvet and sheets.

'Avery, I don't care if they're a bit dusty,' Alice said, leaning against a cupboard.

'This is going to be difficult as it is,' he replied, glancing back to her as he opened the wardrobe. 'We don't want you or the baby getting an infection from the rat or mouse urine that's more than likely all over that bedding.'

'Oh,' she answered, knowing she would have been none the wiser without Avery pointing it out and would have happily slumped down onto the bed in the state she had found it.

With the moonlight now flooding the small bedroom, Alice could see a photo of a smiling couple in a frame beside the bed. For a moment, her mind drifted, wondering what had become of the happy couple, but she was soon brought back to reality by the contraction she could feel building inside her.

'Shit!' she spat, clutching at her stomach. 'Avery, I need to get out of these trousers... now!'

'Ah ha!' Avery said, pulling a pile of neatly folded sheets from the cupboard and giving them a quick sniff to check if they smelt of damp or mould. 'Not exactly laundry fresh but better.'

'Avery!' Alice snapped.

'Just breathe, Alice,' be began, unfolding a mix of pastel coloured and floral printed sheets. 'It's too early to push just yet. Let me get the bed ready, and then I'll give you something for the pain.'

'Just fucking hurry,' Alice said, leaning back against the cupboard while the pain of the contraction rippled through her.

Matt found the room at the front to be dark shadowy bathroom, not surprisingly nothing but a dry hiss escaped the tap when he gave it a turn.

'Oh well,' he said quietly to himself, turning the tap back off again.

Now that he knew the house was empty and safe, he didn't want to alert anyone or anything of their presence unnecessarily, so with a click, he turned off the torch. A beam of light in an otherwise dark countryside would be a dead giveaway and they had enough going against them as it was without advertising their bolthole. It was then that he remembered the front door was still ajar, so he made his way back along the landing to the staircase. He was half way down, when he heard the distinct scrape of a foot on the tiled floor below him. Although he was positive it wasn't one of the newly Dead from the camp that had found their refuge, it didn't give him much comfort to think of the slow Dead lurking in the shadows either. He debated turning his torch back on but decided against it. If one of the Dead had found them, the last thing he wanted was more of them being drawn to the light, particularly with Alice in labour.

With an annoyingly loud creak, Matt finally stepped down off the last of the stairs and into the still living room. Without his torch, he could now see the thin beams of moonlight that struggled to force their way through the dirty cracked windows to form small pools of cool light on the tiled floor. Suddenly, he caught a streak of reflected light out the corner of his eye, but before he could react, a long blade sliced through the air to hover just under his chin.

'Where the fuck is Alice?' a young woman's voice from the darkness came.

***

Twenty minutes earlier and Liz had been waiting patiently in the cart for Imran and the others to return from the camp, hopefully with their friends in tow. She looked over at Anne and Justin asleep, bundled up together beneath a blanket and smiled to herself. It had been simply miraculous that they had found them both alive and with Liz's own rescue added to this list of the miraculous, they were certainly in God's debt. She just hoped their favour would last just that bit longer and let them get the rest of their friends back too.

Delilah suddenly made a snorting noise and began to stamp one of her hooves in irritation. Moving over to look through the front slit, Liz tried to determine what was affecting the usually steady mare.

'Damn,' she said quietly, as the bright headlights of a large vehicle appeared round the corner.

It was one of the armoured vehicles from the camp and it was traveling at quite a speed along the lane towards them. Instantly, thoughts that Imran and the others had been discovered flooded her mind and she turned to shake Jen awake.

'Jen,' she said urgently.

'What? What is it?' Jen asked, startled and a little disoriented to be woken up.

'Company,' was all Liz could say as the bright headlights broke over the cart, sending a thousand tiny beams of light through every crack and seam of the wooden cover.

However, the roaring engine did not stop and they were not discovered. Whoever was driving had either not noticed the cart with the two horses nestled in the shadows of the pine trees, or they had other, more important things on their mind.

'Jesus fucking Christ!' came a shout from the vehicle as it sped by.

'Alice,' Liz whispered.

Whoever had just thundered past them had had Alice with them.

'Jen, I've got to go after that vehicle,' Liz said, reaching for her sword.

'But Imran said to wait here,' Anne butted in, tears already filling her large eyes. 'He said to wait...'

Liz cupped her sister's face in her hand.

'Whoever just went past has Alice with them,' she began looking into her sister's eyes. 'I've got to get her back, Anne. Jen will look after you till Imran and the others come back. I promise it'll be alright, okay.'

Even though Anne didn't look convinced, she silently nodded her head.

'I'll be back as soon as I can,' Liz said turning back to Jen. 'Please… keep them safe.'

Jen nodded, instinctively putting her arms protectively about the two children.

Within seconds, Liz was out of the cart and unhitching Samson. After two ungraceful attempts, she finally managed to pull herself up into the saddle, and with a sharp flick of the reins, she gave chase. Using the compacted snow left by the armoured vehicle, Liz was able to let Samson move a lot faster than she would normally have dared. Kicking up the snow as his hooves thundered after the retreating vehicle, Liz could tell Samson enjoyed being able to really let go and run as fast as he could. At one point, she saw two of the Dead shambling aimlessly in the middle of the road, but she flew past at such speed, they were far behind her before they even had time to react.

She was surprised when she saw the bulky shape of the armoured vehicle parked at the side of the road barely half mile down the lane. Pulling Samson to a halt, Liz quickly made an equally ungraceful dismount, almost falling on her backside in the process.

'Come on, boy,' she whispered, stroking Samson's muzzle to calm him.

After such a short burst of speed, Samson was twitchy, stamping his hooves and sending large plumes of fogging breath into the still night air. He had tasted the freedom of the gallop and he was eager to get going again, but now she needed him to be still and quiet.

'Shh, Samson,' she said, looking into one of his large glossy eyes as she continued to calm him. 'Shhh.'

Eventually, the stallion let his nervous energy bleed away and he was soon the content calm beast Liz was used to. Leading him over to a tree, she tied him off, and with one last comforting pat, Liz made her way past the armoured vehicle to the front door of the overgrown house. With a click, her blade slid free of its sheath, ready to defend or to kill as she walked through the open doorway.

Stepping into the dark dusty living room, Liz used a technique Charlie once taught her. Closing her eyes, she allowed her senses to open up and listened to the sounds of the house. Above her at the back of the building, she could hear the muffled voices of two people talking and she was sure one of them was Alice. Why she should have been brought here, away from the convoy, Liz could not guess, but at least she had found her friend and yet another miracle had been tossed her way. To Liz's right she could hear some light scratching, but dismissed it as probably mice or rats nesting in one of the walls. They were certainly no threat, but footsteps above her that were making the way from the front of the house and along the landing to the top of the stairs caught her attention. Slipping deep into the shadows under the stairs, Liz waited. Whoever was coming down had heard her move and had altered his own pace accordingly. He moved with caution and purpose now, because he knew someone awaited him in the living room and was now on his guard. The only choice Liz had was to act first and act fast. The man had barely taken his foot off the last step before she sent her blade whispering though the air towards his throat.

'I said where the fuck is Alice?' Liz repeated, pushing her blade a fraction closer to the of the soldier's neck.

Matt opened and closed his mouth, shocked that the young woman had him exactly where she wanted him within seconds.

'She's upstairs having her baby,' he replied, 'Who are you?'

Liz looked at the man, trying to gauge whether he was friend or foe. They already had one soldier who had risked his life to save some of their number, perhaps another of them had followed suit.

'Liz,' she finally said, lowering her blade to push past him and run up the stairs.

'You're in big trouble, lady,' Liz said to Alice, waltzing into the room, her eyes brimming with tears of relief.

'Jesus!' gasped Avery in surprise, almost falling over himself to get to his rifle.

'You took your time,' Alice said though pants. 'It's okay, Avery… she's a friend.'

Liz could hold out no longer and rushed forward to hug the friend she thought she might never see again. Kissing her forehead, Liz watched as the man who Alice had called Avery, loaded a hypodermic with a clear liquid.

'Do you know what you're doing?' Liz asked the man.

He simply looked at her as if she was asking a stupid question and carried on wiping an antiseptic swab over the crook of Alice's elbow.

'It's okay, Liz,' said Alice, wincing as the needle went in. 'Avery's a doctor or micro biologist or something, so he knows what he's doing. He's… ooh…ooH…OOHHH.'

Whatever Alice had intended to say about her new friend, Avery, was lost as a powerful contraction stole the words from her.

'Sounds like it's time to push, Alice,' said Avery positioning himself at the foot of the bed and lifting the sheet up over her knees. 'When I tell you, I want you to bear down like you're trying to go to the toilet, okay?'

'Mmm,' Alice said, clamping her mouth closed to prevent any more dangerous cries escaping her.

Alice looked over at Liz and grabbed her hand tightly.

'I'm scared,' she managed to whisper before she felt the undeniable need to push take control of her every thought.

Liz knew Alice was petrified but together they would get through this. At least they actually had the luxury of a doctor to help with the birth. That alone was something they'd never dreamed of all those months ago when they had realised they were both going to have children. Alice let out another strangled cry and Liz turned to the doorway where the soldier stood.

'Did you close the front door?' she whispered, worried they could be swamped by the Dead at any moment.

'Yes,' he replied, his face full of concern as he watched Alice trying to suffer in silence. 'I'll go and keep watch though... just in case.'

With that, Matt turned and left Dr Avery and the two women to it.

Sooner than he had expected, Matt heard the high pitch wailing of an infant coming from the bedroom above him. Running back up the stairs, eager to see the baby, Matt paused briefly before knocking on the bedroom door and pushing it slowly open.

'Everything okay?' he asked, popping his head round the door to see a beaming but tired looking Alice holding her baby boy wrapped in a floral bed sheet.

'Yes, it all went quite smoothly,' Avery replied, wiping his hands on another of the sheets, 'considering.'

Alice looked from Matt to Avery, tears filling her eyes.

'I can never thank the two of you enough,' she said through her tears. 'You both risked your lives to save my baby... thank you... thank you.'

'Hey,' said Matt, walking over and crouching down by the side of the bed to look at the baby in her arms, 'it was nothing, Alice... a walk in the park.'

'Phil's going to be so pissed he missed the birth,' said Liz, her little finger gently stroking the baby's face.

'Well, when we get back to Lanhern, you can tell him all about it,' Alice replied softly, looking in wonder at the miracle in her arms.

'It'll be sooner than that,' Liz replied dragging her eyes away from the baby to look at Alice, 'He's with Imran, Patrick and Leon. They've gone to the soldier's camp to get our people back.'

'Oh, my God, Liz,' Alice said, her face collapsing with worry.

'It's alright, one of the soldiers is with them, Steven Blackmore, Penny's friend from school,' she replied, unsure of Alice's reaction.

'Steve's alive?' Matt interrupted.

'Yes,' Liz said looking from one worried expression to the next. 'What's the matter?'

'We drugged the soldiers,' Avery said softly, 'and the Dead came while we were escaping.'

'The unconscious soldiers were sitting targets for them,' Matt added, 'and now...'

'And now the camp's full of the Dead and they're walking right into it,' said Liz, the horrific realisation hitting her. 'I've got to go!'

'No, Liz!' said Alice, reaching for her, but Liz was already half way to the door.

'Wait,' Matt said grabbing her arm. 'I'll go.'

Liz pause for a second, weighing something up in her mind.

'No,' she replied flatly, 'I need you to stay here to protect Alice and the baby.'

'Liz,' Alice interrupted.

'No, Alice, it's the only way to keep the both of you safe, so I have to go.' From her tone, Alice knew it was pointless to argue with her. Liz's mind was made up. 'And if I'm not back by morning, Anne, Justin and a woman called Jen are waiting with Delilah half a mile down the road in the direction of the camp. Go get them and tell Anne that I love her and that... and that I'm sorry.'

'No, Liz!' Alice cried, 'Wait!'

However, Liz had already left the room and even as Alice's words faded into the night, they could hear the thunder of hooves from outside the house.

***

'Something's not right,' said Steve in a low whisper, 'there's no-one stationed on watch in the Jackal.... I don't like it'

'No, wait, here comes someone,' replied Patrick, tapping Steve on the shoulder and pointing to the shadowy figure of a man stumbling towards the vehicle.

The group slowly crept along the driveway, keeping deep in the shadows of the dense thickets that, like everywhere, had grown wild and unchecked along the roadside verge. With their backs pressed against the foliage, they had made it to within five or so meters of one of the armoured vehicles and were surprised to find it unmanned. Phil placed his hand on Imran's arm and gave a nod in the direction of the approaching soldier. Knowing what was being asked of him, Imran took position. Down on one knee, with the string to his bow pulled taut, Imran took aim on the man's head. After a deep breath to centre him, Imran let his fingers gently slip from the string and watched as the arrow flew towards the target. With a cracking sound, much like that of a dropped egg, the arrow appeared lodged in the man's temple. For what seemed like an eternity, the man seemed to sway back and forth on his feet, his body unable to realise or perhaps accept the sudden change in state from one of the living to one of the dead. However, the body couldn't deny reality for ever and just as Imran considered reaching for a second arrow, the man fell face first onto the tramped down snow.

'We'll need to move that Jackal if we want a hope in hell of getting the holding truck out of here,' said Steve turning back to Phil. 'I'll release the manual brake and then we can push it to the side of the road. That should give us enough room.'

'We should check for weapons too,' Phil whispered. 'It might even things up a bit.'

With a nod, the five men ran to the Jackal, keeping low and out of sight. As they passed the solider Imran had killed, Leon stopped and began searching him for weapons. When the other four reached the Jackal, Steve jumped up into the driver's seat while the other three went to the rear and waited to push.

'What the...' he began, his hand coming away wet and dark as he slid across the seat.

Moving his hand up to catch a pool of moonlight, a tight knot began to form in his stomach. The fingertips, his palm and half way down the sleeve of his right arm were now covered in thick cooling blood. As the knot tightened within him, Steve looked from his hand back to the Jackal interior. It was then that he noticed the thick blood dripping from the ceiling onto the seats, forming a slowly spreading puddle.

'Shit!' he said to himself, knowing this could only mean one thing.

'Guys, we got a problem,' Leon whispered.

Looking back at Leon, Patrick, Phil and Imran could clearly see what he meant. During the search, Leon had turned the man's body over and even with only the moon for illumination, it was clear to see the soldier had been dead long before Imran's arrow had plunged into him. In the silver light, they could see that much of the flesh had been torn from one side of the soldier's face, exposing part of his cheekbone and jaw. One of his eyes had also been viciously ripped out, leaving only a stretched shred of optic nerve in its place.

'His pulse box thing is gone,' Leon whispered, pulling aside the man's blood drenched collar, 'and no gun either.'

'Right, no time to be subtle now,' Phil said, standing away from the Jackal. 'Steve, just start the engine and drive this thing out of the way. If the Dead attacked the camp, we need to get this done as soon as possible.'

Agreeing with Phil's urgency, Steve began to flip the switches that would start the mechanical beast, but nothing happened. Repeating the procedure just in case he had done something wrong, Steve tried again, but still nothing.

'Come on, you piece of crap,' Steve mumbled as he tried a final time to no avail. 'Shit!'

'You're going to have to push it, after all,' Steve whispered back to the four men. 'It's out of action.'

Not waiting to be told twice, the men braced themselves against the rear of the Jackal and straining, began to push. At first, their boots slipped on the compacted snow making it seem impossible, but then, ever so slowly, the vehicle began to move forward. Once the momentum had been built up, the weight of the vehicle, the slight slope of the driveway began to work in their favour, and before long, the Jackal was wedged deeply in the roadside thicket. Jumping out of the driver's seat, Steve ran back to the other four, wiping his blood-covered hand on his trouser leg. He was a metre away from them when he saw a shadow separate itself from the darkness and run at full speed towards Patrick.

'Look out!' he cried, as the figure threw itself at Patrick's back.

But unlike Steve, Patrick spent the last eight years with the Dead and even as he felt the body impact against him, he was using the momentum to throw himself forward. The Dead man didn't stand a chance. This was one meal that would be denied him. As Patrick landed in the snow, he twisted in the Dead man's grip and thrust his hand sharply up into the ravaged flaps of a torn throat. Latching onto the man's trachea, Patrick began to push the face with hungry snapping jaws away from him. When the struggling Dead man was at arm's length from him, Phil stepped forward, grabbed what was left of the man's hair and yanked his head even further back. With a cracking sound, the Dead man's vertebrae ground together until with a snap something gave way. It was then that Phil pulled a long hunting knife from his belt and stabbed down on the crown of the man's skull. Instantly, the unnatural life left the Dead man's limbs and he slumped to the ground.

'Thanks,' said Patrick, taking Phil's offered hand, to help pull him up.

'This doesn't look good,' said Steve. 'Whoever just buggered off in the other Jackal has made sure no one from here would be following them... well... no one alive anyway.'

'We need to get that holding truck out of here, now,' Imran added, looking around in case more of the Dead soldiers appeared.

'Right,' said Steve. 'Leon and I will go to the Med lab to get the pregnant woman and my mate, Matt.'

'Alice,' Imran whispered, 'her name is Alice.'

'Oh, okay... sorry,' Steve replied. 'Leon and I will go get Alice and Matt. You three, try to get the holding truck started.'

With a nod, the men split up and darted off into the shadows.

Steve and Leon walked with caution through the camp towards the Med lab. With each step, they expected the gore covered Dead to attack, hungry and merciless. All about them, the once pristine white snow bore the tell-tale signs of the recent carnage that had descended on the camp. Great swaths of the snow were now splashed with spilt blood and dotted with unidentifiable chunks of flesh.

'Jesus,' murmured Leon, as he stepped over what looked like part of someone's hand.

Each time they heard movement, the pair would freeze, their hearts hammering loudly in their chests as they peered desperately into the shadows, afraid the instrument of their death was lurking just out of sight. From at least one of the small tents, they could hear something noisily gorging itself and they knew it wouldn't be long before this act of feeding would increase their danger by one more Dead soul.

Steve tapped Leon's shoulder and pointed to the Med lab. Unbeknownst to the pair, in Matt's haste to escape the camp, he hadn't ensured the door had closed properly behind him and even now, it swung slightly ajar in the cold breeze, making a clicking sound each time the lock failed to connect. Glancing quickly over to the Holding truck, Steve could just make out Phil climbing up into the cab while Imran and Patrick walked round to the back of the long vehicle.

'Shit,' Steve mumbled, noticing the bloody handprints over the Med lab door.

Looking over to Leon, whom stood ready, his feet apart and a sharp gleaming knife in each hand, he knew now was a good a time as any. So, reaching slowly forwards, Steve's hand closed over the blood splattered door handle, stopping the door mid-swing. Taking a deep breath, Steve pulled the door towards him, revealing the bloodbath within. The once sterile and shining surfaces now dripped with clotting blood and stinking viscera. Whatever had happened here had left the Med lab looking more like an abattoir than a medical facility. The Dead had had a feeding frenzy and the two bodies that had been on the bunks seem to have had much of their flesh and internal organs violently ripped from them. At least these two had still had the safe guard of the pulse detectors on their necks to prevent them from coming back. One of the corpses had an arm that was just about still hanging to its torso by a few threads of muscle and on it, Steve could see the medical insignia that identified the body as that of one of the doctors. Which one, Steve had no idea. Such was the mutilation the person endured at the hands of the Dead.

The second body was clearly that of a man and had faired fractionally better than his comrade. However, with his back arched painfully upwards and his skinless face a mask of horror; it was clear this man had been aware in his final moments of the hands that plunged deep into his stomach ripping free a tasty morsel. Steve prayed that this was not Matt, but it was hard to tell. So, stepping over chunks of various organs he couldn't name, he moved closer to the body. Staring down at the bloody remains, Steve tried the fit the image of Matt onto the corpse's face. The body was approximately the right size and what was left of the skin was the right colouring, but without a face and scalp, it was impossible to tell.

'Your mate?' Leon whispered, stepping gingerly over a lump of something on the floor.

Once again, Steve looked down at the body, turned back to Leon and shrugged his shoulders.

'I don't know,' Steve replied softly.

'Well, at least he didn't come back, man,' Leon said, shaking his head.

'Not much of a consolation,' Steve thought to himself, averting his eyes from what looked like a partly chewed ear on the floor.

It was then that Steve noticed the third body in the lab. Slumped in a corner and covered with a sheet, this corpse showed no signs that it had been attacked by the Dead. When Steve pulled the sheet back to reveal Dr Morris with a thin, but fatal, slash across his throat, he knew the scalpel blade he'd tossed Alice had at least managed to even the score a little. Perhaps Alice and her baby had even managed to escape this slaughter. He hoped so.

'Come on let's...' Steve began, turning to Leon as he stood.

Stepping through the doorway was Clarkes, or rather, what was left of him.

'Look out!' Steve shouted, as Clarkes lunged clumsily towards Leon.

Spinning to meet the danger head on, Leon let one of his knives fly from his fingertips. Before the knife had even met its target, he was reaching for its replacement from the channels sewn into the front of his jacket. However, just as the knife was about to hit home, Clarkes slipped slightly on the wet floor, causing the knife to land harmlessly deep in his cheekbone.

'Fuck!' snapped Leon, taking a small step back from the Dead man reaching for him.

Clarkes had been a real A-grade bastard in life and deep down, Steve was not sorry to see what had become of him in death. The wounds inflicted on the man during his attack had obviously caused him to bleed to death. Much of the flesh from his throat up to and including his bottom lip was now gone, together with the all-important arteries and veins. A ragged tear of skin and bloody flesh ran from the corner of his mouth to just under his ears, exposing his blood smeared jawbone that was dotted with lumps of sickly yellow fat. In fact, if not for a few remaining tendons keeping it in place, Clarkes' jaw would surely have fallen away from his face entirely. With a cry, Leon suddenly launched himself at the Dead solider, his blades gripped tightly in the hands he held high above him. With a 'thunk', Leon's fists connected with the side of Clarkes' head and for a split second nothing happened. Then, as the knives ripped through his Dead brain, the arm that had been reaching for Leon fell uselessly to his side. Piece by piece, Clarkes' brain began to shut down and within a few seconds, his body collapsed to the floor, truly dead this time.

'Let's get out of here,' Leon said, removing each of his knives from Clarkes' head with a swift tug.

'Yeah,' Steve agreed. 'Alice and her baby aren't here. Let's hope the others have had better luck.'

Stepping over Clarke's body to leave the Med lab, Leon suddenly pulled Steve down into a crouch.

'What?' Steve whispered, looking about him for more danger.

Leon silently pointed over to the holding truck where two, very much alive, soldiers stood with their rifles pointed at Imran and Patrick. Standing by the two unexpected arrivals, Hills and Streiber, was also a woman. She had clearly been on the wrong end of a good beating and even from where Steve sat, hidden from view; her vacant glassy expression told him that she had been forced to endure more than she was capable of coping with.

'Shit!' Steve muttered, wondering what to do now.

***

'And Steve said it's pretty standard to drive…' said Phil to himself, as he climbed into the holding truck cab and looked at the alien controls.

Like Steve and Leon, Phil, Imran and Patrick had crept through the camp thinking that at any moment the Dead would lunge at them from the shadows. Thankfully, despite the mournful calls that drifted to them on the breeze, they had only encountered the bloody evidence of their passing. As Phil was the only one who had driven anything larger than a family car, it was decided he would drive the holding truck. Now that he was sitting there trying to figure out what the various dials and levers were for, he realised there was a world of difference between this monster and the old butcher's van he used to drive.

Outside, Imran and Patrick had gone to the back of the truck to check on the civilians. Relieved that the door was still bolted from the outside, the pair hoped their friends, safely locked away, had been missed by the Dead that had brought such rampaging slaughter to the rest of the camp.

'Keep watch and I'll check out inside,' Imran whispered to Patrick. 'Fingers crossed…'

Slowly, Imran pulled back the bolt and swung open the door. Holding the door wide, an oblong of silver moonlight seamed to spear the darkness within. Stretching across the floor of the truck and partway up the end wall, it highlighted the body of a man with one arm raised above him. It was only when Imran looked closer that he could see the raised arm was actually handcuffed to a ring on the wall above. Imran did not recognise this man but from what Jen had told them, the convoy had been collecting people for the last few days. Whoever this poor soul was, he had surely been stolen away from those he loved just like the rest of the Lanherne group.

Stepping into the truck, Imran let his eyes become accustomed to the dim shadows and it was then that he could see the people for whom he had been searching. Like the unknown man, Cam, William, Damian and Rich, together with another male stranger, had all been restrained with handcuffs. The women and children of the group were also thankfully there. Nicky sat slumped against Rich with a floppy looking Samantha in her drooping arms, while Penny was lying on the floor, her hand reaching out to Alex who was lying motionless nearby. Little Jimmy, Samantha's brother, had also collapsed on the floor near Bailey, for all intense and purposes looking like a pair of puppets with their strings cut. There was also another woman on the floor, Imran did not recognise her either, but as her hand seemed to be stretching towards one of the unknown men, he assumed she was the woman Jen had told him about that had decided not to try to escape but stayed with her husband. Imran's first thought was that they were all dead and at any moment, they would jump up on mass and attack. But as he stood there, the bow in his hands ready to consign his friends to the oblivion their deaths deserved, he realised there didn't seem to be any signs that these people were dead at all. The soldiers would not have killed them. They had spent too much time collecting this precious cargo and even if they had not been fed and watered, surely it hadn't been long enough for any of them to die of thirst. Stepping further into the shadows, Imran knelt down next to Penny.

'You better not bite me, girl,' he muttered, moving his head slowly down to her chest.

What he heard there made a smile creep slowly across his face, a heartbeat, slow but steady, pounded in her chest. Moving over to Alex, he was relieved to find the small child was also only unconscious. What made all of them lapse into this fairy tale slumber at the same time was beyond him, but at least they were all alive and safe.

'They're all okay,' Imran whispered, turning to Patrick. 'They seem to be knocked out but...'

Imran's words faltered. There, standing in the doorway, was a soldier with a rifle pointed at him.

'Well, what the fuck do we got here?' said Hills, casually targeting a point on the young man's head. 'Drop it, Raghead.'

With that one word, Imran knew they were in trouble. If this was the sort of man who still bothered to pass judgement in a world where the Dead walked and life was so fragile, he didn't hold out much hope for getting out of this with just a discussion. Slowly, Imran lowered his bow to the floor. From the disturbed look in the man's eye, he could tell this man was just waiting for an excuse to blow his head off.

'Outside, Robin Hood,' Hills snapped, jerking his rifle towards Imran.

With his hands behind his head, Imran walked past the soldier and back out through the door. As he had expected, there was another soldier with a rifle pointed at Patrick who was on his knees in front of him. Surprisingly, there was also a woman in torn clothes hanging back slightly behind the second soldier. Imran glanced at her, catching her eye. She had been badly beaten and it didn't take a genius to guess by whom. As their eyes locked, she pulled the tattered remains of a sweatshirt tighter about her and Imran saw a strange mix of shame and rage dancing behind her eyes.

'What the fuck have you two cunts done?' Streiber spat, forcing the muzzle of his rifle under Patrick's chin. 'You think you can just waltz in here and shit all over her Majesty's forces? Well?'

'We're just getting our friends back,' said Patrick, trying to tilt his head away from cold metal of the rifle. 'The Dead were already in the camp when we got here.'

Like Imran, Patrick knew a man who revelled in the dark pleasures of life when he saw one. These men were unhinged in a dangerously sick way, their grasp on sanity dancing precariously on a knife's edge. He would put nothing past them.

'Now, that's where I think we've got a bit of a problem,' Streiber began, glancing over at Hills with a strange smile on his face. 'See, in that truck there is some fine pussy and we've gone to a lot of trouble to find it, you understand me? Now you calmly say you're here to take it back? I don't think so, you fucking pair of shits!'

With the last word, Streiber swung his rifle round and slammed the butt hard into Patrick's face. With a flash of pain, Patrick's head jerked backwards and he tasted his own blood in his mouth. Spitting a mouthful of blood onto the snow, Patrick looked up at blankly the man who held his life in his hands. He knew no matter what he did or didn't say, this man had already decided his fate.

'You're in for a world of hurt, boy,' said Hills, ripping off Imran's Kufie cap and chucking it into the darkness. Leaning in close so he could whisper in Imran's ear, he continued, 'Streiber and I cut our teeth dealing with the likes of you over in Afghanistan. I know lots of fun games we can play. Believe me, you'll wish you were dead by the time I've finished with you.'

Suddenly out of the darkness, a streak of silver flashed through the air. Catching the movement out the corner of his eye just in time, Hills jumped aside. However, his reaction had been a fraction too slow and Leon's knife sliced through his left cheek.

'Fuck!' he said, his free hand clasping the side of his face, where already his blood was flowing freely.

Now was the moment Marie had been waiting for. She did not know who these two men the soldiers had at gunpoint were and did not care. All she knew was that now was the time for her to reap her revenge. She would see them pay for what they had subjected her and her husband to and even if it cost her life, she would have their blood.

With a wild scream, Marie threw herself onto the back of Strieber. Shocked that the broken woman had dared attack him, Strieber reached behind him to pull her off. However, with a strength borne of bloodlust and hysteria, Maria held tight. As he tried to shake her off, Strieber turned his head to look back at the wild banshee latched onto him, as he did so, his eyes widened in fear. Held tightly in her fist was a small tube looking blade and it was flying towards him. With a satisfying pop, the potato peeler sunk into the flesh of Streiber's neck but Marie was not finished and even as the man cried out and twisted beneath her, she yanked the blade free and plunged it in again. Again and again, her arm rose and fell and as Streiber's blood sprayed over her, she turned the flesh on his neck to a bloody pulp. Finally, his body could take no more abuse and he collapsed to the ground. Even now, Marie was unable to stop her rampage and she simply transferred her attention to his back, stabbing his already dead body over and over again.

Finally, a single shot rang out and Marie was thrown from Streiber's back to land in a tangle of limbs beside the man she had just killed.

'Move and you're as dead as that bitch,' Hills snapped to Patrick and Imran.

Slowly walking over to Marie, Hills kicked her body so she rolled over onto her back.

'Fucking bitch!' he spat, levelling his rifle on her head.

He knew she would come back and her hungry corpse was just one more problem he could do without right now. Pulling the trigger again, Hills sent a single bullet through the woman's head and already dismissing her from his concerns, he turned back to the men he still had to deal with. It was then that he noticed two more men running towards him from the direction of the Med lab. Torn between targets, Hills brought his rifle up to fire at the two approaching men. Because of this, he was not aware of the large man throwing himself from the roof of the holding truck until it was almost too late. Swinging back just in the nick of time, Hills lifted his weapon to fire on the falling man and as the man's heavy body collided with his own, he managed to get off a single shot.

'No!' shouted Imran rushing forward with Patrick.

Without thinking, Imran grabbed for the dropped weapon Marie had used and with an animalistic cry, he launched himself at the soldier. Before Hills could fully pull himself clear of the man on top of him, Imran was on him. With a punch, Imran's hand connected hard with Hills' chest.

Suddenly, a tight sensation began to spread across Hills' chest and for some reason, he couldn't seem to catch his breath. The young man's punch hadn't been that powerful... something was wrong, something was very wrong, he just knew it. Looking down, he simply couldn't understand what he was seeing. A circle of red was seemed to be spreading across his chest and at its centre was the wooden handle of the potato peeler. The kitchen utensil had been buried in his chest up to the hilt and as his lungs began to fill with blood and his sliced heart began to fail, Hills wondered what would happen, if he pulled it out. However, he would never find out, because seconds later, his heart stopped beating and one more monster was consigned to the darkness.

'Imran,' said Patrick.

He was looking at the hand he had used to roll Phil over onto his back gently. It was wet and covered in Phil's blood.

'Well, don't just sit there,' Steve said running over with Leon at his side. 'Pick up his legs and we'll get him to the Med lab. We need to stop the bleeding.'

With Steve's words, Imran and Patrick snapped in to action. Imran was about to reach down for his legs when Patrick moved him aside.

'No time,' he grunted, pulling Phil's large body up into a fireman's lift. 'Just watch for the Dead, and close the door to the truck. No one else is dying tonight.'

Taking a deep breath, Patrick gripped tightly onto Phil's hand and legs and walked purposefully, if a little shakily to the Med lab. Even through his jacket, Patrick could feel a growing wet patch of Phil's blood on his shoulder and hoped there was something they could do to save the brave foolish oaf.

'Here,' said Steve, ripping a sheet from one of the beds to cover the gore splattered examination table. 'Lay him down. Leon, Imran, start looking for something to stop the bleeding, a sewing kit... anything.'

No sooner had Patrick lowered Phil's head down onto the bed, than Steve had ripped open the injured man's jacket to see how bad the wound really was.

'What do you think?' Patrick said, looking hopefully at Steve for answers.

'I'm not sure,' Steve replied, knowing he held a man's life in his hand, a man who only a few hours ago had risked his own life to save Steve. 'There's an exit wound on his back, so that means the bullet went right through'

'And that's good, yes?' Imran asked, thrusting some sterilized wadding into Steve's hand.

'Depends on what damage it did on its way through, I guess,' answered Steve, dividing the wadding and applying half to each bullet wound. 'That's where my medical knowledge ends. I guess we'll have to sew him up and just hope for the best.'

'We can't just hope for the best,' Imran said, looking at the pale and drawn face of his friend. 'We can't let him die.'

'Oh, I wouldn't worry about that,' came the cold voice of Sergeant Blackmore standing in the doorway, his rifle pointed at them.

Immediately, everyone in the room froze.

'Thought I'd gotten rid of you already, boy,' Blackmore said, glaring at his son.

'Sorry to disappoint you,' answered Steve, quickly glancing down to make sure he was still keeping the pressure on Phil's bullet wound.

'Nothing that I haven't come to expect from you,' Sergeant Blackmore continued, contempt dripping from his words. 'Since the day your useless mother brought you into this world, you've been one big disappointment to me...'

Steve looked at his father, hate rolling off him, as he tried to find one good memory of the man, but he couldn't.

'You know, when the Death Walker plague came I was actually pleased,' Sergeant Blackmore continued. 'Humanity finally had a chance to rid itself of the useless, the crippled and the weak. I even thought it would make a man of you, but I was wrong. You're weak... I should have left you on the mainland like that pathetic mother of yours.'

'Oh, go fuck yourself!' Steve spat.

With the words, Steve had always wanted to say to his father finally spoken, he knew the circle was complete. His own father, who had given him life, was now going to take it away again and he could do nothing about it. Sure enough, Sergeant Blackmore raised his rifle and his finger began to apply pressure to the trigger.

Suddenly, Sergeant Blackmore took a sharp intake of breath and made a small stumbling step forward. With a ragged cough flecking blood on his lips, he looked down in surprise at the long blood smeared blade that appeared through the front of his chest. With a grunt, Liz kicked the Sergeant's heavy body forwards, letting him fall to his knees. While he fell, the end of her sword slowly disappeared from his chest as he slipped down its length.

'I hope for Penny's sake that you're nicer than he was,' Liz said, smiling as she stepped over Sergeant Blackmore's still body. Her smile dropped when she noticed Phil.

'How bad?' she asked no one in particular, pushing past Leon to take Phil's hand.

'We don't know,' Imran replied, seeing her tears that threatened to fall. 'There might be damage inside, but we just don't know how bad.'

'Right,' Liz said, wiping a tearful sniff on the back of her sleeve. 'Get him to the holding truck and we're getting out of here.'

'But Liz, that doesn't help Phil. We don't know what's going on inside,' Patrick calmly added, placing a hand on her back.

'It does if there's a doctor half a mile down the road with Alice and her baby,' Liz replied, looking from one stunned face to the next. 'Come on, let's move, people, we've got a friend to save.'

'Man, your woman is fierce,' Leon said to Imran, shaking his head with a smile.

'You should see her when she's not pregnant,' Imran replied. 'She's fucking unbelievable!'

***

EPILOGUE

FIVE MONTHS LATER

'Oh, stop being such a baby,' Avery said, his fingers gently feeling the swollen glands in Phil's neck. 'I've told you, it's just the flu. Everyone else has had it, so now it's your turn.'

With the examination done and prognosis given, Avery's hands fell from Phil's neck to rest on his shoulders, one of his thumbs working a soft circle on Phil's exposed skin.

Liz looked over at the two men sitting at one of the long refectory tables, one who she loved and one whose kind nature had already begun to work its way into her affections. That the two men had found in each other something they had been searching for made a soppy smile spread over her lips. She glanced over to catch Alice, who had paused in her folding of laundry to watch the two men, smiling also.

'Aww, sweet,' Alice mouthed silently to Liz, pouting her lips and nodding in Avery and Phil's direction.

Liz was glad Phil had finally found someone to share his life with, the way she shared hers with Imran, and now of course, with Saleana too.

When she found Phil, pale and bleeding in the Med lab she feared they would lose him and even as the thought came to her, she thought her heart would break. It wasn't until she almost lost him that she realised just how important Phil was to her. Not just because like all those at the Lanherne, she looked to Phil for strength and guidance, but also because she had so few friends left in this world she simply couldn't bear to lose another. Getting Phil back to the holding truck had been tricky and even now, the short journey was still a blur of swinging clubs, flashing blades and the falling Dead. Only moments before, she managed to sneak through, unmolested by the Dead, to deal with Sergeant Blackmore. Minutes later, the Dead converged on the camp en mass, drawn to sounds of the living. She remembered Patrick lifting Phil's body back up onto his shoulders while the others formed a circle of protection around him. Countless arrows had flown through the moonlit camp and sliver knives spun with deadly accuracy to find their unholy targets. She herself let her blade slash and flit through the air with desperate abandon, sending any of the Dead that came too close back to the oblivion that nature demanded. They had made it to the holding truck unscathed, unbitten and alive. Steve had jumped up into the cab and as soon as he knew all were on board, the mechanical goliath roared into life, crushing any of the Dead in its path under its powerful wheels.

For a while, it had been touch and go for Phil. Avery, although managing to stop the internal bleeding, knew the operation had certainly been conducted in less than ideal circumstances and was afraid of complications and infection. He stayed by Phil's side in the holding truck the whole journey back to Lanherne, watching over him day and night, administering constant care for a man he didn't even know. When Phil finally woke, Avery's smiling face full of relief was what greeted him back to the world of the living.

'Earth to Liz,' Imran said, snapping her back to the present. 'Someone wants a feed.'

Looking up at Imran, the memories of darker times disappearing like smoke from her mind, she smiled. Held protectively in his arms was an unhappy looking Saleana.

'Who's on watch?' she asked.

Since having Saleana, she seemed even more determined they would never again be caught out by the living or the Dead. Never again would anyone breach the walls of Lanherne, even if it meant more on watch than they strictly needed.

'Patrick, Gabe and William,' Imran replied. 'Leon and Cam are watching Damien and the others are in the field.'

'Okay,' she replied, with a nod, satisfied all was well.

'Come to Mummy, darling,' she then cooed to her daughter, opening her arms to receive the precious cargo. 'I know, I know... isn't Daddy terrible, eh?'

'Hey, don't gang up on me,' Imran said, reaching forward to kiss Liz on the forehead as she began to breastfeed Saleana.

'Get used to it, buddy,' she replied with a wink. 'mothers and daughters... special bond... us against the world...'

'I thought that was supposed to be mothers and sons,' said Alice, resuming the mammoth task of sorting the huge pile of washed clothes.

'Ignore her, Imran,' said Liz, shifting Saleana's position slightly. 'She's saying that because she's only got a boy. What does she know.'

'Only a boy?' Alice replied arching her eyebrows. 'Look at him, he's gorgeous.'

Alice nodded over to Charlie, angelically asleep in Sister Josephine's arms, who was also dozing.

The invasion of Lanherne had hit the Mother Superior hard and even though everyone managed to get back safely, the whole experience left her somehow frailer for it. Avery assured her that is was perfectly natural for a woman of her age to feel the way she did and that the best advice he could give her was that she should just listen to her body. If it was telling her to slow down and rest more, then that's exactly what she should do. There were now enough people at Lanherne that she didn't have to worry about keeping on top of every detail. She should sit back and try enjoying life for a change. As soon as he said it, Liz knew he might as well ask the sun not to rise than ask the feisty Mother Superior to slow things down. So it was nice to see her relaxed for a change and able to take an afternoon nap when she needed it.

'Yeah, okay,' replied Liz rolling her eyes, 'he's gorgeous.'

'Ladies, ladies,' Steve said, walking into the refectory his hand around Penny's shoulder as she carried a distant looking Danny, lost in his own world of his making. 'I'm taken... sorry.'

'Dump him, Penny,' said Alice with a grin, 'you can do better.'

'Yeah, I'm thinking about it,' she replied, letting Danny down to the floor and waving a small stuffed giraffe in front of him, trying to engage his interest.

Immediately, the small boy ignored the stuffed toy and waddled over to Sister Josephine and Charlie.

'No, Danny,' Penny said softly, 'don't touch, you'll wake them up.'

'Oh, he's alright,' said Alice, waving off Penny's concern. 'You're just curious, aren't you, Danny, eh?'

Surprisingly, Danny turned, looking blankly at Alice when she said his name, but he soon returned to looking at the sleeping baby that lay in Sister Josephine's arms.

Shrugging her shoulders, Alice raised her eyebrows in surprise. Any reaction from Danny was so rare that even the slightest recognition of those around him was noteworthy.

'Still no sign of Matt and his sister?' Alice asked Steve, reaching for a pair of socks that had fallen from the pile of clothes onto the floor.

'No, nothing yet,' Steve replied, shaking his head.

After everyone had collected in the holding truck, ready for the off, Matt surprised them by saying he wouldn't be going with them. He promised himself he would return to the island base to get his sister, Karen. With no other survivors from the squadron to contradict him, he could his spin any story he liked about what happened, and he assured them he would make it clear that Alice's baby had not survived the rampaging Dead that had wiped out the rest of the camp. Therefore, after emptying the Jackal of the weapons, he bid farewell to Matt and the Lanherne group and left them with the promise he would return to the mainland one day and seek out the sanctuary they had built for themselves. Alice certainly hoped so, because she owed the man more than words could ever express and he deserved to live out his life in a community held together by trust and love, rather than one bound by fear.

'Well, the base will be down on manpower since losing our squadron and the one sent to the power station, he might be finding it difficult to get away,' Steve continued, pictures of the cold steel corridors with their CCTV cameras watching every corner of the base, coming to mind.

'He'll find a way,' said Penny, stroking Steve's arm reassuringly. 'I'm sure of it.'

'Hmmm,' mumbled Steve, lost in his thoughts before snapping back and giving Penny a weak smile and a quick kiss.

Alice and Liz exchanged glances once again, each knowing what the other was thinking and smiled. With the smile still on her face, Liz let her eyes roam over the group in the Refectory. It was when her eyes fell on Danny, that it started to falter. Something was niggling at the back of her mind, and then small boy slowly reached up to touch Sister Josephine's arm. As his small fingers touched her sleeve, her arm fell limply to side. Then Liz knew.

'Alice!' Liz whispered, horrified at what could be happening.

Almost as if in slow motion, a smiling Alice turned to look follow Liz's wide-eyed stare and in a split second, she could see her world falling apart.

'Charlie!' She screamed, throwing herself over the table to get to her son before the unthinkable happened.

Shocked into action, Penny darted forward to pull Danny away just as Alice plucked Charlie from Sister Josephine's arms and spun away with a startled Charlie crying in her arms. A heavy silence enveloped the adults in the Refectory as each of them realised Sister Josephine had finally been taken from them. She had died peacefully in her sleep.

'I'll do it,' Phil said, solemnly stepping forward as he pulled a long knife from his belt. 'Before she comes back... she deserves better.'

'No wait!' Avery said, reaching for Phil's arm.

Phil turned back to Avery, looking quizzically down at the hand holding him back.

'Avery?' he asked.

'Just a few minutes,' Avery replied. 'Please Phil... please trust me.'

'What is it, Avery?' Phil said knowing it must be important.

'I don't think she's coming back...,' Avery replied softly.

'What do you mean, Avery?' Phil said taking the man's hand in his.

'It's the flu,' he began, looking from one questioning face to the next, 'I think the anti-virus given to Charlie may have mutated. I think it became air-born and I think we've all been infected. The flu we've all had was actually the new virus battling with the Death Walker virus that was already in our bodies and I think it won, Phil. Don't you see, if she doesn't come back, none of us will and we'll be free... it'll be over.'

As the meaning of Avery's words sunk in, Imran instinctively reached his out his arm and pulled Liz and his daughter to him. He could feel her heart pounding in her chest, and when she turned her head to look up at him with tears of loss in her eyes, Imran lent forward to kiss her softly on the forehead.

'It'll be alright,' he whispered. 'Whatever happens, it'll be alright.'

Then as one, everyone in the room turned to look at the still body of Sister Josephine and waited for nothing to happen…

The End

Last Days With The Dead: Book 3 of the Lanherne Chronicles is out now

5893382R00126

Printed in Great Britain
by Amazon.co.uk, Ltd.,
Marston Gate.